She buried that thought as soon as it rose. Even if it was fairly safe here, the reflex was too strong. *Think on something safer. Something that will help you survive.*

Her fingers relaxed, undyed nails tapping the silvery metal of the Gates. *Clear enough, at least, and it's likely to become no clearer for the waiting.* It would be chill in the mortal realm, but she wouldn't feel it, not with the warming breath and her own half of sidhe blood. Besides, it was easy enough to steal clothing.

For a moment she toyed with the dangerous idea of losing herself in the mortal world, abandoning the sidhe to their own problems. There *was* a valley or a city that would hide her somewhere in the wide, wide world. The Queen would no doubt forget her after a while.

Unless she did not.

PRAISE FOR THE WORKS OF
LILITH SAINTCROW:

Dante Valentine

"She's a brave, charismatic protagonist with a smart mouth and a suicidal streak. What's not to love? Fans of Laurell K. Hamilton should warm to Saintcrow's dark, evocative debut."

—*Publishers Weekly*

"Saintcrow's amazing protagonist is gutsy, stubborn to a fault and vaguely suicidal, meaning there's never a dull moment.... This is the ultimate in urban fantasy!"

—*RT Book Reviews* (Top Pick!)

"Dark, gritty, urban fantasy at its best."　　　—blogcritics.org

Jill Kismet

"Nonstop rough-and-tumble action combined with compelling characterization and a plot that twists and turns all over the place. Saintcrow...never fails to deliver excitement."

—*RT Book Reviews*

"Loaded with action and starring a kick-butt heroine who from the opening scene until the final climax is donkey kicking seemingly every character in sight."

—Harriet Klausner

"Lilith has again created a vibrant, strong female heroine who keeps you running behind her in a breathless charge against forces you just know you would never be able to walk away from completely unscathed."

—myfavouritebooks.blogspot.com

"This mind-blowing series remains a must-read for all urban fantasy lovers."　　　—bittenbybooks.com

Bannon & Clare

"Saintcrow scores a hit with this terrific steampunk series that rockets through a Britain-that-wasn't with magic and industrial mayhem with a firm nod to Holmes. Genius and a rocking good time."
———Patricia Briggs

"Saintcrow melds a complex magic system with a subtle but effective steampunk society, adds fully fleshed and complicated characters, and delivers a clever and highly engaging mystery that kept me turning pages, fascinated to the very end."
———Laura Anne Gilman

"Innovative world building, powerful steampunk, master storyteller at her best. Don't miss this one....She's fabulous."
———Christine Feehan

"Lilith Saintcrow spins a world of deadly magic, grand adventure, and fast-paced intrigue through the clattering streets of a maze-like mechanized Londonium. *The Iron Wyrm Affair* is a fantastic mix of action, steam, and mystery dredged in dark magic with a hint of romance. Loved it! Do not miss this wonderful addition to the steampunk genre."   ———Devon Monk

"Lilith Saintcrow's foray into steampunk plunges the reader into a Victorian England rife with magic and menace, where clockwork horses pace the cobbled streets, dragons rule the ironworks, and it will take a sorceress's discipline and a logician's powers of deduction to unravel a bloody conspiracy."
———Jacqueline Carey

BY LILITH SAINTCROW

GALLOW AND RAGGED
Trailer Park Fae

BANNON AND CLARE
The Iron Wyrm Affair
The Red Plague Affair
The Ripper Affair

DANTE VALENTINE NOVELS
Working for the Devil
Dead Man Rising
Devil's Right Hand
Saint City Sinners
To Hell and Back
Dante Valentine (omnibus)

JILL KISMET NOVELS
Night Shift
Hunter's Prayer
Redemption Alley
Flesh Circus
Heaven's Spite
Angel Town
Jill Kismet (omnibus)

A ROMANCE OF ARQUITAINE NOVELS
The Hedgewitch Queen
The Bandit King

AS LILI ST. CROW

THE STRANGE ANGELS SERIES
Strange Angels
Betrayals
Jealousy
Defiance
Reckoning

TRAILER PARK FAE

Gallow and Ragged:
BOOK ONE

LILITH SAINTCROW

orbit

www.orbitbooks.net

Orbit
Hachette Book Group
1290 Avenue of the Americas, New York, NY 10104
www.OrbitBooks.net

Printed in the United States of America

RRD-C

First Edition: June 2015

10 9 8 7 6 5 4 3 2 1

Orbit is an imprint of Hachette Book Group, Inc. The Orbit name and logo are trademarks of Little, Brown Book Group Limited.

The Hachette Speakers Bureau provides a wide range of authors for speaking events. To find out more, go to www.hachettespeakersbureau.com or call (866) 376-6591.

The publisher is not responsible for websites (or their content) that are not owned by the publisher.

Library of Congress Cataloging-in-Publication Data

Saintcrow, Lilith.
    Trailer park fae / Lilith Saintcrow.—First edition.
        pages ; cm.—(Gallow and ragged ; book 1)
    ISBN 978-0-316-27785-3 (softcover)—ISBN 978-0-316-27783-9 (ebook)—ISBN 978-1-4789-0396-3 (audio book download)
    1. Fairies—Fiction.   I. Title.
    PS3619.A3984T73 2015
    813'.6—dc23
                                            2014046001

For L.I., as promised.

Then he began to gaze about
and saw within the walls a rout
of folk that were thither drawn below
and mourned as dead, but were not so.
—SIR ORFEO, AS TRANSLATED BY
J. R. R. TOLKIEN

A DIFFERENT BEAST

1

⊃╫╫⊂

Summer, soft green hills and shaded dells, lay breathless under a pall of smoky apple-blossom dusk. The other Summer, her white hands rising from indigo velvet to gleam in the gloaming, waved the rest of her handmaidens away. They fled, giggling in bell-clear voices and trailing their sigh-draperies, a slim golden-haired mortal boy among them fleet as a deer—Actaeon among the leaping hounds, perhaps.

Though that young man, so long ago, hadn't been torn apart by gray-sided, long-eared hounds. A different beast had run him to ground. The mortals, always confused, whispered among themselves, and their invented gods grew in the telling.

Goodfellow, brown of hair and sharp of ear, often wondered if the sidhe did as well.

The Fatherless smiled as he watched Summer wander toward him through the dusk. She was at pains to appear unconcerned. His own wide, sunny grin, showing teeth sharper than a mortal's, might have caused even the strongest of either Court unease.

Of course, the free sidhe—those who did not bend knee to Summer or her once-lord Unwinter—would make themselves scarce when the Goodfellow grinned. They had their own names for him, all respectful and none quite pleasing to him when he chose to take offense.

Summer halted. Her hair, ripples of gold, stirred slightly in the perfumed breeze. Above and between her gleaming eyes, the Jewel flashed, a single dart of emerald light piercing the gloom as the day took its last breath and sank fully under night's mantle.

Someday, he might see this sidhe queen sink as well. How she had glimmered and glistened, in her youth. He had once trifled with the idea of courting her himself, before her eye had settled on one altogether more grim.

The quarrel, Goodfellow might say, were he disposed to lecture, *always matches the affection both parties bore before, does it not?* The Sundering had taken much from both Courts, and that bothered him not a bit. When they elbowed each other, the space between them was wide enough to grant him further sway. Carefully, of course. So carefully, patiently—the Folk were often fickle, true, but they did not have to be.

He let her draw much closer before he lay aside his cloaking shadows, stepping fully into her realm between two straight, slender birches, and she barely started. Her mantle slipped a fraction from one white shoulder, but that could have been to expose just a sliver of pale skin, fresh-velvet as a new magnolia petal. Artfully innocent, that single peeping glow could infect a mortal's dreams, fill them with longing, drive all other thought from their busy little brains.

If she, the richest gem of Summer's long, dreamy months, so willed it.

"Ah, there she is, our fairest jewel." He swept her a bow, an imaginary cap doffed low enough to sweep the sweet grass exhaling its green scent of a day spent basking under a perfect sun. "Where is your Oberon, queenly one? Where is your lord?"

"Ill met by moonlight, indeed." She smiled, just a curve of those red, red lips poets dreamed of. There had been mortal maids, occasionally, whose salt-sweet fragility put even Summer to shame, and woe betide them if any of the Folk should carry tales of their radiance to this corner of the sideways realms. "And as you are an honest Puck, I have come alone."

"Fairly." His smile broadened. "What would you have of me, Summer? And what will you give in return?"

"I have paid thee well for every service, sprite, and have yet to see results for one or two dearly bought." Summer drew her mantle closer. She did not deign to frown, but he thought it likely one or two of her ladies would take her expression as a caution, and make themselves scarce. They would be the wisest ones. The favorites, of course, could not afford to risk her noting such a scarcity, and so would stay.

"Oh, patience becomes thee indeed, Summer." He capered, enjoying the feel of crushed sweet grass under his leather-shod feet. A fingersnap, a turn, as if it were midsummer and the revels afoot. "As it happens, I bring word from a certain mortal."

"Mortal? What is a mortal to me?" Her hand dropped, and she did not turn away. Instead, her gaze sharpened, though she looked aside at the first swirling sparks of fireflies drawn by her presence. There was nothing the lamp-ended creatures loved more than her own faint glow by night. Except perhaps the Moon itself, Danu's silver eye.

"Then you do not wish to hear of success? O changeable one!"

"Puck." The fireflies scattered, for Summer's tone had changed. In her sable mantle, the golden hair paler now as her mood drained its tint, her ageless-dark eyes narrowing so very slightly, the loveliness of Summer took on a sharper edge. "I grow weary of this."

"Then I shall be brief. He has worked another miracle, this mortal of science. There is a cure."

She examined him for a long moment, and the Goodfellow suffered it. There was a certain joy to be had in allowing her to think he quaked at the thought of her displeasure. Far greater was the amusement to be had in knowing that the Queen of the Seelie Court, Summer herself, the fount of Faerie—for so the bards called her, though Goodfellow could have told them where a truer fountain welled—had very little choice but to dance to his tune.

She turned, a quarter profile of hurtful beauty, her black eyes flashing dangerous. The stars in their depths spun lazily, cold fires of the night before any tree was named. If an ensnared mortal could see her now, Goodfellow thought, he might well drop of the heartshock and leave the trap entire.

"And what is the price for this miracle, sprite?"

He affected astonishment, capering afresh, hopping to and fro. Under the grass was sere dry bramble, and it crunched as he landed. "What? I am no mortal tailor, to double-charge. All you must do is send your own sprite to collect it. The mortal longs for any breath of you, he entreats a word, a look, a sigh."

"Does he?" Summer tapped one perfect nail against her lips. There was a rosy tint a mortal might mistake for polish on its sweet curve, and it darkened to the crimson of her smile as her mood shifted again. *Changeable as Summer,* the free sidhe said. Unwinter was far less capricious, of course...but just as dangerous.

"Welladay." Summer's smile dawned again, and she turned away still further. "Does his miracle perform, he may receive a boon. I shall send him a sprite, dear Goodfellow, and our agreement stands."

"My lady." He cut another bow, but she did not see the sarcastic turn his leer had taken. "You do me much honor."

"Oh, aye." A girl's carefree giggle, and she moved away, the grass leaning toward her glow and the fireflies trailing. "I do, when the service is well wrought. Farewell, hob. I'll send him a familiar face, since mortals are timid." Her laugh, deeper and richer now, caroled between the shivering birches, a pocket of cold swallowing a struggling swimmer.

"Mind that you do," Goodfellow said, but softly, softly. He capered once more, to hear the dried brambles crunch underfoot, like mortal bones. He spun, quick brown fingers finding the pipes at his belt. He lifted them to his mouth, and his own eyes fired green in the darkness. Full night had fallen, and silver threads of music lifted in the distance—the Queen was well pleased, it seemed, and had called upon the minstrels to play.

He stepped *sideways*, pirouetting neatly on the ball of one foot, and emerged in a mortal alley. It was night here, too, and as he danced along, the breathy, wooden notes from his pipes arrowed free in a rill. Concrete whirled underfoot, the mortal world flashing and trembling as he skipped across its pleats and hollows. They did not see, the dull cold sacks of frail flesh, and only some few of them heard.

Those who did shuddered, though they could not have said why. A cold finger laid itself on their napes, or in another sensitive spot, and the gooseflesh walked over them. None of them suited Goodfellow, so he ambled on.

A little while later, a mortal chanced across his path—a sturdy youth, strong and healthy, who thought the Fatherless a common, staggering drunkard. With the pipes whispering in his ear, luring him down another path, the mortal boy did not realize he was prey instead of hunter until his unvictim rounded on him with wide, lambent eyes and a sharp, sickeningly cheery smile.

Yes, Goodfellow decided as he crouched to crunch, hot salt against his tongue, bramble *did* sound like mortal bones, if it was dry enough.

Pleased by his own thoroughness, he ate his fill.

SIMULACRUM

2

❊

Jeremiah Gallow, once known as the Queensglass, stood twenty stories above the pavement, just like he did almost every day at lunchtime since they'd started building a brand-new headquarters for some megabank or another.

He was reasonably sure the drop wouldn't kill him. Cars creeping below were shiny beetles, the walking mortals dots of muted color, hurrying or ambling as the mood took them. From this height, they were ants. Scurrying, just like the ones he worked beside, sweating out their brief gray lives.

A chill breeze resonated through superstructure, iron girders harpstrings plucked by invisible fingers. He was wet with sweat, exhaust-laden breeze mouthing his ruthlessly cropped black hair. Poison in the air just like poison in the singing rods and rivets, but neither troubled a Half. He had nothing to fear from cold iron.

No mortal-Tainted did. A fullblood sidhe would be uncomfortable, nervous around the most inimical of mortal metals. *The more fae, the more to fear.*

Like every proverb, true in different interlocking ways.

Jeremiah leaned forward still further, looking past the

scarred toes of his dun workboots. The jobsite was another scar on the seamed face of the city, a skeleton rising from a shell of orange and yellow caution tape and signage to keep mortals from bruising themselves. Couldn't have civilians wandering in and getting hit on the head, suing the management or anything like that.

A lone worker bee, though, could take three steps back, gather himself, and sail right past the flimsy lath barrier. The fall would be studded and scarred by clutching fingers of steel and cement, and the landing would be sharp.

If he was singularly unlucky he'd end up a Twisted, crippled monstrosity, or even just a half-Twisted unable to use glamour—or any other bit of sidhe chantment—without it warping him further. Shuffling out an existence cringing from both mortal and sidhe, and you couldn't keep a mortal job if you had feathers instead of hair, or half your face made of wood, or no glamour to hide the oddities sidhe blood could bring to the surface.

Daisy would have been clutching at his arm, her fear lending a smoky tang to her salt-sweet mortal scent. She hated heights.

The thought of his dead wife sent a sharp, familiar bolt of pain through his chest. Her hair would have caught fire today; it was cold but bright, thin almost-spring sunshine making every shadow a knife edge. He leaned forward a little more, his arms spreading slightly, the wind a hungry lover's hand. A cold edge of caress. *Just a little closer. Just a little further.*

It might hurt enough to make you forget.

"Gallow, what the hell?" Clyde bellowed.

Jeremiah stepped back, half-turned on one rubber-padded heel. The boots were thick-soled, caked with the detritus of a hundred build sites. Probably dust on there from places both mortal and not-so-mortal, he'd worn them since before his marriage. Short black hair and pale green eyes, a face that could be any anonymous construction worker's. Not young, not old, not distinctive at all, what little skill he had with glamour pressed into service to make him look just like every other mortal guy with a physical job and a liking for beer every now and again.

His arms tingled; he knew the markings were moving on his skin, under the long sleeves. "Thought I saw something." *A way out.* But only if he was sure it would be an escape, not a fresh snare.

Being Half just made you too damn durable.

"Like what, a pigeon? Millions of those around." The bullet-headed foreman folded his beefy arms. He was already red and perspiring, though the temperature hadn't settled above forty degrees all week.

Last summer had been mild-chill, fall icy, winter hard, and spring was late this year. Maybe the Queen hadn't opened the Gates yet.

Summer. The shiver—half loathing, half something else—that went through Jeremiah must have shown. Clyde took a half-step sideways, reaching up to push his hard hat further back on his sweat-shaven pate. He had a magnificent broad white mustache, and the mouth under it turned into a thin line as he dropped his hands loosely to his sides.

Easy, there. Jeremiah might have laughed. Still, you could never tell who on a jobsite might have a temper. Best to be safe around heavy machinery, crowbars, nail guns, and the like.

"A seagull." Gallow deliberately hunched his shoulders, pulled the rage and pain back inside his skin. "Maybe a hawk. Or something. You want my apple pie?" If Clyde had a weakness, it was sugar-drenched, overprocessed pastry. Just like a brughnie, actually.

Another shiver roiled through him, but he kept it inside. *Don't think on the sidhe. You know it puts you in a mood.*

Clyde perked up a little. "If you don't want it. How come you bring 'em if you don't want 'em?"

Insurance. Always bring something to barter with. Jeremiah dug in his lunchbag. He'd almost forgotten he'd crumpled most of the brown paper in his fist. Daisy always sent him to work with a carefully packed lunch, but the collection of retro metal boxes she'd found at Goodwill and Salvation Army were all gone now. If he hadn't thrown them away he had stamped on them, crushing each piece with the same boots he was wearing now. "Habit. Put 'em in the bag each time."

She'd done sandwiches, too, varying to keep them interesting. Turkey. Chicken. Good old PB&J, two of them to keep him fueled. Hard-boiled eggs with a twist of salt in waxed paper, carefully quartered apples bathed in lemon juice to keep them from browning, home-baked goodies. Banana bread, muffins, she'd even gone through a sushi phase once until he'd let it slip that he didn't prefer raw fish.

I just thought, you're so smart and all. Ain't sushi what smart people eat? And her laugh at his baffled look. She often made little comments like that, as if…well, she never knew of the sidhe, but she considered him a creature from a different planet just the same.

"Oh." Clyde took the Hostess apple pie, his entire face brightening. "Just don't stand too near that edge, Gallow. You fall off and I'll have L&I all over me."

"Not gonna." It was hard taking the next few steps away from the edge. His heels landed solidly, and the wind stopped keening across rebar and concrete. Or at least, the sound retreated. "Haven't yet."

"Always a first time. Hey, me and Panko are going out for

TRAILER PARK FAE

beers after. You wanna?" The waxed wrapper tore open, and Clyde took a huge mouthful of sugar that only faintly resembled the original apple.

"Sure." It was Friday, the start of a long weekend. If he went home he was only going to eat another TV dinner, or nothing at all, and sit staring at the fist-sized hole in the television screen, in his messy living room.

Ridiculous. Why did they call it that? Nobody did any *living* in there.

"Okay." Clyde gave him another odd look, and Jeremiah had a sudden vision of smashing his fist into the old man's face. The crunch of bone, the gush of blood, the satisfaction of a short sharp action. The foreman wasn't even a sidhe, to require an exchange of names beforehand.

I'm mortal now. Best to remember it. Besides, the foreman wasn't to blame for anything. Guiltless as only a mortal could be.

"Better get back to work," Jeremiah said instead, and tossed his crumpled lunchbag into the cut-down trash barrel hulking near the lift. "Gotta earn those beers."

Clyde had his mouth full, and Jeremiah was glad. If the man said another word, he wasn't sure he could restrain himself. There was no good reason for the rage, except the fact that he'd been brought back from the brink, and reminded he was only a simulacrum of a mortal man.

Again.

A MORTAL FAILING
3

It looks clear. The Gates shimmered slightly, cold metal under Robin Ragged's fingertips. Triple her own height, cruel spikes along their tops frozen with hungry, thorn-carved flowers, they hummed a low warning scrape-noise at her.

She drew back into shadow, afternoon sun rippling as the border between *here* and *there* slid. As long as she stayed just within touch of the Gates, one foot carefully on either side of the dividing line, she wasn't trackable even though she was technically outside Summer's realm. Had Robin a choice, she wouldn't have picked *this* point of egress—but the Queen had ordered her to make haste.

The shadows *there,* in the gray mere-mortal world, all had teeth. Low doglike shapes with moonlit eyes twisted, their slim muzzles lifted between wavering seaweed fringes. If there was any doubt of the watch kept on the Seelie Gates, it was now assuaged most heartily.

Robin whistled tunelessly, concentrating, a silver quirpiece— an hour's worth of work, a paltry insurance against pursuit— clutched in her free hand. Her palm was sweating. Mortal sweat, perfuming the air around her in long shimmering strands. Her skirt fluttered a little, eternal Summer breathing against her left ankle, a chill almost-spring wind touching her right. Dusk was the best time to slip through unremarked, but too far into nightfall was dangerous.

She could not wait for dawn, the rising sun that would keep most Unseelie at bay. One of the Queen's mortal pets had sent word, so Robin was sent to fetch and carry.

Again.

The Gates were not open, but the postern just to the north of them admitted or released any Seelie who required it—at least, any Summer sidhe not sickened by the damn plague. The Queen wouldn't tread the path leading to the other side of the Gates for another short while. Sooner or later she must, and who could tell if the infection running rampant outside Summer would enter once the actual Gates were flung wide?

Nobody knew, and even the mortal-Tainted of a scientific bent—now petted and cosseted in the hopes of finding a cure, instead of ridiculed and relentlessly pranked by their more sidhe-blooded betters—couldn't tell for certain. There was only one assurance so far, and it was that those tainted by mortal blood weren't prey to the sickness. A quartering of mortal or more seemed to keep the infection at bay.

Here on the borders, safe in the interference, it was perhaps the only place Robin could allow herself to think that the blackboil plague could be a blessing in disguise if it cleared away the proud and malignant. Still, if the fullborn sidhe were all gone, what did that leave for the mortal-Tainted, even the most blessed of mixtures, the full Half?

Once the wellspring was gone, would the smaller freshets dry up? It was an article of unquestioned faith, how the fullborn kept both Courts sideways to the mortal world.

Which still left those with only a measure of sidhe blood in an uncertainty. Maybe a new plague would spring from the old. Or would they simply escape into the mortal world and leave Summer and Unwinter both, not to mention the Low Counties, as fading, dry-leaf memories?

She could have refused to tread outside Summer's borders. But there was Sean, now at the Queen's dubious, thorny mercy. The Queen would not let her Robin loose without a silken thread tied to the leg. What else did Robin have left? Her sister was dead, and well so, for it meant she could not be used against the Ragged; grief was a luxury to be shelved so she could *do,* and just perhaps find a way to slip the leash.

She buried that thought as soon as it rose. Even if it was fairly safe here, the reflex was too strong. *Think on something safer. Something that will help you survive.*

Her fingers relaxed, undyed nails tapping the silvery metal of the Gates. *Clear enough, at least, and it's likely to become no clearer for the waiting.* It would be chill in the mortal realm, but she wouldn't feel it, not with the warming breath and her own half of sidhe blood. Besides, it was easy enough to steal clothing.

For a moment she toyed with the dangerous idea of losing herself in the mortal world, abandoning the sidhe to their own problems. There *was* a valley or a city that would hide her somewhere in the wide, wide world. The Queen would no doubt forget her after a while.

Unless she did not.

Sean. The child's face turned up to hers, his golden hair smoothed by Robin's own fingers every day. Her shoulders hunched, and she suppressed a shiver. All the stars of Summer's dusk, and his soft voice following hers as she taught him the constellations. Would it be easier to be fullblood, and able to set down a pretty mortal child and forget it? Regret was, as far as she could tell, only a mortal failing.

15

Half were oft presented with the choice of being like the sidhe, or like the mortals. As far as Robin could tell, neither side of the coin lacked tarnish.

I'm stalling. She cast a look over her shoulder, an impatient toss of her curls. Fields sloped away behind the Gates' bars, a sweet green valley opening up and each copse of trees drowsing under golden afternoon sun too richly liquid to be mortal. The Queen would be in the orchard today, because the pennants were up, snapping and fluttering on a brisk hay-and-apple wind. Thomas Rinevale would be harping; he was high in favor at the moment. The ladies-in-waiting would be draped across silk and satin pillows, and the Queen would be resting in the tent, her white cheek against her pale hand, smiling just slightly and very aware of her own beauty as Sean brought her another cup of *lithori* or a bunch of damson grapes.

If the blackboil plague breached the Court, that white skin might be raddled in days, and that golden hair a snarl of dishwater. Her graceful slenderness would become a jenny-hag's bony withering. Eventually, Summer might choke out a gout of black brackish fluid, and expire, her eaten body collapsing into foul wet dust.

A comforting thought, and one Robin kept despite the danger. She turned away from Summer and faced the mortal world again. Everything now depended on luck, speed, and her native wit. Her whistle became a high drilling buzz, lips pursing and her hair lifting on a breeze from neither realm. Robin Ragged's blue silken skirt snapped once, her heels clicking as she stepped with a jolt fully into the mortal world, slipping through a rent in the Veil just her size and shape. Her fingers left cold metal, the Gates' thrum disappearing like a train rolling into the distance, and the alley closed around her. Bricks, garbage, the effluvia of combustion engines and decay.

For all that, it was an honest reek, and she welcomed it as she took a few experimental steps. The world rippled around her, cautious as it always was to accept a child of the sideways realms, then firmed like gelatin.

She made it to the alley mouth, peered out into the city. Night gathered in corners. It was the perfect moment of dusk, when the tides between all the realms, sideways and mortal, turned and the interference made it difficult to track *anything*, much less one ragged little bird with a whistle that trilled into silence.

She cocked her head. She'd gone unremarked.

At least, she *thought* she had, until the ultrasonic cry of a silver huntwhistle lifted in the distance, and she thought perhaps *they* had been watching far more closely than even the Queen had guessed.

It was whispered that Unwinter himself had loosed the plague, and even now reveled in its destructive force. Certainly Summer had openly hinted as much, when the black boils began to cut a swath through the unaligned. The free sidhe often named themselves the lucky ones who bowed to no master—at least, not fully, though there was always the Fatherless.

Don't think about him. If all goes well, you won't see him tonight. He won't even know you've been out and about.

Robin slid out of the alley and set off down the deserted street, cars humming in the distance and every nerve in her body quivering-alert.

Now let's see how well I run the course. Her heels tapped the sidewalk as she lengthened her stride, her much-mended skirt whispering and her curls bouncing. She was not so foolish as to think fear of any reprisal from Summer would keep her whole should Unwinter's hounds have orders to bring the Ragged to their liege.

She was, however, just arrogant enough to think perhaps she

could outrun them, and if all else failed, there was always the song, its thunder under her thoughts a comforting roil.

Dusk closed around her, and Robin hurried.

>‖<

She doubled a time or thrice, turned counterclockwise in a deserted intersection, and worked closer and closer to familiar ground. The trashwood that had seemed a fairytale forest once was untidy stumps and clumps of refuse choking a small pond that used to be a blue eye, but the path up the hill was still used by something. Maybe animals, or homeless mortals. Her heels didn't slip on the greasy, frozen dirt, but she went carefully anyway, stopping often to listen. Night's wings had folded.

Everything here was familiar. She hadn't chosen this place, and didn't like the idea that it was a message from the sidhe who had found her skinny-dipping in the pond so long ago and opened her eyes to the sideways realms. Deciphering what such a message could mean took second place to the consideration that it was familiar ground, since Robin knew every inch of the trailer park. It would be difficult to trick her with glamour or pixie-leading here.

The entire place was abandoned now, maybe because of the fires evidenced everywhere by the gaping toothsockets of scorched, empty concrete foundations between slumping, gutted tin-walled boxes that had once been something akin to homes. Chill, forlorn menace eddied and swirled about the trailers lucky enough to be intact; she ignored it. She'd laid some of the glamours here herself, safeguarding the Queen's pet.

One of the trailers listed uneasily on its pad, but it was eerily solid underfoot as she climbed the back stairs, finding the stable ones by touch and memory, ignoring the illusory ones and the traps just waiting to clutch an unwary ankle. The flimsy door was locked, but she whispered the password and twisted the knob, stepping through into dim electric light and close, sweating mortal warmth.

"Who's there?" A pale, fretful voice.

"It's Ragged," she answered, gently enough. "You sent word."

All the internal walls had been taken out. Sidhe chantments had coaxed roots to support the place; it was far more solid than it looked. At one end there was a camp bed with sweat-yellowed sheets, an ancient radio tinkling away with mortal music, and a chair; the remains of a bathroom halfway down the trailer were still functional, but there wasn't even a curtain for privacy. The rest of the space was crammed with tables and shelves, computer screens with odd designs glowing through their blank stares, glassware of odd shapes and Bunsen burners with their blue flames, alembics and three microscopes, two refrigerators for his "samples," and various other weird mortal accouterments.

Hunched at the far end was a skinny mortal man with glittering eyes. He leaned against the table and scowled at her, lank, greasy hair falling over his face. Rounded bird-shoulders in a dirty white lab coat, trembling hands, Robin might have been shocked at the change in him if she hadn't seen it happen so many times before. The wanting consumed them from the inside out, when the Queen took a mind to dazzle a male of any realm, sideways or no.

Still, the mortals burned away so much more quickly.

"I thought *she* would come." Petulant, a whining note in his tone. No wonder he sweated; it was stifling in here. "I've done it, I did it, all she asked."

"She wanted to come," Robin lied. "But it's not safe, Henzler. She sent me to hear you."

"I already sent the vials." He edged forward, into the light. "They're in a black bag. I gave it to *him*."

For a moment she thought he meant Unwinter, and every

inch of her skin chilled hard-taut before she reminded herself that Henzler wouldn't be alive if the shadowy king had visited. The whole point of hiding the mortal scientist here was to keep him safe from Unwinter's prying, especially if Unwinter was the source of the plague.

Robin sighed. "She will be displeased. You were *told*—"

The mortal—there was no hint of sidhe about him; he was purely salt and decay—made a short stabbing motion with one hand, something in it glinting. "You keep telling me lies. I know he'll take it straight to *her*. Then she'll come for me. I can do so much more. She'll see."

"What did you give, and to whom?" At least she was the entire length of the trailer away from him. "So I may know what to tell her when she asks." *And woe betide us both, mortal—you for letting the prize out of your fingers, and me for carrying ill news.*

"The glasses went with the boy." The mortal shook his head, spattering drops of sweat across the glassware on tables to either side of him. "The boy with the knife."

Oh, for the love of . . . It wasn't as bad as she'd feared, but frustration still sharpened under her breastbone. Her throat ached, and she suddenly longed to let the song loose. It would sweep all this jumbled mess away, and ease the man's suffering in the bargain. If he had given up what Summer had contracted him for, he was all but useless now, and he would not see hide nor hair of the Queen again. He would sicken and waste away, perhaps take refuge in insanity, a mortal butterfly dipped in dwarven filigree. Consumed, only a husk remaining to clatter in a thoughtless sidhe's hair.

Her stomach, weak mortal thing that it was, roiled at the notion. Not three months ago he'd been a thoughtful, dark-haired mortal man with wire-rimmed glasses, his sober mien handsome in its own way. A scientist, probably with a good job—Puck had mentioned him as a teacher. Now he was a pixie-led mess, picked like a fruit, a single bite taken and the rest flung away.

There was nothing to be done. "Very well. I shall leave you in peace, then." There was no way to douse the fire Summer had kindled in him, and he would not thank her for trying.

They never did.

"No, wait!" Henzler stumbled forward, and she saw without any real surprise that the gleam in his hand was a jagged bit of glass, sickle-shaped and wicked-sharp. Who was he planning to use it upon? "Does she speak of me? Does she say anything, anything at all? When is she coming? I've done what she wanted, done it twice now. *When is she coming?*"

You lost any chance of seeing her again when you handed the cure over, mortal. Robin's breath wanted to fetch up into a sigh; she denied it. Four in, four out, even and slow, for a mortal could be dangerous with the amorous fit upon him and the song was Robin's only defense.

"I do not know, sir Henzler." Courteous enough, and she stepped sideways, her hand searching for the doorknob.

He stopped, stock-still. "I'll wait." His face was now a crafty child's, under hanks of limp hair. Now she could see his legs were bare, covered with pinch-scabs, under a pair of stained boxers with smiling penguins cavorting across the cloth. "I'll wait, and I shall build her more marvelous dolls. Little tiny toys, to creep into blood and breath and brain."

He's even talking like a sidhe now. Her gorge rose, she denied it, and wasted no more words on the moontouched mortal.

Outside, the chill was a balm. Even if the place still reeked of smoke and refuse, it was a cleaner smell than inside the glamoured trailer. From the outside, it was a ramshackle, empty cavern, listing dangerously, everything about it warning passerby or poacher away.

She scrubbed her hands together, once, twice, and listened intently. It was quiet.

Too quiet.

Robin turned counterclockwise once, and hurried for the main entrance, her heels making soft sounds against cracked, weed-clotted pavement. Each dip and rise was familiar-strange; she could remember riding a borrowed bicycle along its humped back, so long ago. Of all places for Puck Goodfellow to hide the Seelie Queen's precious little morsel, why had he picked here? Merely to upset one little Ragged? She was not worth such effort from the closest thing to a leader the free sidhe had, even if he *had* brought her to Summer.

Who knew what Puck ever meant or intended? She hunched slightly and hurried more, faint tendrils of vapor rising from her bare shoulders into the night air. She either had to find the Goodfellow and his cargo, or slip over the border and bring the news to Summer that the Fatherless had absconded with something valuable.

Neither option was appealing, even if it was Summer herself who had traded with Puck to provide some of the chantments and glamours around her mortal toy.

Robin stopped, her head upflung, brushing back her hair and feeling at small items caught in its long flow—the bone comb, two long, thin pins, a ribbon tied about a matted lock to the left of her nape. Chantments in solid form, but she was no warrior to carry weaponry. There was nothing in her hair that would help at the moment.

Especially since another silver huntwhistle sounded. Far to the south, but its high, chilling cry sent a wave of almost-panic through her.

Whatever you're going to do, Robin, you'd best decide now.

AN ARRIVAL
4

⊶╫⊷

Falida Street lay deserted, shadows swirling uneasily as the streetlamps flickered. Ripples danced, flickers weaving between the lampposts. A weary mortal might think them fireflies out of season, or gossamer traceries of violated night vision. They moved against the wind, sometimes clustering, and if the mortal was sensitive, he might even hear chiming and high, sweet giggles.

A thrill ran along the shivering air, and the streetlamps died one by one, their bulbs fizzing softly. The tiny dots of light dilated, each a palm-sized sphere. Their colors changed almost at random—crimson, emerald, sapphire, each hue spreading through its neighbors before being replaced by another.

The last streetlamp, on the corner of Falida and 217th, struggled to stay lit. When it finally winked out, the bobbing, weaving lights turned cold blue. They clustered, and their tiny piping chorus took on a darker tone.

Pixies always collected where the Veil was thin, and this night was no different. Any of Summer's realm or the free sidhe would make themselves scarce as soon as that chill pale azure spread. Even a mortal might have sense enough to flee.

The darkness swirled. One moment, nothing, the next, it *appeared,* and the pixies scattered shrieking in their sharp, tiny crystal voices. One or two weren't fast enough to escape the breath of chill accompanying the tall, bulky shape, and their lights snuffed out, tiny bodies thudding onto pavement and decaying quickly, sending up coils of autumn-leaf vapor that vanished through the flux of the Veil.

The killing cold etched frost onto the cracked sidewalk; the black horse pawed with too-slender hooves, a chiming ringing down the dark street. The equine head was subtly wrong, too.

A horse should not have carnivore teeth.

Caparisoned in moth-eaten velvet, its rider in silver-chased armor, the horse pawed again, then stilled as the rider's spike-helmed head lifted and cocked. A faint green glow limned them both; the rider sniffed deeply.

So did the horse, its nostrils each bearing a greenish spark in their depths. At the rider's breast a small silver huntwhistle gleamed, a tarnished star. His gauntleted left hand, its six slim fingers all bearing an extra joint, rose to touch it as he inhaled again, a wet snuffling sound. The horse blew out a cloud of frost, small droplets hanging crystalline in the air around them.

The pixies hung back, scurrying into hiding-holes in the sickly sidewalk bushes and the closest free earth, a weed-infested vacant lot that sighed under their tiny hands and the buffets of their membranous wings. The windows facing Falida Street, every one with bars, chopped the sidhe's reflection into several, an army of Unseelie riders, each with a struggling star at his chest.

Horse and knight both froze. Another deep sniff, as the wind veered. The pavement groaned as the cold intensified, and the rider caught a breath of spiced russet fruit. He tilted his head, and heard, not so far off, the tapping of frantic heels.

"Ragged." A chill, lipless whisper, somehow wrong. The pixies cowered, their dismay grown so vast it was now silent, more and more of them flicker-vanishing through the Veil in search of a more salubrious place.

The tiptapping of heels intensified.

The elfhorse let out a shattering neigh and bolted for the western end of Falida, just as headlights sliced an arc across its path. An old woman clutching the wheel of her ancient, rusted Ford Fiesta let out a high piercing scream as *something* boiled across her windshield, a suffocating black bird of terror beating in her mortal brain. The car veered wildly, bumping up onto pavement and scraping its side along a fire hydrant, and when the emergency personnel came, the verdict was sudden heart failure, tragic and completely ordinary.

The Unseelie rider was long gone.

A BRUEGHEL PAINTING
5
⊃╫╠⊂

Panko bought the first round without taking the smelly cigar end out of his mouth. He puffed at them constantly off-site, and the fume was enough to make a man choke. Here at the Wagon Wheel, though, there was no differentiating it from the omnipresent fug of burning cancersticks anyway.

Jeremiah took a long pull off his beer and ran an eye over the crowd. Flannel, thick shoulders, the red-faced mortal women with their hair teased high. Friday nights were crowded and loud, especially during Two-Dollar Hour at this particular watering hole. Panko was a cheap bastard, but it didn't matter. Here was as good a place as any.

"So I *told* the bitch," Panko yelled over the surfroar of the crowd. The jukebox was roaring, too, overwhelmed by three deep at the bar and elbow room at every table. "I *told* her. Didn't I tell her?"

"I wasn't there!" Clyde yelled back. This was an old, old conversation, and Jeremiah wasn't called upon to do more than nod whenever Panko's flat, dark gaze slid his way. Which it now did, measuring his response.

Jeremiah nodded. Took another long draft of beer. It foamed

on the way down, and he found himself wishing for wine. White wine, tart and crisp with apples, and Daisy's special soft laugh when she was half drunk and he slid his hand up her leg.

His chest seized up again. Jeremiah drank faster, broke away from the bottle and had to take a deep breath, hunching his shoulders further. Five years and counting. Weren't sidhe-blooded things supposed to forget? *The only long memory is for a grudge,* Paogreer the slick-skinned grentooth had said, tapping his cane on the glassy floor of Summer's Hall, marking time as the dancing revel spun and shook before them.

No room for gratitude in that sidhe's chest, Jeremiah had replied, and kept his hand away from the glass badge pinned to his chest with an effort. The Armormaster did not dance. Even then he had been wondering how to free himself of Summer's clutching white hands, but it had taken Daisy to make him attempt it. He'd done his best to keep away from her for a few months after he left Court, so the Queen wouldn't suspect she had been abandoned for a mortal.

If Summer had suspected, it wouldn't have been just a car accident for Daisy.

Jeremiah blinked, brought himself back to the present.

"I *told* her not to go in the basement. But she does, even though—get this—she's *scared* of it." Panko's broad face twisted up. He always had a tan, even in the dead of winter, his skin remembering years of working outside.

Clyde came in on cue, with a braying horselike laugh. Panko's wife was a neurotic, if he could be believed.

Daisy had been scared of the dark, too. Like any reasonable person. Jeremiah took another mouthful of beer. How much would he have to drink before he could expect the hole in his chest to shrink a little?

There's not enough booze in the world. He kept his expression neutral, despite the recurring thought that if Panko's wife *was* neurotic, it was living with the man that had done it.

"Christ." The flow of Panko's familiar story snagged. "Would you look at *that*."

He didn't want to look. The noise in the Wagon Wheel had changed, too, a sharper edge to the sibilants, a breath of wonder. So Jeremiah raised his gaze, and saw nothing but the usual tired old mortal faces clustered around their tankards and glasses, cracked skin and frizzy hair; the entire fucking bar looked like a Brueghel painting on a Friday night.

Except her.

He almost choked on his beer. The markings up his arms sent sharp tingling bursts down to the bone, racing up until his shoulders stiffened as if he'd been struck.

Same slim outline, same shadow of dancer's musculature on the back left bare except for the spaghetti straps of a blue silk dress. The skirt was flared, calf-length, and the calves were the same satiny paleness. The way of standing was the same, too, hip tilted, most of her weight on one foot. She was reaching across the bar, and the wrist was the same as well. But it was the mop of honeygold hair with its red tint that would only come out in sunlight, looking a bit washed-out in the bar's half-glow, cut in an inverted V, longer as it fanned forward, taming and shaping that slight springy natural curl, that did it.

All the breath left him in a hard rush. If he hadn't been sitting down he might have fallen. The markings on his arms burned, spiked flame spreading like oil down his entire body. But this was a cold fire, like meeting the Queen's laughing, innocently murderous gaze.

Daisy was dead, rotting under a blanket of earth in the too-green graveyard at St. Pegasus. Hallowed ground, he'd insisted.

He couldn't bear the thought of it otherwise.

"Huh." Clyde let out a grunt, like he'd been punched. "Wonder where she blew in from."

Jeremiah's hand, freighted with beer bottle, locked halfway to his mouth. His entire body flushed hot, cold. Hot again, sweat prickling up his arms and at his lower back. He smelled of exertion, fresh air, and a faint sharpish apple-rotting because he didn't know what Daisy did to make the clothes turn out sweet. That was a mortal chantment, and one he'd never bothered to find the secret of.

The bartender shook his head, swiping his hand back through greasy black hair and standing up a little straighter. He was a whip-thin Chicano, and his face had never held an expression other than resentful boredom the entire time Jeremiah had been drinking here. Now he looked mystified, and his mouth dropped open a little.

The woman turned to look toward the door, and the curve of her cheekbone stopped Jeremiah's heart. The earrings were gold hoops, dwarven work, and they took a russet from her hair.

His beer bottle hit the sticky tabletop. Fortunately it was empty, so it only clattered, lost under the din. His fingers had gone numb.

"You okay?" Clyde sounded nervous for the second time that day.

Tingling ran along Jeremiah's skin, scalp to sole. Left on the bar where the woman had leaned was a single silver circle, perfectly round, a glowing moon.

Quirpiece? Here? He pushed his bar stool back, the scraping lost. Another sound lost, too, under the rollicking of the jukebox and shrieking drunken laughter. Pool balls clattered in the long room off to one side, and Jeremiah heard a metallic thread stitching underneath a bright carpet of human noises.

A silver whistle's cry, high ultrasonic thrill-singing. Too off-tone to be one of Summer's forays, and in the wrong season besides, but undeniably sidhe. Since it was not All Soul's or St. George's, it likely wasn't the anarchic free sidhe, either.

Which only left one possibility.

Unwinter, hunting.

The tingling turned into a prickle, stopping just short of pain. He shoved through the crowded humans. It was too warm in here. He was sweat-clammy, heart pounding like an overworked engine. He reached the bar, scooped up the quir-piece just as its shine sent a hard dart of light winging into the far dark corner.

A bottle shattered. Someone cursed, and a woman screamed. The quir had done its job, muddying the girl's trail, and turned scorching-cold in his palm. Jeremiah ignored it, as well as the sudden tip-shift of the crowd's mood, and lurched after her. The crowd pressed carnivorously close, and someone shoved him. *"Watch where you goin'!"*

Jeremiah stepped sideways, dropped his shoulder, and drove toward the entrance. A flash of redgold as the swinging doors opened and she ducked out. There was no doubt—her stumbling attempt to flee said it all.

She was prey.

The silver whistle unsounded again, too high for any mortal but the gifted or sidhe-touched to hear, and every living thing in the bar tensed.

The mortals couldn't hear that sound…but they could certainly feel it. A flare of violence, wine-red, closing over his vision, and he dove for the door, his weight turned into a battering ram.

The inside of the Wagon Wheel erupted. Fists, elbows, bottles. Another female scream, cut short with a crunching sound.

A chair broke, and Jeremiah ducked under a clumsy strike from a squat bearded man.

The ripple of violence spread, confusing the woman's scent. Russet gold and blue silk, a faint blooming of... what was it? Cherry? Strawberry with sandalwood? Spice-fruit, as if she was part nymph.

That was one relief. She didn't smell like his purely mortal, salt-and-sweet Daisy. She reeked of sidhe, even through the quirpiece's struggle to mask her. Breaking her trail with a mortal whirlpool because the riders were close behind—but riders of which Unseelie faction, and why? Was it Unwinter himself riding, one last hunt before Summer's Gates opened and he was confined to the dark of the moon or the Blighted Lands? Or was it simply some of his knights a-riding, for no other reason than the joy of it?

It didn't matter. She wasn't Daisy. She couldn't be Daisy... but still. He knocked one man aside, ducked another flung beer bottle, threw his arm up as someone tossed a bar stool. It was nothing but reflex; the leg almost clipped his skull, but the cursed sidhe speed was still with him. Everything slowed down, droplets and shards of glass hanging in struggling air, faces contorted with rage.

Jeremiah *moved*.

TO SELL HERSELF DEAR
6

⋈╫╟⋉

It was a risk, leaving the quir behind. Robin pawed in the pockets of her mended skirt as she bolted down the street, finding little that would aid her. Of *course* it was an Unseelie knight following her; she had caught a glimpse of him, helmed and gauntleted and smoking with Unwinter.

She had *also* seen the play of greenblack sickness on the horse's mane. A plagued rider. Panic beat high and thin in her throat, cold sweat tracing down her back with one chill bony finger. At least it was not Unwinter himself, though that was cold comfort indeed.

If she could just slip away, or find an entrance-point, she could be over the border and back in Summer in a trice. Returning empty-handed was better than *this*. All she needed was a few moments' worth of quiet—but that, apparently, was just what she was not about to be granted. The silver whistle-cry lifted behind her, eager and searching, and she would have cursed whoever had betrayed her—*had* it been Goodfellow?—down to the seventh generation if she could have spared the breath.

If someone hadn't betrayed her, she might be simply unlucky. It was, she supposed, just barely possible. During their season, the Unseelie hunted where they would, and they always liked to do Summer a disservice. Unwinter grudged the Queen her glory, it was said, but perhaps he had just grown tired of her fickleness. Sometimes Robin wondered if the Sundering was a lover's spat now ossified, King and Queen at each other's throats by proxy. They were wondrous well matched, from all Robin could tell.

Her skin still crawled. The reek of the mortal tavern clung to her. It was a good attempt at camouflage, but not enough to discourage a Court Unseelie. The riding hunters were far too thoroughly practiced, the lords of the lesser Unseelie accustomed to all the various ways prey sought to escape.

If the plague was Unwinter's, and the rider suspected what she was about... well, best not to think upon it. Best just to run.

Am I formally under the Hunt? No, there was no warning, no riddle—maybe it's simply that I am of Summer and he is not?

It would be terribly ironic if she fell prey to a plague-maddened sidhe who bore her no personal ill-will.

Still, the quir had bought her some precious time, and it might yet buy her more if the rider descended on the tavern while she slipped away. There was some risk to the mortals inside, but enough cold iron around them to interfere with the worst of the dangerous things the Unseelie could do. A few of them might be led or glamoured, or brushed with sadness.

I had no choice, she told herself as she ran, and shut it away. There was no energy to waste now.

If she could not flee, and could not tear the Veil and step into Summer, she was left with only one choice. For that, she needed her breath.

Her voice made sidhe nervous, especially those who preferred the mortal world. She could, she supposed, have sung moon-touched Henzler a song, and left him a corpse freed of Summer-yearning, then hied herself over the border bearing news.

But killing the Queen's pet would be disastrous if Summer had, against all appearances, another use for him. So Robin had decided to quarter the area, seeking Puck. This was what she had to show for her caution—running down a mortal street with the hounds on her heels, the thud of hoofbeats behind her, and her quirpiece probably lost. She could make another with small trouble, but it was such an *annoyance*.

She flung the breakaway, a small crystalline globe laced with hair-fine, dwarven goldwire, and it shattered satisfyingly behind her. Sidhe magic flashed, a breath of apples and a plume of perfumed smoke rising to possibly divert, or maze and pixie-lead, pursuit. If the hounds were overexcited, or if luck was with her, they would chase the breakaway's bouncing until they ran it to ground, by which time she would have a comfortable few lengths' worth of time to find a doorway.

She suspected, even as she put on another burst of speed and her heels clattered, skirt swinging and her hair tangling wildly, that it had not taken.

A false gift the raddled bitch gave me. Or not, but the rider is close and gaining. Gulping heaving breaths, she cast about for a place to make her stand. A rider and hounds—if she brought down the rider, the hounds might well scatter. It would take the song, and she would need her lungs full. He would attack without giving her a chance, if he could, if she was not under Unwinter's Hunt and he was not bound by those ancient codes.

It was possible, she supposed, that he might not know who she was. That he would think her just a nymph gone astray or a mortal-Tainted sidhe of Seelie country on some personal errand. If he recognized her, the rider might well try to silence her before she could assay a rill of notes. A knife or a bolt to the throat would discourage Robin's song most wonderfully, and she dreaded the thought.

Without the song, she was all but helpless.

Why is it this is the only time I am certain I wish to live?

An alley beckoned. There was an entrance-point just beyond, but she couldn't run the risk of the song warping her into Twisting or worse if she tried to step between here and Summer while holding off an Unseelie. He wasn't merely one of the fullborn but Lesser sidhe, he was a highborn fullblood Court lord; he rode silvershod and had the hounds and the blackboil plague; it all added up to Robin Ragged dead before moonrise.

Dead, or Twisted and unable to sing. Or even plagued, if mortal blood no longer was insurance against the illness. Which would be worse?

You know very well what would be worse, Robin. Be canny, now. She nipped smartly into the alley, pounded down its length, and whirled. Set her back against the weeping bricks and focused on her breathing.

No breath, no song. Control the breath, control the song. In, then out, slow. Four counts, Robin. Always four counts, or their close cousins. Four in, four out.

Her ribs heaved. Her heart hammered. Footsteps and hoofbeats, and the hounds belling as they realized their prey was treed, or at least had ceased to rabbit-run.

I do not so much mind dying. I merely hate being hunted. It was a lie. She did very *much* mind death, especially in a filthy mortal alleyway. Robin clutched the wall grimly. Long practice clamped down on her starving lungs and dry throat. She spat, once, twice, braced her shoulders against cold weeping brick, and prepared to sell herself dear when the rider finally appeared.

VENGEANCE ENOUGH
7

⇥╫╾

A flash of bright green, a pattering of glove-soled feet, Good-fellow ran softly along the edge of a rooftop on Colchis Avenue. The Veil momentarily swallowed his lithe leaping; he reappeared across the street without breaking stride. Hurry-ing, hurrying, his ageless heart beating a little more quickly as he heard the huntwhistles trill in the distance. Those piercing cries, both like and unlike the Horn the whistles were copied from, sent shivers of delicious wine-dark anticipation down his back. Not *precisely* fear, because foxing such a hunt was merely an enjoyable evening's sport for one such as he, but oh, the fun. The *interestingness* of it all, a merriment of the type he liked best, with blood and screaming at the end.

Was she clever and swift enough to escape? She should be. She never disappointed. Ever since he had found her bathing in a mortal pond, rising from the water nymph-slim and river-haired, she had warmed him clear through. And oh, what a voice she had! To hear the Ragged sing, and watch the destruc-tion that followed, was always a fine event.

Hoofbeats, chiming against concrete. Riding silvershod, the Veil twisting like seaweed around its bulk, the rider below shot away, after a ghost of cinnamon hair and white arms. Around the elfhorse, the hounds were curls of smoke-vapor, their lamp-lit eyes winking as they vanished and reappeared, eddying in the dark knight's passage.

Not for long, though. As he ran, Puck's brown fingers dipped, and the pipes were in his hand, a familiar weight carrying secret delight. He put on a burst of speed—the knight veered, a sharp turn and plunging into a section of run-down warehouses.

Puck slowed, skipping diagonally across a rooftop and blinking through the Veil once again. What was this? Something else trembled in the air, a different scent than he had expected.

Where is she going? What does my tricky girl have up her sleeve, eh?

So changeful, just like a woman. The sidhe had their own fickleness, but a female was something else. With that voice of hers, dangerous in her own right, too. The Ragged needed careful care and grooming before she would fall from the tree at precisely the right angle, and into the waiting—

The knight veered again, penetrating a tangle of indifferently paved streets. The mortal world decayed far less gracefully than Summer. Unwinter, of course, never decomposed further than its lord's mood would permit. Puck's own realm held thorn-tangles and bogs as well as sunlit glades, except for those areas bordering Unwinter. The Low Counties, the broad part of his kingdom between Summer and Unwinter, were plague-ravaged, but could be rebuilt. A necessary sacrifice, but still one Puck disliked.

Aha. There.

The breakaway glimmered, bouncing happily away. Some few of the hounds bolted after it, doubling back on themselves when the rider, indifferent, plunged after the fleeing girl. Puck's frown deepened, and he quickened his pace. The breakaway should have worked. Why had it not?

Look closer, look again. He tried, but the Unseelie, scenting his prey closer and closer, spurred his beast with silver rowels. Puck blinked, catlike, as he leapt from one roof to another, and skidded to a stop cat-quickly, as well, a-tiptoe and quivering as a plucked string.

Black spots writhed over the knight's armor, and his glow was not the pale fire of Unwinter's Court. Instead, the green tinge was sickening, not an attractive pallor but the corpse beginning to decay in liquid runnels against bleached, worm-eaten bones.

A plagued rider. Strong and quick, and one even the Ragged's voice might have a difficult time dissuading.

He needed the Ragged, but to risk his precious self against a carrier of that sickness...well. Hesitation, one glove-soled foot in empty air, perched on the crumbling edge of a warehouse's tarpapered roof, the entire city wheeling around him as the Veil trembled, responding to his uncertainty. The sickness was virulent. He had cause to know, did he not? The mortal had wrought well.

As Puck hung there, betwixt and between, a new clamor intruded. Hooves lashing, bell-like, against pavement, and a short, sharp cry.

Was it her? All his plans a-tumble, and he would have to dance a different path to his goal.

Cursing inwardly, Puck decided, and plummeted to earth, landing lightly and running silent as a will o'wisp. If the rider had, against all expectation, robbed him of pretty Ragged's fine voice, Goodfellow would play a tune or two on his pipes, and that would be vengeance enough. Plagued or not, they could still die when he breathed across the tubes.

Any sidhe could.

A MORTAL QUOTIENT

8

The bouncer stared over the swinging door, jaw dropping. Jeremiah hit the wooden panels at a run; one smacked solidly against the mortal and sent him flying. Gallow was already past, a fine evening mist just beginning to solidify into rain kissing his sweating face and hands. The scent was sharper to the right, but he jagged left on instinct. A sidhe who could craft a quirpiece could also craft—or barter for—a breakaway, and if the huntwhistles were so close he could hear them through a mortal brawl, it was time for her to use every trick she could beg or borrow, not to mention steal.

He was rewarded with a shadow slipping down the street, a flicker whose flying hair caught a stray red gleam from a streetlamp. She was flagging, stumbling, and that changed the equation somewhat. Perhaps she didn't have the endurance—and running in heels, even if you were sidhe, was probably enough to slow down even the fleetest.

The hunter's whistle came again, to the north, probably over on Colchis Avenue. He marked it and continued, running lightly as he hadn't done for years, skipping every few steps to avoid the crazyquilt of cracks—*break your mother's back,* though his nameless mother was long dead—in the sidewalk and keeping as far as he could to the shadows. The rain would help, and there was no ribbon of scent on the cold, iron-tainted breeze. The breakaway lay glittering on the pavement, sucking in traces of her presence, its other half bouncing merrily away to distract and mislead.

He could still hear hoofbeats plucking at the night; the shadows communicated them over his skin. Silvershod, slender hooves. A rider whose eyes would be cold moonlight, whose laugh would be chill, and whose armor would be chased with sharp, hurtful runes, either blazing with sick white or bloodred.

The hounds commenced belling again, howls and yaps made of sharpsilver ice, and Jeremiah cursed internally.

He could have stopped there. Drawn aside into the shadows and let the hunter pass him by. But the girl had stopped, too, her hair dewed with jewels of rain. She nipped into an alley, her steps slowing.

It was the worst possible choice. Running until your heart gave out was preferable to halting and hoping they would ride past. Sometimes they did find new prey when one proved too quick and determined. Not often, but more often than you could successfully hide.

It was a simple choice. Halt and conceal himself, because he heard the hoofbeats drawing closer and there was a chance the horseman would break through all deception? Or involve himself, again?

The whistle sounded again, savage delight in its trilling. The mortals wouldn't hear it unless they'd already been touched or hooked; they would simply feel a chill.

Mortal-Tainted and sidhe alike would hear, know, understand. And fear.

He was already moving. The alley was raw with the smell

of garbage, greasy crud sliding under his workboots. A good choice to go to ground, perhaps, if she had been eluding one of the Lesser, not one of either Court.

The Lesser, of any allegiance, did not ride silvershod. They had other means, from a kelpie's dragging to a boggle's ghost-cold fingerings.

Gallow halted just inside the alley's mouth. His breath was coming fast but not hard. Not like the woman with her back to the brick wall, fingers spread against it, chin lifted and the skirt of her dress draggled around her knees as if she'd fallen into a puddle. How far had she run tonight?

Pointed chin, high cheekbones, wide-spaced blue eyes. Pale. An aristocratic nose. There was an echo of Daisy, but it was filtered through the hurtful beauty of the sidhe. Her spice-fruit smell carried a tang of iron.

She was mortal-Tainted, quite possibly a full Half. Like him. If she was less than that most salubrious of mixtures, of course a horseman would run her down without even this attempt at escape.

She clutched at the brick wall, her pale hands starfish-spread as if she intended to splinter her fingernails scratching her way through. Ribs flickered under her dress as she panted, and her hair was now weighed down with dampness. The gold hoops dangling from her ears peeped at him, and the first hounds skidded behind him on the street and sent up a racket. The cry of prey cornered filled the night, turned the mist-rain drops to diamonds.

He turned. Groundfog rose in the middle of the street, luminescent fingers sprouting precisely between double yellow lines. The hounds took shape, sliding through Veil into the visible. Fogbodies, reptilian heads on short but flexible necks, and eyes like tilted silver coins. The quirpiece twitched in his palm. He stuffed it in his pocket, and felt the familiar tingle racing up his arms.

Too late to ignore it now. His off-duty jacket—leather, and studded with shiny but false-metal mortal rivets—creaked as his arms moved, the markings on his skin mortals would mistake for tribal tattoos writhing madly. The air hardened between his hands, and his calluses rasped against sudden solidity.

Summoning a dwarven-inked lance was easy. Mastering its hunger was the difficult part, but he'd had the best of teachers, between the former Armormaster's fire-whip and Jeremiah's own innate stubbornness. He had sometimes even left Daisy sleeping in their bed and gone out on moonlit nights to practice, sweating-cold in a flood of sterile light behind their trailer.

Now, like riding a bicycle, the control never went away.

Fog cringed and thickened, birthing more dogbodies. One darted forward, and Jeremiah's body moved without thought, the not-quite-physical weight of the lance leaping of its own volition, playing through the arc that would end in a strike home in insubstantial flesh. The fog-hound cowered back, flushing red for a moment as the leaf-shaped spearhead quivered into being, a metallic fiery gleam flooding back along the shaft until it jolted home in Jeremiah's hands. It finished through the tasseled end, streaming dripping moonglow that vanished before it hit the ground.

"Show yourself." The words burned his throat, hard with command. "Come forth, I bid thee."

A point of brilliance coalesced above the fog, then spread. The smell of rotting apples and salt accompanied it. First came the eyes—green with a silvery overtone, their pupils hourglass-shaped. Then the crown of the high-peaked helm, a narrow head set on broad shoulders. Plate armor, heavy shoulders, chestplate ribboned with moonglow in the shape of a tree that didn't grow on this side of the Veil. Plated thighs, greaves, spurred boots. The horse took shape, too, dappled-gray smoke bearing weight. Silver-eyed, the horse stamped. Its mane ran with greenblack, and that was wrong.

Still, things could change with the greater sidhe sometimes. They just liked to pretend alteration was a mortal quotient.

The lance resolved itself into complete solidity and hummed between his hands. As usual, it felt right. *Too* right. His palms moved, everything coming from the hip, and the lance's end hit the ground in salute. The point jutted an accusing finger at the drizzling rain, hungry moonglow from its tassels threading into the pavement.

The helmed rider simply stared for a few moments. Jeremiah waited. The woman let out a sharp breath, and he could hear her frantic pulse. A bird's wings, fluttering inside an iron cage.

The horseman pointed one long, gauntleted hand, his extended finger one of five opposed by a quadruple-jointed thumb, all too slender and tapering to be anything but inhuman. A highblood wight, one of Unwinter's lords, and he pointed not at Jeremiah but past him. The message was clear.

Move aside, and I will let you be.

Which told him this was no ordinary hunt. He had another chance now, to step aside. Except there was no guarantee. If he had injured the horseman's pride, he might be the next quarry. Within that mailed glove, there was a hand that might not keep its promises.

Seelie or Unseelie, there was always that risk.

"Don't," the girl said breathlessly behind him. "Oh, please *don't.*"

What, *don't get yourself involved*? Or *don't get hurt*? Probably too late for either, but he appreciated the thought.

She looked like Daisy; he wanted at least to hear why she was being chased before consigning her to the huntsman's problematic mercy. That was an acceptable reason to get himself involved, wasn't it?

The horse neighed, a ringing sound, queerly flat, a misshapen crystal wineglass stroked by a rotting finger. *That* was wrong, too. It should have been a crystal bell, tightening every nerve. Spots of greenblack on its mane shifted, spreading.

"What the fu—" He never got to finish, for the horse lunged forward, hooves clattering. The lance jerked, pulling his body behind it; the street chimed as the lance's end braced itself against concrete and its head darkened, the silver-dripping ruddiness changing to a dull gray.

Cold, deadly iron.

His feet were pushed forward, boots skidding. Caught, planted solidly just like the lance's tasseled end, and he recognized the motion, a pikeman's defense against the greater weight of cavalry.

He had been a knight once, too, but the truth of life was you couldn't count on having a horse when you fought. Or anything else. Except the weapon tattooed into your flesh, carried everywhere with you. You couldn't lose a dwarven-inked weapon, no matter how hard you tried.

Even if you wanted to.

Crunch. The horse hit, turned to leprous greenish mist as the iron broke its smoky hold on this side of the Veil. The lance flashed all along its length, and Jeremiah was ready. Knees dropped, body twisting back and to the side as the iron head tangled in the net of glamour and vapor, striking the solid heart—the knot that kept the horse on the mortal side of the sideways realms. The lance-shaft rang, a high, hard sound as it extended and flicked, a lizard's tongue, shearing through half-physical strings.

The horse went down in a thrashing pile of mist and crunching bone. Jeremiah stepped aside, flicking the lance; it popped and black blood flew steaming. He took two quick, almost-skipping steps back, which placed him deeper in the throat of the alley. For better or worse, he'd chosen his ground; if there were any flying units—harpies, or even blackbird *moraghs*—he would be bottled. On the other hand, he could defend here against both flying and foot, Seelie or Unwinter, for a long time. Should he care to do so.

The horseman rose from the mess, his helm smoking with fury now. *Definitely* a highblood wight. Jeremiah set himself, the lance's endcap clicking as if on parade. The girl heaved out a small retching sound behind him.

About . . . now. He wasn't disappointed. The sword rose up, a slender scimitar-shaped sidhe blade with the moon in its metal, and he had plenty of time to strike if he could just *move* quickly enough. Throwing himself sideways, against the brick wall, which cracked like a piece of wet laundry snapped by a pair of capable hands. Adrenaline ran down his nerves and muscles, golden wires pulling a puppet along.

The girl blurted a warning Jeremiah didn't need. He'd already seen the battle in his head, options and choices narrowing to a single unavoidable conclusion.

That was the true gift of the lance, and its best-kept secret. Even the former Armormaster hadn't mentioned its possibility to Jeremiah during the harsh training to bring metal and haft to heel. A weapon such as this did not merely help a man fight. It also showed, as far as it was able, the outcome of a battle.

Where you could see, you could *change*.

Brick dust shook from his jacket as he leaned into the motion, the lance splitting air and smacking aside the downsweep of the horseman's blade. The horseman's strike spent itself uselessly, grinding against the shaft, and the lancepoint punched through plate with an agonized scream, matched with a curlew cry of effort escaping Gallow's lips. The shock grated home, and the blood-tinted satisfaction of performing the movement perfectly turned everything red for a moment before Jeremiah wrenched the blade free. He didn't want to leave the iron in contact with sidhe flesh any longer than he had to.

Instead of merely going to his knees like any other defeated foe, the horseman screamed.

The deathcry pushed Jeremiah back, broken glass tinkling to the ground in sweet cascades through the retreating fog. Cracks and veins of black tore through the armor, as if the sidhe had been stabbed with a mercury blade instead of honest iron. The smell exploded—wet fur and a maggoty reek. Jeremiah skipped back nervously, suddenly aware of the twitching in his muscles. He hadn't fought in a long time.

Not since the week before he'd let himself get truly involved with Daisy, instead of just occasionally passing the diner she worked at, seeing her coppergold head through the window, and feeling his heart wring itself dry.

That shouldn't have killed him! We didn't even exchange names! "Wait—" A hopeless word. There was probably no more useless word in any language. "*Shit!*" Just as useless, but far more gratifying.

The girl let out a sobbing breath. His stomach threatened to reject both mortal beer and peanuts, the smell was *that* bad.

Stranger and stranger.

He whirled, the lance coming up, and eyed her as the fog retreated in thick tendrils. The dogs slunk back, whining as the

Veil claimed them again. He didn't need to worry about them now. One bared its teeth and snapped, halfheartedly, before it shredded into long thin trails of steamsmoke.

The woman stared at him. Her eyes were even bluer now, matching her dress. She still looked like his dead wife, but shock had robbed her of the glare of sidhe over her features. Some would say that glare was *perfected* or *refined*.

He'd call it *false*. A pretty, pretty lie.

He didn't want to talk to her after all. It was just a coincidence, and he'd saddled himself with one more death.

"You're free now." The words were ash against his tongue. "Go in peace."

The lance vibrated in his hands. The last of the dogs' lamp-like eyes winked out, and he was suddenly aware his fingers didn't want to let go. It would be easy to take a single step forward; the point that could strike home through Court-crafted armor of either kind would make short work of her flesh. The light would go out of her eyes, and maybe her body would rot the way the horseman's had.

That thought freed his hands. The marks on his arms hurt, power returning to its home under his skin. He turned on his heel, and saw the oilslick of foulness that was the horseman. The last vestige of fog vanished. Fallen stars of broken glass littered the dark street; sirens howled in the distance. The diffuse roar of city traffic came back.

"Wait!" The girl skipped and scrambled behind him, footsteps clicking. He made a fist, shoving the feeling of the lance away. If he turned around now, she ran a good chance of feeding the weapon's endless hunger.

That was another wrongness. There had been no shock of life ending, torn away and pulled into the lance's thread-thin, eternally thirsting core.

"Go away." He stepped over the stain. Down where he had run from, the streetlamps glowed and ran with the reflection of blue and red—police cars. Ambulances. A fire truck. "Christ."

A shocked inhalation. If she was Court-raised, the mild mortal blasphemy might be a physically painful insult.

He didn't care. He kept going, willing the tingle in his arms down, and set off for the lighted end of the street to find Clyde and Panko.

LEE TO GIVE
9

>╫<

What in the name of Stone and Throne was that?

Her mouth all but hung ajar. Robin clutched at the bricks, fingers cramping and her calves aching. Her sides heaved and burned.

He was just a shadow, tall and broad-shouldered, green eyes alight and his hair black even in the shadows, ruthlessly short. The lance had appeared from nowhere, but he wasn't full sidhe. She'd smelled a tinge of mortal on him even through the burning gunpowder of anger and the reek of blackboil death. The lance was a sidhe trick, a thing of cold moonlight and solid silver except when it dulled to cold iron, which meant he had some mortal blood, and he had killed a plagued Unseelie rider. What manner of man, mortal or sidhe, did that and simply walked away?

Go in peace.

She should. Her teeth would be clicking and clattering had she not clenched her jaw tightly enough to shatter them. Her breath had finally returned, and with it the mortal discomfort of cold and damp faded.

The slippery, loose fearfulness of having just narrowly escaped death at the needle-teeth of possibly plagued Unseelie hounds, however, would not disappear so quickly.

She collected herself as well as she could, smoothing her hair back, her gasps evening out as a measure of calm returned. Her heart hummed in her wrists and throat. She examined her arms and legs as well as she could in the dim light, and found no trace of plague. No rash, no black stipples. Pale, smooth, unmarked, uncontaminated. Her skirt dropped back below her knees with a sweet low sound, draggled with water and spattered with less-wholesome things but still intact.

Just like her skin. Still healthy.

Harsh breath caught in her throat. Robin stared at where he'd stood. Appearing out of nowhere, like a glamour sung into being by a Loremaster, an illustration of a courtsong or a riddling tale. Disappearing just as quickly, his boots smacking heavily on the pavement, as if he did not know the lightfoot, and his voice a harsh growl.

Go away. Christ.

She edged for the mouth of the alley. The sidhe rider was gone, only a stain on the concrete marking his untimely passing. It reeked of rotting fur and spoiled fruit, maggots squirming, and she held her breath until she was past. She flitted across the street, drifting from shadow to shadow as her rescuer clumped inelegantly back toward the tavern and the bright flashing lights. Mortals swarmed like disturbed bees, and she reached the safety of the dimness on the opposite side of the vibrating stain of bloodspill and death.

She paused, irresolute, on the sidewalk. Her trail was well and truly broken now. It wasn't necessary for her to go back *quite* yet. She could very well salt this tale with a little more flash and bring it to Court, with the information that a green-eyed warrior breathed in the mortal world who could face a high Court Unseelie rider boiling with the plague and slay him—not as effortlessly as the Queen plucking an apple from a branch or bespelling a witless mortal man, but still. News of one who could stand against the plagued would be worth something, wouldn't it, even if she had failed to bring back what Summer sent her for?

You're lying even to yourself, Robin. You're curious.

More than curious. There was a plan, hovering in the back of her nimble brain. A way to free herself, and possibly Sean, from those graceful, clutching six-fingered hands, perfumed with mortal desperation and the sweetness of apple-immortality.

For Summer was eternal. Or so it was held, in the Seelie realm.

A small clicking sound made her start. Robin whirled, and the humpbacked shape in the shadows rattled a dark leather cup at her. Dice clicked like bones inside, and her mouth went dry.

"Hullo, my dearie," Puck Goodfellow murmured. He stood, easily, shedding the layers of shadow and glamour. "It appears you need no rescue from the hounds. How interesting."

Robin's fists clenched. Her heart had almost started out through her throat. "Puck!" More sharply than she intended to, her tone high and chill; the brown-haired youth eyed her warily. He wore leather, from softshod feet to leggings and laced jerkin, his bare arms moving with supple muscle under barkbrown skin. The leaf-bladed dagger at his hip glinted dully, and if the light had been better, she would have seen his hourglass pupils and the high points of his ears.

Goodfellow did not dress much to match mortals, if at all. If he wore a glamour, it was only to approach his prey more easily.

Robin backed up, two short, nervous steps, and regarded him.

"I was seeking you, to bring you a gift." He spread his narrow, capable hands, keeping them well away from both dagger and the pipes hanging from his belt. "It occurred to me you might be followed, so when the whistles came I followed. Mayhap I would have done you a good turn."

Mayhap you set the dogs on me yourself. I wouldn't put it past any free sidhe, and you least of all. "You're far from home, Goodfellow." She was damp, she realized, with fear-sweat and poisonous, mortal acid rain. Or maybe it was the plague, settling against her skin. "And what you carry is Summer's, not a gift you have lee to give. She will be glad of its return." She resisted the urge to check her arms again. Tainted, Half or below, didn't take the plague.

At least, they hadn't yet. There had been gossip about Ilara Feathersalt, shutting herself up in a faraway bog because she saw a spot or two, even though she had a mortal great-great-however-many grandmother. Or maybe that was merely rumor, and she left Court because Summer had finally tired of Ilara's beauty being compared to hers—or vice versa.

Robin had herself glimpsed Ilara's gray-veiled slenderness stepping into a pumpkin-shaped carriage drawn by flame-manes one early, misty morn behind the Eldar Circle's looming white stones. No trembling, and no breath of foulness had marred the lady's form, but her exit had caused a buzz throughout the Court.

Goodfellow's small laugh was another dry, bony sound. He tossed a small black silken bag; her hand flashed out and caught it. The glass ampoules inside clicked together; she examined them. Each one was sealed with colorless wax, containing a thick fluid that sparkled like firefly pixies. She muttered a chantment to rob them of the noise of clinking together and tucked them in her left-hand skirt pocket. There was time enough to shift them later, and she finally raised her gaze to Goodfellow's. "I shall tell her of your aid. She will no doubt ask its price."

The Fatherless grinned, sharp white teeth gleaming. "Oh, my Ragged, perhaps I am curious, curious sidhe. Perhaps I know who your dark knight-errant is, as well. What would you pay for his name and a warning?" The free sidhe grinned even wider, his irises firing in the gloom, a glow no mortal would see unless they were near to shuffling off their living coil. "Or will you hurry along now that you have your little baubles for Her Majesty?"

Baubles. As if he doesn't know what's in these. Robin folded her arms defensively. "I don't think you have anything of value. I might even suspect you of setting the Unseelie on me; isn't that a free sidhe's favorite pastime?"

His face fell. The gleams of his eyes filled with more dangerous sparkling, though, a foxfire that a mortal might be led by. "You wound me, darling Robin. We share a name or two, and I was your guardian into Summer. You should be more charitable."

His right-hand fingers now played with the leather-wrapped daggerhilt. Robin kept those extra-jointed fingers in sight, and backed up still more. Her earrings warmed slightly, the golden hoops brushing her cheeks. "I *am* charitable, free sidhe. I'm not singing." She edged out into the street.

No, the Ragged could guess why Ilara had left, and kept the knowledge close in case it should be useful later. The Feathersalt's lover Braghn Moran, tall and fair-haired, had been ensnared by Summer herself, and was now wasting away for want of the Queen's affection. Summer had taken another into her favor, fickle as always, and perhaps Ilara disliked to see the wreck of her former paramour. And Sean, poor Sean…

Her throat threatened to close. *Pay attention, Robin.* Now she *had* to step over the border into Summer soon, or Goodfellow would carry tales. If he did and someone listened, Robin might be trapped at Court until the Queen decided to send her on another thankless mission.

The next one might not end so well.

"His name is Gallow." Goodfellow leaned back against the wall, hooking his thumbs in the woven-leather belt. A show of disdain or relaxation, or both. "He has not been moved to take an interest in a sidhe in many a long year. I wonder why he did so for you, my dove?"

Gallow? What an ill-starred name. "Perhaps he thought the rider was hunting him." It was pale, inadequate, and as a parrying blow, very much not up to her usual standards.

Goodfellow regarded her narrowly. His expression softened, just a fraction. "You are shaken, and white as milk. Come, I know a place you may gather yourself, and—"

And place me under an obligation? I think not, mischievous one. "No, though your kindness is more than I deserve." A pretty, empty phrase to match his own. *Gallow, Gallow... Have I heard that name? Not that I can recall.*

"Robin." He sounded serious now, his even, light tenor tinted brown as bark. "I mean you no harm." The tone dropped, became intimate. "I have never meant thee harm."

Ever since she had surfaced from the pond and seen him crouching near her clothes, regarding her with bright interest, he had been in the habit of making such comments. There was a time she had been mortal-stupid, and thought perhaps he meant them—but caution had been ingrained in her even then.

Male meant *danger.* Any girl raised in the trailer parks absorbed that warning early and well.

"Oh, certainly not." The sarcasm dripping from her words

could have turned the slow drizzling rain to ice. She retreated even further, but he made no move. "Would you have taken my sister to Summer, too, had I begged thee harder?"

His face closed like a door. "Mortal is as mortal does. She was lucky to be left in this pale realm. Tell me, how is your changeling friend? Still warming the Queen's bed, and yours still cold?"

It actually hurt below her breastbone, the dart striking true and a bite of disgust that he would think her so crass as to use a mortal child so. Still, she had not survived Court by allowing her face to show every wounding word.

"Warm enough, Robin Goodfellow," she heard herself say. "Warm *and* wide enough, but *you'll* never know."

With that, she fled. She did not aim for the entry point so near to this alley. Let the free sidhe carry all the tales he would. Robin Ragged had decided, between one breath and the next, to have further words with this green-eyed Gallow.

TERRITORY TO BE GAINED
10

⟫╫⟨

Summer exhaled sleepily, under an indigo canopy gemmed with strengthening stars. A white tower rose, its sides pierced with slender windows, and in one, a golden gleam trembled. Silver lute strings plucked by soft ageless fingers, their nails faintly blushed with the pink of a tender rose's heart, and amid the quiet music, a mortal breathing.

He sat on the nacreous marble floor below the window, her cascading green mantle almost swallowing him whole. The heart of Summer essayed a lazy rill of music, one bare white foot peeping from underneath a mantle's fold. The loveseat was of frayed red velvet, but you could not see the bloody fabric under the green. The Jewel on her forehead flashed, once, as the balance tipped, evening into night. The flower-carven walls, glowing softly, bathed the entire host in spectral light, moonglow captured by the tower's top and slowly released when Summer willed it. Low couches covered in velvet and watered silk held those few honored enough to attend, and sigh-wrought draperies wrapped each wall and sconce, not to mention the shell-glowing lamps and the couch legs, in cobweb-fine mist.

She played, the Queen of all she surveyed, and looked out upon the night. Those high in favor at the moment amused themselves in their own quiet fashion, the highbloods feigning interest in books or each other, soft whispers traded behind slim, cruelly beautiful hands or fans made of multicolored gossamer wings and tiny bleached bones. The ladies-in-waiting, their skirts spread according to arcane etiquette, alert to each small change of Summer's expression, draped themselves in languid poses. Braghn Moran, Ilara Feathersalt's erstwhile paramour, held a moonwrought chalice while a masked brughnie squeezed freshly picked cloister-grapes in her knotted, bark-brown fists, the feathers on her mask quivering. Chantment dropped from Braghn's lips, turning the stream of amber fluid into thick honeyspice mead.

Summer's other favorite, a lean, black-masked rogue rumored to be Arcad Shallowdraft, held a gold-trimmed tome weighing as much as a kelpie. He did not bother to pretend to peruse its fantastically colored pages, choosing instead to study the mortal boy crouched in the folds of Summer's mantle. The eyeslits of the sidhe's beaked mask showed hot crimson sparks, and some of the ladies-in-waiting tittered among themselves. Imagine, to show jealousy of a mortal so openly! Especially a mortal tainted by association with that Half girl, the russet-haired one Summer sent hither and yon.

But it pleased Summer to let it continue, and when she set the lute aside to invite the golden-haired boy onto her seat, the rogue had the grace to look away. Soon his identity would be revealed, and a delicious play would have been wrought, and they would politely applaud.

For now, Summer smoothed the mortal boy's hair while he gazed adoringly at her. "Little Sean," she cooed. "And how is my little sprite, my little joy?"

"Your Majesty..." The boy stumbled over the words, blushing. So charming, when the mortals flushed with their hot salt-sweet blood. A changeling held his place in the mortal world, and would until Summer tired of him. It was inevitable.

"Oh, little sprite." Pearl-white, sharp teeth flashed between her carmine lips. "Speak again."

His tumbled curls parted under her snowy fingers, and he shuddered like a pony under the brush. A hush fell—even among the sidhe, silence sometimes falls at once on a gathering. Mortals called it *a god passes among us,* but the sidhe have a word for it—one mortals cannot hear, even when spoken.

The high, sweet music of a mortal child's voice broke it, clear as crystal. "When is Robin-mama coming back?"

Silence deepened, as every sidhe in attendance tensed, waiting to see what Summer would make of this.

She laughed carelessly, but a darkness passed briefly over that ageless-beautiful face. Pinpricks of light in her black, black eyes winked out, something moving in the depths of her gaze. "Oh, she is on an errand, flapping her ragged wings." Summer exhaled a sweet-drugging breath over the child's head. "She's quite forgotten about *you,* little one."

The boy's face slackened, drooping, but he brightened when Summer toyed with his hair afresh. It was so easy to divert the mortal mayflies, and so pleasant. If this one was returned to the mortal realm he would lead a shadow-life, longing for the Court he would remember only in dreams; when the changeling who held his place was brought home and fêted, its sojourn and celebration would end among the Queen's apple trees, or in some corner of the sideways realms not yet Summer. The blood would flow hot, loosed by the flint knife only a queen could wield, and wherever it sprinkled would be forever under her sway.

Each mortal pet was, in the end, only territory to be gained.

Soon the child was gamboling merrily among the ladies-in-waiting, who petted and cosseted him under the Queen's gaze. The rogue drew close, whispering in Summer's ear as she drank from a moonwrought chalice, and if her laughter rang a little harshly, none dared to remark upon it.

Quite a few of the assembled sidhe smiled cruelly at the thought of Ragged Robin's return, even as they fed the boy ambrosial bits and crowned him with glossy chantment-wrought laurel.

SHADOWCOIN

11

>|||<

Four ambulances. Cops everywhere sorting out the mess. Broken car windows and other detritus crunched underfoot. One car was a fuming hulk, firefighters still dousing it with foam or fog or something. Jeremiah watched, the marks on his arms tingling as the lance, unsatisfied, ached for release.

There were bodybags. Three of them loaded into coroners' vans. The quirpiece had done its work well, and a crowded bar on a Friday night was never too difficult to tip into chaos. Lowered inhibitions, petty pride, and rough words were fertile ground for any seed of mischief.

He stepped back into shadow, his skin alive with twitching adrenaline. His truck was at the other end of the parking lot; Panko's ancient Volkswagen van listed slightly to the right half a block up the street. He couldn't see Clyde's motorcycle; a fire engine was blocking the view.

He searched for Panko's familiar wide broad bulk, or Clyde's muttonchops and baseball cap. Nothing yet. The quirpiece was a cold weight in his pocket. By morning it would be crumbling mud, or leaf sludge. Of all the uses such a sidhe chantment could be put to, this was one of his least favorite.

It was amazing to watch human beings cooperate in the face

of disaster. Sidhe response would be...otherwise. The humans, they swarmed to comfort one another and repair the damage. Someone wept in huge messy gulps, while someone else made soothing sounds.

He kept looking, unwilling to leave his vantage point until he saw a familiar face. Maybe it was his mortal half forcing him to tarry. Maybe it was the traitorous ache in muscles he hadn't used in a while—construction kept you in shape, but combat was another thing entirely.

Clyde, his head wrapped in a white bandage, stood stolidly at the edge of a knot of people corralled in a corner of the parking lot away from the action—the lightly wounded section. His hands hung loose at his sides, and his bald spot glowed under the assault of light, circled by white gauze.

Jeremiah eased forward. There was no crowd of onlookers; the Wagon Wheel was at the end of a street packed with warehouses, well after quitting time. Everyone who was likely to gawp had been involved. Nobody even looked at him.

Except Clyde, who glanced up dully. "Gallow." He blinked, and his face settled back into sullen shock.

"Clyde. Jesus. Panko?"

The foreman pointed at the coroner's van.

"No." Jeremiah didn't have to work to sound shocked. "What the hell?"

"Someone had a knife. Where'd you go?"

"Ended up outside." Just like a sidhe—lie with the truth. "I thought, that girl..."

"What girl?" Clyde scratched at his cheek gingerly. His gaze was very far away. Maybe shock, or just too exhausted to respond. A stripe of drying blood on his cheek smudged as he rubbed at it with his knuckles. His hand dropped back down again, a limp, callused fish. "Cops took my name. Fuck."

"You didn't do anything." Fat lot of good it would do, though. The truth never shielded anyone. Not in this world, certainly never in Summer or Unwinter...and, he'd bet, not even beyond the Second Veil itself, in those realms even the fullborn feared to tread.

"Yeah, well." Clyde shook his head. "One minute, everything's fine. The next, Jesus. All hell breaks loose."

He would probably be repeating that for a while. A mortal trick, seeking acceptance through repetition. Just like pacing outside a hospital room, wearing a rut in the linoleum as your wife tried to breathe with the aid of mortal machines, her fragile body shattered by mischance.

Jeremiah shut his mouth. Stood close enough to feel the other man's heat. Death smelled like brass, and tasted of the bitterness in his throat now.

Just like a sidhe to spread this chaos. She'd been trying to escape, but...

Had she even thought of the trouble a quirpiece would spread in a human hole, with alcohol lowering inhibitions and—

That's not the real point, Jeremiah. He winced as his conscience pinched him. He had probably led the rider right to her, and wasted the lives she hadn't even thought about ruining. That was the trouble with being tainted by the Fair Folk, the Strangers, the Gentle Ones.

You could never be innocent.

"Jesus Christ," Clyde kept repeating, rubbing at his face.

Jeremiah agreed completely.

>≒H≒<

One in the morning, the entire trailer park still and quiet. Porch lights burned, and the serious domestic disturbances had either finished over dinner or wouldn't get under way for another hour or so. He eased his truck down a long shallow grade and back up, going slow out of habit. Their trailer—only his now, since Daisy was gone—was at the top of another slight rise, the very last on a loop of crazycracked concrete. The garden she'd worked so hard over was a shambles, vines clutching at the fence he'd cobbled together, weeds thriving.

The Garnier place next door was dark. Melody had thrown Paul out a week ago, and the man was probably still on a bender somewhere. He'd be crawling back after the weekend, repentant and filthy. In the meantime, it was quiet, and the Garnier kids were probably enjoying it that way. On the other side, Mama Loth's ancient cave of a trailer listed, looking like the next good wind would blow it away.

The old lady wasn't sidhe, but she wasn't quite mortal, either. The world was more crowded than mortals ever dreamed, even if they spun themselves stories out of hints and moonlight. If the religious or the door-to-door salesmen came through the park, they often avoided Loth's home. Those who didn't had a certain hard gleam in their gazes, a certain aggressiveness in their stride—but after they mounted her steps and knocked at her rickety screen door, there was no more trouble from them.

Ever.

Loth's sagging rocker on the gap-boarded porch moved a little, pushed by the unsettled breeze. Behind them, the field sloped down to a stand of trashwood, and there was even a grove of pale young beeches behind the scruffy bushes. The field was reasonably level and studded with refuse, but he hadn't stepped out to practice in a long time.

Tonight might change that, though. The urge to hurt something, even just empty air, itched under his skin.

The truck rumbled into its oil-spotted parking space under the listing carport Daisy had laughingly called "the arbor."

She'd planted climbing roses, and coaxed them up the supports...but they were dead now, brown leaves and thorns reaching their bony knotted fingers for the roof.

He twisted the key, drew it loose. The engine shut itself off.

The cops hadn't asked him a single question, assuming he'd already been spoken to. Clyde thought he'd been swept outside in the chaos of the fight. Panko's van still crouched back near the Wagon Wheel; there was nobody to come pick it up. At least, not unless the cops could find someone who cared. Panko's neurotic wife was never going to be mocked for fearing the cellar ever again.

Monday morning at the jobsite was going to be awkward at best. Should he dislike himself for dreading the disruption of the routine, inevitable questions, mortal curiosity hemming him in?

Jeremiah scrubbed at his face, thin skin moving over bone. Stubble scraped his fingers. Daisy would have been frantic with worry at his lateness, standing in the door outlined in golden light, her hair a mess of ruddygold curls because she would have been pushing her hands back through it and—

Stop it. He opened his left fist. The quirpiece glinted; he walked it over his knuckles like a gambler's shadowcoin, felt the sardonic scowl twisting his mouth down. The truck's engine popped and pinged, metal cooling.

The lance's marks itched. Restless and unsatisfied.

"She looked like Daisy." His own voice startled him. When he looked up again, the truck's windows were fogged. How long had he been sitting here, staring at the gleam of the quirpiece, flipping over his knuckles one by one, his hand moving without any real direction on his part? Round and silver, its surface brushed with faint scratches, it caught a stray gleam from the porch lights.

He should have left it in the bar. In the morning it would be a dead leaf, or moss. He would likely never see the redheaded sidhe again. Gone like a whisper, gone like the wind.

Jeremiah opened the truck door, climbed out. Stamped up his porch stairs. He still remembered Daisy bringing him cold beer while he measured and sawed and hammered, and her delight when he'd finished. You'd've thought he'd built her a palace.

"I would've," he muttered as he twisted the knob. It was never locked. Without Daisy here, there was no reason. He couldn't have cared less if someone stole anything inside; her few bits of jewelry were under a chantment and safe enough. "If she'd wanted one."

The living room looked like a tornado had hit it. Clothes, fast-food wrappers, the television with its big blank hole in the screen—his fist still smarted a little, remembering that night. It had made him stop bringing hard liquor home.

A low glow came from the kitchen—they always left that light under the cupboards on, since Daisy was so frightened of the dark. He never turned it off now; it was the only thing that greeted him. The whole place smelled dusty, sour, like nobody in here breathed the air.

Like an open grave.

He slapped the quirpiece down on the counter next to a stack of plates slowly congealing together. He'd long since stopped washing them, only occasionally rinsing off a spoon if he needed it.

The fridge was bare and white inside. Not even a bottle of beer. He'd found out the milk was turned this morning, and revulsion crested inside him again as he thought of it.

Milk turned. Means the sidhe've been around. Or just that I left it in there for a month.

He swung the fridge door closed. Stood in the half-dark, emptiness pressing against him from every side. It was a struggle not to find something to break before he trudged back to the bedroom, his shoulders aching and the rest of him shaking with tired rage.

FOR THAT WHICH MATTERS
12

⟩╫⟨

She spread her fingers against the skinny, age-blackened door. A slight tingle against her palm told her he was home, and she pushed just a little. The wood flexed, trembling, and she stepped through it like the curtain of *seeing* it was.

"*Stone!* What are you doing here?" He looked stretched, with a wight's long fingers and lean hungry face; no matter how much he ate, Parsifleur Pidge would never fatten. His skin was old bark, complete with moss in the crags, and his hole was dank and stuffed with odds and ends.

"I wish to leave an item in your care." Robin didn't dare give him more. Confusion would help her here.

She dug in her pocket, ignoring Parsifleur's cry of dismay.

The glass ampoules were there, a quick sparkle against her fingers. The amber fluid inside them coruscated, and she glanced at the Twisted woodwight, who was rubbing his twig-like hands together. Outside his hole, there was a rumble—the subway, a giant dozing worm-beast who occasionally dreamed.

Parsifleur's blue-sheened eyes were wide and wet, and the bright rags hanging on his wasted frame quivered. It could be that her visit made him concerned.

Or it could be something else.

"You may cripple over the border and take these to Summer Herself for a reward, Pars." The smile skinning her lips back wasn't nice, but it was certainly gleeful. "Aren't you happy about that?"

"Don't want to. Don't want you here. Go *away*." He was actually *wringing his hands,* and Robin's skin rippled into gooseflesh.

She did not feel the cold, much—no Half did short of deep-ice or a steppe's keening, once they had breached Summer or Unwinter's borders or discovered the warming breath. So it was something else, and Robin stilled. The music under her thoughts did not dim, but it took on a sonorous quality she did not quite like. While she watched Parsifleur's uneasy fidgets, the feeling grew worse.

"Please," the Twisted sidhe half moaned. "*Don't* stay. Always trouble following on your wings, and warrior I am not."

"I return so often because you're trustworthy, Pidgins." *But you may not be.* "Keep this for me, and it shall be good night, Stone bless, and good riddance."

"I'll not!" His skin creaked, moss shivering free as he lunged. He spread himself against the door, skinny arms wide and thin legs braced. "Go. Flee. Not this way. *Other* way."

Right into the arms of whoever visited thee before me, Parsifleur? She shook her head, a single curl falling in her face and tossed away by the motion. The small package burned against her fingers. "Now, why would I wish to go into the dark, Pidgie?"

For the *other* road from his hole was into the subway's maze. The cold iron there was perhaps why he had twisted as he had, but she did not care enough to barter for such information. It was enough that he couldn't use chantment against her, being

Twisted, and besides, she often brought him bits of living oak to ease the pain of crippling.

He *owed* her.

"Please!" The water swelling in his eyes might be a clever ploy, but who could tell? "They must have scented you. They'll come back—go, *go*!"

Come back? Does he mean Unwinter's kin came visiting? Later she would think she should not have hesitated, her mouth opening slightly and the song blooming deep below her throat. It came from a place other than breath and biting, past tasting and swallow. Parsifleur must have seen it on her face, for he cowered against the door of his bolthole...

...so his was the life they took when their curved, silver-chased flintblades pierced the veil of seeming and found flesh.

Robin stumbled back over piles of oddments, her heels sinking in and her ankle threatening to twist before she saved herself with a fishlike sideways jump. Parsifleur hung against his illusion-shell door, the light in his wet eyes dimming as his mouth worked weakly, and the song burst from her throat full-born.

They were cold pale barrow-wights, not bark-skinned *or* Twisted as poor Pidge had become, their eyes alight with Unwinter's will and their grasping fingers clasped about hilts chased with moon-gems. It made no difference, for the key shifted and Robin's song dropped a full octave, becoming a river of sharp-edged sunshine that blasted the illusion-door and the solid concrete wall on either side with considerable force. There was a rumble, a high keening, and twisted steam-threaded bodies flopped as Robin inhaled, backing up still further in a quick, light-clattering shuffle. Here, with enough breath and a means of escape to hand, she was slightly more sanguine about her chances.

Still, such a broad spread of the song's force would not last long. Robin was no warrior. Fleeing was always better, using the song to distract or stun so she could escape.

And yet.

Orange-veined and smoking, the ruin of Parsifleur Pidge crumbled to the floor of his hole, and she spared another few counts of precious breath to sweep through his remains and make certain. The song crackled, full of the hot sough of a forest fire's breathing under the organ notes. It was all she could do, burning the wood-spirit that remained, however twisted by the cold iron that had been driven through his ley, so that he could not be taken by Unwinter and forced to serve as part of the Hunt.

Or worse, the Sluagh's ghostly cavalcade.

Then she had to breathe again, sucking in smoke-laden air and conscious of the rumbling silence that was full of little hisses and twitches as the wights found they were not quite torn from living's embrace just yet.

Not until she could gather more air, and bring more killing sunshine into this dark hole.

"*Ragged,*" one of them snarled in the darkness. "*He wantsssssss you.*"

No need to ask who. Only Unwinter would send barrow-wights. *He'll have to catch me first.*

She did not say it. *Save the breath for that which matters,* the first lesson she learned in Summer's beautiful, treacherous Court. Now her lungs were full, and her shoulders hit the weeping concrete wall next to the back door. If she killed now, any reinforcements arriving later would have trouble tracking her over cold iron, and she could use her own quirpiece's echoing to find the trail of the knight who had saved her earlier. All things should be so simple for the one who had crafted it, and she, unlike most sidhe, did not have to worry about the chantment fading with dawn's cold rise.

Later, though. First, the Ragged Robin had to survive.

They came for her, their eyes lunar sparkles in the cold dimness, and Robin's back, scraping against the wall, ran with prickles and danger, again. The sensation was useless, so she discarded it and opened her mouth completely, letting her throat relax and the music swell out. As long as she was breathing, they would not catch her here.

The hot salt water on her cheeks was a weakness, and she denied it, even as she sang Parsifleur's assassins into dissolution. All but one, and that one was her own self, scrambling through the escape-tunnel on hands and knees, hoping the wights were the only pursuers she would face tonight.

It does not matter, Robin. Run now, and pray for absolution later.

There was no absolution to be had, but Robin ran.

A REVERSAL OF ANGER
13

⫯⫯

Morning sun striped his face. He kept forgetting to close the blinds. Jeremiah Gallow woke flung on his back, a chill running through his bones and the sudden sense that he wasn't alone filling his head with tingling danger-heat.

He sat up in one motion, the lance sending jabbing warnings up his arms. The bedroom was deserted, as always, but there was...

He sniffed, cautiously. Recognized the salt and crisp goodness.

Bacon? And a woman's voice, speaking softly. A crackling.

Jeremiah shut his eyes. Rubbed at his face again. He didn't dare to think her name.

He stepped blindly into his boots, stood up from the frowsy bed and its yellowed sheets, moved down the short hall floored with cheap nylon carpet. Daisy's sewing room opened off to the side; she'd sometimes talked about what would happen if she caught pregnant. They would turn the sewing room into a nursery, blue for a boy or pink for a girl. He would train the child to be free sidhe—though he never told his wife so—and she would quit her job at the restaurant; he'd go for management so she could stay home or just simply glamour what they needed. He might even tell her, after a while, what he was.

The living room was full of sunlight, too. The French door to the back was wide open, the clawed and broken screen pulled to. The smell of a hot griddle rode the golden air.

The living room was still a mess of trash bags and dirty clothes, but she was down on her knees, the blue dress pooling on harsh orange-patterned nylon. Slim, delicate fingers patted at the hole in the television's face, and her hair was a glory of reddish curls. Her soft speech sharpened a little; cracks and slivers of glass eased together seamlessly.

It was no mortal tongue. Pure sidhe, the Old Language falling from her mouth like rain. Chantment.

Other glass slivers hopped up, melding themselves into the hole. It shrank, a reversal of anger, and she kept patting as if the television were a small shivering animal needing to be soothed. Her shoulders were pale flawless cream, and the coffeemaker clicked on in the kitchen. It began to gurgle and sigh, providing a counterpoint to her soft melody.

His mouth was dry.

The last sliver of glass hopped obediently from under the couch. How had it gotten *there,* of all places? It whooshed across the room like a dart, and she smoothed it in. Then she ran her palms down the huge, ancient television's curved face, stroking. The almost-smoky fragrance of sidhe magic blended with the sudden good smell of coffee and the outright-luscious reek of bacon, and the glass screen flickered once. A moonlit flash, and she peeled her hands away with a half-pained flick of those long, pretty fingers. Unpainted nails, soft skin, and as she glanced toward the kitchen those reddish curls bounced and slid.

She rose, and the blue dress fell. Barefoot, her calves shaped like a dancer's. Muscle moved smoothly under that satin skin as she reached the kitchen, and Jeremiah made a sound deep in his throat.

He couldn't help himself.

"You're up." A husky contralto, not Daisy's sweet cracked soprano. The coffeemaker gurgled afresh, in counterpoint. "I thought you'd sleep later. But the salt pork must have called you."

He picked his way across the living room. She moved in the kitchen, and there was a hiss of something hitting the griddle. Dishes dried on a rack next to the sink, and the stove was scrubbed gleaming-clean, as if Daisy had just stepped away.

The sidhe—she *had* to be mortal-Tainted, like Jeremiah himself—picked up Daisy's plastic turner, the exact one she always used for pancakes. Her slim shoulders were stiff, as if she expected him to shout. Her free hand, resting on the pale blue counter, curled into a half-fist.

He found words, finally. "Who. The hell."

"Robin." She half-glanced over her shoulder. A slice of pale perfect cheek, a glimpse of her aristocratic nose. A dimple, just as quickly lost as she turned back to the griddle. It was a huge, balky electrical thing, easily older than Daisy. "Robin Ragged, if you're feeling formal."

The kitchen window let in a hot bar of spring sunshine. It burnished her naked shoulder, and Jeremiah's throat was dry as the Mojave. In this light, no mortal-Tainted glamour would hold up completely. He would see her face when she turned to him. Leaden, he waited.

"I thought this was the least I could do." She flipped the pancakes expertly. Reached up and opened the cupboard for a flowered plate. She'd washed dishes, too; not a single dirty one remained. The coffeemaker kept gurgling. "He almost had me, last night. I owe—"

"There is no debt." The words bolted free. "I was equally at risk." Now *there* was a lie, and it stung his lips.

"Nevertheless." Now she sounded amused. "I didn't bring sugarpowder, but there's syrup. You had no buttermilk."

I had no milk at all, and no bread either. No salt. There's iron buried under my doorstep. "You're at least Half. You *have* to be. Why were you running?"

Her shoulders came up slightly. She piled the pancakes on the plate, turned away to pick up a fork, and spun on her bare heel to face him. Her skirt moved with a low, sweet sound, and her face...

No. She wasn't Daisy. Still, there was the same nose, and the chin. The beautiful cheekbones. No fading, no intimation of mortal death or sagging on her. "Tainted, but straight Half. I'm under commission, and I...My talents are not like yours."

"What, you're Twisted?" Yet there was no twisting on her. A reflexive insult, to keep her at arm's length. "What was wrong with that knight? We didn't even exchange names. And he was—"

"Rotting with blackboil. Yes. This won't stay hot forever." She all but shoved the plate into his hands, and he took it numbly. "He was *plagued*. How do you take your coffee? Black?"

He took it with milk, like any self-respecting sidhe. But he merely nodded and retreated. The table had been cleared, papers stacked haphazardly at one end. One of the good blue linen placemats sat there; a sparkling jelly glass held a few weedflowers from the field behind the trailer. She must have dug in a drawer for that placemat, and the sudden fury that shook him made the marks itch on his arms, all the way up to his aching shoulders.

Plagued. But sidhe don't take ill. Not like that, anyway. There's poison, and the iron-burn, but neither looks like that.

She busied herself in the kitchen, making little sounds but no longer humming. He stared at the steaming pancakes. Perfectly golden, perfectly round. A ceramic dish Daisy had used as an ashtray held pats of butter, each individually wrapped and probably stolen from a restaurant. The blue ceramic was scrubbed clean, no trace of cigarette remaining.

Robin Ragged. Not a bad name, but not one he'd ever heard of either, and probably not her *entire* name. He hadn't given his, either. Well, he wasn't taking a debt; he didn't have to give even a use-name.

She tripped blithely around the end of the breakfast bar with a smaller plate. A mound of crispy bacon tangled like tentacles. She set down a coffee mug as well, one he hadn't seen since the morning after the accident, when he'd filled it with milk and sat, stunned. In this very chair, as a matter of fact. "There. Do you want a glass of milk? I brought orange juice, too."

"How did you…" Yet he knew how she'd made it over his doorstep. The quirpiece. He glanced instinctively at the counter, to see if she'd left the leaf or stone it had been made from, and his breath caught in his throat.

She followed his glance. The quirpiece sat, glowing-mellow, still silver. Still *real*.

"I have some small skill as a Realmaker." Now her bright cheerfulness faltered. Her eyes darkened to indigo now, the irises flooding with dusk. "It makes me…valuable."

She said it like it meant *dangerous*. It probably did. The halfbreeds who showed promise as Realmakers were customarily snapped up by both Courts before their third birthdays, changelings sometimes left temporarily in return, except the

Realmaker children weren't returned, and their placeholders not sacrificed in the usual way but buried alive.

So how did this girl know how to cook mortal food? Bannock and apples would have been more a Court-raised Realmaker's forte.

"I wasn't taken until I was twelve, and I...have no shadow." A pretty way of saying there wasn't a changeling buried in an oaken cask somewhere in Summer, quietly moldering. Her face set itself, a shade less lovely in that moment. "Anyway, I'm under commission now. Summer may possibly be grateful for your aid, and she'll reward you. If you want it." A quick nervous flicker of her tongue as she wet her lips. "I'd caution you, though. Court isn't safe nowadays."

Of course, she wouldn't refer to Summer by her formal name, even with the *Queen* before. Only a fullblood would do such a thing. And Court, safe? A bubbling chuckle rose up like acid in him. "It never was." He stabbed at the pancakes. They didn't turn into anything else, so he cut a bite loose, lifted it cautiously to his mouth.

"No butter?" She sounded disappointed.

Belatedly, he realized how rude he was. It wasn't like he cared. Still... "Bring a butter knife. And have some as well."

She examined him for a long moment, weighing. Of course, if she was Court she would be looking for the hook in the words. It was a hard habit to break.

A habit he had never broken. Except with Daisy, and even then not completely.

I'm used to men keeping things close, Jer. Said very softly in the dark haven of their bed. *It's all right.*

Had he been stupid to believe her?

"I'll have some milk," the sidhe-girl said, finally. "And make you more." With that, Robin Ragged turned with that quick birdlike grace, her skirt whispering again, and hopped into the kitchen as if something chased her.

Was it just his imagination? Was it just her coloring making him think of Daisy? Reddish hair wasn't *that* uncommon.

Now he had the urge to get up, go back into the bedroom, and look for the photos. At least then he wouldn't have the feeling that his wife's face had grayed out of his faithless sidhe memory, replaced by this stranger's.

No. She looks like Daisy. How many redheads would, though?

Jeremiah settled himself to eat. She didn't chantment again, and the morning must have been part-cloudy. The sunlight dimmed, and he found himself staring at the quirpiece's bright gleam. A Realmaker. Robin Ragged. Barefoot in his kitchen. Looking so much like his dead, rotting wife his heart squeezed down on itself like a clockwork toy in a high-gravity well each time she tilted that russet head of hers.

>╫<

She settled gingerly in Daisy's chair—the only other seat at the table since he'd smashed the other two to flinders one drunken night and thrown them out the sliding doors. There was a whole pile of junk back there, scattered over the half-finished deck.

The glass of milk held a faintly bluish tint, compared to her skin. She toyed with it, and when she finally took a dainty sip, something in him relaxed slightly. The bacon was just crunchy at the edges, the way he liked it. The coffee was passable—not nearly strong enough.

It was a relief to find something she *didn't* do like Daisy Snowe had.

She was silent as he ate, drinking her milk in tiny hummingbird nectar-sips. Watching him, those dark blue eyes fathomless.

A thread-thin golden chain holding a teardrop of a locket glittered at her throat, probably true metal if she was a Realmaker. The single piece of jewelry nagged at him, but he couldn't think of why. He studied the line of her jaw as he chewed, the arches of her cheekbones, the fragile notch between her collarbones. Even when still she looked restless. A delicate, feathered exotic in his dirty heap of a house. Had he looked the same way to mortals, ever?

Not half as pretty, Gallow. Next to Robin, Daisy would have looked washed-out, pale, worn-down.

Good thing she's not here, then, right? The old dull fury tried to rise; he pushed it down. He hadn't even looked at another woman since Daisy's death; why was he even curious about this sidhe now?

Finally, he mopped up a last lake of amber syrup, suppressed a belch, and took a hit off the fresh cup of coffee. He'd forgotten what it was like to eat a real mortal breakfast.

When he looked up, she was studying him in turn. A faint vertical line showed between her arched eyebrows, and her mouth at rest was a sweet curve.

"Robin." He set his fork down precisely, took another sip of coffee. "You can call me Gallow."

She nodded, her shoulders easing. "I don't mean to be trouble. I really don't. I thought the quir would break my trail and the rider would—"

"A man died in there." Harshly, because he still tasted the bacon and the sweetness of maple blood. "But I suppose that doesn't matter."

"Died?" She looked puzzled, before her entire body drooped. "You mean a mortal? In the tavern?" Disbelief, very prettily played. Some part of it might even be genuine. "I thought the Unseelie wouldn't..." A catch, as if her throat was full.

It wasn't them; it was the chaos you caused. And it was more than one, but I didn't know them. "His name was Panko." The ash of his anger burned his own tongue.

She nodded. Slowly, coppergold curls falling forward. "Panko." Repeated it. "Panko. I will remember."

It wasn't what he expected. Most sidhe would've been honestly befuddled by his harshness. Mayfly mortals died. It was what they *did.* The sidhe died, too, of violence or of an old age measured in geologic spans. Except pixies and ivyfalse brughnies, of course, but even they didn't care much for a human life.

Remembrance was a mortal trick.

"Panko," she murmured again. "I'm sorry. He was your friend?"

"Coworker." Then, because she might not understand, "Yes, friend." The concept of work and paycheck really didn't sink in for most sidhe, either.

"Oh." She watched him for a long moment, then rose swiftly. *Robin* was a good name for her; she hopped like a small bird. "I didn't know. I'll be going, then." She turned, scooped the quirpiece off the counter with swift grace, and was headed for the door.

Maybe she thought he'd require bloodgilt. Jeremiah's hands lay on the table, flat and loose. As if the tattoos weren't itching, digging in, whispering how easy it would be. The lance could slide free, pinning her in place against the wall, and he could feel its hunger as it took yet another life. He could even tell himself it was payment for Panko, whose wife would have nobody mocking her for fearing the basement now.

Once he'd killed here in his very house, there was no reason to stay and pretend to be mortal any longer. And yet...all he had to do was sit still until she crossed his threshold, and he could be free of the whole mess. Except the questions and the lies on Monday. He could stay as he had been these past months. Hell, these past years.

Playing at being mortal. Playing at mortal grief.

His own voice surprised him. "Don't." He made it to his feet, creaking like an old man, a warm lump of breakfast weighing him down. "Don't leave."

She stopped, shoulders set. He could see the mending in the blue dress now, rips and tatters closed with exquisite needlework, probably chantment. At Court, would she wear the same dress? The glory of her hair and those eyes would be her passport; she wouldn't need—or be allowed, more likely—finery. No cobweb lace, no cloth-of-gold, no draperies made of sighs. No damask, no sweeping train, no mantles.

Not for a half-mortal.

Was *Ragged* a use-name? Had she chosen it to make a badge of her mortal shame?

"You haven't had breakfast," he finished lamely, even though she'd taken the milk. If she was Court-raised, she might well need nothing else... but she'd said she was older when she was taken, right? It didn't matter. After breathing the air of either Court long enough, the mortal appetite became a shadow of itself. A changeling left to mark a place, halfway between.

She still did not turn to look at him, and he suddenly wanted to cross the distance between them, take her shoulders, and *make* her. Because with her back to him it was as if Daisy was leaving, stepping out the door again to go to the store.

Just a quart of half-and-half, you like your cream so much. We're almost out. She'd laughed, hitching her purse up on her shoulder... and later, the call from the police. The wreckage, the hospital's machines, and the brassy final reek of death.

"I'm under commission. I've lingered long enough as it is." Her shoes were by the door; it was a moment's work to step into them. Still, she hesitated. "I thank you for your hospitality, Gallow. I'll offer advice, too, though you don't recognize any debt." One foot slid into the low black Cuban heel, muscle in her dancer's calves flickering. "There's a plague about, stalking the sidhe. Bar your door and carry iron with you. *She* is unhappy, there is conspiracy, and things have grown dangerous of late." Her second shoe, and Jeremiah was nailed in place.

It was all so much noise. "Don't go," he managed. "Please."

She looked back over her shoulder. "If you knew me, you wouldn't ask me to tarry." A shadow of sadness, and it copied the weariness of mortality so exactly that for a single crystalline moment she looked like...not Daisy, but his wife as she might have been with a sidhe's gloss. "Take care, Gallow."

He took another two stumbling steps forward, but the door opened. A flash of blue and brown, and she was gone. She hopped over the cold iron buried under his threshold and disappeared into morning sunshine.

Jeremiah sagged on his feet. The tattoos itched unbearably. The entire trailer smelled like bacon, pancakes, the indefinable sweetness of a place a clean, beautiful woman has just been breathing. He filled his lungs several times. Even the faint mildew of the laundry pile had retreated, replaced by fresh air.

He finally piled all the dishes in the sink. The coffee was still hot, so he poured himself another cup. He settled on the couch, right next to a mound of dirty laundry, and stared at the blank glass face of the television set as if it would tell him something.

A CERTAIN SATISFACTION

14

⊃╫⊂

Thin sunshine could not warm a sharp breeze redolent of exhaust and rotting wood. It skipped across St. Martin's Avenue, lingered at a stone wall, and licked at a shadow darting up the moss-stained wall-face in a lizard-flicker. Once it reached the shelter of branches overhead, the shadow thickened, and Puck Goodfellow braced himself on an oak tree's huge, brittle arm. The wall itself was wide enough that he could walk along it, ignoring the sharp, unpleasant nipping sensation stabbing his quick feet.

On the other side, cool greenness beckoned, but he did not leap down. Willows trailed their spiny fingers, the grass soaked with mineral-smelling water and other substances, bright spots of plastic gewgaws or—more rarely—actual blossoms, dying but held fast in cones, and the stones. Some upright, some a-tumble, some set flat in the earth, they hadn't changed since the last time he had occasion to prance along this confounded heap of stone.

Although green, this park gave him no pleasure, because of the gray bulk rising in the distance. Atop its highest spire, the hated symbol of singularly joyless invaders spread its bony arms, worked over and over again into the colorful windows and repeated on some of the stones.

The sideways realms were wide and varied, between the place of mortals and the Second Veil's shimmering, deadly barrier. In another few years, Summer's Gates would move, according to its whims, and another city would hold its garlanded mouth. Unwinter had entrances everywhere, and the free counties over-lapped anywhere they could, but Summer…well, perhaps it craved mortals to contrast itself with.

Or perhaps *she* did.

It was mere chance that the Gates lingered here. Although, of course, the Goodfellow liked to think chance favored him, as he was in a certain way her eldest. They called him the Fatherless, when they thought he could not hear.

It pleased him to think most believed it.

He squinted, spotting a fir's dark drooping, and danced into its shadow just as she appeared, her russet head down and her skirt fluttering, tugging at her knees while the breeze fingered her bare arms and teased her curls.

A Half would feel none of the stabbing from such cursed ground.

The fir's shadow was a balm. He climbed and leapt, the tree sleepily waking enough to breathe fragrance over him. He settled comfortably where he could see a particular stone, next to a notch made in the trunk's thick bark by his little knife. Marking a tree did not make it heartsblood, of course, but there was still a certain satisfaction in knowing even here, at the edge of a cursed churchyard, he could in time spread his influence down through living sap and spreading roots.

She brought no flowers, her hands bare and empty as she trudged up a slight rise, stepping off the narrow strip of cracked paving. Her heels did not sink in the wet loam, but she stepped delicate as a doe, unwillingly, until she reached a stone no different from the rest—the very one Puck could see through a convenient parting in the fir's green robe.

He knew the name that would be chipped on the stone. Sometimes he fancied this was the Ragged's idea, to lay such bones in hatefully consecrated soil to keep them from... disturbance. They would not be half so pretty now as they once were when a mayfly mortal's brief blossoming had enchanted the eye and hand.

Puck settled himself more comfortably. His feet had stopped stinging. Clasping the branch with both palms, his knees widesplayed, he smiled his sharp white smile and wondered if the Ragged would, as she sometimes did, weep at her mother's grave.

This time she did not, and she did not linger overlong. She did whisper something the breeze almost failed to carry to Puck's waiting ear, but he pursed his lips and blew a little. The air itself was happy to carry tales, for a sidhe such as himself.

"Mama, I'm sorry."

Puck's grin widened, his green eyes twinkled, but he waited until the Ragged had disappeared over the far rise—she was, it appeared, making for the entrance to Summer in the weedchoked lot on 176th, and using this place to break her trail most handily.

Then, when he was sure she could not hear him, the Fatherless threw back his head and laughed, a merry, boyish chuckle that chipped a few pebbles from the top of the stone wall and blackened the moss on the side that faced St. Martin the Redeemer's Church.

MORTAL WORTH

15

⌖

Leafshadow and droplets of golden Summer played over Robin's skin, the sweet breeze lifting the hem of her skirt. Here there was no pavement to bruise a sidhe's feet, just good honest cobbles, and the air was silken with a warm afternoon breeze. The orchard was full of whispers, laughter, and the plucking of a sidhe harp, high-pitched and thrilling, the notes carrying bright spangles through dappled shade.

The first surprise was that *she* had arisen from her couch, and come to meet Robin in this dell. Over the slight hill, behind a screen of cloud-flowered trees, the Court was a murmur and a singing, laughter like silver bells cruel and wondrous.

The bark of every tree held carvings, faces twisted with fear or remorse, none of them serene. At least, it was easy to pretend they were carvings, if one did not look too closely.

The tall, pale *Belle Dame sans Merci* paused, swaying like a young willow. White skin, crimson lips, the dazzlement of utter beauty in her heavy silken indigo mantle—did she feel cold, the Queen of Summer? Who knew why she did as she did?

Who had the right to ask? She was the fount, and Sidherie flowed forth like her golden hair. At least, so the harpers said, flattering; none now dared speak of plagued Unwinter and the peasants of the free sidhe catching blackboil ill.

Sometimes Robin suspected...well, why flatter Summer so, unless she needed the reassurance?

Her features betrayed none of this dangerous idea. Her thoughts had grown bleaker of late, a thing Robin had not thought possible.

"Dearest Robin," the Queen murmured, and her robe rustled. Beside her, staring adoringly at her so-perfect profile, was a boy with corngold hair. A changeling kept his place in the mortal realms, and sometimes the young man would tilt his head as if listening to the faraway music of his life passing outside the sideways realms. Straight nose, a lush mouth, wide blue eyes. The Queen had preferred her toys to be *brun*, and Sean's arrival at Court had been via a stealer with long grasping fingers, Archane the Quiring. *A beauty for you, my liege.*

Who could guess what the Queen thought—maybe that Archane was currying favor too openly, or that he presented the dazed child not as Summer's by right, but instead something only he had the power to convey?

Sing him a song, Robin. Thank him for this gift. And oh, the Ragged had.

Then, as the boon for her service, pressed by Summer to take a reward, she had asked for the boy. For some short while, she had even been allowed to keep him as a mortal pet, until the Queen—maybe bored, maybe simply cruel—had paid the boy special attention one afternoon, caressing his cheeks and breathing in his golden hair, the drug of her presence turning him glaze-eyed and lost while Robin stood frozen, her face a mask.

Watching.

Sometimes Robin had thought of finding the changeling and singing it to death, returning the little one to his mortal family. She had not. *One more day,* she would promise herself. *What harm could one more day do? Is it not better here than in the pale mortal realm?*

Because he was wide-eyed and charming, and his laughter was like bells, and because he called her *Robin-mama,* and sometimes, on her narrow pallet, they would sleep together, the boy sucking his thumb and Robin dreamless, for once. The top of his head smelled of dust and a haze of golden healthy mortal youth, just like another, remembered child.

His warm living weight reminded her of other nights spent listening to mortal breathing, wondering why she was so different.

Strange, her mother had called her. *You take after your father,* she sometimes whispered. The anonymous father who had left with the death of a mortal summer fading into russet fall. Mama pregnant and finding herself the mortal Daddy Snowe, a proud peacock of a delivery driver. Mama swearing Robin was his, that she was just premature, and Daddy Snowe seeming to accept this until the whiskey rose in him and he called Mama a slut and Robin a slut-child.

Her earliest memories were of his loathsome bellowing, and Mama's soft sobs.

When the younger baby was born, looking just like her older sister, Daddy Snowe believed Mama and began to shower Robin with attention, too, but by then the damage was done. Not only that, but Daddy Snowe's hugs and too-heavy hands, his furtive glances and the way his breathing turned heavy around young Robin...She feared, without knowing precisely what she was afraid of.

At twelve, Robin Ragged had traded herself away to the Summer Court, because knowing everyone would be happier if you were gone was all the incentive a lonely young Half girl needed. Of course Puck Goodfellow had wanted her to join the free sidhe, but they often lived in the mortal world, and Robin, dazzled by Summer's pavilions and greenery, wanted nothing more than to escape the gray drudge of mortals.

Maybe she should have driven a harder bargain. What girl, mortal or sidhe, knows her worth at twelve small orbits around the mortal sun? Whatever else, Puck had found her, and brought her to Seelie. *You would not like Unwinter, my primrose dear.*

All of which brought her here, standing before Summer and realizing once more that Court was a trap. Just a little prettier than a trailer and an older man's pinching fingers, that was all.

"A rider and a knight named Gallow by the Fatherless. An interesting tale." The Queen's snow-white hand caressed Sean's bare shoulder, and the boy trembled. He wasn't more than eleven, but already tall. He slept on Summer's couch now, and brought her honey with milk every morning in the favorite's golden horn. Eyes for nothing else, and sometimes the tight-fitting velvet breeches showed the stiffening of a prepubescent boy's dim, unconscious desire.

Robin tasted sourness, but did not look away. She held Summer's gaze, that black ageless stare you could drown in. "I thought you would wish to hear it."

The Queen did not waste words. "Where are the ampoules?"

"Safe." Robin almost grimaced, thinking of Parsifleur's death. A muscle in her cheek perhaps flickered, but she schooled her expression just in time, and it was lucky the Queen had bent her gaze to Sean's lowered head. Some balance had tipped while Robin ran thither and yon in the mortal world, and he no longer recognized her at all.

Robin-mama. Feeding him bread and honey, thinking perhaps his teeth would not take to it, but they were still pearly and straight. And milk she had fetched every morning and night. His laughter when she made small bits of chantment glamour to amuse, and his greeting when she returned to what passed for a nursery, the brughnies she bargained into caring for him in her absence chirping a hello. His chubby arms, lifted, and the mortal scent of his hair as she opened the casement at night, teaching him the constellations of Summer's dusk.

If he returned to mortals, what would he grow into? The poison was in the wound now. It was all too easy to imagine him crow-gaunt and scab-picked as Henzler, burning with a desire that would never be slaked. Hollowed out for a sidhe's careless, momentary amusement.

The Queen's gaze fell across Robin's face like a blow. Those black eyes, with the little crystalline lights swimming in their depths, under the beautifully arched brows and the fillet holding her golden hair back, the Summer Jewel burning against her smooth ageless forehead, that cherry-red mouth a pout. "You could not bring them? Oh, Robin."

"The Unseelie are about, even watching the Gates. And I am only one, while they are many." *Make of that what you will.* She did not watch the white hands caressing Sean's shoulder. Instead, she turned her attention to a single creamy apple-blossom. This particular tree held a face with its moss-stuffed mouth wide open, seeking to scream. Another changeling forever Summer, roots holding ancient chantment fast.

The Queen considered this. Robin kept breathing. Four counts in, four counts out.

Sean made a small piping sound. The snowy fingers, momentarily tipped with wicked bloodred nails, had dug in.

Even glamour could wound, if strong enough.

"Ah, forgive me," Summer whispered. "I did not mean to hurt."

Robin's heart would have leapt like the traitorous mortal-tinged thing it was, but if it had, the Queen would hear. Those nails could draw blood instead of simply bruising. So Robin examined the blossom, and concentrated on the thought of the plague spreading over that flawless skin. The golden hair becoming dishwater snarls, the supernally lovely face a hag's withered grimace.

A marvelous consideration, indeed.

Finally, Summer sighed. "Very well. Go forth and bring this Gallow to me, little Ragged. When will you bring me the ampoules?"

Now. She met the Queen's gaze, and smiled. A wide, warm, inviting expression, as her breath continued in its steady cycle. "When Sean is returned safe, young, live, and whole to the mortal world and his safe, living, whole mortal parents, with no geas or ill-will on him or his relations forever, then, O Summer's Queen, I shall bring them."

She turned on her heel, and the hiss behind her was of a bright green asp. Robin treaded her measure forward, steadily, her shoes crushing the springy turf. *Four in, four out.*

Does she strike me down, the plague may take them lock and stock, for all I care. And she'll never find the ampoules; she'll never think to look in my pocket. It's altogether too simple. They'll throw my body in the bogs or the Dreaming Sea, perhaps, or into a mortal alley to rot.

"You have overreached yourself," the Queen said softly, chiming ice in every word. "I will not forget this, *Ragged.*"

Nor will I. If Summer released Sean, then it would be time for Robin to set her wits to delivering the ampoules and escaping Seelie lands alive. At least Robin would have freed him, would have done *something* worthwhile.

For once.

So her reply was a simple statement of fact. "I go in search of the black-haired knight who may kill a plagued Unseelie, Summer. As you have commanded."

Too risky to use the postern near the Gates, even at midday, and she didn't want to use some of the other routes, including the one near her mother's grave. Saving those for pressing need—for later, when she might have to slip in and out of Summer without any of the Court glimpsing her and carrying tales—was the wisest course.

It took a short while for the shaking to go down, but in this copse at the very edge of Seelie there weren't even any dryads to see. They were all out among the fields, or sleeping inside their boles.

Which meant Robin could lean against a fir's trunk, bark rough against her forehead, and think about what she had just done.

Nobody else had witnessed Robin's intransigence. Her song was held in great caution, and Realmakers were valuable. It would be foolish to think Summer wouldn't punish her anyway. There was a faint vanishing chance that the Queen would be distracted by another pretty toy, and only think to torment her Ragged when she grew bored.

Then leave. Give her the ampoules, return Sean to his family, and disappear. The mortal world is wide.

It was, but Summer was always reachable, no matter where the Gates made their home. The Veil was everywhere, if you had some of the sidhe in your veins. There was Unwinter to fear as well, and the free sidhe possibly catching sight of her. Rumor flew like the wind. Hiding in the mortal world was chancy if Summer truly wished revenge.

Was it better than Court? The velvet, the silk, the glances, the harpsong? The tall white towers of Summer's Keep and its greenstone walls, the stars in their net of purple dusk? Sweet-smelling, soft and beautiful . . . and deadly.

What part of the Keep wouldn't hold the ghost of a small blond mortal child? *Robin-mama*. Her presence might remind Summer of an insult during Sean's mortal lifetime. Surely Robin could slip away until he was no more than dust in one of their graves?

Just like another child, buried—or a woman who was little more than a child herself, helpless and soft and broken, now sleeping under mortal earth. Robin squeezed her eyes shut. Solitude was a luxury, to be used to the full.

So she thought about the most hurtful thing of all.

I got me a man, Rob, and I want the rest of it, too. Please? You know I can't have no babies, but maybe that root magic Mama was always on about... You know what I mean, don't you?

Don't you?

Her fingers still remembered the throbbing of the chantment she'd bargained so hard for. Waiting in the rain at their usual meeting spot, an hour and a half sliding past unremarked, no quick familiar footsteps or raucous young laugh. No breath of cigarette smoke, salt, mortal, and the same White Musk perfume Mama had favored.

She'd waited as long as she dared, slipped back into Summer to attend Court, escaped again when she could...and found the grave. Not even near Mama's, but whoever the nameless mortal man was, he'd laid her to rest where no sidhe could work nasty chantment on her bones.

Stop it. A deep breath, another, and Robin straightened. *You're not doing yourself any good.*

A selfish thought. A selfish sidhe.

Perhaps once Sean was returned to his mortal life and family, perhaps once he had lived a long, full life and was buried safely, she might feel as if she had mitigated some small part of that selfishness.

In the meantime, Robin Ragged told herself, there was work to be done, the Veil to pierce, and pursuit to be eluded.

SENSE AND BREATH
16
⊰╫╠⊱

Monday morning, while dank and cold, wasn't as bad as he'd feared. Except for the hangover, pulsing inside his head like a troll's spiked club. He'd gone back to hard liquor for the first time since smashing the television, but it hadn't helped a single damn thing. It had just blackened the already-dying mortal world, and the amount he'd been forced to drink to reach unconsciousness was nothing short of ridiculous.

Mortal liquor just wasn't strong enough.

Spring had retreated again, as if the Ragged Robin had taken it with her. The day was damp and cloudy, a wet wind and near-constant drizzle not quite enough to coat his blue truck's smear-cracked windshield. He didn't even have the quirpiece to look at.

Clyde took one look at him, sniffed suspiciously—probably catching wind of the sour reek of metabolizing whiskey—and put him on hauling duty, where he wouldn't hurt himself.

Or anyone else.

So all the chill raw day, Jeremiah heaved up and down. He didn't break for lunch, either, just kept carrying, pushing a wheelbarrow, moving. Steel, brick, bags of concrete, refuse to be carted to the chutes and thrown with a grunt and a nasty feeling of satisfaction. The work was an anodyne.

Like the liquor, it didn't help enough.

There is plague about... Carry iron with you. Good advice. Especially since the rider pursuing her had fallen apart with a green fume of sickness and leprous rot.

They did not sicken easily, the sidhe. Iron would do it. Longing also, perhaps, or poison. But any type of illness, a cold, a plague? That was a mortal thing.

Not my problem. Neither was the redheaded sidhe-girl. So she resembled Daisy, so what? There were other women who did, too. Mortal *and* probably otherwise, red hair and blue eyes, and fragile, pretty faces.

Jeremiah lifted the bag of concrete mix. Flipped it easily into the wheelbarrow; you had to be careful or the paper would tear and then there'd be a mess. When he straightened, Clyde was bearing down on him, hard hat shoved back and worry printed all over his seamed face. "Gallow!" he bellowed, jabbing his heels into the flooring. The building quivered, but only from the wind singing through it.

What now? He waited, empty-handed, feet braced.

A burning draft of fried food and worry followed Clyde's solid frame, brushed Jeremiah's face like the chill breeze. The foreman must've gone around the corner to McDonald's for lunch. Jeremiah wiped at his forehead as if he was sweating, rubbed his hand over his cheeks and chin to hide his expression.

"What've you *done*? Was it the cops the other night?" Clyde's stubble and fine white mustache was dusted with dirt; he'd been monkeying around with the bottom-level guys. "If you got something on you, now's the time to book it."

For a moment, Jeremiah thought the man had gone moon-touched. "What?"

The man stopped two feet from him. He was out of breath. "Got two Feds in my office. They asked for you by name, flashed some badge. Christ, what'd you *do*?"

"I haven't done anything." As far as law enforcement knew, Jeremiah Gallow was a nonentity, not worth noticing. He paid taxes, yes—but a simple glamour had taken care of giving him a human identity. There was no reason for any mortal authority to take notice of him. "Is it about Panko?"

Clyde's face screwed up like he smelled something foul. "How should I know? They're in the office. Sylvia gave 'em coffee. I said I'd come and find you."

Jeremiah's nape tightened. The marks on his forearms tingled slightly. "I'll go see. Maybe it's taxes."

"If you have to bail..." Clyde was, at heart, a decent man. Rare enough in any realm.

Jeremiah shrugged. "I haven't done anything," he repeated. "I don't know."

"Well, go on down if you're gonna." Clyde turned on his heel. "You didn't clock out for lunch, either. Don't make paperwork for me."

"Fine." Jeremiah followed. The iron in the building resonated, singing its cold song as the breeze picked up.

The elevator heaved and shuddered its way down. Jeremiah trudged toward the office, the bite of almost-worry under his breastbone sharp and unwelcome. His right hand wormed its way into his jacket pocket, the calluses on his fingers scraping rough corduroy.

Daisy had picked this dun coat out for him. Heavy and graceless but sturdy as hell, leather patches at the elbows, found on sale. Thrift stores were her favorite places. The broken-down, the beggars and half-drowned kittens, the cheap and the castoff overwhelmed her gentle heart. Maybe that was why she'd settled for him.

The right-hand pocket held three iron nails. A little bird had warned him, and unwilling gratitude warmed the inside of his ribs.

If he hadn't been touching inimical mortal metal, he might not have seen it. The office—a temporary trailer listing just a few degrees out of true, less well-built than Jeremiah's own—hunched against the damp. Warm electric light shone from its windows...and up the wooden steps lifting toward the door were smears of phosphorescence, weak in the gray daylight. They glowed a sickly green, and his fingers spasmed against cold iron. The marks on his forearms twisted, writhing under the skin and dragging their tingling claws bone-deep.

Unseelie. Here, in the daylight. But why?

Robin. There was no other explanation. Had the rider been pure Unseelie? A highborn of Unwinter, be it the Hunt or the Hallow, simply wouldn't fall apart at the mere touch of a dwarven-inked lance, even iron-bladed.

It took far more than that to kill *them*. Or the Sluagh.

If the ragged little Robin had been under the Hunt of Unwinter Himself, killing one rider wouldn't have stopped the pursuit. There would have been more of them, and they would have followed her over Jeremiah's doorstep, cold iron or no. Once the Hunt—or, God forbid, the Sluagh—was called, it took more than a single piece of cold iron to bar passage.

There had only been the one, though. No names exchanged, no bloodgilt to be asked. Why would Unseelie brave even cloud-filtered sunlight and ask about *him*? He hadn't been Summer's Armormaster for a long while, and any sidhe with a grudge against him would have found him before now—and found him willing enough to answer.

He kept moving, the same heavy mortal footfalls. Regret and chill forgotten, every sense alert, he made no attempt to alter his gait. They would have heard him long before now. Let them think him stupid or oblivious.

He eased his hands free of the corduroy pockets, letting go of the iron regretfully. Now that he was on guard, glamours wouldn't be nearly as effective. His workboots thudded on the rickety steps. It was ironic—a construction site full of cold iron, and the Unseelie had been ushered to a tin can of a trailer that wouldn't seriously hamper anything they wanted to do.

The doorknob was slick and ice-cold; he twisted it and stepped in.

Immediate darkness enfolded him, wet illusion clinging and cloying. He ducked, and the spat curse went over his head, its wingtips brushing past his hair and sending a rill of ice down his spine. *Fullblood. Great.* The marks on his arms gave a flare of cold heat as he drove forward, the lance resolving and striking lightning-quick.

Most flying curses were sight-line; he swept the lance, the blade striking home in something soft as dark-glamour fell away, spent. The inside of the office was a shambles, paper exploded everywhere; the lanceblade sinking in just under the ribs of a tall, black-clad noseless scarecrow of a sidhe, all the visible slices of its skin patterned with the violet tree-ring markings of lightshielding chantment.

They had planned and prepared for coming out by day, and asked for him by name. The intervening years fell away, and he was the Armormaster again, calculating as he moved, the lance part of his breath and bone.

Sylvia the secretary lay flung back over her desk, her throat cut and a bright jet of arterial spray painting the corkboard where project-resolution timetables and OSHA notices were tacked up. The stench of a mortal battlefield rose—copper blood, adrenaline sharp against his palate, the reek of loosed bowels.

Sylvia had two cockatiels waiting at home in her apartment. She kept the coffee hot and didn't complain when the boys dirtied the bathroom in the office trailer. She walked around in a cloud of Loveswept perfume and chain-smoked in her office, a merry defiance of company policy. She could find any document in seconds flat, stall an inspector or find a hard hat, "lose" an asshole's paycheck, or nag a worker into Doing the Right Thing. Now her pudgy middle-aged body, thick legs indecently splayed under her usual tartan skirt, slumped in the final indignity of death over her thronelike metal desk.

Jeremiah twisted the lance, ripping it free. *Two, there's at least one more. Get your weapon free. Move. Move!*

Another Unseelie hit him from the side, the wicked edge of a flint knife kissing his jacket and scraping the tough material with a ripping sound as Gallow twisted, right boot stamping down and driving him away from the strike. The blade was probably poisoned, and if it touched skin he'd be in trouble.

The butt of the lance flicked out, catching the second nose-less bastard right in the middle of his elongated face. Watery greenish ichor sprayed, and the smell of freshly cut grass filled the trailer, fighting with the stink for supremacy. Jeremiah snapped his own curse, and the second Unseelie went flying. The sidhe smashed into the flimsy bathroom wall and kept going, fetching up against the toilet with a sickening *crack*. The mirror shivered into pieces.

Bad luck, but for who? The lance flicked again, catching the first Unseelie in the throat as he sprawled, snarling, one maggot-white hand clapped to his side. The shock of a life ending grated up the haft, and the lance made a hungry keening that trembled the flimsy windows in their sockets, vibrating along every edge and settling in Jeremiah's back teeth. Sick heat boiled up his arms, following the channels of the marks, and his jacket smoked with sudden heat.

The Unwinter sidhe were in dusty black suits, their eyes holes of darkness. If there was half-and-half left in the dish near the coffeepot—and Sylvia made certain it never ran out, yet another reason to admire her—it would be soured by now. Nausea twisted like a fish under Jeremiah's breastbone. The door had swung shut, and he didn't have time to reach behind him to lock it.

The second Unseelie rose from the ruins of the bathroom wall, broken drywall settling over him in a pall of fine white dust. "*Gallow*," he whispered, and the sound turned air to ice, Jeremiah's breath pluming in the sudden chill. Paper stirred, rustling, and the lance shrank. Close-quarter fighting was not good with a reach weapon; it was too confined in here.

Still, any blade would have to do when faced with a scion of Unwinter.

Each sidhe wore belts with heavy twisted silver-gleaming buckles. Rings flashed on the live one's fingers, a pale golden gleam. Barrow-wights, then, fullblood but not highborn. Dangerous, and deadly—but not very bright.

Jeremiah inhaled smoothly, disregarding the smell. His boots shuffled in paper as he moved forward, lance ready, its tip glowing a dull hot red. Steam writhed along its edge, and it shifted again, wicked sharklike teeth growing from its edges.

He had forgotten how *good* it felt to kill.

"Wight." He spat the word like a curse. The dead sidhe on the floor twitched, runnels of dust eating ageless flesh. In the old times, he would take the rings as bloodgilt. They would jingle on his belt when he walked, and he would trade them for bright bits of moonmetal to tie in his hair. Or he would gift them to *her*, since there was little she liked better from an Armormaster than shinies from an Unseelie's fingers. Or ears.

Or throat.

The barrow-wight hissed, exhaling. They were sneakthieves and assassins, not direct fighters. Were there more? Had to be; nobody would send a trio of mere wights to deal with *him*.

The stupid wight leapt forward, strangler's hands outstretched and a collection of black-flapping curses taking shape in the air around it. The lance jerked, and the swipe ended with its teeth tearing in sidhe flesh, the green scent pungent-foul as fresh-cut grass rotted in marshy swampwater. Curses fell, flapping and wriggling, and intuition bloomed under his skin. There *had* to be more. Nobody would send only a troika of wights to—

The world halted, then turned over. A huge noise, almost soundless in its immensity, and Jeremiah *flew*. The explosion rammed him through the trailer's wall, the lance screaming as its feeding was interrupted, but the flush of power up its haft and through the marks was enough to shield him from the worst of the blast. Landed hard, rolling, his jacket smoking afresh and the lance retreating into insubstantiality as a column of fire rose. Black smoke billowed.

There goes our safety record, he thought hazily, before instinct tucked his head and he hit the side of a handy pickup truck. The impact left him stunned, nothing broken but blood bursting briefly from his nose and ears. The world took a breath around him, settling back into its rightful dimensions with a thump.

The construction trailer exploded again. Flames writhed, fat ropes of yellow and orange. Probably from a fireglobe; it would burn everything it could reach down to ash until the parameters of the curse laid inside it had been reached. Nine feet, or twelve, or twenty-one.

No mere wight, even a highborn one, could bargain for a fireglobe this intense. They had to have help from fullborn higher in the Unwinter Court.

Who among either Court would want him dead *this* badly? Or was Robin supposed to be with him? Why would they want *her*? She was *definitely* of Summer. You only had to look at her to see as much. Under commission, she said—so she was working for the Queen herself. What games were Summer and Unwinter playing now?

Jeremiah braced himself against the side of the truck, his ribs heaving as he dragged in breath after breath, staring, wiping at the blood on his upper lip. A swift pain piercing his ears was membranes healing. It had been a long time since he'd tasted his own claret.

Have to get out of here. There could be more.

For a moment he simply stared, like a witless fool. The mortals would think him dead now. Clyde would be puzzled, to say the least. Shouts and running feet, someone hit an alarm and the noise mounted as the fireglobe took another deep breath and expanded another yard in all directions, hungrily seeking. The smoke sent out questing fingers, burning stuff rained down. Papers, bits of tin and smoking wood, peppering the earth like rain after a hard-baked drought.

The lance trembled on the edge of visibility as he tried to decide if he needed it. Were there more Unseelie around?

If there are, you must draw them away. Be stealthy, Jer. Be smart.

Humming in his hands, its blade leaf-shaped and dappled, the lance burned cold blue before it winked out, retreating up his arms as he forced it away.

Jeremiah shook his head, regaining sense and breath both.

Time to vanish.

WIGHT, KNIGHT, AND HOUND
17

⇒╫╪╪⇐

*W*ith its back to cliffs falling into the Dreaming Sea, a lacework *of wet black stone burned with red at its tips. Scarlet pennons flew from each slender tower and a deep, low mumble plucked at the air. Thorn-tangles shuddered, writhing against the border of the moat; greasy black water rippled as the Watcher within it moved, its oily scaled hide surfacing for brief moments.*

Among the thorns, splashes of crimson and spots of moonglow bloomed.

The Rim rose to the castle's north, piled black stone crawling with wights and honeycombed with their barrows as well as the harpy-nests and crags for the fire-goats. Further up the Rim, the mines crouched, their wide mouths carved with fantastical loops of wyrmscale. Few of the great winged beasts remained, their own mountains at the very edge between Unwinter and the Second Veil's glimmering. The mines below held trollwrights and free dwarves, those without the alliance and network of a fierce clan— and those outcast.

Unwinter turned none away. His was not Summer's aristocracy of beauty. To live in his ashen realm you needed only to swear fealty—and be prepared to fight.

The thorn-tangles at the mountain-feet were pierced by black-rock roads, their glassine faces sometimes full of drifting mist as Unwinter's will moved through his kingdom. A will like the mortal iron, it was whispered, kept the Second Veil back and built this refuge, without Summer's petty games of glamour and reliance on the flint knife.

The thorny Tangles gave way to Dak'r Wood. Sometimes mortals slipped through chance gaps in the Veil and walked its moonglow paths all a-wonder—and no few of them fell prey to those who lived in its fastness. The tribes of the Dak'r—drow, brughnie, smalltroll, gytrash and woodwight, grennik, grentooth, and the nymphs of the shade—were not all carnivorous… but many were, and they bore no love for the shapers of cold iron.

It was in the fens and the Ash Plain that the hunting coursed. The Plain, its pale flax and bleached bloodpoppies ruffled by chill wind, swept itself with long cindersnow fingers, hound and fleet white deer scattering. The fens held kelpie just as the Dreaming Sea's rocky Unwinter shore held sharptooth selkie and singing mergirls—and it was on that shore the night-mares stepped from pale foam and crashing spume, stamping on the beach and tossing silvery fish high before catching them afresh in their wide, obsidian-toothed maws. It was these mounts, silvershod and fleetfooted, the very few boon companions of Unwinter rode. The rest of his knights made do with shadowy elfhorses—and other beasts.

Thrumming resonated through Unwinter, the roads a shifting plucked string. Sleek wet heads rose from crashing surf or mirrorglass fen; the cindersnow on the Ash Plain became a pinprick-stinging hail. A wind slid through the Dak'r and the Tangle; winterheart nymphs and blue-glowing pixies scrambled to escape, retreating inside their homes. Wights drifted to the edges of their barrows, burrows, or boles, peering out with bright curiosity—or naked fear.

Inside the mines, trollwright and dwarf alike paused. The music of hammer and anvil took on a sharp, chiming edge, the glass knife that would shatter in the wound quivering restlessly, the wicked-barbed silverine arrows whispering in their bundles.

Production of those weapons had quickened of late, though if the plague continued its ravages, there might be a shortage of hands to wield them.

A deeper flame bloomed at the heart of Unwinter's Keep, the black pile on the cliffs. Some whispered that Summerhome was a pale copy of this citadel, but never very loudly.

The bridge-mouth opened, its tongue dropping silently. Ruddy glow leaked through Unwinter's Gate, a cold fire. Shadows clustered, and the Watcher in the moat stirred to a frenzy, lashing about until, from one of the high, dust-draped towers, a shriek sounded.

It melded with the thrumming, and Unwinter quaked. Hounds belled and bayed, hooves rang against the Bridge, and a sortie rode forth at Unwinter's bidding. It was late in the season for a hunting, but Summer had not opened her gates yet.

Consequently, even though afternoon held the mortal world sideways-below-above under an unforgiving glare of that awful day-eye the mortals loved so much, the lord of Unseelie sent them hence to slip through blood-bought gateways and into shadow, waiting for dusk.

Wight, hound, and knight, they rode in pursuit.

SMALL CATHY

18

⊶╫╳

It was both familiar and strange. A chill wind under a leaden sky, the thin-skinned trailers shivering. During the day, only the elderly or the very young rattled around inside the tin cans. Broken cars and toys scattered in small weedy approximations of front yards, plastic sun-bleached and pollen-roughened paint baked onto metal by long, slow summers of decay.

The smell of it threatened to grease-soak her skin. Fried food on ancient ranges, crusted inside ovens that had to be propped shut, backed-up drains and sharprot mildew that never fully faded no matter how much bleach you used. Cat piss, desperation, and twice-boiled coffee. Sagging porches, plywood-patched siding—even the pavement was veined with age, like the back of an old mortal's hands.

Robin flitted at the edges of the trailer park, keeping to the weeds and winter-naked saplings outside anyone's yard. What was a sidhe, even a mortal-Tainted one, doing *here*? He was no pixie, to find a home in even the smallest bit of free soil or even pockets of the Veil itself.

There was a stand of birch saplings and other small trees struggling across a trash-strewn field behind his home. They were not awake, even with a sidhe living so close. Hadn't he spoken to the trees? Of course, the entire trailer park and its surroundings might be razed to make way for something even mortal-uglier, the living earth sleeping fitfully under concrete. He might well decide it wasn't worth the effort, or the heartbreak when such careful work was undone.

Maybe such a decision was even wise.

She circled, her unease growing. It wasn't until she finally stepped fully out onto the paving near his home, committing herself, that she realized she had been noticed.

A wan mortal child, probably no more than six or seven, peered through the slats of a broken fence. Bright blue eyes, but a sallow face, pinched and uneasy as Robin herself felt. No coat, her tiny feet only in ragged dirty socks, the child crouched in long damp grass, anemic weeds brushing her hips and elbows. She stared, and behind her, the listing trailer next to Gallow's looked dark and dead. Was the power shut off?

Robin remembered standing outside another trailer, long and long ago, her fingertips on rusting barbed wire as she listened to the arguing behind her, rumbling from a dark cave of a brown and white tin shack. The child's gaze was direct, and sad, and very, very sharp.

The little ones see the most of a sidhe, they said. *They are not yet blind and deaf.*

So Robin paused. "Hello, small one." The greeting left her before she considered its price, and she winced internally.

"You're pretty," the child said flatly. Male or female? Fey as a brughnie, with messy pale hair still sleep-tangled. Not a slattern's mane to be elflocked into mischief, but fine silk begging to be combed and set right.

"Thank you." Robin did not point, but she allowed her gaze to drift over the child's head, back down. "Is that your house?"

"Yeah. Daddy came back again." The child shrugged. "He drinks."

Robin nodded. "Mine did, too." *Or rather, Daddy Snowe did. If he had only a little, he'd be friendly.* She was suddenly aware of looming over the child and sank down into a crouch, peering through the fence as if she were a small one herself, her skirt brushing the ground around her. "Does he…"

Does he hurt you? But then, no child would tell, would they? Robin never had.

Still, the girl—now that she was this close, Robin could see *female* instead of just *small*—stared wide-eyed, as if she'd heard what Robin was about to ask.

A sharp, bright pain lanced through Robin's chest. She shook her head, thin tendrils of steam rising from her damp shoulders, and glanced down, finding a small white pebble half hid under a brown, dying weed. She grubbed it up, rolled it in her fingers as if it were a pearl from the Wailing River past Brughnie Wood. Chantment flowed, her tongue stinging slightly as she whispered a few words in the Old Language, will taking shape in breath.

When she opened her hand again, a sullen gleam nestled in her palm, traces of wet earth still clinging to it. The rock looked different now, crystalline. "What's your name, little one?"

The girl hesitated, *don't speak to strangers* warring with *obey the adult.* Robin hunched her shoulders, to appear smaller.

"Cathy," the child finally whispered. "What's that? It looks magic."

You're far wiser than your parents. "It could be, small Cathy. Does your father drink ale? Beer?"

"He does. What is that?"

Would you understand, if I told you? Mortals grow early into disbelief. "Does he drink it from a can, or a cup?"

"Bottle. They have a deposit. Five cents." Still wary, but the child stared at the small glowing stone.

"I see." Robin nodded again. "List well, then. Don't put this in soda. But the next time you bring him a bottle of beer, you can put this in, no matter how small the neck. It will fit. You can even put it in his coffee cup."

"Is it bad?" Immediate distrust.

Poisonous, you mean? It's well that I'm not another sidhe; that would be a very valid question. "It's not. He won't even notice, but he'll never drink ale again. Or anything else that makes him shout, or be mean, or..." *It will make him dog-sick to drink, and he'll stop soon enough.* Her throat full, she swallowed hard and continued. "Or anything that makes your mother cry," she finished.

That was evidently the right thing to say, because the girl's face eased. She shot a wary glance over her shoulder, and her dirty hand wormed through the fence.

Robin grabbed her wrist, dropped the bollstone into the small palm, closing the fingers around and breathing another syllable or two of chantment. It was as strong as she could make it under such circumstances. "Remember, small Cathy, not in soda."

"Okay." Disbelief warred with cautious hope. "You *are* magic."

And you are mortal. "Don't tell a soul. It will break the spell."

"Okay." The girl's eyes were owlish, and she pulled her clenched fist back through the fence. "Here."

A flicker of small fingers, and a flash of blue. It was a ring, blue plastic, glowing slightly with its own inner light. "For you," Cathy whispered. "Th-thank you."

A fullborn might take insult from those two words, or might consider the lack of them an affront, too, as it suited them. Robin merely nodded, picking up the small, sad payment. Maybe instinctive, maybe a young mortal's generosity—or maybe it was that small Cathy knew, even so young, that nothing at all was ever free.

Robin watched as a pale head bobbed through the weeds and up shaking stairs that had probably once been handmade with care. The door slammed, but not before Robin heard raised voices. A woman's, angry, and a hangover-blurred man's, pleading.

She straightened, scuffing the empty dirt-socket she'd pulled the pebble from. If little Cathy was quick and canny, she might well be able to slip the boll into a cup. If not, the chantment would fade on the next full moon.

Oddly, Robin's heart had lightened. Perhaps Cathy had a sister who would be grateful of the peace, too.

She turned, and almost-danced her way to the end of the fence, where the weeds leaned over into Gallow's yard—if you could call hardpacked dirt and brambles a yard. His driveway was gravel, and the rosevines climbing over a trellis serving him as a carport looked blasted as well.

That was what had been bothering her. She'd forgotten the blue truck that had crouched here the other morning, just as worn-down and dirty as the rest of the place.

Robin nipped into the carport and stood for a moment, glad of the roses. They were good insurance against Unwinter. Her hand still tingled from chantment, scraps of the Old Language clinging to her fingers as she touched the vines to steady herself, wondering why her eyes were so dry and smarting.

Oh, Robin, you fool. He's not home.

Had she stopped to consider, she might have expected as much. What had she been thinking?

Oh, come now, Robin, you know what you thought. Half

distracted is as good as pixie-led. Parsifleur's last despairing breath and Sean's empty-eyed adoration even while Summer's nails dug into his young skin filled her head, mixing with a pair of bright blue, too-wise eyes. Robin halted at Gallow's doorstep, as if struck.

She leaned forward a little, and found it was true—he had buried cold iron under the threshold. The other day she had been able to cross, for the quirpiece was hers, and could be considered an invitation. Today, the tingling along her skin crested painfully. Still, she continued apace, and the knob turned under her touch as it had before, a lock glad to help a sidhe along. There was brief discomfort as she crossed the barrier, but then she was inside. So she *was* invited, after all. Perhaps he had not thought to bar her specifically? He seemed too canny to miss such elementary self-protection.

Maybe there was simply nothing here he valued. The trailer, without his breathing weight in it, sagged dull and dispirited. She paused in the kitchen, for the dishes had not been washed, and studied the glass he had taken his milk from. She peered down the hall that led to his bedroom, but some clear instinct kept her from treading further.

What was she looking for? These rooms seemed oddly familiar, and his kitchen, strangely, had been arranged just the way she would have thought a proper kitchen should be.

A proper *mortal* kitchen, like the one she had slaved in for Mama and Daddy Snowe. *Girl can't even make biscuits right. Come here, little girl!* The crack of leather snapping against itself.

Robin shuddered, brought herself back into the present. The sidhe were brutal, but even their violence had a cold glamour Daddy Snowe had lacked. The more she saw of mortality, the less she liked that half of her heritage.

Sometimes she wondered if any of the tall, pale Court lords could be her father. Whoever he was, he was long gone, and no doubt had already forgotten his mortal paramour's brief blooming. Even so, Mama had been brushed by the strange glimmer of sidhe from couching with one and breathing in his drugging breath; she had little trouble attracting another man to take care of her.

Now Robin wondered why Mama had stayed with Daddy Snowe's violence and insults. It was a puzzle, and one she was no closer to solving for time spent thinking on it.

Even when the cancer had ravaged Mama, she had still looked wan and beautiful, though Robin had only seen as much through a rain-soaked window as the woman who birthed her lay on a hospital bed, the stentorious rise and fall of machines breathing for her a doom-knight's footsteps without a bell-ringing edge to their accordion flex.

And I felt nothing, did I? Too sidhe for it, I suppose. That night she had also run across Puck Goodfellow again, just before she stepped over the border into Summer. He had asked her errand; she had returned that it was none of his business though she thanked him for his worry and fled.

It had perhaps not been wise to snap at him, but he appeared to take no umbrage. Who could tell when he would, though?

'Tis not your concern now, Robin. Where could this Gallow be, and dare I wait here?

She turned counter to the sun, a full circle once, twice. It was habit, to confuse any pursuer with a simple trick. You could sometimes tell a mortal who knew of the sidhe by the little measures—tying knots, tangling fringe, turning or pacing, or a single item worn seams-out. Mortals had forgotten much about the sideways realms, a fact often bemoaned when the malaise of boredom gripped the Court. It made mischief easier, though less satisfying since they refused to credit the Good Folk for their misfortune.

Three times she turned, and as usual while she did so, she found the answer.

Or, if not precisely an answer, a direction.

Coworker. Friend.

Well, he had a job, then. Just like a normal mortal. Why?

Who cared? The important thing was, where there was a job there was paper, and where there was paper there was...

"Address," she said, and the wide grin that broke over her face felt strange. A few moments' worth of searching the breakfast bar and its small mountain of tossed paper garnered her several pay stubs, and she almost-danced with joy, again, as she tucked one into her skirt pocket and left his front door locked behind her.

⋊║⋉

She shouldn't have danced, for the sky threatened rain and a long weary time later she found the address was only a building full of stupid mortals, with no spice or trace of sidhe about them. She perched above the alley where they stepped out into the cold to breathe on what the brughnies called nagsticks—the cigarettes, each puff freighted with sickness. The iron of the fire escape was only slightly uncomfortable, her mortal half useful after all.

They spoke of "job sites" and "targets," "quotas" and "administration," but none of them mentioned Gallow the knight. They also didn't reek of turned earth and cold iron the way he did. Just paper, and mortal salt, and burned coffee.

She drew the paper out again and looked at its numbers and squiggles, most of them fairly incomprehensible. More than three was "many," more than seven was a dance, more than

120

thirteen simply a crowd. Numbers were a mortal magic, and one frowned upon at Court. She'd forgotten them gladly once she realized she never had to attend school again. How Puck had laughed at her when she asked if the sidhe had schools.

Now she wished she hadn't forgotten. She knew there were certain numbers that mortals would take as almost-names, but which ones? A name she could follow, but the incomprehensible numbers just confused and sickened her. Disgusted, she slid the paper back into her pocket.

"Gallow," someone breathed, and a chill trickle went down her back. Robin scrambled noiselessly for the roof, and pelted lightly across its tarpapered flatness.

She was in time to see the black-clad barrow-wights drifting out the front door, pale and insubstantial in the cloud-choked sunlight. Inside, though, they would appear real enough to stupid mortals. If they were out by day, they would have lightshield tattoos covering them, violet tree-rings that faded as they were spent shielding Unseelie from the day-eye.

She went to her knees, ducking under the lip of the roof, her heart hammering and her breath coming in short gasps. More wights, in *daylight,* and bearing his name like a tracking-banner.

So he was being hunted, too. Almost certainly because of last night's act of charity. Or had it been generosity on his part? He certainly was a grim one, parsimonious of *any* cheer.

Yet he had appeared from nowhere, and killed. Had it been for her sake? Or had he business with Unwinter? Habit forced her breathing to even out, and she sought to control her pulse. There was no need to act the stupid rabbit when she could be a fox. Or better yet, a hawk lacking jesses and hood.

Did she dare to follow the wights? They would no doubt like to snare her as well, and she had little faith in her ability to withstand Unwinter's...*persuasion,* should she be brought before him. That was, of course, if they caught her breathless and did not kill her outright.

Should she find Gallow before they did, what would she say?

Even as she debated, she knew it was too late. They had already vanished on a breeze laden with cinders, and she found herself sweating lightly, peeping over the roof's edge at the gray city. Every alley a trap, every tree a spy, every building a dark, closed face.

It was essential to keep moving. A wandering Robin would be more difficult to catch. If she stayed in daylight she would have an edge when facing any of Unwinter's minions capable of lightshield chantment; and the plagued would not dare even this milksop daylight.

Or so she hoped. She also hoped, as she ghosted noiseless above the roof while the mortals inside drank coffee, stared at glowing screens, argued, and cheated at their "jobs," that she would have a better idea before sundown.

LOCKED AND SILENT
19
>⧲|⧳<

Jeremiah left his truck behind at the jobsite—dead mortals didn't drive—so it was two long, weary bus rides and a mile's ramble before he stopped at the corner and peered down his street. Midday, and the trailer court lay silent under the drizzle. The Garnier house was quiet and dark. Mama Loth's rocker tilted back and forth, squeaking a little as the breeze pushed at it. The glass windchimes on Loth's porch tinkled a sad dissonant melody.

He crouched in the lee of Bob Haskell's dead, ancient van with a stag painted on its side, its four flat tires melding with the patched concrete. The stag was the only spot of color on the street, its painted sides somehow heaving even as it lifted its disproportionate head. Behind it, the artist had tried for mountains that looked more like low blue loaves of bread. The grass looked like wisps of smoke, and Jeremiah was suddenly aware he reeked of fire and bloodshed.

He exhaled softly. Nothing appeared out of order. If they could find him at an iron-laced jobsite, though, could he assume his home was safe? Or even the admin building downtown?

Then again, an attack on his burrow would be foolish; they

couldn't guess what he had lurking in the walls or ceiling to trap the unwary.

Five minutes. That's all you're allowed.

He stepped out of cover and sauntered down the street, an iron nail clutched in his left fist, every sense quivering-alert. The doorknob gave under his hand, and all was as it should be. It even smelled right—dust, dead air, the lingering of Robin's perfume.

"I should have known," he muttered once, while opening dresser drawers that still held a breath of violet sachet. In the end, a single backpack contained everything he needed. The spare pair of boots, two pairs of jeans, underwear, a few shirts...and the weapons. The two knives, slender-hilted with curveleaf blades. He'd left behind the long, slim box strapped to the wrapped cylinder of a quiver when he left Court, and now he regretted it. A bow kept the enemy further from you than the lance.

He paused, and swept Daisy's jewelry from the top drawer of the dresser into the Crown Royal bag she'd kept potpourri in. She'd never wanted much—it got caught on things, got lost, she said. He knew it was because they scraped by. He could have done so much more, but Daisy said it was good enough.

He'd believed her. Now he wondered.

Four and a half minutes later, he stepped out onto the porch and glanced at the carport. It stood like always, the thorny vines reaching up like a throbveined hand. He swung the door shut as an afterthought, and stopped.

Little green buds covered the tough blasted vines. They were tipped with pinpricks of swelling crimson.

All the breath left him in a rush. He actually clung to the doorknob, memory rising under his skin. Daisy on the step, laughing, her hand up to shade her eyes. Daisy coaxing the rose vines, Daisy warm and silently sleeping on moonlit nights.

Why was her face suddenly a haze? Just the coppery hair and her rich, young, beautiful laugh.

His fingers slid off the knob. It was spring. There were tiny razor-tooth leaves clinging to the vines as well. No mystery, just that the roses had finally decided to come back. Sometimes they did. It had nothing to do with anything sidhe. Just chance, luck, coincidence.

"Right," he muttered, and his fingers flicked. The door locked, the deadbolt shot home. Let it stand or let it burn, he had everything he needed.

Except he didn't. He hefted the bag onto his shoulder and checked the sky. Still gray and spattering drizzle on the mortal earth. At the site they would be poking through the wreckage, either cursing the loss of half a day to disaster or secretly excited at the break in routine.

Halfway down the street, he glanced back. The little flashes of red in the carport mocked him, and the trailer already looked abandoned. Mama Loth would watch his carport and the yard as the days lengthened, spitting into her Folgers can and occasionally nodding a counterpoint to the conversation in her head. Garnier, once his wife let him back in, would take care of the mowing and scare off any mortal nosing around in the evenings. The rent was paid automatically; there was enough for at least a year and a day in that account.

What else did he have to spend it on? Worse than dead leaves; at least the leaves had some value as they decayed to feed the next generation of trees.

Gallow left his mortal life locked and silent, and vanished.

MERCY IN HIS END

20

꘎꘎꘎

"Tap, tap, who is home?" Drumming his fingertips on the thin door, as the trailer rocked slightly. It was much sturdier than it appeared, but he had laid some of the glamour and chantments here himself, and they obeyed his poking and prodding. "Who is that nibbling at my house?"

No answer. Puck twisted the knob, stepped into a hot bath of mortal illness and dim red light. Chemical stink filled his nose, and he stepped fastidiously around broken glass scattered on the floor.

"Only the wind, the child of heaven," Goodfellow murmured, and stepped leaf-light and lively. A skip, a hop, and he was atop a laden table. Rinds of cheese, nutshells, takeout containers—free sidhe brughnies had brought the mortal pet enough to dine on and to spare, and much of it had gone to rot.

They lost appetite when Summer's sickness was upon them.

The mortal curled on his narrow pallet, shirtless and frowsy-haired. His shoulder blades were tiny wings, the knobs of his spine almost piercing stretched-tight, yellowed skin. Hugging his knob-knees and muttering to himself, he rocked back and forth slightly, and his movement caused an echo in the trailer as well.

The branches and vines coaxed through the walls now exuded a sweet, drowsy resin—the mortal had lashed at the walls with something sharp, not caring where he cut, and it was the sapblood that flowed so steadily. Long strings and ribbons of amber festooned every corner, slowly thickening. Perhaps they would even reach the mortal's bed, did he slumber overlong, and wrap him in a crystalline cocoon. The pungent analgesic would lull him, and he would not even feel the digesting juices.

Such was the revenge of free earth. Slow but steady, and turning all to advantage.

From his perch, Puck surveyed the ruin. The glass containers and the microscope the mortal was always muttering at were broken, scattered across the table. The privy stank, clogged with Stone alone knew what, and the strange spinning-machines the mortal used to "separate" fluids lay in twisted pieces still smoking from the fury that had crushed them. The glowing screens were all smashed, too.

Henzler's soft mumbling stilled. So did his rocking motion. A rabbit, crouched in the snare.

"Hello, mortal." Puck balanced on the table, his feet placed *just* so. Mortal filth disgusted him, and yet this particular sack of sweetsalt blood had been useful. Perhaps mercy could be granted here. A quick movement, a sigh, and this small pile of chantment and glamour could close about itself. Eventually, this entire decaying place could become free earth, with Goodfellow's influence already at its core. They did not know how he spread his own borders, either of the so-lordly in either Court. Perhaps Unwinter suspected, for he was a canny beast.

Even the most fell of beasts died before a hunter with enough patience, though.

The cot creaked as Henzler moved, pushing himself up and turning slowly, swinging his legs off the bed. His bare feet were now horn-callused as a brughnie's, though not nearly as charming *or* useful. Yellowed nails curled around the end of the knotted toes, weeping sores covered his stick-legs. His wide dark eyes, pupils swollen in the dimness, held the firefly-flickers of the moontouched. Were Summer to see her pet now, she would turn away in loathing.

Puck almost chuckled at the thought.

"Boy," Henzler breathed. "Little boy." He had clawed at his own cheeks, and Puck decided to be magnanimous.

"You have served well, mortal. I promised you a reward."

Henzler waved one clawlike hand, half-moons of grime tipping each finger. "Where is she? Did she send word?"

Puck's good temper frayed slightly. Asking for Summer, when the Fatherless was before him? Still, he had decided mercy would please him. So he rested one narrow brown hand on the hilt by his side, and smiled broadly. His ear-tips wiggled, twitching with pleasure that had nonetheless lost some of its luster.

Perhaps there was a way to repolish it. "Oh aye, she sent word. You are fortunate, indeed."

The mortal leapt to his feet with surprising speed. His scarecrow limbs trembled, and he bounced two paces toward Puck, kicking glass out of his way with abandon. Part of a container rolled and shattered, but he paid it no mind. "What? *What did she say?*"

Puck did not move. He observed the man's trembling fists, his knobbed knees. "She's ill, and not expected to live past sundown. She sends her regard, and does not know you made the rot that killed her, with your glass baubles and spinning-machines."

Silence, broken only by the faint tinkling drip of sweet narcotic resin. The mortal's thin mouth trembled and fell open. So fragile, and so easily wounded.

Yes, that sweetened his pleasure nicely. Puck's mouth had filled with its own juice, anticipating. His wide V-shaped grin gleamed, a flash in the ruddy glow, and the mortal lunged for him.

Desperation made them strong, and quick. Puck leapt aside, his left hand sinking into the wall, claws slicing effortlessly as he folded in half, bringing his legs up. A cat-flexible spine twisted, crackling, and he propelled himself across the trailer. The cot crumbled underneath him, its legs shattering, and he hissed, again like a cat—they were such elegant creatures, after all.

The mortal stumbled for him, shrieking blindly, and perhaps the moontouch insanity was like the plague in its own way, for it made him quick. Clasped in one shriveled hand was a wicked curve of mortal glass, its edge ground fine-sharp and its handle wrapped with black electrical tape. It whistled as it clove the air, and Puck leapt nimbly again—but the crumbling metal and fabric of the mortal's sleeping-couch pitched, and the glass-edge striped the sidhe's arm.

One lean brown fist flashed in return, a crystalline dagger singing, but the mortal had skipped nimbly back. The luck of the moontouched was on him, too, for he did not grind his bare feet on broken glass.

"You killed her!" the mortal roared, and Puck hissed, a grinding, serpentine noise too big for such a narrow chest.

The sidhe darted forward. Any of his kind, facing him, might have retreated, for when Goodfellow drew his wicked, glittering little knife, green venom collected on its pinpoint tip.

Dying of wyrmsting was a thing to be feared.

The mortal scientist, however, had another piece of blind luck. His hip struck one of the tables, and its legs screeched. His arm, windmilling wildly, struck a tiny glass bottle full of colorless liquid, with a wick protruding from its top. It flew in an insanely perfect arc—

—and hit Puck Goodfellow's snarling, twisted boyface with a shattering crunch. The boy-sidhe howled, and the mortal, perhaps understanding that not even luck would save him now, blundered for the door. His free hand, sweat-slick and shaking, pawed at the knob.

Puck howled afresh as colorless alcohol mixed with thick, dark ichor, stinging and blinding. He was barely aware of the mortal flinging the thin door open and scampering out into weak, cloud-choked daylight. He rolled on the floor of the hovel, shrieking, pawing at his face with his free hand.

Henzler blundered down a rotting, cracked pavement strip, tearing two toenails loose as he ran. His throat burned with screaming, his eyes blinded by daylight he hadn't seen for quite some time, and his feet slapped both concrete and thistles threading their way through cracks with equal force.

Behind him, the cries from the trailer ceased. It took much more than a few shards of glass and some mortal solution to damage the Fatherless.

Puck bounced out of the trailer, landing soft as a whisper on the steps, loping in Henzler's wake. He was utterly silent now, his grin no longer pleased but instead grim good cheer, his soft boyface striped with swiftly healing cuts bleeding thick sapphire-blue ichor. He did not hurry, for the boundaries of this dilapidated village were his to command.

The mortal would not get far, and there would be no mercy in his end, now.

NO SMALL PROPOSITION
21

꒣╫꒦

It was late afternoon, and she was weary. Robin moved among the mortals with her head down, seeking cover, if not comfort, in their mass of gray salt and sourness. When night fell, she would have to find a hole to hide in, or...

Perhaps she should have stayed at Gallow's abode, and not sought him elsewhere? Yet if barrow-wights could find the same job-building she had, would his burrow be safer at all? Could she risk returning to the knight's trailer? She could not decide, and she kept walking. Moving was better than staying still, and there were hiding places well within range once dusk threatened.

Which of them, if any, would be *safe*?

The best was a place she had never visited since finding it, preferring to keep its secret locked within like a highborn sidhe's truename. Was the danger extreme enough to warrant using it? For once used, no place was safe ever again.

Not from Unwinter, and she thought it rather likely *he* might take a personal interest in matters very soon.

Another of her narrowing options was the waste and wrack of Tanglemire Park, where the free sidhe held little truck with either Court. She was not hated among them, but neither was she loved. Still, even those who rode a-hunting sometimes hesitated at the borders of their holdings.

That hesitation would give Robin precious time, and breath to spend.

Had she already decided? She found herself stepping from pavement onto long, sere grass, her heels almost catching in a blown-down section of chainlink fencing. Her calves ached slightly, mortal weakness only, since the heels were full of surefoot and passage chantment. She made for a stand of birch trees—they had been manicured once, long ago, but the free sidhe had diverted mortal interest in this slice of land for a while now. Bracken and bramble, greenness under the brown of winter's weathering, thorn and thistle all shouting the presence of the Folk to all who cared to look.

Who would, in this time? They lamented, in Summer, that they were not recognized anymore.

Anyway, birches were good. Hopefully no other had found shelter there, for the wind was chill and unsettled. With Unseelie about and so active, the free and those who held even nominal allegiance to Summer would be seeking safety. Those whose fealty lay with the King of Unseelie's gray and red, well, they would do well to seek, too. Crimson in tooth and claw was Unwinter, and Summer held them to be the darker half of sidhe, almost Twisted in the Sundering between the Courts.

Still, the Seelie Court was just as dangerous. The difference was the perfume they laced the poison with.

She was about to step into the grove when a chill rippled through her. She turned, inhaling sharply—

—and let the breath out, dangerous song unsung, staring at the slim boylike sidhe who grinned with his sharp white teeth.

"Puck," she said, as the air neared the end of its outcycle, and did she imagine his slight flinch?

She decided she had. He *had* been dogging her steps in the mortal world of late, and even more so now that she was playing fetch for the Queen. Sometimes he took an interest in Court affairs, but not often, and given his taste for mortal boyflesh—for eating, not for sport, most said, though the two were often commingled among the sidhe—Robin did not think him likely to be wanting much of her except mischief.

He had brought her to Summer, of course. Maybe he felt proprietary, or was simply bored.

His name echoed uneasily, fell flat against sere grass. The hard consonant was crisper than she liked, and the birches rustled uneasily. Maybe they felt her; even if they were ghilliedhu they might be sleeping until the Queen opened the Gates. Or they might be a-wandering away from the tree that housed what might be called a soul.

Did they have them, the beautiful sidhe? It was an open question.

"At your service, my lady Robin." He grinned even wider, and cut her a fine, if unpolished, bow. It had to be a mockery, for she had seen him act with the latest Court manners when he pleased to do so. "'Tis fine to see your face again so soon. And whither are you bound this cold evening?"

Nowhere you may see me tread. "On business, Goodfellow, and thank you for your interest."

The browns and greens melded him into a clutter of bramble and blackberry vines as he crouched, his hands carefully kept from the leaf-sheathed dagger at his belt. The age-blackened reed pipes, bound with thin flexible bands suspiciously resembling dried tendons, were just as dangerous, but he spread his long-fingered hands, only four and a thumb on each hand but each with an extra joint, in the leaf and mulch. Hourglass-pupiled, flash-green into yellow eyes winked through his tumbled hair, and he laughed. "You may thank me for more than that, Ragged. I have a riddle for thee."

. She backed up two paces, wondering if she dared step inside the birch grove *now*. "I do not recall asking thee for one, good sir."

"Nevertheless. Why do you not leave the changeling to the Queen's graces, Ragged? You could be free. *Truly* free."

That's twice he's mentioned Sean. Will I have to kill him? It was no small proposition. Goodfellow was ancient even among the Folk, called the Fatherless in certain quarters—though never to his face.

Robin-mama. And all the stars of Summer's dusk. Were they worth the risk of enmity with one this old and strong?

Her expression hardened, and when she spoke, each word was chill. "That would make me faithless as your own good self, Goodfellow. What business have you here?"

"Ah, the lady who disdains me is the lady I love." He sang it, queerly accented but musically enough, and she did not recognize the tune. No doubt if she had it would have been a cruel jest, and her skin was thin enough just now.

"Sing another measure, Robin Goodfellow, and I shall sing one in return." It was not a true threat, but it was satisfying to see him blanch slightly. As if she did not know that very little would stir Puck's heart to the cruel mercy of his kind of affection.

He unfolded from the ground with queer, flowing grace, and had she not been accustomed to the strange movements of sidhe flesh and bone she might have been nauseous at the alienness of his articulation. When he spoke, though, there was no fear or laughter, and his voice could have been a mortal man's, with even a mimicry of tenderness in its timbre.

"I'll bring you Gallow, dear Robin, if you want him."

She measured him from top to toe, and found him just the same as ever. The question was, dared she trust his word, or was it a silken lure? There was no love lost between them, but neither was there *open* enmity, and he had stood almost-godfather in presenting her to the Queen. No, Puck the Goodfellow treated her just as he treated all others, granting where it pleased him and snatching away as well.

In that, he was like Unwinter, and like Summer herself. At least he had given her the cure ampoules...and as far as he knew, now, she had handed them over to Summer.

Almost alarmed at the turn her thoughts had taken, Robin backed away another step. Her skirt fluttered on the edge of the freshening breeze, and now that dark was rising as well, the wind had teeth. Muzzled for the moment, but soon they would bite.

"Do not flee me, Ragged." Puck performed a capering little jig, dry blackberry vines crunching under glove-soled feet. "It pleases me to bring to you the Armormaster. That is what the Gallow was, before he left Court. Did you know?"

Armormaster? Broghan the Black wears the glass badge now, and none speak of who preceded him. Maybe they've forgotten.

Or maybe he displeased Summer, and left. Which might make this Gallow more of an ally than she had thought. The Armormaster set the guard on the Keep, and was the arbiter of duels. And he could be challenged by any who sought to wear the glass badge, or make a name for themselves. It was unlike any of them to simply leave Court unless banished— perhaps that was why he wasn't spoken of, and he would take Robin's tidings as a gladness, that he was to be readmitted to Seelie?

She shrugged, carefully enough. The sun dipped below some

of the frowning buildings overlooking the tangled woods, and the distant sound of traffic held a thread of silver.

Yes, maybe even Unwinter himself would be riding tonight. Perhaps following hard on the heels of a ragged bird.

"Come, Ragged. A neutral place, and I shall bring thee a princely gift. For no other reason than it warms me cockles to see the Glass-Gallow face you. No doubt you have words he should hear; he and I are acquainted of old."

Glass-Gallow. And merely acquainted. At least he's not claiming to be friends. Once I have Gallow himself, or have delivered my message, I may return to Summer. At the moment, it seemed a better option than any other that had presented itself the whole dreary day. "Name the ground, Puck." For his choice of traps would tell her much.

"The Rolling Oak. At the very least, if I am not true, you shall have an ale and perhaps a means to divert ill-luck."

The Oak was free ground, and one of the few places that perhaps could break her trail. She did not wish to cross its threshold unless things became truly dire, but the wind chilled further as light drained from the sky, and Robin Ragged was suddenly aware of just how weary she was.

She calculated distance, probable meanings, and Puck's sudden interest, and arrived at a very depressing conclusion.

I might as well. What does it matter?

"The Rolling Oak." It was neither a confirmation nor a denial, and she backed up still further. No hummock turned her ankle, no bog clutched at her shoes. Perhaps it was an omen, or merely good luck. "Perhaps I shall see thee there, Goodfellow."

"Ah, my lady Ragged, perhaps you shall." The unholy glee on his slim brown face would have given her pause, but she had already fled into the birches, taking the chance that they would halt or turn any curse he spat at her retreating back. His last call, though, shivered the naked branches overhead. It was an old song, and no doubt he sang it to taunt her, for at the end of it was a death.

"*For my love promised to meet me, and will she be untruuuuuuue...*"

The rest of its chorus burned inside her as she reached the edge of the park.

And lo, my love, she came too late.

And oh, my love, was you.

LONG AND LONG
22

⌖

It would have been easier with something to practice a sympathetic chantment on. Something she had worn or breathed upon.

But of course it couldn't be easy, not for him.

Dusk found Jeremiah on Challer Avenue, where the old Garden Faire had stood. A meeting place for free sidhe and mortal-Tainted, it had once been a throbbing hub on the edge of the Gobelins. The market—and its goblin Doges— no longer stitched themselves to the alley alongside, perhaps because the coffee shop was now a burned-out husk, with only a faint lemony tang of sidhe remaining. Violence still tingled in the blackened walls, and he ducked past the faded festoons of caution and crime-scene tape.

The massive mahogany counter the long-haired ghilliedhu girls had clustered at was a shell, the walls dappled with smoke and water damage. No sign of Ardie Meg, the brughnie proprietor he had once almost considered a friend; no sign of anyone else. Just the vibration of screaming and smoke—and a very faint, almost unsmell of bitter almonds.

Unseelie, again. Scavengers, or besiegers? Had open war

been declared on free sidhe without him knowing? Of course, if he'd known, would he have cared?

Not before today.

No, Gallow, be honest. Not before Friday night.

He told that sneering little voice in his head to fuck off and eased around the long shoal of burned and shattered mahogany, his boots making the floor wobble alarmingly. He'd thought this place was built on concrete, but maybe that was glamour. Exhausted ghosts of cinnamon steam and faint breaths of coffee-smell rose, brushed his cheeks and the backs of his hands.

There was a scorch in the back hallway leading to the little-used restrooms, scorch-smear clawing down from the ceiling. Up near the top the wall was eaten away, and he sniffed cautiously, smelling the peculiar fading ozone of an electrical fire. This wall was shared with a mortal bar that faced onto 73rd instead of Challer; perhaps some catastrophe there had spread.

Wood and field burned easily, and so did their spirits. He shook his head, deciding it didn't matter, and headed for the bar.

The shelves behind the mahogany wreck were twisted and warped. He crouched right where the cash register had been, and reached back. He had to actually put his head under the bar, into the smoking darkness, and for a moment the thread of screaming and fear rose to overwhelm him.

Yes, a mortal fire. Brughnies didn't burn like ghilliedhu or other wood-spirits, so Ardie might even be alive elsewhere. Who knew? They were homefast wights. They didn't like to move, but would one stay here?

His fingers closed around oiled black canvas. He pulled it free, gently, and his fingers sensed no breakage. He didn't breathe until he had the little bag safely cupped in his hands, straightening his legs so he could check the interior again. No movement, and his instincts weren't tingling.

Still, it wouldn't do to stay here, now that he had what he sought. The few small tokens he'd taken from Summerhome might possibly be useful. It was a wonder they hadn't been found by scavenger or fortune-hunter.

If Ardie was still alive, she was underground. Good luck finding her; brughnie though she was, she owed Gallow a favor or two. There went his best chance of finding what he wanted without cost. Still, if Ardie had left this here...either she was dead, or she guessed Gallow would come back for it, and did not dare to brave his wrath if he found it gone.

Daisy had been here once. Just once.

You and a mortal, Ardie had sneered, her nut-brown face screwing up with distaste. *Don't bring her to the Folk places, Gallow. You know better.*

He'd waited long enough none could accuse him of leaving Summer for a mortal, but he still knew better than to bring one to places sidhe frequented. If anyone still bore him a grudge from his Armormaster days, well, Gallow was hard to harm, but a mortal girl was not. In the first flush of being able to openly court Daisy he'd been silly as a pixie and twice as scatterbrained.

Pixies. Now, there was an idea. If he could get them to concentrate long enough—

The air changed. Jeremiah's head snapped up. The little bag slid itself into his pocket, and he was out from behind the bar in a flash.

"Over Hill and under Sea, what do I now see before me?" A high, almost girlish giggle, and Jeremiah's skin chilled. "Come to pick the bones of the dead, Armormaster?"

"Goodfellow." He didn't sound surprised, at least. "This was once a nice place."

"Not long ago, as mortals reckon." A slim boyshape melded out of the shadows in the back corner, where the great clock had stood, its small gilded figures hopping out to chime the hours. If mortals entered this place, they would have noticed the clockface was blank—except at night, when the full moon rose and glowed through the skylights. Only then the clockface would be a sleeping woman's, the eyelashes and pores drawn with a hair-fine brush, the mouth slackly open and sharp teeth visible.

Now the clock was shattered, and the spirit sleeping inside it loose to ride the night winds. Bits of ebony and glass crunched as the boy skipped forward on glove-shod feet. Brown leather molded itself to his slenderness; his hair was a raggedly cut cap of chestnut streaked with fine bits of gold. His ears came up to sharp points, poking through the fine smooth strands, and a leaf-sheathed dagger rested at his hip.

It was either very good fortune, or very bad, to meet him here. Gallow's weight shifted back, carefully, and the boy's eyes peered from under his messy hair.

Bright and changeful between yellow and green, those eyes, thickly lashed and beguiling, with hourglass-shaped pupils. His pipes hung at his silver-buckled belt, and his extra-jointed brown fingers dipped, stroking their soundless mouths. Goodfellow swept a graceful bow, doffing an imaginary cap. "Hail and well-met, brother mine. Did you come for coffee? The brughnie's hospitality hath grown cold of late. Seven days ago it was scorch-hot, a mortal fire burning quickly and snuffed too late."

A week, and just a bad-luck fire, not an attack. That was likely all Puck would give for free, and could be a lie as well. The marks on Gallow's arms tingled. "What is a free woodland spirit here for? Picking bones as well?" *Let him think me carrion, if he's stupid enough.*

Which Puck was emphatically not, and likewise did not take umbrage at. An almost-insult for an almost-insult, and all even.

It felt so familiar, measuring his words against the arcane rules of sidhe etiquette.

Puck's smile widened a trifle. "Oh, searching, brother. One of our wayward girls has gone so much further astray than usual."

"Who's missing now? And why would you seek for her here?"

Goodfellow laughed. The sound was a crystal bell, wrongly tuned. He capered sideways. "You've grown dull among mortals, Gallow, and you reek of barrow-wight-death. The Unseelie ride hither and yon, striking down all in their way. Have you heard of the plague?"

"Some little of it." Gallow eased the backpack on his shoulders, a loose rolling motion. "The Folk do not often fall prey to sickness."

How quickly the odd speech of the sidhe fell back into his mouth again. Then again, Goodfellow might not answer if you spoke to him with what he considered impoliteness. It was rarely politic to piss off one of the truly unaligned.

"Oh, times have changed. Are about to change more, if you are a-wandering without your mortal doxy." Goodfellow grinned, and the pearly edges of his teeth were sharp enough to cut his whistling laugh as it slid past them. "Did you tire of aging flesh?"

Rage rose, red wine turning to vinegar, but Gallow forced his hands to remain loose. Still, he traded insult for insult, openly this time. "What sidhe are you hunting, then, Goodfellow? A woman? Hardly your usual quarry."

"Boymeat is sweet, but this is not for eating. News has spread that His Majesty, unhallowed be *that* name, seeks a certain winged sidhe-girl. The reward is vast." Goodfellow cocked his selkie-sleek head. "So vast I almost think it a risk to tell you. For if once Gallow rides in pursuit, how can one little bird hope to escape?"

It can't be. If Puck was looking for her, and musing aloud that Unwinter wanted her caught, it would be better if Gallow was there when she was found by *anyone*. "If you don't tell me, I'll hear it on the wind anyway. To see you hunting here in the ruins, Goodfellow, makes me think that I should perhaps simply ride in your wake."

Amazingly, the boy laughed. "And I thought you would take convincing. Come, let us taste some ale. You are not the best drinking companion, but the ash in the air makes my eyes misty. It must be my age."

Gallow's shoulders relaxed a fraction. "It would be an honor."

The boy's smile widened, too far to be human. His eyes twinkled with sheer sickening goodwill. "Then come. I shall show you where to ask questions, and require no tithe. It suits me tonight. How long has it been since you tasted proper ale?"

I think I prefer Coors. But oh well. "Long and long, Goodfellow. Lead on."

>⧾<

It was not a short walk, and night had risen with cold, penetrating rain on a moan-soaking wind. He knew where they were bound halfway there, but still he walked with Goodfellow, whose light banter had vanished. The silence might have been a warning.

In any case, the Rolling Oak was as good a place as any to begin his search afresh.

The entrance was a shopfront that looked vaguely foreign from the outside, and would give mortals a subtle chill. Except for the lonely or suicidal; those would feel a pull right through their marrow, a false promise of relief.

Inside, it was close and warm, full of the smell of wet earth, burning applewood, and splashed ale. The fume of candles in squat lanthorns, the barely perceptible spice-tang of sidhe flesh with only the slightest tinge of mortal blood to tarnish its edges, meat roasting on a spit, the rich illusion of coffee. Down three age-blackened steps, brushing aside the branches— wood coaxed from the walls, leaves pale from lack of sunlight surviving by drinking in the aura of strange and delicious and making little whisper-chuckle sounds as they fingered each patron.

Bark-skinned sweet-loving brughnies and woodwights at the bar, kobolding in a corner sharing a keg the size of a fat pony, the flittering that was pixies with their gossamer shrouds and the gleam of their wicked-sharp teeth. Hobs and grenteeth and jennies or jacks of every shape and size, galleytrots and churchgrims with their snouts in brass bowls on the floor, their sad wise eyes half closed. And more. It all closed about Jeremiah Gallow, and he took a deep breath.

Puck capered for a dark corner, pale mushrooms crawling the wall in pained corkscrews. Here the black vinyl booths were sticky, and the tabletops spattered with scorch and other marks scrubbed at the end of the night with bleach and muttered chantment. A kelpie, broad shoulders straining at a dark coarsewoven shirt and his ropy hair long wet draggles, hunched in one, staring into a bowl of smoking fly-covered chunks of wet glistening meat still twitching from its former owner's agony.

In the furthest booth, a russet gleam. A pale flash—but she relaxed as Puck swung away. She had her back to the wall; the Rolling Oak had only one exit. Unless she planned to brave

Peleaster the Cook's wrath, and in the smoke-hell of the kitchen such a thing was not to be done lightly.

She studied Jeremiah as he settled across the table from her. A single glass of silty red wine, with a faint glow in its depths. Ever-grape, called *lithori*. Expensive, but what could a Realmaker not afford if she chose it?

His palms were damp.

"He brought you." The same contralto. The same tilt to her head, and her fingers played with the glass's stem. Its top was a tulip, frozen cunningly in sidheglass. "I thought him..." A shadow across her face.

You thought him a liar? Wise of you. "We happened to cross paths." *He may be seeking to sell you to Unwinter, but you're safe enough for the moment.*

A tangle-haired brughnie girl, her green coarsewoven skirts hiked enough to show her knobby barklike ankles and bare horn-toed feet, slammed a foaming mug of nut-brown bitter down before him. She whirled smartly away, and Jeremiah winced inwardly. Now Goodfellow had stood him a drink. The debt was slight, but it could be a wedge. Yet he could not be impolite, so he lifted it and took a long draft.

When he wiped his mouth, the tingle of good sidhe ale all through him and his nerves suitably bolstered, he bumped the backpack below the table with his boot. It was a reassuring weight. "Ragged." He accorded her the courtesy of a surname.

She nodded slightly. Her eyes were close to indigo now, and he thought she was perhaps weary. Through the smoke and fug of the Oak's closeness, he could not catch a breath of that cherryspice perfume, and he dared not lean forward to try.

"Gallow." She accorded him the same. "I bring word. *She* wants you."

He dropped his gaze, staring into the mug's blind eye. *A messenger? She said she was under commission.*

"The Queen." Her voice had dropped, but she said it slowly, in case he was stupid enough to not take her meaning. "It pleases her to have your presence in Summer."

It does not please me. "She can go to Hell." He could not help himself, glancing up to take a sipping glance of her face.

He couldn't pretend she was Daisy, but he couldn't look away, either.

Her expression had not changed. She studied the *lithori*, with a slightly distracted air. "Do you think such a place would accept *her*?" It could have been an incautious sally, or a warning.

He shrugged. Why did they have to talk about Summer? He wanted to ask her...

...what? What did he want to say? *You look like a mortal I once knew.* An insult to any reasonable sidhe. There had been no hint of changeling on Daisy; it was impossible. *All* of this was impossible.

Wondering why Daisy's face was now a haze in his memory was, too. He was just like every other faithless sidhe. Would there come a time when he could go a day, a week, a month, without thinking of her?

Except he had just gone an entire afternoon doing just that.

Eventually, Robin pressed on. "You've seen the plague. They are dying, Gallow."

"So are mortals." A bitter cut.

"Panko. I remember." She nodded, those curls falling forward. The sun in her hair had diminished, a smolder now. "The mortal-Tainted don't take the sickness. It began to grow marked last year, and the Queen did not open the Gates until the very last moment, and then only a quarter of the way. She cannot do so this year without risking a withering." Her gaze drifted over the Oak's interior, much as a warrior would study terrain.

She remembered a dead man's name, at least. It was more courtesy than he expected. She was drawn tight as a harpstring, and she was indeed weary. Only a desperate woman would trust Goodfellow—and why had *he,* of all people, brought Gallow here, hinting at Unwinter? Did it serve him to make mischief? Had he told this Robin whom she resembled?

The bigger mystery was, of course, *why* she resembled his dead wife. Coincidence, just maybe.

To put his hands in her hair, make a fist, feel the slippery silkiness—

He took another long pull of the ale as she continued her soft recitation.

"Unwinter suffers the most, since his land is open to all. The Free brush against the sickness and take it more often than not. Mortal blood affords some immunity. Half are safe, and above to a quarter of mortal blood. 'Tis the fullblood who fear, and those who were yesterday so proud of their aristocracy now dig for peasant ancestors, hoping to find some insurance." She took a small mannerly sip of her wine, set it down again with a click. "When the Gates open, of course the danger to her Court is greater. Yet I ask myself, Gallow, what will happen to Half and less, when Summer and Unwinter are gone?"

I don't care. His lips were numb. Maybe it was the ale. "It cannot be that dire."

"It is. Unwinter is *ravaged,* the Black and Low Counties unwonted quiet. The rest of the free spaces before the Second Veil, who can tell? The freefolk—those allied with Unseelie are feeling the blackboil bite more often. Cures are sought everywhere. Some delay the sickness, but cannot halt it entirely. Rumor flies hither and yon...." She shook herself, studied his face again, earnestly. "*You,* though, faced a plagued rider and lived. It makes them strong before it kills them."

I don't care. "Where do you come from?" The sweat was all over him now, his heart hammering. The marks on his arms tingled, ran with excruciating sensitivity. "Who are your folk? Are you part *ghillie?*" They were held to be beauties, the ghilliedhu girls.

She shook her head, impatient. "Shall I convey to *her* that you heed her summons and come soon as you may? Returning with me would be better, but... should you not wish to, Gallow, I will do what I may to sweeten her temper at the news."

It was a handsome gesture, and one from a Half who no doubt felt a debt to him even though told otherwise. Which was not usual among the sidhe.

He opened his mouth to ask again, to *demand* she tell him, but her gaze sharpened. She sucked in a quick breath, paling, and he did not have to look to guess at what had drifted through the Oak's low, wide door. He could smell them, since they used no glamour to mask themselves here. Clammy rotten dirt, decaying linen, pale metal at throat, wrist, finger, and belt. A chill went through the Rolling Oak, and there was a general rustling movement as the Folk within collectively stiffened.

The lone wight moved aside, and others pressed behind him. The branches at the door shriveled to blackness, and behind the bar the half-giant, half-drow Kosthril the Mammoth's four arms dropped to his sides. His long, narrow nose twitched, and the bartender made a scraping, rumbling noise deep in his barrel chest.

NO PART OF THIS

23

⸙

Robin's fingers turned to ice. They curled around the stem of the wineglass—she had chosen *lithori* not because she preferred its sweetness, but because it held flame so well.

Six wights, and if there were so many coming into the Oak, there were no doubt others outside. *Four counts in, four counts out.* "There will be trouble soon," she said softly. "If you do not wish to accompany me to Court—"

"I'll go." As if the words stuck in his throat. His eyes had lit with green fire, and a fine sheen of sweat dewed his forehead. "You knew I would."

I knew no such thing. There was little time for argument. She slid out of the booth, wine slopping inside the bowl of the glass. Still, it rankled a trifle. "I did not."

He was already on his feet as the first pixie screamed, a tiny crystalline tinkle. His hands made an odd movement, as if clasping a slender stave not yet visible. "Stay behind me."

Not here. "Go through the kitchen. I shall—"

"Do as I tell you, woman."

The music below her thoughts sharpened. She turned on her heel, inhaled smoothly, and the first wight's gaze settled upon her, chill as Unwinter itself. She would have unloosed a phrase of song, but Gallow's hand closed about her bare arm, warm and hard, and he shoved her. The *lithori* went flying; she had the presence of mind to whistle a piercing, drilling note that ignited its shining arc. The whistle peaked, and a flaming whip hit the wight ghosting through the crowd.

Pixie screams shattered, the Unwinter hunters howling as well. She held the whistle as long as she could, whooping in a breath after the *lithori*-fueled flame, silvery at its edges, twisted dried-leaf as its impetus died.

Gallow moved forward, his boots slipping slightly in a foaming tide of ale—who had spilled their drink? It didn't matter, though her own shoes slid a little, too, the battleground turned treacherous in more ways than one.

Had she thought to protect *him*? A moonlit lance resolved out of empty air, filling his cradling hands, and flicked serpent-tongue, its head shifting between narrow needle-blade and a broader one that glowed red as true iron, shearing off half a wight's face.

The wights had swords and curses, but Robin had her breath back now. Her throat swelled, a net of throbbing sonic gold catching black-flapping maledictions, crushing them, stripping smoke-veined wings. The bartender, a four-armed drow-giant mix without a clanplug dangling from his large green ear, rumbled again.

Under a suddenly gold-stippled roof, the former Armormaster danced. Half-turn, lance sweeping, a wight's black brackish blood rising in a perfect arc before splattering on a ghilliedhu girl who shrieked and cowered, steam rising from her white, white skin. The weapon flickered through shade and glow, striking and reversing, and for a moment Robin almost forgot to breathe.

He advanced, and the lance flicked again as one of the wights leapt, its smooth noseless face twisting as it hissed. A crunch, the barrow-wight spitted neatly and flung toward the bar, where the 'tender snarled and brought one of his club-like fists down. There was a splatter, a crunch-popping, and the ghilliedhu girls fled en masse, flocking to the door in a tangle of white limbs and long wood-colored hair.

Tables and chairs scraped; the brughnies burrowing into the woodworked walls and the bartender spreading his four arms wide again, muscle flickering in his torso under his tasseled leather vest. *"No more fight!"* he yelled, in the peculiar half-throat accent of the outcast drow, and his eyes flared with yellow glow.

Robin inhaled, trying to decide which one of the wights she should aim the song for. If she misjudged, she might well harm Gallow.

He leaned back as their curved silver blades whispered from blackened sheaths. One darted in from the side, and he stamped, dropping his shoulder and somehow avoiding the wicked gleam of a short curved bone knife. He hit the wight with a *crunch,* and the butt of the lance popped out, catching this one just below the ribs with a sickening, bonebreaking crack.

The remaining wights scattered. Pale gilt gleamed at their wrists and fingers; one wore a fluid rune-scored torc and halted as Gallow stepped to one side, almost mincingly, his black hair slightly mussed despite the fogwater from outside weighing the cropped strands down.

The lance-tip made a tiny circle in the air, its hum a silver thread stitching the chaos together. Pixies and ghilliedhu girls still screaming as they fled, the pixies clinging to long hair, the kobolding massed in a corner, watchful. The brughnies had scattered, more than one straight up the wall, hanging from the ceiling as they craned their very flexible necks to witness. Other sidhe crept or cowered, pressing into corners and crannies.

Puck, of course, was nowhere to be seen as his mischief—whatever of this he'd planned—ran its course. She found herself breathing deeply, wondering why Gallow did not strike again. The wights were drifting apart; they might be able to flank him unless Robin could gain a clear—

He seemed to be waiting for something, caught in curious stasis. Perhaps for the torc-wearing wight to speak, in its throat-cut whisper.

"*The Ragged,*" it said, slowly and distinctly. "He *wantsssss her.*"

Scalding ice flamed over every inch of Robin's body. She took a single step back, finishing her inhale, the music under her thoughts sharp and dissonant as it prepared to loose itself from her throat.

"The Ragged is no part of this." Jeremiah Gallow gave a bitter breathless approximation of a laugh. "I find myself of a mind to do you a mischief, to repay the one your kinsmen wrought upon me."

What?

Her own confusion was echoed by the wight, which made a fluttering little motion with its strangle-fingered hands.

"*Sylvia,*" Gallow said, and struck again. The lance described a sweet-whistling arc, shearing the torc-wearing wight in two. It blade lengthened, curving impossibly *backward* and glowing red-hot. Black blood burst as the remaining barrow-wights leapt for him, and glimmering droplets of sweat flew from Gallow's brow as he moved with the impossible, blurring speed of the sidhe. Choked cries rent the air, and those collected gasped.

The lance blurred as it sang, a low, hungry keening. Halting, a hook instead of a knife, slicing down and pulled back with a small jerk. The last wight howled as its arm, sheared from its body, dropped to the floor. Their cut-grass reek was overpowering, everywhere; Robin's nose was full and her eyes ran with sting-hot liquid. Her mouth gapped, her throat kept clear and ready despite the stuffiness.

"Return to your master, and tell him that Gallow does not serve." Level, furious, and very deep, his tone sliced the hubbub. "Free or Court, none commands me, and *I repay.*"

The wight fell down, wriggling, its right hand clutched against the spurting wound that had been its arm moments before. The stink of charring rose—even if it survived, the iron would poison-burn it into a crippling Twist.

The lance vanished. Jeremiah Gallow turned on his heel, his greenleaf gaze finding hers. "Come."

"There are bound to be—"

"More outside, yes. Can you sing?"

Why do you ask? She nodded. "If I may breathe, I may sing." Despite the thick reek in the air, she could breathe well enough.

"Good. Keep their curses off us." The lance vanished, and the thing writhing on the floor hissed an imprecation. Gallow stepped aside, scooped up his backpack, and shrugged into it. He finished by catching Robin's arm again. A malformed curse struggled and writhed on the floor as well, a quick stamp of his heavy workman's boot and it made a ripe-melon sound of breakage. "Through the kitchen."

"Peleaster?" The Rolling Oak's cook was never of a sweet temper, and it was all the warning she could muster and still keep her breath in reserve.

"I might almost welcome killing again, should I need to."

What else could she do? She followed.

And wondered who *Sylvia* was.

>╫<

He had seen her sing, and seemed curiously unmarked by the experience.

Though Peleaster the Cook was not happy, his great bulk shuddering through the smoky hell of his kitchen and bubbling brew-vats, the fume of violence on Gallow had actually kept Peleaster's roaring to a deep throbbing, an out-of-tune orchestra instead of an earthquake.

They spilled out into a narrow alley, Robin blinking furiously as the smoke grew even more caustic, billowing in thinning strands around them. One of the Cook's tentacles, a fibrous gray-greenish thing, slammed the door behind them with cracking force.

Robin coughed, cleared her throat, brushed at her skirt. Gallow coughed, too, leaning against a brick wall pitted by only Stone knew what. The Cook, in his fury, nevertheless had spat them out a long way from the Oak.

For a few moments she simply savored the air—tinged with smoke, wight-death, and exhaust, but she was still alive to draw it.

Gallow retched, bending almost double, and she patted his back awkwardly. It was different from touching Sean, birdbones under fragile skin. This man was hard with muscle, and twice now he had fought before her.

It was enough to make a woman feel charitable.

She glanced about, alert for danger as he shuddered. Did he often do this, after battle? Some did. A mortal stomach rebelled at death, as the saying went.

Where will we rest tonight? Perhaps he knows of a place. If not... "It will soon be midnight." She patted his back again, smoothing his heavy, scarred coat. She carefully avoided touching the backpack; the lance, with its frightening shapeshifting, had vanished. It had looked like dwarven work, but its winking out of existence troubled her slightly. She did not bother much with weapons, unless it was her voice. "We must find shelter."

He nodded, straightening and wiping his mouth with the back of one hand. "Yes. You...That's quite a song you have, Robin."

She shrugged. Perhaps he would fear her now. She couldn't explain that the music only came *through* her, if she would let it. Robin Ragged could hum, very softly and for a short period of time, but singing let the golden music loose, and she had little control over its form. Whoever her sidhe father was, perhaps he had been a musical beast.

There was no need to tell this man any of that, though. She fell back upon the almost-rehearsed sentences she'd settled on long ago to explain the bare minimum. "I sing it at *her* command, and to save my own life. That's all."

"That's probably enough." He declined to elaborate further, though, and did not step away from her hand. Instead, she let it drop, a pale bird shot down.

"I know a place." Why was she offering so much? "Not far, and lacking a roof, but safe enough for us to rest. Unless you wish not to—"

"I'll go with you. Come dawn we can slip over into Summer." He'd caught his breath, and regarded her now, his gaze level and disconcerting. She was nervously aware of his size, and his strength. It made her step back, carefully, slowly, as if he were a troll's kin she didn't wish to startle.

Maybe, in the dimness, he mistook her movement for agreement, because he followed. Which meant she had to halt, step aside, and pass him, heading for the alley's mouth. The awkward dance ended when he caught her wrist, warm mortal-Tainted flesh like her own. To those not sidhe-touched, they would seem feverish.

You're so warm, Rob. Curling around a thinner, younger child when the power was cut off, sharing that warmth. Before the song began showing itself with the first vague stirrings of puberty, she had hummed at night while Mama and Daddy Snowe fought. Comforting another had comforted her.

Was that why she had asked for Sean?

Gallow's fingers were gentle. "Robin." Testing the name.

"Gallow." She tugged away. "Come, we must hurry. Peleaster may not tell them anything, but it's safest not to trust his mercy. One does better trusting his temper, which has probably been sorely tested tonight."

"True." He didn't try to catch her again, simply followed meekly in her wake.

THE TRUE DANGER
24

⟩╫⟨

Nestled in a greenbelt on a run-down residential street, thickly fringed with holly and laurel—good wood, and healthy— was a mossy stone that vibrated ever so slightly when Robin brushed her fingertips against it. Jeremiah looked again, and realized that it must be a meeting of two ley lines. The earth had arteries, and the lines of chantment, however tangled by mortal iron, were part of that great net.

No wonder the stone looked like its roots ran deep. This *was* safe—probably much safer than his own house right now.

No reason to be nervous. Just . . . he'd grown used to sleeping in a bed.

"Do you know the warming breath?" She knelt, gracefully, and looked up at him. In the shadows her hair reminded him again of Daisy, though everything else was different, and he had to suppress a guilty start.

The Half and Tainted learned the breath early, if they didn't begin using it instinctively. Of course he knew. "Ah. Yeah. Yes, I do."

"I'd suggest using it tonight. I don't dare chantment a fire. It might draw attention." Little traceries of steam rose from her bare shoulders. The sidhe ran warm, except the riverkin and trolls. Even the drow had fire in their blood.

Before he knew it, he'd dropped his backpack and slid out of his coat. "Here."

"There is no need for—"

He draped it around her. She wouldn't need its shelter, but he'd already given. No reason to take the chivalry back. "Call it a gesture, then. You fought with me."

"Only because I feared for myself." Her mouth twisted down, bitterly. "Or so many would say."

"Would they be right?" He squatted easily as she scooted back, settling against the stone.

"Perhaps. I would ask you a question." The coat was ridiculously large on her, and its shabby wornness only made the gloss of sidhe beauty on her more incandescent. Now she was shadows and silk, her eyes blue glimmers and the russet in her hair lost. Very little light from the streetlamps penetrated this hollow. The jagged slices in the coat's material where the wights had almost caught him had vanished in the dimness.

He nodded, watching her pale throat as she swallowed. "Ask."

"Who is Sylvia? You slew them in her name."

It jolted him into sudden alertness. "They killed her earlier today."

"I am sorry." She dropped her chin, probably staring at the ground. "Panko. And Sylvia. I will remember."

"They aren't yours to avenge." Now he sounded harsh. It was only because there was a dry stone in his throat. She *had* remembered, something exceptional from a flighty sidhe. Even Half aped forgetfulness sometimes. Or it rubbed off from the highbloods.

Like a disease.

The unsettling idea that he might not truly remember Daisy's face occurred again, circling like a lazy broad-winged curse.

"Very well." She went still. Her hair fell forward, shadowing her face. She could probably sleep there, propped against the stone. He should keep watch, but it had been a hell of a day.

Even highbloods needed surcease.

"Robin Ragged, I would ask you a question." *I've earned at least that much.*

"Ask." Did she sound wary, or half amused? Or both?

"Do you have a family? You were older when you were taken...." He let it trail away. A question and a half—perhaps she would bargain.

What would she ask in return?

"My mortal kin...they didn't want me." Softly, very softly. Of course, now that he'd heard the song swelling from her— no, not *song*. Pure music, a swelling of organ notes, deep and throbbing hurtfully in the bones, as her lips opened and her face changed, transfigured. She probably could have sung the horseman an injury or two, but she'd been running, and tired—and probably breathless as well. "A free sidhe found me, told me of the sideways realms, and stood almost-godfather to me. When I was brought to Summer she accepted me as a gift." A long pause. There was almost certainly more to that story. "I am...grateful, that Unwinter didn't find me first."

He might find you yet. Or both of us. "I am, as well." He wanted to ask more, but she sighed, a weary sound like and unlike Daisy's. "Rest. We're safe enough here."

She nodded, and was gone, slipping over sleep's border. Sagging against the rock, she tipped her head to the side, and for a few moments he struggled with temptation. It wouldn't be a bad thing to approach her; she could probably use the warmth, right? Even if she couldn't, there was such a thing as a knight's right to a damsel. Among the sidhe, such a thing wasn't the crime it was elsewhere.

Christ, she reminded him of Daisy. He hadn't had a woman since, sidhe or mortal.

Jeremiah, you're a bastard.

Despite the damp, the ground here was dry, covered with sere grass and crackling dead leaves. A good scent of spiced cherries, threads of smell mixing with the cold exhaust breathing of the city around them, and he pillowed his head on his backpack. Moved around a bit to get comfortable. Stared up into the branches. The trees leaned over, secretive, the hollies darker than the laurels.

Robin's breathing was almost inaudible. Her feet, in those same black heels, lay on the grass. Her shins were bare, she hadn't curled up, but his coat would keep the worst of the dew off.

Night outside was full of noises, creaks and whisperings, stealthy movements and the sense of vulnerability from sleeping without a roof. A very mortal feeling.

It took him a long while to fall into blackness.

>≬‹

He must have thought Summer would never change. Why else would a strange fluttering void open under his heart when little details caught his gaze? The gnarled trunks of the Queen's apple trees, with their carved-agony faces, under white drifts of blossom, had gained a few millimeters of girth. Some had gained new faces, too, but there was no flash of skin hidden deep in the cracks of brown bark. As usual, imagining the rough wooden tickle as the tree absorbed its prey—or Summer's— sent a chill down his spine.

The grass was just as green, and the paths were just as flour-white. The blossoms were just as fragrant, and the four white and greenstone towers of Summer's Keep pierced a sky softly blue and endless. Dew lay on the long grass. It was the morning of the world, and yet little things bothered him.

No brughnies a-gathering herbs in the shadowed dells, no pixies humming in the grass collecting ice-bright drops of water-breath. No fetches shimmering between shapes, no riverfolk gamboling or woodland sprites dancing as they did all day. There were gleams in the shadows of fernbrake and leafshade—eyes watching, of course, as Robin walked before him. The sidhe sunlight was a flood of gold, turning her hair to a furnace and burnishing her dress as the skirt fluttered, kissing her knees. Muscle flicked under her flawless skin, and he couldn't imagine she was Daisy, because his wife had never walked like this. No, here in Summer her mortal imperfections would have shone, burnished to a high gloss...and would he have felt the lack if he'd taken her back to the mortal realm afterward and seen her fade?

He'd awakened at dawn to find his jacket tucked securely around him and Robin perching on the stone she had slept against, chin up and her entire body expressing wariness. And she had insisted he step over the border into Summer first, as if she were a gallant.

Or a bodyguard.

Now she walked before him, her head up, looking neither left nor right. Either her surroundings were familiar and so, ignored...

...or she was *very* aware of everything around them, and chose not to appear so.

There were no ghilliedhu girls dabbling in the streams, no naiads poking their sleek heads up to see who was passing. As they began up the gentle slope of Hearthill, he realized what else was missing.

"No birds," he murmured. All of Summer was in a breathless hush, and he began to feel even more uneasy.

If that was possible.

Robin didn't pause, but she did turn her head slightly. "Perhaps our liege wishes silence." Each word weighed carefully. Of course, her voice could kill, and here the air would be conscious of the fact.

That very air carried tales here, too. Gossip, rumor, all the games of fickle near-immortals. It was enough to make him reconsider, but he'd decided to follow her, so . . .

What else had he decided?

She gave him one sidelong glance as she dropped back at the foot of the glass stairs, each riser reflecting a different color. Even a mailed fist would not break them, their fragility a lie.

Just like everything else.

The great silver-chased doors were open. Now he preceded her, and he tried to figure out what that look had been. Warning? Something else?

The rotunda was just the same, its misty starlit dome full of secrets and whispers, its floor a gold-chased map of Summer's domains, shifting and wavering as the sidhepaths moved according to whim and their own quixotic laws. He glanced down, noted Copperswood and Fall Reil had switched places, and stepped squarely onto Darweil with a certain queasy satisfaction.

That had been his first duel, so long ago. Fresh from the railway cars and the scrabble of mortal streets, drunk with the possibilities of the sideways realms, and full of petty pride.

He had not always been of the Summer Court. Maybe he should have told Robin as much.

Three steps up, and the doors—still giant, but smaller than the front ones—chimed softly as they slowly opened, flower-like petals of gemmed metal. The light behind them was bright noon, dazzling after the rotunda's dusk.

So *she* wanted to impress him? A lowly Half-mortal knight who had spurned Court and vanished, leaving behind the glass badge?

Just how desperate was the plague? Well, the Gates were still unopened. Summer couldn't delay much longer, though; the spring would curdle.

The Great Hall, for feasting and ceremony, soared away from him on all sides. The glare was *her* first mistake, and the second was one he did not realize until much later, even though he witnessed it.

White stone, with green veins shifting lazily through its flow. The columns, fluted and delicate, held the massive carven roof high, and there was a slight tinkling. Apple-blossom scent filled the air, as well as the perpetually falling petals—he had wondered, for a long time, where they all came from, and decided it was a glamour so old it sustained itself with little trouble.

Beware the mask, old gnarled Fuillpine had once sneered at him, *for it becomes truth.*

Fuillpine had died on the lance, a duel engineered by Summer, for whatever reason. Perhaps she didn't like his cynicism. Even now Jeremiah's arms tingled, the marks shifting madly under his coat. He was neither warm nor cold, will holding temperature in abeyance.

Just like any sidhe.

The petals stayed on the floor, pristine snowdrifts, until they were bruised or stepped upon. Then they vanished, puffing up ghosts of delicious scents to match the apple perfume. As soon as they were marred, they died, mortal as any of his coworkers.

The hall was empty, except for *her,* at the end, her reclining couch on the low dais. White as snow, carmine lips, the green Jewel on her forehead singing to itself, as usual. She was robed in twilight, shimmering heavy fur and velvet, as if she felt a chill.

He took in the changes with a swift glance—there was a column of amber beside her couch on the dais with its star-pattern. Looked like a statue. Naked, a youth with a proud but immature erection, his hands lifted as if he pleaded. There was a marvelous accuracy in the carving, as fine as the bark of the trees in *her* wood.

The draperies had become dusty blue instead of the deep heart's-blood red of his youth, and there was no tinkling music. Had *she* even dismissed the minstrels?

Good God. Summer without her constant music. It beggared belief.

Robin, behind him, barely faltered. Still, the hesitation between two of her steady steps was as loud as a shout in the hush.

The ageless, beautiful face glowed as the Seelie Queen lay on her side, watching them approach. "Here he comes," Summer murmured, her voice just as beautiful as ever. Just as soulless. "A champion, one who faced plagued Unseelie and triumphed. Hail, Armormaster."

That is not my name. He restrained himself with an almost-physical effort. He remembered those exquisite fingers against his sweating flesh, her quiet laugh when he spent himself, shuddering with loathing.

Perhaps *she* remembered as well. She had not called him to her bed often, and even at the time he'd had enough sense to be glad of that. You had to be half insane to couch with Summer; still, she had her ways of enticing even when a man wanted nothing to do with it.

His throat was dry, but he managed to sound crisp and calm. "Greetings to Summer." Barely polite, not delivered on one knee, and brief. He settled his backpack higher on his shoulders and halted before the dais, gazing up at her. "You sent your errand girl, and she brought me. Speak."

Even he couldn't believe he'd said it. It was a relief to find his body, for once, not noticing the Seelie Queen's nearness. Maybe Daisy had inoculated him against *that* disease.

Robin halted, two steps behind and to his left. His skin chilled, suddenly. After seeing what her song could do, only an idiot would turn his back to her.

Robin Ragged wasn't the danger here. Still, if Summer ordered her to sing him into death, would the Ragged do so?

The true danger in this room snuggled into the mound of gorgeous cushions in every shade of blue piled on that end of the reclining throne and smiled pacifically at him. "First I shall send the errand girl away. She has something to collect for me." Those perfect lips, the smile spreading, white teeth peeping between the carmine eagerly to see what she was regarding so intently.

It was Robin's turn to speak, but she took her time. When she did, it was the soft dulcet honey of a woman past rage. "Have you met my conditions, O Seelie's glory? Is Sean returned to the mortal realm, whole and well?"

Summer's smile widened, fractionally. "I would have, but a poor, poor mortal boy insulted one of Seelie's greatest knights." One pale hand lifted languidly, stroked a velvet-clad hip before pointing at the amber boy, glowing with his own inner light. "I could not deny such wrath from a prince of the Blood."

Sean? The sudden urge to glance at Robin rose up in him, died away. Was she bargaining for a lover caught in Summer's snares? His throat was full of hot ash. There was a ghost of her scent clinging to the collar of his coat; he suddenly longed to shed the rough heavy cloth and leather patches.

Of course Robin had a lover. Those eyes, and that hair. Who wouldn't want her? The danger of her voice would only add spice to it, an edge hidden in a woman's softness.

Summer's eyes narrowed fractionally, their blackness turning hurtfully brilliant and sharpening, tiny star-motes dying in a river of ink.

Whatever he expected, it wasn't the slight sound of weight shifting. A woman turning on a Cuban heel, and there were determined little clicks.

Receding.

"Ragged Robin, Robin Ragged." Summer's smile had widened. "Bring me the ampoules, and I may find a way to return our Sean to flesh."

No change in the footsteps. Jeremiah did not dare to glance over his shoulder. Instead, he watched Summer.

The Queen's countenance didn't alter, a picture-perfect rendition of calm. It wasn't an actress's expression—a mortal actress, after all, would know on some level that she was lying. "Robin." An edge below the silken tone now. "If you leave, I may have to put him away in a storeroom, with dust and cobwebs. Do you think he's alive in there?"

Robin halted.

Jeremiah almost winced. Either Summer was overplaying her hand here, or Robin was just like every other fickle sidhe.

Which one would it be?

GAVE YOU AN ANSWER, DO

25

⇥‖⇤

*A*ll the stars of Summer's dusk. She blinked several times. The hot water collecting in her eyes didn't brim over. Instead, Robin swallowed twice. Maybe *she* thought it was indecision, for the Queen of Seelie spoke again, a little more harshly.

"What is it to be, Ragged?"

Cold fire all through her, scalp to toes. For a moment she considered finishing her smooth inhale—four counts in, to make certain she had enough—and loosing the full range of her cursed song on Summer herself.

What is it to be, Ragged?

Then continuing, singing until every particle of the Queen of Seelie was ground finer than dust. Could she do it? There was precious little the song couldn't destroy, if she gave it enough breath.

A rather fitting expression of your entire life, don't you think? The few times the song had burst free in her mortal childhood were nightmares best kept locked in a dungeon.

Even as Robin considered it, there was a better idea. Though that was hateful, too, wasn't it? The ease with which she considered what would hurt her enemy most, and leave Robin's sorry skin whole.

Daddy Snowe would be proud. How often had he regaled a silent, adoring Mama with tales of how he'd "got one over" on anyone who crossed him?

Her pulse thundered in her ears. Of course *she* would hear it, and probably Gallow, too. So Robin let the tears brim over, two slug-tracks on her burning face. Let Summer think her weak enough to weep from sorrow instead of rage.

Robin whirled in a tight half-circle, her hair fanning out in a heavy wave.

When she faced Summer again, it was a little surprising that Gallow hadn't turned. He was of course entranced by the beauty of the Seelie Queen.

Just as Sean had been. Men did not see past that loveliness. She almost regretted tucking Gallow's coat about his shoulders and keeping watch this morning. Almost regretted holding a little boy and teaching him the constellations. Sean never cried, never threw a tantrum like some mortal children.

Robin-mama! Little hands raised to greet her, and his wide-open smile.

"I go to fetch you a gift, my Queen." Amazingly, the words didn't turn to bitter saltpeter in her mouth. Robin could have congratulated herself on sounding so carelessly polite.

"The ampoules, Ragged."

"Yes." She was looking down, she realized, at the toes of her shoes. Scuffed and black, their gloss a sidhe chant that would renew itself. They had given her good service, a gift from Morische the Cobbler before he had left for the mortal realm. *Let me go, Ragged, and I shall give thee hooves that will not falter.*

Except they had. She had stumbled in the dance somehow, either in caring for a full-mortal boy...or in letting Summer know she cared.

Still, Morische had left with his life; perhaps that counted for something.

"Gallow was my Armormaster, and the finest to wear the glass badge." Summer moved slightly, and a rosy flush simmered through the floor. "He shall keep you safe, dearest Ragged, while you fetch what is mine."

Amazingly, Jeremiah Gallow spoke again. "I will keep her safe. But I do not serve."

A long, trilling, thrilling laugh. "You've grown defiant. Yes, Gallow-my-glass, you shall watch my little bird. After all..." Summer clapped her hands once, and the flush through the glassine floor faded. "She is your kin. You married her sister."

Keep your lying tongue from my sister, you sidhe whore. The inhale filled her, breath in a bellows, and her throat relaxed, ready to let the music through.

Gallow stood before Summer, his head cocked slightly to the side. "I don't recall such an occasion."

"Did you think your mortal dalliance had gone unnoticed? You left Court for little Daisy, who gave you an answer, do." It wasn't precisely a smirk on Summer's fair face.

The most horrible thing about it was her relaxed, easy smile, the utter transparency of her satisfaction.

All the air left Robin's lungs in a rush. "Daisy..."

"She didn't have a—" Thankfully, then, Gallow shut up. He froze as if turned to stone, and for a moment Robin had the strange idea that Summer had encased him in amber, too.

"Where was mortal Daisy bound, the night she died?" The Seelie Queen stretched luxuriously. "And who did she happen to meet there? I'll tell you this much, Gallow-my-glass, she met a sidhe."

"Who?" The word was a croak.

Robin's throat was dry as Marrowmere sands; she could not

make a single sound rise. *Is that what happened? Is that why I could not find her, until I found her grave?*

"Oh, I think I'll tell you, when you bring the Ragged back to me, with her precious cargo." Summer nibbled at her lower lip, teeth so sharp-white against the crimson. "Don't delay. I must open the Gates soon. Wide and wild shall be spring's return."

"And when you do, the plague will spread." Robin had found her voice again, and each word was a weapon, the song trembling right behind it. "It will claw at pretty white flesh, and—"

The amber column trembled. It rocked back and forth, singing a high distressed note, and almost, *almost* fell.

No. Please, no. She couldn't sing—her throat had closed completely.

"If you do not bring the ampoules, dear Ragged, I may not be able to free our Sean." She yawned, patting at her mouth with one hand. Her nails, long and wicked, were now glamour-dyed with moonshine, white bearing a faint blush of peach.

Gallow had turned and was bearing down on her. Robin struggled to breathe. If she could just get enough air in, she could let the song loose, and...

...then what?

His hand closed about her arm with bruising force, and Gallow the Armormaster dragged her from the hall. Summer's laughter, high and sweet and tinkling, accompanied them all the way through the rotunda, and spilled away down the stairs just as they did.

AS PLANNED
26
⊱╫╳

High morning in Summer was busy with bees drunkenly careening from flower to flower, pixies trailing scatterdust as they played among the zipping buzzes. After a great hush earlier in the day, joy had stolen out of Summerhome, filling the flour-pale pathways with a secret, brimming glee. Naiads basked on the shore or cavorted in the crystalline water, the nymphs and dryads had taken up their dancing again, and delight brimmed in every flower-cup.

The fount of this joy swayed between two rows of apple trees, white silk fluttering in a playful perfumed breeze. Decked with long indigo velvet ribbons, her hair pulled back in an elaborate cable-braid, it pleased Summer to appear a simple nymph. The Jewel on her forehead flashed, sonorously, and as she reached up to a low-hanging branch, her quick white fingers found a red fruit nestled among the creamy blossoms.

A shadow lengthened on the other side of the tree, and yellowgreen eyes peered at her. "Oh, lovely one, take care. These trees belong to Summer."

Her soft laugh rustled every leaf. Some few paces behind her, two ladies-in-waiting halted, their heads bent together as they gossiped. The taller, black-haired lovely was Brenna Highgate, and the chestnut-haired other was the fair lady of Dunhill, both in sky-blue and simple holly crowns, since it was still, technically, *not* spring yet. A little further afield, two fair-haired Seelie knights in gold-chased armor stood, no doubt alert.

Puck's fingers caressed the hilt at his side, but he stayed well in the shadow. Pixies flitted among the leaves, chiming, and soon there would be a drift of blossom in every corner of the orchard, flushing to heartsblood and sending up a heavy reek of spice and copper.

Once the Gates were open.

"They do," the Queen murmured, examining the red fruit. No blemish, no stain, marred the perfect rind. "What news, Goodfellow?"

"Unwinter quakes, my lady. Wights and knights have issued forth, and all to catch one small bird. No doubt she is hopping through the brambles as we speak."

"No doubt." White teeth peeped between crimson lips. "What else?"

"Oh, gossip flies on the wind. There are some who say the Ragged has a mighty protector, but who it may be, none knows."

A small, satisfied smile played over Summer's face like sunrise. "Ah. And our pet, the mortal of science?"

"Very fine." Puck's own smile was no less satisfied. "He asked of you, lovely one."

A fractional shake of her golden head. "He has little of value left to give."

Puck's expression did not alter, though he could have noted that in point of fact, the mortal had *nothing* left to give, not even his life. But that would spoil the game. "There is other news."

"Oh?"

"Haahrhne." The name sent a chill through the orchard. Both the ladies-in-waiting shivered and cast glances over their shoulders. A few paces away, the knights stiffened, scanning for danger.

The Jewel on Summer's brow darkened, and she frowned, just a little. "You *would* speak that here."

"I hear the sickness has breached his halls, Majesty. And that he himself may ride forth ere long, to seek its source."

Summer's smile broadened. Her teeth flashed, and she bit, with a satisfying crunch, into the fruit. She sucked at it, a slight flush rising up her cheeks as it withered, and each tree in the orchard stirred uneasily again.

The rind crumbled, turning black and paper-thin. Her suckling did not cease until the fruit was no more than a smear of ash, flakes lifting from her white hand as she flicked the remains away. Full-glowing now, her lips were a sweet curve, redder than any red. "As planned," she murmured. "My thanks, Goodfellow."

"And mine, my lady." He drew back into dappled leafshade as she turned away, and her laughter as she joined her ladies was a silver bell. "As planned indeed," Puck whispered, and faded from sight into a deeper pool of dimness. Only the smears of his glowing irises remained, painted on the air for a few moments before winking out, and his own merry laughter was a faraway cackle that startled the swarming pixies.

No few of them dropped, their tiny hummingbird hearts halted between one moment and the next, and the tinkling of their deaths was lost under Summer's gaiety.

HEART OF THE RIDDLE
27

⋊╫⋉

*L*ies. *All of it.* Gallow's teeth ground together, hard enough to crack one or two of them. He dragged the stumbling girl along, cursing himself for a fool. Summer's laughter died as he strode down the flour-pale road, small curls of white vapor rising from his footsteps.

Was the girl glamoured to look like Daisy? Poison in a sweet sidhe wrapper, russet hair and a blue dress a bait he'd swallowed whole.

Except for the picture, he would think all of this a game, even the rotting Unwinter knight. The picture he'd found after the memorial service—a very young Daisy on the steps of a trailer, a yellowing Polaroid. And next to his dead wife was a gaptooth child, another girl. Older, just a little, but both of them held the promise of beauty. Anyone could see it. *They'll grow up to be stunners,* an observer would say, squinting at the fading image.

Their arms around each other, their hair clearly redgold, but the older girl...well, the half-nervous smile, the way her thin knees rested under her dress, the pearliness of her teeth all shouted *sidhe.*

At least, now that he knew what he'd been looking at, they did.

"Is it true?" He skidded to a halt just at the edge of the orchard and suddenly realized she was gasping to breathe. A mortal man might have cared. Jeremiah just hitched his backpack higher and grabbed her other arm. Shook her, so sharply her head bobbled. "*Is it true?*"

Tears slicked her cheeks. Was she crying for the boy? Goddamn sidhe and their little games.

"*Damn you, answer me!*"

Robin's sob, bit in half, hit him like ice water, right in the face. Her hair bounced, curtaining her expression, and suddenly she was Daisy during one of their few fights. *Hit me if you gotta, Jer. Just don't leave me.*

As if he would. As if he would raise a hand to *her*. Daisy's flinching told him much about her early life, the things she didn't speak about, and he had let them lie.

Robin's flinch spoke the same language.

"Christ," he breathed, unmindful of the way the blasphemy shriveled into blackness and fell to his feet, shredding in the sunshine. "Come on." His grip did not gentle, and she still didn't struggle. Just let him bear her along, like a breathing, pliable doll.

All in all, he supposed, it was pretty much how he'd feared walking into Summer again would go.

><|><

They stepped over the border into a chill late-spring mortal morning, the uncommon bite in the air making much more sense now that he'd seen the Gates firmly closed. This particular exit was ancient and well-worn, and he might have been more worried about someone watching it if not for Robin's pallor and her gasping.

Even while weeping, splotches of red on her cheeks and her nose pink-raw, she was still beautiful. It was pure sidhe, and its similarity to Daisy both curdled his stomach and started an ache down low where a man did most of his thinking before he learned better.

If he ever did.

There were bruises on her bare, milk-pale arms, rising swift and ugly. Deep red-black, the marks of his fingers clearly visible. Even though she could probably hurt him past Twisting him if she opened her mouth and let that massive orchestral noise loose, he'd still bruised a woman.

A sidhe, though. Did she count as defenseless?

Once you started thinking like that, were you any better than a murderous highborn, or a drink-maddened mortal?

Just look at her. Or better, don't. It'll only get you in trouble.

He glanced at the sky, took in the terrain. A dead-end street, juicy-greening blackberry bushes with long tearing thorns making an arch over this small doorway in a concrete wall. The door itself was closed, age-blackened wood and tarnished metal buried under the vines. No prying, watching eyes he could see, and it was daylight. Still, going blindly for a familiar exit wasn't wise.

Losing his goddamn mind in front of *her* hadn't been wise either.

Robin's gasping quieted, little by little. She flinched when he tried clumsily to wipe at her wet cheeks, and the tiny cowering movement was so much like Daisy's a hot acid bubble rose under his breastbone.

It was that flinch that made it truth. Even a Realmaker couldn't be glamoured this thoroughly. She even *smelled* right, Half and mortal flesh both.

What were the chances of seeing her in that bar? What were

the chances of anything, now that both Summer and Unwinter were involved?

Now that he had to, he was thinking about the accident again. A long straightaway of dry pavement. A single oak tree across a ditch. A parched autumn night, no frost, nothing to make Daisy's car—a reliable sedan he had bargained for in a dusty lot off Shreves Avenue—veer, jump the ditch, and ram into the only obstruction.

Her body, tumbled across the field. *No seat belt, Mr. Gallow. Did she often drive without it?*

No. Never. Numb and shaking, had he really only thought it was ill-luck? Chance? Misfortune?

I'll tell you, Gallow-my-glass, she met a sidhe.

Which could mean anything mortal-Tainted, a quarter sidhe or above.

The Polaroid he remembered, tucked safely in his dresser, had a heart drawn on the back in pink nail polish. Sloppy and childlike, he could almost see one of them biting the full lower lip they shared, tracing its contours in some ramshackle rotting tin can of a trailer, while screams throbbed in the kitchen or bedroom.

How he had wanted to give her more, but the sum of Daisy's dreams was a trailer of her very own. *We can't afford a house,* she'd said, with a peculiar smile. *This is good enough.*

Stupidly, he had thought she was right. Now he wondered who had taught her not to want, because it would be taken away.

She never mentioned a sister, either. She didn't talk about her past, and neither did he. Better to say nothing than to lie—maybe she had thought it was better to say nothing than to tell the truth. Had she known what he was?

Since you like your milk so much. But nobody believed in the sidhe anymore. Still, with a Half sister...

It was no use. Daisy was gone, mortal clay, and no skill or chantment would bring her back to answer any questions.

Robin, still pale, wrenched herself from his grasp. He could have kept her, if he didn't mind bruising her afresh. Maybe she thought to flee him, but she only took two staggering steps, bent over, and retched, a deep, awful noise that nonetheless carried no vomit to the pavement.

Had she loved him? *Sean.* A young mortal boy.

She spat as if to clear her mouth, and slowly straightened. Her eyes were closed, her head tipped back, and the beads of sweat on her neck were diamonds.

"I'm sorry." Harshly.

Whatever reply he'd expected, it wasn't her bitter laugh. She hugged herself, tightly, thin traceries of steam rising from her bare shoulders. "Why? *You* did nothing." She was hoarse, too.

At least she wasn't singing.

You're right. I did nothing. Curse me for a fool, twice and thrice over. The tingling and itching up his arms receded, but the effort left him sweating afresh. "This...Sean. Did you love him?"

She regained her breath, shook her head. "What use is love?" Each word low and rough as a cat's tongue. "He was a baby, just a *baby*. I fed him. I bargained brughnies to care for him. I...I taught him..."

She ran out of words, and Jeremiah realized all at once what she meant. "Ah." The curdling in him went away, and fresh loathing rose to take its place. Had he really thought she would...and that relief, deep down in him, because...why?

You know why.

In any case, it was time to move. "Come."

"I will *hurt* her," she said quietly. "I will *kill*—"

He did not remember moving; he found his hand clapped

over Robin's mouth as her wide, dark blue eyes rolled. He had her arm again, in case she decided to struggle, but she went limp.

"Hush, now." As if there was a rock in his own throat. "Don't swear an oath that will get you killed, woman."

He could almost hear her reply. *What do you care?*

There was the heart of the riddle.

He didn't know.

SIDHE ENOUGH

28

꒰╫꒱

She held her tongue while he dragged her along. There was a small diner nearby, one of the twenty-four-hour variety, full of grease, fluorescent light, and mortal desperation. The waitress—a just-past-teenage girl with deep shadows under her eyes—looked at Robin's bruises and probably assumed...several things.

The Armormaster ordered for both of them, and Robin stared at the cup of pallid boiled liquid that passed for coffee. A chipped rim, settled on a table tacky-wet and wiped with bleach water she could still smell.

If she hadn't bargained herself away so young, perhaps she would have been a waitress, too. Backsore and hole-eyed, the vigor of youth drained away by drudgery and her sidhe half still sleeping. Instead, she was here.

Mother, gone. Her sister, gone.

Sean, gone.

Robin was not fool enough to think Summer would ever restore him to flesh. Was he struggling to draw breath inside that stone-resin prison? Nausea thumped into her middle, and she fought the urge to simply put her forehead on the mortal-dirty table and weep afresh. This time, the tears would not be rage, so she denied them.

Gallow watched her. What had he made of all this?

When she spoke, it was a surprise to hear her own soft, throaty tone. "He was stolen away." Her hands lay on the table, discarded gloves. "*She* told me to sing the thief a song, and I did; then I...I begged him as a boon. I thought...I do not know what I thought." Soft and measured, as if each word was not a knife to her heart. "I taught him the names of the stars. And *she*..."

The Armormaster shifted, uncomfortably. "He was dead the moment he was taken. All of us were."

Is that what you think? "It would be a relief if that were true."

"Maybe." Then, the question she had been dreading. "Is it true? Daisy Snowe. Daisy Elaine."

She blinked. *It's a common name. All common names. Just like mine was before I chose the truer ones.*

"She had a mole." He touched the underside of his jaw, on the left side. "Here. And her toes—the second and third were the same length. She sang gospel while she was in the shower, and her favorite flowers were—"

"Dandelions," Robin whispered. "We had a song about them, when we were little. I used to hum it to her when..." *When they were fighting. Or when Daddy Snowe was yelling and Mama sobbing.* Daisy in her arms, a heavy weight, she rocked her sister while the noise battered their flimsy bedroom door.

You're so warm, Rob.

Just as she'd rocked Sean, kissing the top of his head where the smell of Seelie, salt dust, and mortal child concentrated in his tumbled hair. Running through the orchard with Robin at his side, fleet of foot and laughing while she watched for pitfalls.

Gallow sagged against the cracked purple vinyl of the booth. He'd gone quite alarmingly pale. Robin returned to herself with a jolt, staring at him. Was it even possible?

I have me a man, Daisy had said, *and I want the rest of it. Please, Rob.*

Robin studied Gallow afresh. Yes, Daisy would like him. Strong-jawed, those pale eyes, and the broad shoulders. He was the very antithesis of short, pretty-faced Daddy Snowe. You had to look harder at Gallow to find the sidhe on him, behind the scornful mortal dross he wore like a cloak.

It didn't seem to be a glamour. Everything about him simply denied comfort with a vengeance.

"Was she happy?" She curled her fingers around the mug, soaking in the warmth. "Did you... Were you kind to her?"

"Kind?" His laughter was as bitter as hers, as if he had a mouthful of rot. "I would have died for her. I would have given her anything she wanted. I tried. But maybe I wasn't *kind.*" A muscle in his cheek flicked. His stubble was coming in, a charcoal brushing. "I'm not mortal enough for kindness." One corner of his mouth tilted up, just slightly. "Neither are you, it seems."

How would you know? It shouldn't have stung, but it did. She dropped her gaze back into the coffee-sludge. "*She* wants the vials."

"What vials?"

"The plague." Robin wet her lips nervously. "There is... a cure. An inoculation. Summer snared a mortal of science to make one. He sent word that he had succeeded. I was sent to fetch it from the one who told her of its existence. That's where..." *No, Robin. Be careful. Don't allow Puck further into this game than he already is.* "Unwinter's knight almost caught me. Then... you."

"Ah." He didn't ask if the Unseelie had somehow loosed the plague in the first place. It was the obvious question, and no sidhe would wish to be too obvious. "And you bargained with *her*?"

"I told her I wouldn't bring the ampoules back until she released Sean and guaranteed his family, with no ill effects..." Abruptly, she was aware of how childish it sounded. Had she thought she could outfox a creature so old? The very Queen of Seelie herself?

"Stupid." He drummed callused fingers on the tabletop. The place was slowly filling, mortals straggling in to eat whatever passed for food here. Hissing in the kitchens, almost the same as Peleaster the Cook's steaming hell—but not quite. She had explored the Court kitchens more than once. It had never sounded like this.

This *inimical.*

Robin was used to hating the mortal world. Now, she realized, she hated Summer, too. Would she find a home in Unwinter, then? You could not trust an Unseelie to honor a bargain, the Summer sidhe said, and their King was darkness itself. His pride had caused the Sundering, 'twas said, but before that he had been Summer's Consort, a match for her indeed.

Robin had only glimpsed Unwinter's cheerless country once or twice, and had no desire to ever see its cinder-rain and crimson spatters again.

A shudder worked through her. There would be no place to rest, not for a long while. The man across from her was most likely an enemy, too, even if he had been kind to Daisy, and for one simple reason.

You could not trust anything male once Summer had set her gaze upon it. From the lowest cur to the highest fullblood knight, they swelled below the belt and Summer led them neatly by the protuberance. What would this Armormaster give to worm his way back into Summer's favor?

Perhaps he had simply amused himself with Daisy during his banishment.

Gallow finally spoke again. "You must have cared for him." Quietly, as if it didn't matter. "Where are they, then?" He glanced at the front of the diner, the flyspecked windows filling with gold as the sun rose through mist. *She* could not keep the Gates closed much longer—that much was true. When they opened, she was renewed, and that renewal spread through each realm in its own fashion.

"What, I'm to tell *you*?" Robin shook her head. "No, Armormaster. I would like to live a little longer."

"What for?" Soft, but cruel. He probably would be flattered to know he sounded like Summer herself. But he shook his head, as if realizing his rudeness. "I mean—"

Vengeance. "Does it matter?"

"Oh, it does. I wouldn't kill you, Ragged." Flat and convincing, it had all the ring of sincerity. "Not unless I knew..."

Knew what? An idiot's question. When he knew she had the vials, and that Summer would welcome him into her arms and couch again, Robin Ragged would be dead indeed. She had only her wits and her song, not to mention the few small trinkets she carried, to aid her in surviving.

His eyes had paled another shade or two. That was all.

"Breakfast!" The waitress slammed plates down on the table between them, and Robin forced herself not to flinch. Steam lifted from something that was supposed to resemble eggs, and the pancakes were uneven blobs, probably burned on the side facing down. There was bacon, too, full of salt goodness, but revulsion filled Robin's belly.

There were two glasses of milk, anyway, and at least *that*

smelled fresh. Pale, of course, having been processed, but still better than the rest of it. She reached for the glass, realized it was smudged. More pointless revulsion.

"Eat while you can." He looked down at his own plate.

Eat this? Are you mad? She forced herself to take a sip of milk, her skin crawling at the thought of mortal effluvia still on the glass.

She was sidhe enough for that, at least.

Maybe she could be heartless, too.

FOR JOY OR SORROW

29

∋⊣⊦∈

anton Station echoed with midday traffic. Silver pig-buses nuzzled at the big dun sow of a building, and even though the interior was tired and old, it still held Art Deco reminders. Brass rails and marble flooring, shafts of weak cloud-filtered light beaming down from skylights, the fixtures hanging from the ceiling frosted with dust but still intricately pleasing.

Best of all, the lockers were steel, which meant enough cold iron to make them safe. He found the one he wanted and touched the handle, a single syllable of chantment resounding low and vibrating under the PA system announcing *leaving for Buffalo, now boarding in bay 16.*

"Gonna leave some stuff here," he said, though she hadn't asked. The crystalline tears had dried to thin trails of salt on her soft cheeks. Even with reddened eyes and nose, she was beautiful. The matting of her wet eyelashes, the way her mouth turned slightly down, her blue eyes dazed and wide... it made a man think about all sorts of things.

It's just because she looks like Daisy. Cut it out.

Except he didn't even remember what Daisy truly looked

like. Maybe handling her memory every day for five years had made it fade, like the mortal thing it was.

He dug in the backpack, extracted the spare boots, the Crown Royal bag, and a few other small things. Hung the backpack carefully, propping the boots at the bottom and tucking the purple bag into them. Glanced at her again. She simply stared over his shoulder, watching the mortals as they hurried past. Blinking every so often, and deathly pale.

She hadn't wanted mortal breakfast. A few sips of milk, and that dazed, numb look. Was that why he was so unsteady? Why his hands wanted to shake, why he was hiding Daisy's jewelry here in a steel locker?

"Do you want to leave anything here? It's safe enough." He realized it was a ridiculous question as soon as he asked it; she carried nothing. Her hands were bare and empty.

She shook her head. A little color had come back into her face; she reached up to scrape the salt from her cheeks with her long, pretty fingers.

He touched the backpack again, breathing a word in the Old Language, and another word of chantment as he swung the door closed, using the slam to cover the sound of crystalline ringing. When he turned back, it was to see Robin heading away, into the crush of mortals.

Did she really think to slip him so easily?

He trailed after her, soundless. When she halted, crossing her arms over her midriff, he found out what had drawn her.

A young man with a mass of dreadlocked hair, his coffee-colored hands gentle as they coaxed a fiddle's strings into singing a wandering melody. His eyes were closed, the fiddle case set before him seeded with bright coins and dollar bills. Anything larger would vanish into the busker's pocket as soon as possible, to save it from vanishing into the crowd.

Robin swallowed hard, tilted her head. She swayed a little in time to the music, and Jeremiah recognized the tune. An old, old plaintive song. He scanned the crowd, but there was no breath of sidhe. Too much cold iron here for them.

You know what, Robin? Let's get on a bus and go. Which one? Any one. We'll leave, and Summer…

That was a hideously stupid idea, but still, he was tempted. If he could somehow get to those cure vials, the ampoules Summer wanted so badly, and get Robin away from Summer's murderous clutches in the process, maybe it would ease… well, not his conscience. Something else.

He watched her profile, trying not to hear the fiddle's plaintive calling. *You do me wrong,* the tune went, *to cast me off so discourteously.*

"We should go," he murmured, and closed his hand around her elbow. Her skin was alive with a Half's fever-warmth, and before she shook him away with a single graceful motion, he could marvel at how soft she was.

Her fingers flickered, and a glittering landed in the fiddle case. A thin dime probably older than the boy, its edges worn-down and a subtle glamour threading up from it. Jeremiah eyed the chantment narrowly, and realized it was to lure more of its relatives, from coin to cash, into the case as well. A sidhe-gift, one that would likely make the fiddler more comfortable.

She remembered two mortal names, as well. She wasn't the usual thoughtless, heedless sidhe-girl.

The Ragged was something else.

Robin turned away, and set off through the crowd again. Mortals bumping against every side, their salt-sweat despair drenching him, children hurrying along aside adults who took too-long strides, military men in uniforms and freshly cut hair, slinging their duffels on broad shoulders, harried women and students, those too poor to fly.

When he caught up with her, she had finished scrubbing the salt-tracks from her face, and her blue eyes glittered dangerously. If Daisy had ever looked like that—

"Are you finished here? We shouldn't linger." As if she was charged with *his* protection.

"I'm done. Where are we bound?"

"Elsewhere. To satisfy *her*." Robin's lip almost curled, and Gallow belatedly realized the question could be a suspicious one. Summer was not a forgiving creature.

"Robin." He caught at her arm again. "The musician—"

"I cannot sing for joy or sorrow." She shook her head, removed her arm decidedly from his grasp again. "I found that out when I was young. *He* can, and he chooses to bring delight to his fellow mortals. Such a thing should be rewarded." Her pace quickened; she slipped through the press of mortals like a minnow in a pond. "Don't you think so?"

It curdled in his stomach. She had merely been kind, and was used to having her kindness trampled, whether by sneering or by the greedy. A soft heart to match her sister's, maybe. A handicap in any Court, or in the mortal world itself. "Robin—"

"Come along, Gallow Queensglass." The tears were gone, as if they had never existed. She slipped ahead of him again, and Jeremiah, his hands turning into fists before he shook them out, followed.

GUILT MUST WAIT
30
>╫⊂

An hour later, her stomach was still a hard ball and her shoulders were drawn tight with tension. Downtown, everything was sheathed in concrete, no living green anywhere. Her entire body ached, her heart worst of all, but she held herself straight and proud as the revolving door spun hungrily.

His impatience wasn't visible, but she still felt it, a cold weight against her back as her heels clicked against marble. The Dalroyle Building was pleasantly aged, its outside a granite monument to Art Deco and its inside worn but still shining with faded magnificence. The elevator worked, ancient and wheezing with complaints, and the brass wall sconces were restrained flowers. In some places they'd laid down cheap carpet, but the foyer was still marble and soft lighting, the restaurant opening off to one side exhaling a thin thread of coffee and roasted garlic.

"Why *here*?" Gallow trudged behind her like a clodhopping brughnie, though one of their ilk would have been following its nose to the garlic. And would probably receive a bite or two for its pains, a thought that cheered Robin immensely.

They had visited the bus station, where she gazed longingly

at the ticket window while he stored his bag in one of the lockers. Now he wore his knives, but there was no sign of the pike he carried.

And he was asking her *why here*. Did he think her entirely brainless? "Because this is where I've led you." She tapped down the hall toward the stairs. "If word has slipped out that I was carrying... well, any common hiding place would not be safe."

"This is a hiding place? It's gaudy."

It is not. A sidhe who lived as he did—among mortals, in a trailer, perhaps he found anything else too luxurious. Maybe he hated Court's deadly comforts, and any pleasure or magnificence would irritate him. "It's secure." *And it has quite a few exits.*

"This? Secure?"

"Very." She pushed the stairwell door open, looked carefully through. *Good. Clear, and no pursuit I can sense.*

"What makes it secure?"

Could he truly not tell? "What do you smell?"

He inhaled deeply, coughed. Perhaps his senses had been dulled by living among mortals for so long, or perhaps she had grown so accustomed to danger, the slight glamour many predators employed unraveled under her attention.

"Christ." He sounded a little pale now. "It reeks of brimstone."

Only if you're looking to smell danger. "Sometimes. There are kobold swellings in the basement, and a nest atop."

"A nest?"

"Harpies. There's good prey here, for them." *Among other things, some sidhe and some not. None of them, though, take kindly to Unseelie poaching upon their hunting-grounds.* Her fingers ran lightly over the railing, layers of paint applied again and again chipping and cracking, a scaled hide. Come nightfall the stairwell would be dangerous, too, unless one was quick and lightfooted.

"That's why you waited for midmorning." Breathless now, as he climbed the stairs behind her. "Even nestguard kobolding won't be awake yet, and the harpies—"

"They doze, this time of day." *Other things are awake.* Her calves burned, but she did not slow. "At least, they generally do."

"You're insane."

I won't dignify that with a response. Though several burned and trembled inside her mouth, crowding for release. Her throat rasped with denying the song, too. Up the steps, quickly but not so quickly as to tire. She would need all her speed, soon.

The stairs stretched up, and up, twelve flights and one more. That was where she halted, and spread her hand against a fire door. The paint was a different vomitous green than the others, just a shade lighter.

To a mortal, there would be simply a blank wall. Unless whatever lay behind it was hungry.

She concentrated, and found, to her relief, that the tingle of *too-dangerous-to-risk* did not run along her nerves. "Come."

"No." He caught at her arm again. "I'll go first. I'm to keep you alive."

"Only until you know I have the cure." *Then it's a quick knifing, and back to Summer with your prize.* Their faint kinship would not make him hesitate, not when her death was his ticket back to Court.

Besides, he did not seem the hesitating sort. And he had served Summer once. She knew better than to think such a service was easily cast aside.

Especially for a man.

"You think me faithless, Ragged?" He didn't sound even slightly insulted, merely curious.

What had Daisy seen in him? Had she softened him, or had her death turned all of him to bitterness, as it had done for

Robin? He did not speak on his grief, and she would not either. So she settled for the truth. "I think you a man."

"Is that an insult?"

"No." *Anything male is dragged around by its breeches, and* she *holds the string attached to them. Besides, you served. You need only a look or a tone to understand what she wishes done with me. As do I.* She touched the doorknob, found it ice-cold. As usual. Twisted it and stepped through, shaking away his grasp. It was easier when he was not seeking to paint her with more bruises. He had grown fond of clasping her, it seemed.

The instant blackness was a balm, and she pitched aside, rolling. A clatter of metal, a tearing sound, and light returned, blazing fit to blind, but she had her eyes firmly closed. Gallow shouted, but Robin was already up, counting her steps as she ran down the hall.

This corridor, tucked sideways into the building, lit with bright emerald radiance once the dark-glamour was pierced. Doors frowned on either side, moss growing thick and verdant on the walls, and juicy green vines slid against each other as her nose filled with the scent of living growth. She was oriented by the time she opened her eyes, skipping nervously along the left-hand side of the hall where the safe path was, leaping from rock to flinty rock thrusting up from the matted green-moss floor. Behind her, Gallow cursed, understanding where they were.

A Tangle's lair, and like all such lairs, a place-between.

She found the door she wanted—a half-size, tiny little thing almost swallowed by the moss—and scrabbled at the knob. A shrill piercing whistle between her lips, and it turned easily.

Of course, most sidhe doors opened to a Realmaker. Grudgingly, perhaps, but they still opened.

He would be occupied fighting off the Tangle some while

longer. It would eat if it could, but it probably could not take a canny opponent such as Gallow. If he survived, he would begin hunting her.

The door creaked as she forced it open.

"*Robin!*" Why did he cry her name?

She squeezed through—and there was another reason she'd chosen this method of escape. He was taller and wider than her, and wouldn't fit through this particular passage.

"Robin, *no!*"

I will not stay to let you kill me when you think I have what she wants. I have much to do before I see Summer again.

And I will.

She was through, and tugging the metal ring—not cold iron, for this place was purely sidhe—to swing it closed behind her. A puff of green scent, a blast of warm air, and his cries cut off midway through her name.

He would certainly find her again, if he lived. But Robin Ragged had bought herself a little time.

⋈╫⋈

During the day, the glamours in the ruins of the trailer park were pale and thready, since sun would do the work of keeping Unseelie away. They were broken and scattered now, those various chantments, even those laid with the aid of trinkets from Summer herself. Every trailer that hadn't been smashed was now cracked open like an egg, including the so-familiar one Robin stood before, hugging herself and staring at the wreckage. It did not smoke, though it was blackened and reeking of strange mortal chemicals.

She would have been forced to pick her way into the shattered tin-can home, but the crumpled rag of a mortal body, spectacles fused to his charred skull by a blast of unimaginable heat, had been pulled from the refuse and hung from a street-lamp that would never shine again.

Henzler—or what was left of him—swayed gently in the chill afternoon breeze. They had strung him by his heels, and it was little consolation that he probably was already gone by then. Robin hugged herself harder. It looked as if Unwinter had found him; it did not smell of them overmuch here, but the reek of mortal chemicals and broken chantment was almost too thick to breathe. The poor mortal, probably still screaming whatever name Summer had used to bewitch him with, had hopefully been prey to heartshock.

Heartshock was quick. Much quicker and kinder than any-thing else the Unseelie would do to him.

She could not count on it, though. If he had been alive for even a short while, perhaps he would have babbled about the cure. And, of course, Robin's name or description. Maybe Puck's as well, but that wasn't her concern.

Her concern was not joining the mortal on the gibbet-pole. Henzler had been dead the moment Summer snared him.

We were all dead the moment we were taken. Gallow's voice, unwelcome. He could be tracking her even now, if he had fought free of the Tangle. She had to move.

Still, she tarried, staring at the body as it swung lazily. Like a hideous fruit in a mockery of Summer's orchard.

Her throat filled, she opened her mouth, and the song burst out, surprising her. She hadn't meant to sing, but the wall of noise smashed into streetlight and skeleton-thin corpse, flush-ing fiery gold at its edges. She had plenty of breath. As the lamppost twisted, curling and blackening, the remains shred-ded, black dust working itself finer and finer until she had to gasp, her eyes leaking again and the weird weightlessness of oxygen deprivation filling her skull. She staggered back, almost fell as her left shoe met a plastic bag and had to dig down sharply, scraping against cracked concrete.

Most of the streetlamp was gone. Henzler was truly gone as well. He would not be joining the Sluagh once dark fell, either. The host of the Unforgiven Dead would be denied one more to swell its ranks.

Robin panted for a little while. Holding the song without breath was dangerous; it could just as easily burn *her* to ash. She shuddered, great gripping waves passing through her, and sought to calm herself.

When she could finally stand upright again, she shook her hands out. Guilt would have to wait, again. There was much to be done before she let anyone, Gallow or Unseelie, catch her.

I must visit the dwarves. She winced, shook the plastic bag from her heel, and set out, grim-faced, her jaw clenched so tightly her teeth ached.

WHAT PRICE?
31

⚜

The throneroom was vast, lofty ceilings hung with sheets of red and black velvet. Stone logs, chipped and oozing the slow resin of their tearing from the Rim's cliffs, burned with a bright blue, heatless flame, each shadow knife-edged as it danced with the flickering. Those flames, contained in a shallow, circular firepit, darted toward the runes carved into the lip of the pit and retreated as the angular shapes twisted menacingly. An obsidian-glass floor ran with ghostly clouds below the surface, and some said it was by gazing at their shapes that Unwinter discerned all that befell within his borders—and many other places, besides.

Summer had a Stone, and Unwinter's was the Throne. It crouched patiently at the end of the hall, its spines glistening, and its heartsblood cushions were hard as stone itself. Sometimes it appeared of smooth dark metal, other times of granite, but always, the Throne's sharp, high-rearing daggers exuded that faint hint of crimson moisture.

Even a Throne hungered, and required feeding.

High, narrow doors opened, a crack of ruby glow from outside shivering as it fell against pallid stonelight. A shape appeared, coalescing out of the glow, and it stepped onto the obsidian floor with a tiptapping instead of glove-soled softness.

The shadows deep in the Throne's embrace stirred. A high-peaked helm, chased with silver, lifted slightly, but the armored form of Haahrhne the Hunter, Unwinter himself, once-Consort of Summer, Lord of the Fell Host, did not otherwise move. Two crimson pinpricks kindled in the helm's deep eyesockets.

He did not speak, watching the guest solemnly pace around the firepit. The stoneflames leapt again, hungrily, but the visitor did not falter. He merely made his way to the deep-etched star-compass before the Throne, its carved lines rasping as they slid through the obsidian, and bowed, deeply, doffing an imaginary cap. "Greetings to you, O Lord of the Fell, from a humble traveler." Yellowgreen irises flashed, a darting glance to the Throne, and the guest did not straighten. His ear-tips twitched slightly, though, poking through a silken mat of brown hair.

Unwinter stirred. "*Goodfellow.*" Soft and cruel, the syllables mouthing velvet hangings, making them flutter uneasily. "*You dare much.*"

"Oh, we've no love for each other, that's true." Puck straightened, his slim brown hands kept carefully away from hilt or pipe. "But you're a just lord, and a wise one. Your steward let me pass."

Unwinter did not answer. Those crimson pinpricks burned steadily, unblinking.

Puck did not smile. Set and grave, his boyface looked much older now, and the unforgiving light etched hair-thin lines at corners of mouth and eye.

Finally, Unwinter's gauntleted fingers on one hand twitched. Five phalanges and a thumb, all a joint or two too long and encased in exquisite dwarf-wrought armor, the metal making a slight chiming sound as it moved. "*Speak, then.*"

"The Low Counties are withered. Your realm bears a sickness, too. Do you care to know its source?" Puck stuck his thumbs in his belt, spraddle-legged, and lifted his chin.

I have only to look at who does not suffer to guess the source, Fatherless. Her corruption grows.

Puck nodded thoughtfully. "And rumor, that winged beast, whispers she says the same of you. What am I to believe?"

A slow, chill-grinding sound echoed and boomed through the throneroom. Unwinter laughed, and ice flashed, droplets hanging in the air. Puck's breathing warmth sent steam out in questing tendrils that froze and fell, tinkling merrily.

When the sound faded, Puck's expression had turned hard. "You *laugh*, Unwinter? My own are dying, and yours, too. Summer seeks to blame you, and you laugh."

"Who do you believe, Goodfellow? Do I care?"

"You would scorn me, then?"

"We are not lovers."

"And not allies, either." Puck did not move, even as ice melted on his lashes and in his brown hair. "Yet that may change."

"Ah. Now we come to it." Unwinter did not move, but the chill sharpened. His attention was well and truly engaged now. The hangings and pennants overhead, some of them the rotting remains of the standards of fallen foes, snapped as the breeze turned brisk for a moment. *"What price, Fatherless? I know better than to trust your generosity."*

"I have one of Summer's own," Goodfellow said. "Who will invite you over her borders."

Unwinter stilled. The breeze halted, fell into a hush. Even the stoneflames quieted, dying to a low indigo glow. The crimson pinpricks intensified, bright points of bloody light.

Puck waited. The frozen crystals on his hair grew heavier, and his ear-tips flicked, ridding themselves of tiny ice-globules.

Here in the heart of another's realm, it would be difficult to step sideways through the Veil.

Not impossible, though. There was a faint itching along his arm, where a mortal's desperate glass fang had bitten him. He ignored it.

"When?"

"I shall send word. If, that is, you bear an interest."

"I bear much, Goodfellow. Get thee gone, now. You stink of her perfume."

"And yet," Puck observed, as he turned, "you remember its smell."

Unwinter said nothing, but the cold intensified as Puck marched across slippery obsidian. The narrow doors opened again, the ruby glow swallowed his shadow, and when he was gone, Unwinter was motionless for a long, long while. Perhaps his attention followed the free sidhe as he danced through the Keep's dust-thick, glass-floored halls, and perhaps he took note of the moment Puck cavorted across the drawbridge, ignoring the Watcher's hiss of displeasure from below. For it was shortly thereafter that Puck Goodfellow stepped *sideways* and disappeared, nipping through a fold in the Veil...

...and all through Unwinter's realm, a secret subtle thrill ran, as its lord rose slowly from the Throne.

The hunter had stirred.

WHAT WOULD PLEASE

32

>#|#<

Gallow's breath came high and hard, but he had his balance now. The lance hummed, splattering steaming green ichor, and savage little rips of pain smoked all over him, both from exertion and from the caustic of the monster's blood.

Robin was nowhere to be seen. Of course she thought he was a faithless bastard. He'd bruised her, dragged her, insulted her over breakfast—and an awful breakfast it had been—and she knew Summer's effect on anything with a cock. The fact that desire was mixed with loathing made it all the sharper, and the worst was knowing Robin was probably right. Of course Summer would think Jeremiah eager to worm his way back into her graces, and bring the vials back.

Once he was certain Robin had them, of course, and he had relieved her of them *and* her life. He'd been the Armormaster long enough to know what would please the Seelie Queen. Robin had robbed Summer of a mortal toy before the Queen was done with it, and for that, there was little forgiveness even if the Ragged was a useful weapon.

No doubt, if Jeremiah brought Summer what she wanted, he would be in favor for a short while, until the Queen remembered he had left Court for a mortal. He had been so careful, so cautious, thinking himself reasonably clever, but in the end it hadn't mattered.

Stick to what you're good at, Jer.

From now on, he intended to.

The passageway steamed as he slid along the left wall. The occupant of this place-between—a Tangle, well-fed and grown monstrous foul-tempered—observed a wary distance, its hairy tendrils and tentacles sliding along the right, waiting for an opening. He had greased the walls and himself with its green ichor before it decided he was too much trouble at the moment and withdrew, watchful. A single slip here would cause its many arms to swarm him again.

Robin had squeezed through a dwarven-made door. If it did not take her to a different location in the mortal city, it might dump her in the lightless lands of the little men. Of course, a Realmaker would be held in high honor among them, and she could pay for passage with a chantment or two. He could not, and he had no love for the little ore-snuffling bastards. Every time the lance moved he could still feel their needles in his flesh, and the clan that had given him these hadn't expected him to survive.

Which meant the bad feeling was emphatically mutual. If his retribution for their betrayal hadn't sealed the deal, his time as Armormaster certainly had. Summer loved dainty dwarven adornments, but if she felt cheated or desired a particular toy one of the smallfolk didn't wish to part with, it was the Armormaster who obtained satisfaction.

One way, or another.

Still, he'd got what he went to the dwarves for. Only a Half could survive the Marriage of the Lance. More sidhe, and the iron would burn; more mortal, and the lance would consume its bearer. Jeremiah had the precise proportions to be valuable.

For once.

He forced the lance down, carefully not turning his back to the Tangle's main cluster. He was about to force the small door and try his luck anyway when the steaming green and hairy vines filling the corridor shifted, shivering, and he scented cold blood and old hatred.

Unseelie. Here. His arms itched, but he denied the lance its freedom. Quick and quiet was called for, and that meant ceding the field instead of fighting.

He yanked open the next door past the one she'd disappeared through. It was narrow and tall, and as he wrenched at it, a puff of frigid air belched through. There was a slamming, and the rasping of tentacles.

He did not spare a glance over his shoulder to see what Unseelie was hunting him or Robin now. Instead, he flung himself through, hoping for the best.

He landed hard on concrete, lunging away from the closing portal behind him. A quick turn, the lance springing free again and taking on solidity between his palms, and he found himself facing an anonymous brick wall. Concrete rippled underneath him, and for a moment the world *flexed,* space and space-between struggling to find their proper places. Close enough, and you could ride another sidhe's passage through the Veil, much as a motorcycle could follow a semi down the freeway. Just as easy, and just as dangerous.

He exhaled sharply, ready for pursuit... but the rippling halted between one moment and the next, and he found himself on the outskirts of the city, the interstate rumbling close by, staring at the back end of a minimall. The sun was sinking in a cold spring sky, time as well as space drifting. How many hours had he lost?

Too many. He lowered his arms, the lance sliding into insubstantiality, dissatisfied. Took a deep breath. At least he hadn't been carrying his backpack; he would have lost it to the Tangle.

He should have been angry. She'd played him neatly, a treacherous bitch of a sidhe.

On the other hand, she expected him to be duplicitous as well. Court-raised, she could doubtless fathom no less. Trust was a trap, rarely gained and even more rarely vindicated.

His attitude probably didn't help, either.

His attitude *never* helped. You didn't grow up in a charitable orphanage and make your living as a street rat or riding the rails by taking a *helpful* view of things. Strike first, strike hardest, strike fear into your opponents, protect your pride and do before you're done to, that was all he'd known. It was still easiest, and best.

Daisy hadn't been put off by it, though. She was so sunny, he hadn't had to explain himself... or maybe he should have? Maybe she wanted to ask, but couldn't?

God.

She's gone, Jeremiah. And you just lost another woman.

He could walk away, except...

I will keep her safe. I do not serve.

A sidhe's word was his bond, but... did it truly matter this time? He'd given it before a creature who didn't even understand the meaning of *truth.* True and false were whatever served a sidhe's purposes. A lesson so hard to learn, you shouldn't need more than one teaching. Still, those with the mortal taint often failed to learn it thoroughly enough.

Not to mention the fact that Summer wanted her dead, and he had been Armormaster. So of course Robin thought he would betray her. The bigger question was, had she killed Daisy?

Her own mortal sister?

I was twelve when I was taken.

Had she envied Daisy? A family murder was what he was supposed to think, right? Why else would Summer say it? She wouldn't lie when the truth would do. Still, she'd only said Daisy met a sidhe that night, and there were none who owed Gallow enough grudge to kill his wife.

Or if they did, they would know he would avenge her.

Which left Robin, or Robin's enemies, who were probably numerous.

Daisy never mentioned her sister. She sometimes let little remarks drop about her mother, more rarely about her father—*Snowe,* a cold name Jeremiah had left on her tombstone to keep even her bones safe—but anything else? No. If not for that lone picture he'd found in her jewelry box after the crash, he would have discounted the whole thing as a glamour-lie.

None of which helped him find Robin now.

Well, Jer, you don't have to find her. Simple, really. He could head to the bus station and be gone by the time night unloosed her mantle…

…or he could find the Unseelie, and wait until *they* located her.

Because they would.

Jeremiah ran his hands back through his too-short hair, adjusted his coat, glanced at the sky again, and got going.

OF UNWINTER VINTAGE

33

꘦

The dwarves were filthy, but at least they traditionally took little interest in Summer's machinations. The plague brushed them but lightly, their gates closed even to many of their friends. Robin was no friend, but she was Half and they valued Realmaking, and they knew she would chant for passage.

Black MacDonnell snorted and dug in his nose, extracting something large, hairy, and sooty from deep within his sinus-caverns, carrying it to his fleshy lips. Red lamplight licked the walls, and Robin suppressed a shudder as she surrendered the handful of golden threads—finer than even they could weave, those metalsmiths of dream and wonder, because it was made from mortal hair. "As promised."

He snorted, squinting, testing each strand. His beard, tied into bunches with blue thread, almost swept the stone floor. This far underneath the earth, it was warm, and Robin felt the weight above pressing, pressing, even though there was plenty of air. "Aye. Thought you'd forgotten us, Ragged."

"I could not forget you, MacDonnell," she replied, politely enough. "Do you have them?"

He jerked a chin, and one of his clansmen—Figurh, with

a lazy eye—scurried forward, bearing a pouch in his soot-blackened fingers. *The uglier the dwarf, the more beautiful his wares,* they said, and it was by and large true. They could not stand to make an ugly thing.

"Went to a fair 'mount of trouble to make these, songbird. Worth twice what you've paid."

Liar. "Don't be greedy, my lord." She accepted the pouch, and did not check its contents. Playing her false would mean he disdained her, just as bowing and scraping would mean he feared her.

Neither was acceptable to a chieftain of his stature, or likely to be true. The black dwarves were almost Unseelie, it was whispered, but they were faithful to their word. Or at least, this particular one had a healthy enough respect for her voice to remain relatively so.

MacDonnell snorted and waved a begrimed hand, jewels worth more than a kingdom clasping his dexterous, fat fingers. His neck, probably unwashed since his beard began to show, was clasped with so many fine chains it was a wonder he could turn his head. Bone dipped in gold pierced both his ears, carved in high fantastical curves that gave him an antlered shadow, aping a highborn huntsman's horned crown.

Here in his hall, soot veiled the high, ribbed blackstone ceiling, light reflecting wetly over carvings as fine as those trapped in Summer's orchard. A massive fire roared in the pit in the middle, twisting leaping flamesprites feasting on wood and ethercoal, little piping cries of glee echoing with the snapping of kindling. They paid their board in heat and raw chantment the dwarves used, and some said they sometimes grew large enough to couch with their hosts.

"I'll be on my way then." She paid him a pretty courtesy, her skirt swishing, and turned.

He made a deep grumbling noise. "Stay and dance for us, Ragged. Been a long while since we've seen one of the Fair Court down here."

No, thank you. "If I dance, I must sing, and none of us wish for that." Light and laughing, but she turned back as if saddened. All part of the game. "It pains me to leave you, Chieftain MacDonnell."

"Pretty liar. I would give you jewels, Ragged, and a finer robe than ever *she* has worn."

And no doubt after a week I should be forced to murder you or myself. "Ah, my lord, my lord. You honor a drab little bird." Another courtesy, and she spun again, making her skirt flare the way she knew he liked. His gaze devoured her hungrily from under dandruff-caked eyebrows. "I have no dowry to bring you in return, and so must bid adieu."

This time, he let her go with only a snort. Her shoulders relaxed a fraction as she tiptapped through the Hall's great swinging doors, plunging into the labyrinthine warren of the MacDonnell holdings. From here it was easy—uphill, always up. Turning sometimes left and sometimes right, following the small tingling against her throat—the chantment on the golden chain, a Realmaker's pathfinding, leading her to safety.

For a moment she contemplated what it might be like had she no Realmaking skill, and the prospect left her sweating. If she wasn't quite unique—there were a handful of others in Seelie who could craft chantment that didn't fade, none among the Free, and only one in Unwinter—at least she was valuable for scarcity. Her voice was held in caution for its destructive power, but she might have been traded to Unwinter long ago but for the Realmaking.

Or even paid as Tiend, the flint knife stabbing down and a small corner of the sideways realms forever Summer afterward.

The borders grew slowly, if at all, and sometimes the Queen grew hungry for more.

Thank Stone and Throne Sean had avoided *that* fate. And yet, there was the changeling still in the mortal world to consider, too.

What's to say she won't Tiend Sean anyway, and his changeling as well? If he is alive in there...

Could he be? Closed in amber, struggling to breathe? Who knew?

You need to know. You have to be sure.

"Pretty bird." It was Figurh, trundling along in her wake. "Not that way, stormsong. You mean to leave us by the front gates. You mustn't, you mustn't."

I didn't think they would find me so quickly. "Why not?" She did not slacken her pace, so he had to scuttle, his short legs pumping. His lazy eye rolled, its crystalline iris a point of light in the gloom. Here there was no fire, and precious few torches—they could see much better in the dark.

It was how they grubbed out gold and...other things.

"There are those waiting for you."

"Suitors? For such a spinster as myself? Oh, Figurh Mac-Donnell's cousin, if only it were true." Her heart leapt into her throat, traitor that it was.

Just like the rest of her. Figurh might be half deaf from the ringing of anvils, but she could not be sure there were not other ears in the dark.

"No, little bird." He caught up as she slowed, her pulse smoothing out as well. "Dark ales, miss, of Unwinter vintage. You'd best leave another way."

She added up her options; none that seemed very appetizing. This had been a calculated risk from the start; perhaps Gallow had not drawn off the hounds as well as he could have.

Maybe he had decided not to. She had, after all, left him a-Tangle.

"I have safe passage to the front gates." *Nowhere else. If I step off the path, I am forfeit.* "You have my thanks, but I must leave the way I promised to."

"I could..." He coughed, slightly, and under the soot on his cheeks, perhaps he was reddening. "A safer way. I could show you, Ragged."

For what price? It wearied her, to constantly weigh the payment for passage. Did regular mortals feel this, too? Strange how she'd once thought life among the sidhe would be different. It took so much effort simply to navigate, let alone gain ground.

"You are kinder than I deserve." The lie did not stick in her throat; perhaps it wasn't *quite* a falsehood. "I have no wish to be forfeit today, though, even to your gallant clansman."

"Mayhap he's the one who told *them* of your presence here, little bird."

And mayhap you are, dwarf. Her mouth drew against itself, but she smoothed her expression. "Why would Unwinter care where I go, or what I do? Unless they've a message to send to Summer's ear." The thought that maybe the message would be her own rag of a body, pierced and drained, was not comforting at all, and Figurh's next words did nothing to dispel the chill.

"You may be a message from Summer yourself. I'll take you another way, Robin Ragged, and only ask a kiss and a kind word in return."

"Such a knight you are." She did not bother to slow further. The necklace warmed slightly, and at the next tangled branching of tunnels she chose the third path from the left. From here it was not as confusing. "My poor favor is not worthy of your kindness, my lord."

"*Listen* to me!" The words echoed, so sharp and hard Robin actually halted, letting him scurry, panting, level with her.

She gazed down. While she wore heels, his nose was level with her bellybutton, and he was filthy as any black dwarf could wish to be. His beard was scanty on his cheeks, but his chin and upper lip more than made up for it, and was tangled into elflock-braids. Pearls of sweat stood out on his forehead, streaked the soot and dirt on his cheeks.

"Listen," he repeated, breathless. "There are Unwinter waiting for you, Ragged, outside the front gates. Do not rush so blindly into their arms."

Do you think they'd treat me kindly, if I did? "No fear of that. They hold no love for me, and none for you, either."

"That's where you're wrong. They cluster about our gate. MacDonnell was visited not an hour before you knocked on our side door, and I overheard the parlay. Saying a ransom was paid. Someone knew you would come here, pretty Ragged, and wished you to receive whatever you bargained for, and to leave unhindered."

"Was there a chance I would leave otherwise?"

"With MacDonnell, always." The lazy-eyed little man paled even further. He actually wrung his horny little hands together, griming them further. The rings he wore took no foulness, sparkling clean as all dwarvenwork. "Please, please, Ragged, do not run into their jaws."

She essayed a careless smile, and bent low. Of course he would peer down her dress, but Robin found she did not quite mind. Her lips met his bald, greasy forehead, though she shuddered internally. A healthy heat-haze, like the ripple over a blazing forge, rose from him, and the sour tang of unwashed sidhe-skin. Over that was the much-more-sour reek of outright fear.

"Thank you, Figurh." *For your concern. Misplaced as it is.* "If indeed I find *them* waiting for me outside the gates, I shall remember your kindness in warning me. If not..." She shrugged, straightening.

"Are you so desperate to die?" He actually hopped from foot to foot, his heavy boots creaking.

Maybe. "Not until I have run my course." She patted her left skirtpocket, as if distracted. *Keep the fiction, Robin. It's your best defense now.* "You'd best return to your duties; you'll be missed."

"Not likely," he mumbled. Under the filth and sweat he was pink now. "Thank you, lady Ragged. Should you survive, and need a favor I can provide, call."

"Certainly." *I notice you don't specifically say* any *favor. So much may not be in your power, if I ever come knocking.* In any case, he'd delayed her long enough. "Goodbye, stoneborn."

Five minutes later, the jumble of MacDonnell's tunnels was behind her, and the tall black metal gates worked with his device of hammer and flail reared before her. They were ajar, no warden in sight, and she suddenly wished she could have trusted Figurh's words.

Or anyone's, really.

Chin high, Robin swept for the gates, to become a running hare once again. This time, though, she was prepared.

So she told herself. It did not stop the cold fear-sweat beginning all over her.

WHISTLING AT DEATH

34

>╫<

Finding the Unseelie was easy. They made no effort to hide.

She's too smart to come out this way. Please let her be too smart to come out this way.

Yet this was where they congregated, a cluster of cold intent as the sun settled a mere few fingerspans above the horizon. Not just fullborn barrow-wights, but a knight or two, wrapped in sable and utterly still among the run-down houses. They were not a-horse, not yet, and there were low slinking shapes with silver coins for eyes, flickering through the Veil and back, sliding through shadows.

The rest of the city was bare of Unseelie, as far as he could tell. They *could* merely be waiting for nightfall. Or they could know, without a doubt, where she would be.

A wave of tension passed through him and away. Learning to wait was all about letting those waves come and go, swaying just a little as they rocked you. It kept the muscles warm, not precisely a fidget but not a conscious movement either. Just a respiration, tree branches on a cool breeze.

There was little cover in this decaying residential neighborhood, so he perched on the gabled roof of what used to be a

Catholic school, then a bar—certainly the most ironic reversal he'd seen in a building lately. Now it was boarded up, but enough consecration remained to make it a little safer.

Neither of the Courts cared for Christ's followers and their chantment of cross and incense, wine and blood—not to mention their loathing of the sidhe, and reduction of the Folk to children's tales. Belief, that great mother of chantment, could be used even by mortals, and the Pale God's rituals were at cross-purposes with the chantment of wind and water, tree and green field. The sidhe were not feared and propitiated as they had once been, and they took the affront with ill grace.

Besides, between the peaks of the rooftop, his silhouette was not as noticeable, and he had the height.

Birch and 58th met in a perfect crossroads, west of the school. He could see the uneasiness in the Veil flirting above the cracked pavement—the four arms radiated outward precisely between each compass point. It was the sidhe equivalent of an overpass, a pavement flower that could take you anywhere, even through a dwarven chieftain's front gates.

The sun sank further. If Robin was wise, she would find any exit but this one, and he would be watching a fool made of Unwinter. There was no urgency, only expectancy, a calm waiting.

They simply did not act this way unless they were very sure of their prey. Even the hounds were loose and lazy, rubbing along fences and slinking between swords of liquid golden light.

A dilation. Curious breathlessness, as the gates between day and dusk opened wide. The sun slid low, low, lower, and there was a flash of white and russet, a breath of blue silk.

A last gleam of gold filled her hair, and Jeremiah lost all his breath. Maybe it was just the angle, or the light, but she was…

Robin Ragged stood in the precise center of the crossroads, her head upflung and her shoulders back. Even the dark circles under her eyes and the soot of dwarven realms could not hide what she was—a lightning bolt, an arrow of white-hot electricity, the original a mortal copy had been pressed from.

No. He shook his head, because the hounds in the shadows had tensed. Dusk rose, but too quickly, an unholy darkness filling the streets leading to the crossroads. It would choke off every path of retreat, and there was only one thing, in Summer or Unwinter, that could cause such a glooming.

No. It can't . . . no.

It raced up the road with inky, grasping fingers, digging in the cracks, steaming slightly as its chill breathed up to kill any lingering of spring.

Jeremiah was already moving, slip-sliding down the roof. He heard Robin's contemptuous laugh—had she planned for this? Probably not; she was whistling at death, just like a true sidhe.

Had she given him the slip just to die here, because of a boy sheathed in amber?

He was just a baby . . . I fed him. I bargained . . .

She would not be the first to revenge herself on Summer by seeking her own demise.

No.

A moment of weightlessness. He was falling, flung from the roof's edge, as if all his moments on the jobsite had been a prelude. Just fall, and let gravity do the rest.

He hit already running, and spat a half-measure of curse between his lips. It did not take shadow-form; instead, a silver brilliance streaked along the edges of the phrase, boiling into blazing light. The lance hummed into life, solidifying as he swept it laterally, crunching through a low liquid dogshape with obsidian teeth and mooncoin eyes. Iron flushed along the lance's wicked-sharp edge, a molten-red glow, and the Unseelie hound's deathscream was a high piercing cry that shattered the stasis of the streets.

Robin gasped as he skidded to a stop before her. He barely remembered the intervening space; he spun, and the interlocking fingers of chance and combat made him stop, unerringly, the lance pointed due north.

"What are you *doing?*" she whispered, as Jeremiah shouldered her aside.

Isn't it obvious? Saving your life. "I said I'd protect you." The words took him by surprise. "And so I shall."

"You *idiot.*" It wasn't possible for her to sound more disdainful. "I need no—"

The darkness cringed away from ironglow and moonshine, and a soft chilling laugh rose as the gloom ran together, a quicksilver melding. From the pool of darkest blackness, just on the northern corner of Birch and 58th, the glass of a butcher's shop window shivered to pieces as something birthed itself from its sheer reflective face.

Caparisoned only in darkness, the destrier born on cold stone-choked shores of the Dreaming Sea near the Rim stepped mincingly through, each of its hooves clawed and settling with a thin scream on a cushion of resisting air. Atop its broad back, a rider appeared, sable armor swallowing reflected light from Jeremiah's tiny circle of safety. From the broad spiked shoulders a long velvet cloak swirled, shredding into smoke and greenish steam along its tattered edges; under the dull-glinting helm two red coals fastened on Gallow and the woman who inhaled behind him, her hand reaching his shoulder and digging in. She didn't have the strength to bruise *him,* and the sudden hot sharp spike of guilt in Jeremiah's chest was the silence a moment before a volcano's thundering eruption.

"Robin." He sounded calm, and precise, even to himself. "Run."

The lance hummed, and Jeremiah Gallow braced himself to battle Unwinter himself.

CANNOT CARRY TWO

35

⤷╫⤶

*W*hat is he DOING? She wanted to speak—*idiot, you were not supposed to be here. You've ruined everything.* There was not breath for it, if she expected to slip them both free of this trap. Robin had expected to spring the jaws shut just a hairsbreadth away from her own flesh, then lead them a merry chase.

She had *not* expected the Armormaster to show his face yet.

She sought to push him aside, finishing her inhale, her throat relaxing. Her fingers had dipped toward her left skirt pocket; every scrap of Unseelie attention fastened on her. As if she would give away her advantage so easily. Did they *all* think her stupid?

Arrogance blinds them, Robin. See that you do not share that fault.

Gallow completed the ruin of Robin's fine plan by moving forward a half-step, as the butcher shop's window shivered and starred with breakage behind the tall, dark rider. "I am Jeremiah Gallow," he said, calmly and clearly. "And I challenge thee, Harne, Lord of Unwinter."

He's gone mad. That's the only explanation. Robin reached up, feeling blindly under her hair.

"*You.*" The chill, lipless tone froze the sidewalk in concentric rings as the destrier stamped, a pretty movement made horrifying by its ungainly grace. Its rider lifted one black-mailed fist, metal scraping as he pointed with a finger far too long to be human. "*You dare challenge me?*"

"I said as much." Gallow's lunatic calm didn't crack. "Are your ears stuffed with pixie-weed, that you did not hear me clearly?"

A rumbling sound that might have been a laugh, as the Unseelie—and there were more of them now, pouring through rips and refts in the curtain of the Veil, stepping sideways from whatever place in their realm that lay like gossamer fabric over this one. Robin had to exhale, her fingers slippery under the heaviness of her hair, an awful chilling sense of being naked and vulnerable stroking her nape.

"*How proud you are,*" Unwinter said, and the razor-edged amusement was dreadful. Robin's ears, sharpened by attention to cadence and harmony, drilled with sudden pain, hearing *wrongness.* It wasn't just the grim hunger of a creature that could devour souls wholesale she heard, but something else.

Something she had heard not so long ago, in Summer's dulcet tones.

Apprehension.

The world hung suspended for a long moment, as the situation shifted and wavered inside Robin's head. Unwinter was generally held to fear nothing; it was his iron rule that kept his realm from sliding through the Second Veil, not to mention kept the sneaking, malicious Unseelie under some manner of control. If he had begun to dread the plague, instead of seeking to leverage it…

…well. A very small suspicion—that the illness was not of Unwinter's doing at all, despite what some of Summer's

Court said, or even a "natural" disaster—sharpened still further. Which was very interesting, but nothing she had time to worry on.

Her fingers slid away from Gallow's shoulder, muscle gone hard as tile as he prepared to be a complete and utter imbecile. Perhaps he even had a plan.

Distraction, Robin.

"*Hold your tongue—*" Unwinter began, as if his saying it would stopper her throat. Perhaps it would have, had she not already been lung-full and determined.

The song burst free, a flood of gold that painted the intersection with furious light akin to sunshine. Certainly it was close enough to make several of the hounds cringe and scream, their hides smoking; the higher Unseelie cowered into shadowed cracks. Unwinter too made a noise, but it was swallowed briefly in the light.

Dispelling the force of the cry over such a broad area meant it would fade within bare seconds, but she was already moving. Her fingers tugged painfully at her hair, untwisting the precious bone comb worn against her scalp, and her hand tingled with Realmaking's pins and needles. She found Jeremiah's coatsleeve in the glare, plucking at it with her free hand, a vine's desperate caress.

"*Go!*" he cried. "*I'll hold them!*"

Her throat was still full of the light, and only moments of its flood remained. Hold Unwinter?

Did he seriously think he could?

She tugged again, her fingers sweating and the song beginning to fade at its edges. Shadows crept back in, against the false daylight she had birthed. They tore at its edges, and the sweat was all over her as she held the tone steady. Running out of breath *and* the energy to persuade him to come away.

He shoved her, bruising-hard, again. *"Go!"* he yelled, and though he perhaps did not mean to, he struck her with his shoulder, almost knocking her down. The ivory comb clutched in her fist—four-pronged, its fluid head and carven mane writhing as it scented readiness—twitched madly, struggling for release. Her fingers spasmed open, but she caught the wicked little thing as it sought to jump free—and stabbed her free palm with the four sharp prongs, driving them into the flesh below her thumb.

The pain jolted up her arm, all the way to her shoulder. She did not flinch, but Realmaking and chantment both roared through her. Which meant, of course, that the song died as she pulled the bone pin free of her flesh.

Blood welled in her violated palm.

Creaking, crackling cold rushed in as the light vanished. Dusk returned, dazzled but still ascendant, and the Veil unfolded in origami petals, yet another sideways-realm behind it glowing pearly-bright. A shape loomed, white and curious, stamping as it answered her call.

Chantment wasn't the song under her thoughts, it was *en*chantment, and it stole its force from the will of the one performing it. The less sidhe blood, the more will required—and the more sidhe blood, the more evanescent the chantment. Unless you were of the pure, but then you were at risk of the plague descending upon you with its greenspots and blackboil rot.

But every sidhe of Summer could call an elfhorse, just as every sidhe of Unwinter could summon a twisted, darkened mount.

A slim white elfhorse bowed its head as it finished solidifying, shaking its waterfall of silver tail. Robin, scrambling with a clatter of heels, grabbed at its silken mane and was up in a heartbeat. The four bloody pricks in her palm scorched as she wound her fingers securely in the mane, and a flush spilled through the creature's satiny glow.

As long as she fed it, the mare would carry her.

"Jeremiah!" She coughed, rasping. "Come!"

"*A night-mare cannot carry two.*" Unwinter's grinding laugh killed the last traces of liquid golden light. No few of the hounds were charred lumps, and the rustlings in the shadows were Unseelie no doubt still smoking and steaming. She had scarred no few of them, and they would remember.

It was a pity she could not do more. She could continue to let the song loose in lungfuls, but they would swarm her before long.

Jeremiah stood, balanced lightly in his heavy boots, the lance he somehow carried with him held at the same angle.

"You have a challenge to answer, knight." Gallow's hands were steady, but the weapon quivered. It bloomed with red along its blade—*cold iron*, she realized, shuddering even though she was Half and immune to its effects.

Still, if one were to face Unwinter, iron was a good ally. "Gallow," she whispered. "Come away."

"Go, Robin." How did he sound so certain? "I shall see you soon enough."

Unwinter's laugh tore at the darkening. Night shivered, turned to ink instead of indigo. "*Indeed. You both shall be my guests ere long.*"

Still, she hesitated, the elfhorse nervously sidling as it scented Unseelie.

Jeremiah's patience broke. "For God's sake, *go.*"

It was enough. She touched her heels to the white mare's sides, and the horse shot forward like foam on a breaking wave.

Behind her, the cries began.

THE HORN

36

꙰

Each version of the potential battle flowed together, narrowing toward a certain point. Beyond that, everything was murkmist, whether death or simply confusion-flux he didn't care to guess.

What mattered was the receding hoofbeats, bell-chiming silvershod. And her cry, rising clearly audible on the veils of evening breeze.

"I have the cure, Unwinter!"

Goddamn you, woman, just run. He braced himself, lance sweeping sideways as one of the Unseelie, a tallish knight in red perhaps thinking to make himself a name or gain some favor, pressed forward with a crystalline, curved sword upraised.

The movement should have ended with the red-armored sidhe's swift death. Instead, there was a rumble like thunder, and the sidhe—male, broad-shouldered, helmed with pale gold chased with rubies—dropped as a marionette with cut strings would, hit the crazyquilt-cracked pavement, and began jerking as muscles spasmed helplessly. Too-thin legs clasped in clashing metal sent up tendrils of steam.

All froze as Unwinter's displeasure congealed, and the rest of the assembled Unseelie—sneaking through cracks, hiding in corners, a fresh influx of hounds already crunching and slurping at their sun-roasted fellows—cowered.

"*Now, now,*" Unwinter said, the coals beneath his shadowy helm focusing on Jeremiah. "*He is mine alone. Bring me back the Ragged, and a prize to any who does so.*"

A scrambling in the shadows, a chittering howl, and Jeremiah *moved*.

Unwinter's mailed fist had raised, and the deadly silver curve clasped in it was not a weapon. Jeremiah recognized it—how could he not? The lance screamed a high, keening cry as he finally called upon its true speed and strength.

He wanted no mistakes.

They scrabbled and ran, the Unseelie, but the far deadlier threat was the horn Unwinter was about to wind. It was one of the few things older than sidhe or Sundering, that flute-lipped instrument, and its curve was of no geometry a mortal could look upon without queasy revulsion. It was whispered that Unwinter himself had been the only sidhe to escape its deadly call since the first dawn.

To give that ancient thing a blast of living breath was to call the Wild Hunt in its full strength, both Unseelie and Sluagh— the ravening unforgiven, who could find no rest under any god or master. The smaller horn-whistles the knights carried were copies, and awful enough, their ultrasonic cries chilling every living thing, even those that could not hear it. Unwinter had not ridden the full Hunt in a few hundred years, but if he was about to now, it meant certain death.

There was no escaping the Sluagh.

The lance quivered, straining through air gone brittle-hard as glass. For a paradoxical syrup-stretching moment, brief as a blink and long enough to contain his entire life, Jeremiah

Gallow thought he was too late. Airborne, the lance pulling his body along on crimson-thread strings, a sharp sweet flare of pain in his calf where one of Unwinter's hounds had leapt at a tempting target, a coughing lion's shout—

—and the lance's tip grazed the ancient deadly thing, wrenching it from the plated, long-fingered fist, sending it flying.

The gasp of horror echoing from every Unseelie who had lingered to watch their lord murder him would have been amusing if he hadn't already been straining himself in a different direction, the lance screaming with fierce joy as finally, *finally* its full measure was called upon.

What if it's not enough?

The thought was there and gone in less than a heartbeat. He hit concrete, rolling, his hand flashing out and closing over something burning-cold.

Star-metal, they whispered in corners and hiding-holes. *It fell, before the dawning when First Summer woke and named the trees, when Unwinter was merely a child. Some say the dwarves made it from a lump of sky-molten metal, but they deny it; they say it was already shaped when it landed, and they merely held it until the Sundering and Unwinter's Harrowing, when he rode through Seelie and the mortal realms at will, and all barred their doors at night.*

Up again, his coatsleeve scraped almost to ribbons by the pavement, the lance vanishing into the fiercely burning marks on his arms. Behind him, Unwinter's roar of rage shivered windows, a ring of ice expanding, nipping at Gallow's heels. Running, heart pounding, cradling ancient death against his chest, he put his head down and yelled, a rising cry of effort that weakened the high iron church gate just enough for him to burst through, metal shattering as the flash-chill turned it glass-brittle.

Lingering consecration on the church grounds would slow them, but Unwinter wouldn't stop until he had his horn back.

Which meant Robin was safe. Or at least, safer, because Gallow was now the sidhe Unwinter would want to pursue most.

Time to think fast, Jer.

LIPS INSTEAD OF THROAT
37

⟩╫⟨

Wind roared in her ears. She wrapped her fingers more firmly in the elfhorse's mane and leaned down to make herself a smaller target. Her hand throbbed with wild sweet pain, an exquisite drawing against each nerve's branching channel as the mane crawled into the pinpricks, hair turning to tiny greed-gulping mouths. Hot water stung from her eyes by the wind slicked her cheeks as the elf-mare neighed and turned sharply, obeying the pressure of her knees and shifting weight.

Wratton Street was busy at dusk. Horns blared, headlights glaring at the sudden appearance of a wild-haired sidhe on a white horse. Up the sidewalk, the elfhorse uneasy at the cold iron throbbing under pavement and in the canyon walls of this street, the rider's immunity to inimical metal communicating itself through the creature but not enough. A clatter of silvershod hooves, Robin's sharp cry as they nipped under the Metropolia Hotel's red and white striped awning, a bank of windows suddenly full of smoky forms as the Veil quivered around them.

A hard turn, Robin's body melded to the white mare's. She'd never ridden a horse in her benighted mortal childhood, but Court meant palfreys and easy walkers, and she had been complimented on her pretty seat more than once, with varying degrees of innuendo. Stealing away to call an elfhorse and coax it into a moonlight ride over the scented hills or the sugar-white dunes along Summer's half of the Dreaming Sea was one of the few things she would miss if she turned away from Court.

Or if she was banished.

The long straight shot of Santhorn, up a slight rise, would be accessible at the corner of Wratton and 8th. Just a few more blocks to go, clinging to the mare's back, the horse's flush deepening as its hooves pounded, chimed, rollick-and-rocking back and forth.

Silver huntwhistles pierced the deepening indigo of the sky. If she let the elfhorse have its head and reached Santhorn she stood a chance. At the crest of the hill was Amberline Park, well along with its greening because the mortal hilltop was not full-sideways to Summer's realm; they aligned more often than not, sidhe rubbing through as a knife-edge creases taut paper.

The whistles behind her, curving forward on either side to cup her course, were a silver net as true darkness filled the city's rivers of pavement. Even the pollution of orange streetlight painting the undersides of the clouds couldn't alter that shadowing, a reminder of the time when mortals barred their doors at dusk and would not open them until dawn. More among them heard the sidhe-horns in those days.

Heard, heeded, and feared.

The perfect crossroads in the Marlyle residential section was far behind her now, and there were tiny flashes in her peripheral vision. *What the—*

They were flutterings, each one a point of foxfire. The sidewalk was no longer deserted, the elfhorse needle-threading through pockets of the Veil as the crowd thickened. More horns blared as some drivers saw her and others didn't; there was a crunch of metal as the distraction of her appearance struck like a viper.

I am sorry for it, she thought, wishing the wind would drive the words from her head.

The firefly-dots were pixies, hop-skipping around the rents in the Veil as the horse casually flickered through real and more-than-real with each step. Green, red, blue, their jewel-wings fluttering and their babble a high, excited drone through the sound of Unwinter's pursuit. Why were they clustering about her?

Sorry for everything. For those she had just learned the names of—Panko, Sylvia. For those she had sung into death's arms at Summer's command—riding like this, her arm tingling before it grew numb, she heard them all. She even heard Parsifleur and Henzler, caught in webs not of their making.

Most of all, she sorrowed because she suspected she had just left Jeremiah Gallow to die at Unwinter's dubious pleasure. He had been afoot and challenged the Unseelie King, and it was because everything Robin Ragged made the mistake of caring for withered.

Daisy. Even Mama. And the most hurtful name was also the smallest.

Sean.

Was he still awake and aware inside the amber casing? The expression of horror on his young face—what had Summer done to him *before* she struck, or another sidhe struck with her blessing? Did he know Robin was the reason he had been—oh, of course. Summer would not let a chance to drop *that* information pass.

It was, after all, what mortal playthings were for. Like Mama, abandoned with a baby when mortal summer ended. Robin, just a silent swelling inside Mama's body, was the burden that forced Mama to turn to Daddy Snowe for help, because waiting tables, even with a breath of sidhe upon you, was not enough to feed and shelter mother and child. And Daddy Snowe, suspecting Robin wasn't his, turned to vinegar like cheap mortal wine.

If not for Robin, Mama and Daddy Snowe might even have been happy. Maybe, just maybe, Daisy would have found a way out of the trailer park.

If not for her, Sean might have been returned to his mortal family after a year and a day, his changeling brought back and feted before it was taken to Tiend or given to the apple trees, or perhaps even wicker-burnt on the Dreaming Sea's singing shores if Summer felt the need for spectacle instead of territory.

The huntwhistles drew closer; Robin urged the elfhorse on. How were they managing to surround her? Of course, now they would guess her destination, and if Unwinter had murdered Gallow swiftly, he would be riding in her wake as well, the ecstatic terror of his presence giving his hunters fresh strength.

The pixie-drone changed pitch, and they clustered about her. Was it merely the excitement of novelty—who had ridden openly through a mortal city in many, many years, even as the sidhe counted things? The iron, the smog, the poisoned rain— all these were deterrents, and the fullborn didn't care to risk such things *or* give the mortal-Tainted pride of parade.

The pixies piped at her. Were they intending to lead her astray, or alerting Unwinter to her presence? Flashes of their fluttergauze draperies, tiny sigh-woven shifts as they darted before her, crawling over the horse's mane, smoothing her hands with their tiny paws—three fingers and a dexterous thumb, their particular chantment soothing the numb-tingling.

Stone, I think they're trying to help—

Hoofbeats thundering on either side, the whistles near and chilling. The trap snapped shut, but she was on its lips instead of in its throat. Pixies scattered, chime-laughing, dark wings beating around the edges of Robin's vision. Headlamps swerving, red-jewel brake lights two close hungry eyes before the elfhorse let out a shattering neigh and compressed itself, a moment of lifting, *flying* as silvershod hooves smoked and crunched against a car's roof. The drawing on Robin's veins intensified, the nightmare seeking her immunity to cold iron as steam-roasting rose in veils, and the pixies were turning on the riders behind her, tangling hooves and tugging on clothing, biting with their tiny, fierce, wicked teeth.

Why are they helping? They have no debt to me. They're free sidhe. This is not right.

The park's entrance, a stone arch with perpetually open, decorative gates, loomed before her. Gravel scattered, and the elfhorse gleamed moonlit in the sudden dimness. Pressure released, easing, but the mare suddenly turned, hindquarters bunching, as a mass of pixies flew straight into its face. Rearing, Robin's hands torn free of silver mane, its hairs slicing deep as it sought to keep her.

She tumbled through free air, hit hard. Trees danced, their branches tossing with chiming pixie laughter. A crunch in her shoulder, the world turned over again, and Robin knew no more.

GLEAM IN THE GLOAMING
38

>+|+<

It was a good thing the cursed sidhe speed was still with him.
Scrambling and slipping across the rooftop, he leapt and
dropped into a dripping, overgrown garden. It had started to
rain, of course, because running from Unwinter with the freez-
ing weight of the Horn clutched to his chest could never be
easy. There was slight comfort in the fact that even though he
was likely to die at the Unseelie King's spiked gauntlets, his
deed had been witnessed and would be sung of for a very long
time.

That was rabbit-thought, though. He had no intention of
dying.

He burst through a holly hedge, thorny leaves tearing at his
coat and hair and skin. Slowed slightly, clasping the Horn to
his chest and breathing in the Old Language, the thing shrink-
ing as it took its other form. A silver medallion bounced against
his chest; he put the chain over his head while running, almost
tripped, hair caught in the fine links tore free of his scalp, and
he dropped its burning ice down his shirt.

It *hurt*. The agony scorched all through him, skin in contact
with something inimical, both sidhe and mortal flesh trying

desperately to avoid it. He fell, rolled out of habit, and reached his feet running again, pushing the pain aside.

He was glad he'd put Daisy's jewelry in a safe place even as he cursed himself for not hauling his bow along when he left Court. A weapon with some distance would be *incredibly* useful at the moment—

"Hist!" Movement in the shadows, further down the hedge he was now running parallel to. "Gallow! This way!"

His arms tingled. The lance ached to burst free, but Jeremiah denied it. "Puck!" he gasped, not breathless yet but close. The medallion against his chest was heavier than it should be, warming by too-slow degrees. "*Hide!* Unwinter!"

Puck fell into step behind him, running lightly on gloveshod feet. "You have made a merry mess of many plans, Armormaster. Come, this way."

It was useless to speculate whether Goodfellow intended mischief or not. Any mischief that could be done to his pursuers was welcome, and the free sidhe seemed to have an interest in this affair. If Jeremiah could guess what it was, that was all to the better.

For right now, any aid in escaping what pursued him was to be grasped with both hands.

He followed as the boy nipped through a gate and clambered up the side of an imitation-Tudor house. Across the roof in a flash, and there was an oak tree in its backyard, a fine spreading set of branches just barely tipped with new green. Up into those branches the boy clambered, with Jeremiah right behind him.

This won't shield us. "Goodfellow—"

"Hush." The free sidhe tilted his sleek dark head. "You shall not be Unseelie meat tonight."

Awful nice of you. Can't say I want you to change your mind. But why are you doing this? "I ask the price for this aid."

Puck's sharp white teeth flashed as he laughed, a small whistling sound. "It is not for your sake I bestir myself. Be quiet."

For whose sake, then? Robin's? He swallowed dryly. Maybe the Fatherless simply wanted to pull Unwinter's tail.

It would be just like him. A dangerous game some other sidhe would pay the price for, and mischief merry enough to make any sidhe laugh if they were not the target.

Jeremiah balanced among the branches, finding that the lightfoot had not deserted him, either. His heart thundered until he could spare the concentration to calm its pounding, gapping his mouth so he could breathe softly. Night air, full of subtle flavor—warming earth, ice and rotting things, the tang of exhaust and the blue ghost of evening rain. Tiny cold kisses on his face and hands, and he heard the huntwhistles in the distance.

Puck's eyes glowed greenyellow, his pupils dark hourglass holes. The free sidhe hooked a knee over a branch and brought his hands to his mouth, a swift graceful movement. He inhaled, Jeremiah tensed...

...and the pipes, usually at Puck Goodfellow's belt, gave a long breathy moan like a woman in love's final throes.

It wasn't precisely music, simply a rill like a running stream, sliding at the very edge of hearing. Jeremiah's skin roughened with gooseflesh; he'd heard enough tales of what could happen if those pipes shrieked. The soft skimming unsound tautened into silvery loops, complex and doubling back on themselves as air pressure changed.

The temperature dropped at least five degrees, Jeremiah's breath suddenly a plume of white vapor. Rushing and sliding in the shadows, all around the overgrown garden's crumbling brick wall—had the whole of Unseelie come out to play in this one city tonight?

A high trilling from Puck's pipes. It buzzed and blurred between the clamor and clatter of Unwinter's riding. The Fatherless narrowed his burning eyes, moving with loosely fluid grace as a chill breeze mouthed the tree.

Jeremiah moved as well, riding the swaying. Just like what surfing must be like, he supposed. He and Daisy had talked idly about moving to California one day. Golden sunshine and oranges all year-round, and maybe no sidhe hiding in the shadows... but the Dreaming Sea touched all shores.

There was never any escape.

The cold eased, a little at a time. In the distance, more hunt-whistles. On the other side of downtown—was that where Robin was leading them?

Puck's music died, and the pipes dangled loosely in one brown hand. He cocked his head, yellowgreen gleams winking out as he shut his eyes and *listened,* the sharp points of his ears dewed with condensation, poking up through the droplet-gemmed mat of his hair. He was sweating, too.

So there was something Goodfellow feared. Or the effort had cost him much.

"On the green hill," the Fatherless finally breathed. "Behind the sculpted gate."

Jeremiah blinked. *Other side of downtown—Amberline Park. Of course, that's Seelie, and Summer's touch will make it difficult for Unwinter to set foot there without invitation. I don't think Robin will invite him.*

She might be alive.

It was just possible, he supposed.

Puck beckoned, the entire tree rustled, and they both dropped from the oak, landing lightly. Jeremiah waited as Puck tucked his pipes away, taking deep, cautious sniffs.

Yes, the Unseelie had definitely passed them by. They were

drawing away toward the south, perhaps thinking he'd run for the river and its dubious bar to their passage on a night with no moon.

The Fatherless grinned again, his teeth pearly in the mellifluous shadows. "A good night's work, that. They'll be chasing fog and shadow 'til morning. More I cannot grant you."

That's more than enough. "Amberline Park. Probably where Robin ran."

"Of a certainty. List carefully, Armormaster, for it pleases me to give one more gift this most diverting of nights."

Now it comes. "You have already done so much."

"Aye, and not for thee. Your mortal lover, did you know her family?"

Now, suddenly, everyone wanted to tell him about Daisy and Robin. A popular subject, indeed. He'd thought he'd been so crafty.

Jeremiah forced himself to breathe, staring to the south as if he was still thinking of Unwinter's pursuit. The weight against his chest was cold, and throbbed a little. Was it blackening the flesh underneath? "Summer told me."

"An unlikely tale indeed. I marvel you did not know. Poor Robin; her mortal shadow earned all the affection, with barely a scrap left over. Did you know I brought the Ragged to Summer?"

Now, there was a new twist. Was it the truth? Who cared? "A most auspicious day that must have been." It didn't sound precisely snide or ungracious, but it was probably not the response Puck wanted.

What, precisely, *did* he want? The free sidhe was going to some trouble tonight, and for no profit Jeremiah could see. Which was enough to make him very nervous indeed.

"Oh, aye. She rose from a pond like a nymph, and I saw

the sidhe in her, so fair it threatened to blind the gaze. I asked Robin if she would not remain free, but she would hie herself to Summer, and so I brought her thence. But I wished to tell you, Gallow Queensglass, that Robin and her sister met the day her sister met with mortal fate as well."

Where was she going the night she died? And who did she meet there?

So Goodfellow and Summer both wanted him to believe… what? That Robin had done Daisy some ill?

"Family is as family does," he said carefully. "Is there a destination to these wendings, Goodfellow?"

A shrug, a smile, and the boy finished tying his pipes to his belt. "Simply making conversation while the air clears from the reek of Unseelie. Let us hie hence to our fair Robin's aid."

I don't remember inviting you along. Jeremiah simply nodded. "Lead on, Puck." *Again.*

"With good heart." A capering sideways step, another broad, sharp grin, and Goodfellow scarpered for the fence.

What else could Gallow do? He followed.

>⊦⊦⊰

Flitting from shadow to shadow, Puck flickering through the Veil and back, Jeremiah stepping in his wake and feeling his stomach flutter high up under his breastbone each time the free sidhe pulled them both through another fold between *here* and *there*. They paralleled Robin's course, in case scavengers or other unpleasantness rode in Unwinter's wake, and Jer caught glimpses of the chaos reverberating in the mortal world. Fender-benders, angry mortals turning on each other, sirens blaring, the dapples of red and blue lights as the mortal authorities descended to make some sense out of the sudden eruption of pandemonium.

How long had it been since an elfhorse had been ridden openly through the heart of a mortal city? Unwinter had left his country, too, and led his vassals in hunt. The medallion, a cicatrice of frost against Jeremy's chest, twitched slightly as the Veil shivered around him and Goodfellow.

Now was a fine time to wonder whether he should trust the free sidhe, and follow him so blindly. Especially when the path took them up the side of a skyscraper and out into empty air, the lurching of falling in his stomach before concrete jolted under his feet and Puck brought them out on another rooftop, a cold stinging wind turning their breath to twin dragon-clouds, and quickly sideways as an Unseelie hound's muzzle lifted, the flat glitter of its eyes scorching through several layers of the Veil behind them.

Puck whistled, skipped sideways; the lightfoot bloomed in Jeremy's boots and he followed. Had the other sidhe tried to shake him off? Perhaps.

The sideways-skipping ended with a great gripping stitch in Jeremiah's side and his stomach cramping, and he almost retched as the Veil flexed and popped, the park gates thocking into place just behind him. Puck half-spun, his irises a flash of yellow, and every muscle in Jer's body tightened. He stepped aside, the lance prickling and the medallion turning scorch-cold again, quelling the nausea and muscle tremors while he scanned for Unseelie.

Branches rustled uneasily, most of them starred with new growth. The evergreens whispered, conspirators, and for those who knew how to look, Summer could be seen, a ghost rubbing through the mortal world, sharp and hungry.

Puck's hand fell away from the hilt at his side, and his grin was a gleam in the gloaming. "Well?"

Gallow inhaled, sipping at the faint breeze. Apple-blossom,

mortal night masked by exhaust and almost-spring, new-mown hay, a breath of the baking-bread scent elfhorses carried...

...and a thread of spiced cherries, a flash-impression of red-gold curls and much-mended, fluttering blue silk. When had her scent become so instantly recognizable?

When had he started almost longing to fill his lungs with it?

"She made it," he whispered.

"Indeed," Puck replied. But his tone was grave. "I smell pain, Gallow Queensglass. And blood. Let us search."

SIMPLE BETRAYAL
39

⊃╫╠⊂

Blackness, for a long while.

Cold. And damp. Agony all through her—her head, her left arm, her right shoulder.

There was motion close by. Chiming little voices. Pixies, maybe. A branch snapped, there was a grunt.

Her eyes opened slowly. Crusted blood in her lashes, sticking; she tried to blink it away and took stock. Her head pounded, and she was thirsty. Wet all over—rain pattered between branches carrying only the nubbins of leaves. Against her hip a boulder reared; she was lucky the mare hadn't thrown her *onto* it. Half were durable creatures indeed, but healing from such a thing would be...painful. She might even end up Twisted. Unable to sing.

She might have even wished for as much, if it wouldn't leave her defenseless. Just like any sidhe-gift—you couldn't ever truly win.

But I might. If I can just survive.

Her legs obeyed her, but slowly. Still, she could lift both feet, though she'd lost a shoe. *Must find it,* she thought, the words a soupy haze. Her left arm obeyed, too, and she rubbed at her eyes, gently, with her left hand. The thirst mounted another few notches.

Of course, she had spilled much claret, feeding an elfhorse on such a wild ride.

"Christ." A man's voice. "A shoe...there. Jesus Christ."

"*Must* you utter that ugliness?" Another man, a light tenor, very familiar. She couldn't think. Her hair was wet strings, and she felt at her skull. Still whole, the bleeding seemed to have stopped. Her right shoulder burned, a deep drilling pain intensifying every moment she gained more of her wits. Her right hand twitched, and she bit back a whimper.

"Robin!" The first voice, closer now.

"She came far, and fast." A low, cruel laugh. "Riding like Unwinter himself."

"Robin!" Calling. Who would call *her*, especially in such a tone? Almost as if he feared for—

More movement in the bushes. "You're loud enough to break a trollkin's winter dream, Gallow. Let me hold her shoe, and—"

"No." Short, abrupt. Very close now, and Robin struggled to think.

The next moment, a dark shape loomed above her, and she made a small desperate noise as her body refused to obey, and she didn't have the breath to loose the song.

"Shhhh, it's me." Gallow's green eyes a gleam in the dark, he slid an arm under her. He was warm and real, whole and alive, and she shook against him. He had her missing shoe and bent to slide it onto her dirty foot, brushed the crusted blood from her forehead and eyes, peering at her face. "It's me," he repeated. "Are you all right?"

She shook her head, not trusting this sudden concern. Her side ached when she tried to breathe, and she flinched when he touched her shoulder, his fingers oddly gentle. Tried to push his hand away, but her arm wouldn't work.

Behind him was a slim shape, yellowgreen irises burning fiercely. Puck watched Gallow minister to her, and she could not see the free sidhe's expression.

"Dislocated." Gallow peered at her face, pushing aside strings of her wet, mud-grimed hair. She must look a sight, and the only reason she hadn't given anything away was because she couldn't move her right side and her throat was stoppered by the pain. "This is going to hurt."

She set her jaw and nodded.

A crunch, a brief starry darkness, and she came back to herself, her left hand clutching at her skirt pocket and both Puck and Jeremiah holding her upright. She tried frantically to dislodge them, but the free sidhe's fingers were like iron and Gallow appeared not to notice.

"Lift her over... there. I'll take her."

"What if I wish to?" But Puck surrendered her, with one last brutal squeeze of her left arm. She would bruise there, another blotch to add to the others no doubt blooming afresh all over her. "They will be pixie-led until dawn; more I cannot grant you. I suggest you hie over the border into Summer as soon as the sun rises."

Gallow shrugged. "We'll see. You've grown charitable of late, Goodfellow."

"Oh, aye. Perhaps the Ragged interests me." The boy stepped back. He watched Robin as she sagged against the Armormaster's side, too weary to care much what happened as long as the Unseelie didn't find her. "After all, hers is a marvelous voice. I would that she chose to use it as it should be used, and not simply a toy for Summer's little games."

"I'd hardly call her games *little*." Gallow sounded even more cautious. "Whither are you bound now? More mischief planned for tonight?"

"Much more." The V-shaped smile widened, and among the dripping, half-naked trees Puck looked more solid than ever. He looked, in fact, just as he had the first time she saw him in the trashwood, sharp-pointed ears pricked and his entire body a taut string, regarding her, nostrils flaring, as she rose out of the swimming hole.

What beauty is this? he had said, his first words to her. *And wouldn't she like new clothes, a warm bed, and no more blows or serving?*

She coughed, spat to the side to clear her throat, uncaring of her manners. Puck was still staring.

"Ragged." Now he leaned forward on the balls of his feet. "I've led Unwinter a merry chase for you tonight. Remember it."

With that he was gone, a whistle fading at the edges of Robin's hearing as the bracken and underbrush swallowed him.

"Great," Gallow muttered. "Okay. Nothing else broken, it seems. Can you walk?"

I can. To prove it, she pushed him away and tried to. Her ankle turned, her leg buckling, and he caught her again. Still strangely gentle.

"Let me help. Christ, woman, don't *ever* do that again."

Do what? Lead you astray? Why do you care? Or you don't. She was finally able to take a deep breath, and found her voice was a croak, torn just like her skin and dress. "Had to."

"Of course you think I'm just like every other man Summer casts her eyes upon." He lifted her over a fallen log, steadied her as her feet slipped, and made a small sound of effort as she tried to lunge away and walk on her own. "*Stop* it, Robin. I told Summer I'd protect you, and I told her I don't serve. Both are true."

You're serving her now. "Thirsty," Robin managed. "Hoarse. Thirsty."

"I know. I'll take care of it, Robin. We'll get you milk, then you can sleep. Come morning I'll take you into Summer. I hope to hell you have what she wants."

She clutched at her left skirt pocket. Let her hand fall away. Winced inwardly at what she was about to do. "Must…hide… them." *Come now, betray me, and she'll reward you handsomely.*

"Just be quiet." He moved steadily, despite the brambles grasping both of them. Their thorn-bites were simply pinpricks, unheeded in the general agony. "I'm not leaving you behind."

It was no use. She went limp, and the last thing she heard was his muttered curse as he bent to pick her up. The music inside her head swallowed her whole, and she sank unresisting into its flow.

⨎

A dark, painful time later she surfaced to find him dabbing at her forehead with something wet and cold. It smelled awful, and she tried to push it away, but he ignored her. She was weak as a kitten; the night-mare had taken a great deal of blood.

It was warm, though, and she was clean. The material against her naked skin was mortal-woven, and it smelled powerfully of musky male and sidhe. She blinked several times, staring at the paneled wooden wall, and finally realized where she was.

"We're safe enough," he said, without preamble. "Puck gave us until morning. He must favor you."

Not likely. Yet he'd done her a service and no mistake; consequently, she was hard-pressed to find any explanation for him extending himself so far. She shook her head, and Gallow slid an arm under her, propping her up and lifting a glass to her lips.

It was whole milk, still holding a trace of chill from the refrigerator. Sweet and cool, it poured down her throat, and she drank greedily. When the glass was drained he wiped at her mouth, as if caring for a child. "There you go. I hung your dress up, figured I shouldn't run it through the washer."

Did you go through the pockets? Or just one of them? She nodded, watching him. He settled her back on the thin pillows, cocked his dark head. His hair was plastered down, and he'd scrubbed himself with harsh mortal soap. Its scent was all over her, too, and the fire in her cheeks was mitigated only by the fact that she didn't feel as if she had been... touched.

Was he honorable? Did he only kindle for Daisy's hand?

Or Summer's?

"I'll sleep on the couch." He pulled the covers up. "You know, I should have guessed who you were. She... Daisy had a locket just like that. I... She was buried with it. I put her in hallowed ground under her maiden name, because... well, she always had trouble sleeping. I wanted her to be able to rest."

Of course, in a hallowed graveyard no sidhe would go digging and take bits of her to give Gallow grief. No Half would trace her through Gallow's name, either. An unexpected kindness on both counts; now Robin felt foolish for thinking Daisy would have had a mere-mortal man. Bright and blithe, Daisy was the sun's blossoming eye, and Robin, as ever, was the shadow. Almost a changeling, but not quite.

It didn't matter.

She still watched him, a line between her eyebrows, trying to guess what he wanted.

It occurred to her in stages. The milk coated her throat, a balm soothing fiery thirst. When she coughed, clearing the way, he didn't flinch.

"I'm not *her*," she whispered.

He looked away, at the two dressers standing side by side under the window. Of course Daisy had sewed the curtains;

they were in the shade of peach she liked, and even though the stitching was by machine, they held her sister's touch. The smaller dresser was ancient, and Robin recognized it, wondered if there was a lump of strawberry chewing-gum still stuck to the back of the third drawer down.

The closet was half open, and hanging next to what had to be Gallow's clothes were dresses and two pink waitress uniforms; Daisy's shoes—larger than Robin's, just as Daisy was taller but Robin's bust a little larger—were set neatly below, a pair of cheap navy heels with diamante buckles, thick-soled white shoes for work, a battered pair of blue and yellow trainers.

How many years, and he still hadn't taken down her dusty clothes? Did he think Robin could wear them?

"I know you're not her," Gallow said finally. Maybe he even believed it. "But..."

"I am not my sister." She moved, fretfully, wishing she could get up. The sheets were all but marinated in his scent. "I never will be."

"No. She was mortal." He rose, fluidly. Daisy must not have seen the sidhe in him. Maybe he hadn't been grim, with her. Maybe he had been laughing and carefree as her baby sister.

The familiar twin bite of love and envy, threaded through with stinging grief, darkened everything. Robin couldn't even love her sister completely. Always a shadow, for all that she'd been born first, born incomplete, in-between, Half.

It all added up to born *lesser*.

It stung, of course, a familiar pain by now. Just as she was used to Summer's many betrayals. The Armormaster might not have the stomach to kill her himself, perhaps in honor of Daisy's mortal memory, but he would draw the pouch out of the left pocket of her skirt. Not the hidden, chantment-sealed one, but the one she had been telegraphing since she left the dwarves.

All betrayals, in the end, were so simple. All you had to do was give anyone, mortal or sidhe, the chance, and they would inevitably use it. After all these years, Robin had finally learned.

Daddy Snowe would be proud.

"I'll sleep on the couch," Gallow repeated. "If the Unseelie draw near I'll wake you, and we'll chance the border at night. I have one or two who owe me favors; I should use them. One way or another, I'll take you to Summer; they can't follow us there."

Not without an invitation. Her skin crawled. Perhaps he meant to be kind, but all she heard was that he would be between her and the door, at least until he left to take Summer her prize. If Unwinter found her here, he could even have the benefit of Summer's thorn-decked gratefulness without murdering Robin himself. Whichever way it ended, Gallow won.

Or so he thought.

There was another message in his words.

She was mortal.

And Robin was not. A flighty, faithless, treacherous sidhe bitch, capable of coldly plotting against even those who aided her, a poison spreading to all who breathed near her.

Perhaps, Robin considered, wearily, she should simply become such a thing. Would it hurt less?

He flicked the light switch, plunging the bedroom into darkness. A thin thread of yellow, mortal glow outlined the door, which he swept almost closed. He left the light in the hall on, and she heard him moving around his trailer while her eyes burned fiercely.

He would be gone when she awoke, even if Robin secretly, in some dark, small corner of herself, hoped to be proven wrong. Everything now depended on the Gallow Queensglass, the former Armormaster, betraying one ragged little bird.

A BOON

40

꙰

She finally slept, curled on her side and breathing deeply as the bruises faded on her shoulder. He could almost see them retreating.

I never will be.

The bag in his hands was black and silken, chantment in the gold-threaded stitches to guard its precious cargo. Inside, stitchery divided the pouch around slender glass tubes, sealed around a liquid that sparkled faintly. Tucked in her left skirt pocket along with a crumpled piece of paper—one of his own pay stubs, she'd probably thought to search for him with it—and a cheap blue plastic ring, a kid's gimcrack prize her fingers were probably still slender enough to wear. It was exactly the shade of her dress, and he could see her finding it in the gutter, or on the sidewalk, picking it up like a magpie steals anything shiny.

And one more thing. If he hadn't been looking for the ampoules he'd never have gone digging in her pocket and found it. A metal barrette, the kind that snapped closed when you bent it. Caught in it, wrapped tightly around, golden-red hairs that were not sidhe. Too pale, especially when compared to the glory of Robin's mane.

Mortal hair.

Had Daisy been wearing it the day she died? You could do things with hair; a Realmaker's chantment could be turned to dark uses indeed. Hell, you didn't need Realmaking. Even a pixie could distract a driver, lead a car to jump a ditch and ram a lone tree.

Poor Robin; her mortal shadow earned all the affection, with barely a scrap left over.

It was a hell of a thing to think.

Balanced against it, everything he'd seen. *I have the cure, Unwinter!* Waving herself before the Unseelie to draw their chase. *You fool!* Her expression when he appeared, her obvious efforts to keep him from coming to harm…but she had led him into the Tangle, just like a faithless sidhe. She remembered names, too. Mortal names. A thin ancient dime tossed into a street busker's case, a gift with no price and no sharp teeth.

What to believe? He was already halfway to somewhere he never thought he'd visit again, something he thought had died with Daisy.

Halfway? Oh, Gallow, do not start lying to yourself. Or at least, do not continue.

She sighed, shapelessly. Curled more tightly into the covers, clutching the pillow like a life raft. Daisy had sometimes done that, as if she could make herself small enough to be ignored. When she was ill, or upset, that was how she slept.

Beat me if you got to, Jer. Just don't leave me.

The boy—Sean—was as good as dead in Summer's clutches. Robin was as good as dead once the Queen had what she wanted; when the ampoules were handed over Summer would be just as dangerous as Unwinter's pursuit. He could trade the Horn to Unwinter in return for Robin's life—she wouldn't like his ashen country, but it was better than death. He might even manage to win some other concession from the Unseelie King.

Worry about that later. You know what you have to do now.

Funny, but even in the uncertain light from the hallway, she didn't look a thing like Daisy. There were similarities, of course, but they weren't twins. Looking at her now, her face serene with sleep, her forehead painted with iodine—the wound had been shallow, thank God—you could see the sharper features, the original beauty.

Her mortal shadow.

Small consolation that he found he remembered Daisy's face just fine, and Robin's couldn't take its place. Instead, the Ragged burned through him, a still, secret heat at his core, where the ash and gall of grief had rested. His own personal Unwinter, now broken.

Was it so easy?

It was tempting to think he could take his shirt and jeans off, slide into the bed next to her. Share that warmth, and put his arms around that softness. Let tomorrow do what it would.

You know what you have to do. Time is short.

He uncoiled from his crouch next to the bed. Her dress hung in the bathroom, shedding mud as it dried, sidhe-woven cloth healing itself. The rips in her skirt she could mend with simple needle-chantment. He'd returned everything to her pocket except the ampoules in their black case.

Jeremiah's fingers hovered a bare inch from her shoulder. The living heat of her brushed his palm, a feather's caress. Soon the paleness would be burnished, whole again. She would probably sleep past daylight; Unwinter wouldn't think to look *here*. Only a fool would come back to his own house after being under either hunt.

The pad of his middle fingertip barely brushed her skin. A familiar tightening, down low.

Who would even want Summer, with Robin standing nearby? Even her mortal shadow had been enough to dizzy an Armormaster. The flame itself threatened to leave him ash and cinders afresh, even as he welcomed its touch.

I am not my sister.

"No, you're not," he whispered, mouthing the words. "You're something else, Robin."

Moments later, the bedroom was empty.

So was Jeremiah Gallow's trailer, except for a sleeping Half-sidhe, curled on her side and muttering shapelessly as she dreamed, then settling into healing blackness.

>+|+<

The borders of Seelie were watched, but he had not been Armormaster for naught. A man was only as free as knowledge could make him.

Night under a sliver of milk-pale moon in Summer was warm, hushed, and expectant. He tested the air, rolling it on his tongue, as the shifting border retreated. He had probably been remarked—there were foxfire pixie-lights in the tree branches, jewel tones winking in and out. Were they carrying tales to Puck, too? Or had he simply managed to interest them in the chase earlier?

I should be in armor for this. It probably wouldn't help, though. His armor, chantment-chased, was hanging in a bus station locker, in a tiny purple bag with Daisy's few bits of jewelry.

No time to brace himself. He stepped out into the open, the set of his shoulders military-straight. Falling back into the habit of moving like a sidhe, with that damnable sense of comfort.

Struggling against his true nature wasn't going to help anyone, least of all Robin.

Is that why you're here?

The roads were bone-white, and he skirted the orchard out of habit. The high ground was best, and in any case, the apple trees were more...active...at night. There were no pennants and no bonfire visible through the blackened trunks, so *she* would perhaps be in a pavilion, or even abed.

The thought of waking *her* was equally fearsome and grimly pleasurable.

Summer and Puck both wanted him to think Robin had been involved in Daisy's...death. Which could mean only one thing, and it did not make Robin guilty.

Quite the opposite.

Summerhome rose before him, bleached pale in the star- and moonlight. He had never noticed before how it looked like the bones of some giant creature, its flesh either fallen free through inactivity or outright death. It dozed, and it rotted.

At least in Unwinter the foulness was held in the open.

Thinking on that would only distract him. The Horn at his chest was quiescent, but so cold. Not burning-cold, just mortal ice against his breastbone. His skin wasn't blackening under it; that was one mercy. More than he expected.

I was not always of Summer. Who would remember as much? Maybe not even the Queen.

He climbed the stairs, and found no guard at the door. In his time, such laxity would have been unacceptable. Who was Armormaster now?

Did he care?

Well, for one thing, he might have to kill whoever held that position, if Summer was in a mood to play catlike with prey. It would be nice to know. The thrill along his nerves was danger, and after so long in the paper-thin mortal world he could almost have welcomed it.

Could you be truly living, if you did not know you could be slain?

The doors were easy enough to push open. He strode through the deserted entryhall, and the prickle of unease along his arms and legs crested. No mailed knights at guard here, either. No brughnies hurrying about their duties, no ghilliedhu girls swishing past with their long fingers full of jeweled pins and ribbons to tie in a lady's hair.

Not Robin's, though. Summer would not allow a Half to appear bedecked. The insult was perhaps mitigated by the fact that Robin needed no such decking.

Or driven in more deeply.

The Hall's great swinging doors opened, and this was why no guard had been set. The Hall throbbed with color and light, tinkling sidhe-laughter and a whirl of dresses. The music spilled out, too, bone-keyed harpsichord and silver-dipped pipe, the drums of stretched skin, pounding to speed mortal hearts along, to make them faint and dizzy.

How many years ago had he heard similar music while he wandered, starving and footsore, hiding from the railway dogs? More than a mortal lifetime, long enough that the memory didn't wound him.

At least, not much.

And the smells! Spices no mortal could name, crisp-juicy apples, new-cut grass. A musky tang of sidhe sweat, the merriness of a just-kissed lover's breath, the copper tang of fresh-spilled blood. It filled his nose, enough to reel even his senses... but into the whirl he plunged, an arrow in drab mortal clothing, flying true. His arms itched furiously, the marks moving under his sleeves, straining for release.

She did not recline upon her throne. Summer's Queen, dressed in deep verdant green instead of blue, sat upright, her feathered mask slipping aside as she sighted him and smiled. Candy-red lips parting slightly, her white hand rising, the mask made a dipping gesture, and between one wild beat and the next...silence.

"And who is this?" Her words were edged with frost, even though this revel could only mean that she was about to open the Gates. "Why, it's Gallow-my-Glass, visiting us afresh, come to bring his Queen a gift."

Now, Jeremiah. He halted at the foot of the dais. They had drawn away—hobs and knights, ladies in fantastical velvet and fluttering silk, drogwiles and woodwights, dwarven envoys of the Red clans but none of the Black. Selkies with their shimmer-seal coats and dripping fingers, naiads clothed in riverglitter and dryads of every shape and size—the trolls and giants would be carousing on Hoyland Moor this night, and woe to any who wandered that way under ten feet tall.

"I do bring you what you asked, my Queen, and I will have a boon in return."

"A boon!" Her gaze glittered, avid and hungry. "Oh, you demand payment for a gift, Gallow?"

"No. I demand the life of Robin Ragged." He took a deep breath. "For this I will give thee what I carry, what you charged us to bring, O Summer. None other shall lay a hand upon the Ragged or claim her life. Only myself, and myself only."

She clapped her hands, the mask fluttering, and the Seelie Queen's laughter was silver bells. "Granted, with goodwill! Hear and witness, goodfolk all—the Ragged's life belongs to Jeremiah Gallow, the Queensglass, once-Armormaster."

I'll not spend it to please you. His face showed no sign, merely set itself further. Years of wearing a mask for mortals served him in good stead now.

He reached into his coat pocket, pulled out the bag. "As promised, then." He tossed it, and Summer actually leapt from her throne to catch the small embroidered thing.

Also in his pocket were the three iron nails, and Jeremiah plunged his fist back in, almost tearing the material in his haste. His slippery fingers found and clasped them. "*God's blood!*" he cried, and the world turned sideways as the revel of the sidhe cast him forth. Always, in tales, the blasphemy and cold iron flung one from the sideways realms. A truth hidden in so many garbled stories, but what they never mentioned was the pain.

It hurt, and he screamed.

MOST MARVELOUS MEAT
41
⊱╫⊰

She slept deep, the young one, her hair spread over a mortal pillow and shaming it with rich redgold gloss. The familiar curve of her cheekbone, her long fingers mortal-fragile, the roundness of a cream-pale shoulder.

He stood at the foot of the bed, his irises glowing and their hourglass pupils each bearing green sparks in the top and bottom bells; his teeth lengthened as his mouth filled, again, with the juices of hunger. Sweet, and *powerful*. Not like a salt-rich, terror-drenched mortal.

The most marvelous meat of all was another of his kind.

He cocked his head, listening intently. Nothing but the hushed breathlessness of a mortal night, past witching hour and before gray predawn. No hint of silver whistles or clawed hoof-fall. The pixies would be winking out as dawn rose, slipping back into the Veil-pockets they lived in or fleeing to Summer's bonny swards, weary after a night of good sport. They had performed well, aiding the Ragged's passage and also stopping her from stepping over into Summer's clutches, and he had wanted to be the one to find her. There was a bower within Amberline Park, soft moss and a clear running stream, heavy cream to soothe her thirst and hurts, and a couch wide enough to cradle her dreamlessly. Pixies to twist her hair into braids, and a robe made of sighs and crisp red fall afternoons to cover her, such a robe as she had never been given leave to wear in Summer.

She would no doubt be grateful, Half as she was, for his attentions. Such a little thing he would ask of her in return.

Only to be his.

Instead, she was here. But what a stroke of luck, the milksop Armormaster stealing and sliding over the border! It was, he decided, even better this way. He had noted a troubling soft-ness in the Ragged's treatment of the Queensglass, and vice versa.

It was, he rather thought, time for the Ragged to be taught a lesson.

He turned, softly, softly, and winked through the bedroom door. Down the hall, soft-padding, and impatience rose. If he woke her, she would be half dead, and useless besides. As charming as it would be to maze a dozing Ragged, to see her wander with sleep-weighed lashes and a flush of exhaustion on her cheeks, it would not do.

He had prepared such a *pretty* bower for her, too. Not like this mortal hole, with filth everywhere. Long ago, such a thing—a slattern's hair, a hearth ill swept, crusted food left on trenchers instead of scrubbed off with sand—would have moved him to mischief.

Now it moved him in another direction. The Queensglass should know better than this. If he was to ape a mortal's life, he could at least show some respect to his betters when they visited.

Puck Goodfellow stepped into the kitchen, examined the dirty dishes. His lip curled, and he turned in a full circle, deosil, then another widdershins, while he mulled how best to express his displeasure.

Not as if it mattered, really, since Unwinter now wished Gallow's head on a pike. He was welcome to it, too.

Puck Goodfellow's smile widened, and widened again. His face suffused with dark glee, and he began to hum.

PRIMROSE DARLING

42

⌖

O h, what a merry song I give..."

Someone was singing, a light tenor wandering through an airy tune. Golden light striped her face, and for a long syrupy moment she was a child again. Waking up in Mama's trailer, a sick knot of fear in her stomach, listening to find out if Daddy Snowe was home, Daisy beside her—

There was no small, warm, living weight next to her. The light was wrong, too, from her feet instead of her right side. The singing wasn't Mama's wandering renditions of gospel or Grand Ole Opry ballads, either. There was a hiss, a crash, and low sidhe laughter.

"When I undertake to sail a sieve..." More singing. Quick, light dancing sounds—the trailer shook, and there was another crashing noise. "Oh, how I wish she'd never leave...oh, oh, what a tangled web I weave..."

That's not Gallow. He didn't seem the type to sing in the morning, with his set face and sullenness.

She stretched cautiously. Her arms and legs obeyed her, and she was naked in a bed that took up most of a trailer's master bedroom. Electric light glowed around the half-closed door, no sunshine apparent. Daisy's clothes were in the closet, along with Gallow's, and Robin was head-sore and a little shaky, but otherwise whole.

Did I truly escape Unwinter? And Gallow carried me here. *Why?*

If this was his idea of a clever move, she supposed her own breathing life would be proof of its success. She had not cared enough to question last night, all her failing strength taken up with not giving away her small, slight advantage, her toss of the dice in this murderous game.

The crashing halted, and Robin slowly pushed herself up on her elbows. There was a galumping in the hall, the bedroom door flung itself open, and Puck Goodfellow bounded through, landing on all fours on the bed as Robin scrambled back, cloth tearing. She took the sheet with her, and her throat tingled, but Puck merely grinned, his sharp white teeth gleaming. Electric light from the hall glowed on his nut-brown skin, fired in his eyes, and picked out the grain of his leather jerkin. If not for the catlike crouch and the points of his ears, he could probably be mistaken for a mortal boy.

"Good early morn, damsel, and look at you a-tumble. Did I not know Gallow was in Summer before the witching hour, I would suspect you dishonored by a knight neither of Seelie nor its counterpart."

She absorbed this, staring at him, willing her face to remain neutral. *Where's my dress?* "And you left to guard my dreaming, Goodfellow?"

"Oh, I watched over my primrose darling, never fear. Here you are, still fine and feathered. And delicious."

Does that mean I am prey now? Loosing the song on him was a wonderfully attractive proposition. "My clothes?"

"Ah. Yes." He bounced slightly on the bed, and his pencil-thin eyebrows rose. "Do you need them? I'll wager you are all rose and cream under that mortal ragpile."

"My clothes, Puck. Or get out, so I may find them." *Gallow left. For Summer, Puck said.* The disappointment, however expected, was still sharp and sour against her tongue. *I was a fool to hope.*

Still, Jeremiah Gallow had fallen to her expectations, instead of rising to her hopes. It was all one could ask for, from a man. She edged for the side of the bed, carefully gathering the sheet to take with her. Her shoes were placed neatly on the floor, and she didn't have to look at the bedside table with its purple-shaded lamp to know this was Daisy's half of the mattress.

Sudden nausea cramped her stomach, but she kept moving, slowly and steadily, stepping into the heels and trying not to sigh with relief as their chantment tingled against her skin. Puck whistled, a long, low wolfish tone, and laughed when she shot him a glance that could have been a curse, had she willed it a trifle harder.

He hopped down, and danced for the door. "Your robe is in the water-room, and I've stolen you fruit and lovely heavy cream. Hurry, dear Robin. Morn approaches, and there is much to do."

"Gallow went into Summer." It was early morning yet, the sun strengthening but not yet breaching the horizon.

"Not only that, my primrose Ragged." Puck stamped into the hall, turned and beckoned her. "Can you not feel it?"

She did, as soon as she halted, wrapped in a torn sheet and standing in her heels at the foot of her dead sister's bed. A subtle thrilling all through her, a clock those pure mortal would never hear the ticking of. "She's opening the Gates."

"At true dawn, in less than an hour. Summer fears the plague no more." His tone turned grave. "I wonder how soon she will move to collect the mortal servant who created its pretty black boils for her. What do you think?"

Henzler is dead, though. "For..." *Not just the cure, but the illness itself.* Robin clutched the sheet to her chest. Her locket

271

was gone. Her throat felt naked. Who had taken it? Jeremiah? "Puck... Robin Goodfellow, are you telling me what I think you..." *It can't be.*

And yet. *I did what she asked. I did it twice,* Henzler had crowed. Summer had not opened the Gates last spring, not until the very last moment and only partway. The mortal season had been rainy and chill, and Seelie not fully renewed. Five changelings given to the Tiend last mortal summer, a prodigious number, but necessary, Robin grasped now, to stave off withering.

Summer had *planned* this.

Puck watched her dawning realization, his smile returning in increments. "Oh yes," he murmured. "Summer bargained hard, and bargained fierce, and earned some little of my expertise. She glamoured the one I thought most likely to make what she wished; I installed her pet in a lovely safe place, and brought her his reports. You were to keep a watch on me, all unknowing." His arms stretched out; he brushed either side of the hallway with his ten fingertips, the thumbs folded in with ease no mortal hands could match.

Robin's skin was ice. "She didn't expect it to start killing fullborn."

"'Twas meant for Unseelie alone, my pet. Imagine her surprise." He stepped back as she advanced, holding his arms stiffly out. The bathroom door was to her left; that was where Jeremiah had hung her dress. Not in the closet; it would have fouled Daisy's holy, dusty robes.

She was mortal. He'd said it like a curse. He hated anything sidhe, it seemed, including himself.

Including her, no doubt. He had his place at Summer's side secured now, and may he have joy of it. At the moment, though, there were other matters to concern her.

Why is Puck telling me this? "If you mean to kill me, Robin Goodfellow, either attempt to do so or get out of my way."

"Kill *you*?" Now he looked shocked. "I would sooner destroy one of my precious heartsblood oaks than injure your fine voice. List, dear Robin Ragged. I would tell you more."

She froze. The door was so close. If she opened her throat to the song, she could probably injure him grievously, and with a chance to gather more breath she could quite possibly kill. That had to enter into his calculations; and besides, he could have done her any manner of murder while she lay sleeping.

"He didn't leave you here for me." She felt stupid for even considering that Jeremiah might do so. "And there's iron under the doorstep." The words were soft and broken, because she forced herself to reserve half her breath. "How are you—"

"Gallow Queensglass does not consider me an enemy." Puck stepped back carefully, feeling with his glove-shod feet. The pipes dangled at his belt, and it occurred to her that he held his arms out because he wished to prove he meant no harm. "List, Robin."

"I heed you." Her lips were numb. *Summer* had loosed the plague? To get rid of Unwinter, very well, but . . .

"The tiny glasses you carried will avail Summer naught. The Counties, both mine and Unwinter's, are ravaged, the Realms shuddering, Unwinter full afire with blackboil, and now the Gates of Seelie will open wide as a lover's thighs."

Think, Robin. What does he want from you, to tell you so much? She wrapped the sheet more securely around her, took another step as he fell back. "*That* is why you were at Henzler's, and gave me the ampoules after. And why *you* returned and slew him, or led Unwinter to him. I was sent with a decoy, to lull *her* into false security."

"Oh, aye. Should you turn from Seelie's Queen, Ragged, your voice will always be welcome at my side. I am disposed to be generous; I have not had this much sport for many a long year. When Unwinter and Summer are gone, there will be no bar to us riding the night, and teaching mortals to fear again."

Her jaw threatened to drop. "You…" There were no words. There was not even breath to utter them, or to fuel the song. *But you're fullborn, too, Puck Goodfellow. Why do you not take ill? Or are you willing to risk it?*

"Summer did not wake first, my primrose. I was old before the Sundering, and I weary of their games." His hands dropped, fractionally, and she hoped her face betrayed nothing but shock. "After both Courts fall, no more petty little dances. You and I, Robin Ragged, shall lead the way."

God. Holy… Even the obscenities of her childhood were too pale. *Think quickly, Robin. If you do not, he may change his mind.*

Her chin lifted. The sheet loosened, and Puck's eyelids lowered a fraction.

That was all.

"You are a changeful sprite," she pointed out. "What assurance do I have of your fidelity, Puck?"

"Oh, Robin Ragged, Ragged Robin. Who do you have left? All those dear to your heart have been dispatched, all in a row." So smug, so self-satisfied, and a horrible suspicion bloomed in Robin's chest. "Mother a-wasted, sister a-broken, little mortal boy Summer's plaything, and your faithless knight left you sleeping. Who else should you turn to, if not the only kin remaining?"

It can't be. The suspicion sharpened. *He can't… he can't…*

He must have seen it on her traitorous face. His hands dropped fully, and the boy-sidhe's head made a slight, fluid movement to the side, his leaf-shaped tongue flickering out to wet his lips.

"Dearest daughter," Robin Goodfellow, the Puck himself, said, "my primrose love, who *did* you think you were named for?"

NO LIAR IN THIS CASE
43
⊃╫⊂

Well, that was one way to leave the party. Jeremiah pulled himself upright, blinking, his fingers slipping in weeds, long grass, and sludge. It hadn't thrown him very far, just across the street and into the ditch. Summer would no doubt be piqued at his exit, but at least Robin was safe from the Seelie now. A gift given at the revel before spring's unloosing, witnessed by the multitude, was good insurance. Gallow himself was the only danger to Robin now—and Unwinter. Who would cease to be a danger soon enough, if Jeremiah could just keep his luck and work things right.

Just across the road, Amberline Park dripped with rain, and the east was graying rapidly. If they weren't already riding out to the Gates, they would be in a matter of moments.

His left-hand coat pocket was warm, and the golden chain wrapped against his thumb. He closed his eyes for a moment, crouching in ditchwater, the weeds around him already beginning to take notice of the change in the air, rustling softly. Peeking over the park's low, gray north wall was a ghilliedhu's birch tree, slender and moss-cloaked, quivering expectantly. Its wandering spirit was at Summer's revel, so no worries there.

His thumb drifted over an oval of metal. Daisy's locket had been gold-coated, but this one was true metal through and through, and he thought perhaps Robin's Realmaking was the cause. When she found he'd taken it, she might be angry, or think it a price extracted for her sleeping safely.

It was something different, though. He concentrated, breathing as softly as he could. Here at the edge of Amberline, the interference was enough to cloak him, the Veil rippling and thickening, thinning and snapping.

All he had to do was watch dawn come up. When it did, he could follow the tugging against Robin's necklace, and it would lead him straight to her, wherever she had wandered. Hopefully she was still in his trailer, but if she woke she might well consider it not the safest place in the world.

She might even let him explain before she unloosed that song of hers. He'd earned a little gratitude, but even if she wasn't happy with him, well, once night fell and Unwinter was free to roam, she'd be glad enough of Gallow's protection.

What, you think she'll fall right into your arms?

Well, no. But he could . . . what? Show her he wasn't so bad? Apologize?

I am not my sister.

No, she wasn't. Daisy was mortal, and dead these long years.

Five years. Be precise, Gallow.

Something nagged at him. A thin thread of sound.

He stiffened, rose slowly, slowly, to peer over the edge of the ditch. His feet were cold, but his boots had seen worse on mortal jobsites.

Dammit.

Hoofbeats. Soft, slithering rustles. Snicking of claws on pavement.

The necklace tugged against his fingers.

No.

It tugged again, more insistently. The hoofbeats were a measured jog, not the pell-mell of chase. Jingling of tack, a soft, queerly flat neigh.

They melded out of the Veil, fog rising in thick white ropes from the ground to shield them from the murderous light rising in the east. At their head rode Unwinter, and Jeremiah's knees threatened to go soft for a moment. He realized he was holding his breath, staring at the crowned helm and the hands on the war-horse's silver-dripping reins.

It makes them strong, before it kills them, Robin whispered in his head.

Unwinter himself was afoot. And Robin Ragged was near.

Was she thinking to escape into Summer as well? If she was awake and moving, she knew her precious cargo was missing. How could he explain? Would she give him time to?

Or did Unwinter have her, bringing her body—or what was soon to become a corpse—to Amberline, to toss over the wall and into Summer? A declaration of war, or merely a slap at the Queen he had been a Consort to so many years ago?

The company of Unseelie halted. Mist thickened, swirling, ice crackling under Unwinter's horse. A mocking laugh cut through the vapor, familiar and chilling.

"Hail to thee, lord of Unseelie." Glove-shod feet brushed, and Puck sounded well pleased with himself.

Jeremiah peered over the edge of the ditch. This was a horrible hiding place, and the mist wove around him, its fat flabby corpse-fingers a living blanket along the ground. It was filling the ditch, and his feet would freeze in the water before long. He'd be trapped like the swan in Ell Mercy's lay, and wouldn't that be an awful way to die?

"*Goodfellow.*" Colder than the mist, that voice, and rumbling, too. "*I have kept my end of the pact.*"

"And so have I. Hark, Unwinter, the Gates of Seelie open."

It was true. The dawn chorus of birdsong was rising around this mist-walled spot, liquid streams of gold that were the Gatehinges singing as well. The entire Court would be at the south end of the park, flickering through the Veil as Summer's white hands brushed the metal lovingly.

"*Little good that does me without...*" Unwinter halted. "*Ah. Her.*"

"Give up your chase of my kin, Unwinter, and she shall do what no other has done since the days of your own Harrowing."

Unwinter's silent sneer was nevertheless palpable. "*And you are so certain of this?*"

Birdsong crested. The fog, shot through with rosy tendrils, cringed.

The Gates were open. Spring was loosed on the mortal realm.

The next voice took him by surprise. Clear and very low. "Unwinter, from this dawn to this dusk, I invite you into Summer."

Robin. And... Puck? Wait, what?

"See, see what a good daughter she is?" Puck laughed, and Jeremiah could almost *see* him capering with delight.

I was twelve when I was taken... And Puck, the one to bring her to the Seelie Court. Had she known? Had it all been a game?

Yes. Of course it was a game. He would be willing to wager, though, it was not of Robin's making. She was caught, well and truly. No doubt Puck's offer to free her of Unwinter's Hunt seemed her best option right now, since she would think Jeremiah had thoroughly betrayed her.

How am I going to—

"*I did not know you had kin.*" A slight creaking sound—had

Unwinter gestured? A slipping, a slithering, and a cry of unholy joy. *"Yet it appears you are no liar in this case."*

"Not in this one. Speak, mighty one. You shall hunt my child no more."

"I swear I shall not harm the Ragged, and all mine shall abide by that vow." Unwinter's laughter killed the rising rose-glow in the mist. *"My Unseelie, my nightmare children, let us ride."*

The silver huntwhistles blew, more of them than Gallow had ever heard. He risked standing a little straighter, and saw Unwinter facing two slight, slim figures. Robin, her arms folded about her midriff, transparent-pale and sweating.

She was of the Seelie, and had just invited Unwinter and his host across the threshold.

His plagued, murderous host.

Before her, Puck went up on his toes, then swept the Unseelie King a courteous bow. "Vengeance is yours, lion of the house of Danu."

Unwinter's horse turned; he did not grace Goodfellow with a reply. The assembled Court would be weary from their night of entertainment, and no guards were set.

Summer would be *ravaged.*

"Ride forth!" Unwinter cried, and the rushing, stamping mass of them cleared the low wall in a steady stream, their lord at their head. Robin actually fell, her knees barking pavement with a painful jolt Jeremiah felt in his own legs. He stamped, shattering the ice in the ditch, and Puck Goodfellow halted.

The free sidhe looked about him, suspiciously. His gaze fastened on Robin. "Do you come with me, little elfling?"

She shook her head, bending over, still clutching her stomach as if ill. Of course, she had just committed an unspeakable act. What price would Goodfellow extract for this protection—and for his silence on the matter if Summer began to wonder who had invited Unwinter in?

My kin, Puck had said. Was he really... Did it matter? The Goodfellow was most likely lying for his own gain. How long had Puck planned this moment?

Puck smiled, his face lit with sheer ravenous goodwill, and blew her a kiss. "Then I shall attend to other matters. Come along at your own pace, Ragged."

With that he went over the wall in a single bound, like a springheeled jack, and in the depths of the park a screaming began.

The mist flushed again, burning away as Unseelie leached from the air. Robin, still on her knees in the middle of the road, shook. Was she weeping? In shock? Nauseated by what she had done?

Oh, God. He meant to say her name, but the word froze in his throat just as the ditchwater had crystallized around his ankles. He rocked from side to side, ice groaning and snapping afresh. The long, blasted grass and thistles along the slope, coated with spikes of solidified malice, denied his hands. He scrabbled at his shirt, freeing the Horn's chain; it thickened as he drew it forth, perhaps scenting his desperation.

"Sean..." Robin made a low, keening sound, and it grew in volume. He scrabbled at the slope, but the ditch had turned out to be a false friend after all.

Ice creaked and snapped as the sun rose, and it would be a bloody dawning in Seelie lands. The noise sharpened even through the Veil's thickening, and Robin's agonized cry ended on a single throat-cut whisper.

"Jeremiah!"

The word tingled all along his skin, reached down, and yanked on something blind and old within him. Half were not burdened with truenames that could banish, but still something in him recognized the sound.

She thought him still within Summer's borders. Maybe she wished vengeance, or felt a debt—and the boy trapped in amber, the one she had raised...

He found himself on hands and knees, tearing ice-sharp plants from the side of the ditch in great ragged furrows as he scrambled, finally spilling up over the top. The lance burned, springing free without his volition, but hers was not the life it sought.

Jeremiah Gallow gained his feet, clutching his dwarven-inked weapon, a cold, heavy weight on his chest and ice falling from his hair, eyelashes, hands, pants, every part of him. Each piece shattered and steamed on the crack-scorched pavement.

He had just enough wit to notice a blue and ruddy flicker in the bushes as Robin Ragged vaulted the low wall, following the Unseelie host. Thinking to perhaps save him, even though she had to know he had stolen the ampoules and could only think he'd betrayed her. Thinking perhaps to save the boy, even though Summer would never relinquish a mortal toy to a Half.

And yet, still she ran.

Cursing inwardly, he could only follow.

BETWEEN IMPOSSIBLES
44

Summer cringed under the lash. They were everywhere—trow and drow tearing down the apple trees, biting into the bark and drinking the sapblood as the trees fought back with lashing, ineffectual branches. Ghilliedhu girls fled screaming from satyrs and dark hobs. There were even black dwarves there, though none of MacDonnell's clan she could see.

The Seelie knights held the doors of Summerhome. Some few of them were armored, and brughnies shrieked in the battlements among the dryads and wood nymphs, whose bows hummed. Stink and wrack flooded the white roads, and the sun, which would have been a bar to their passing, was a low white disk in the fog-choked sky.

Robin plunged to the side, her heels clattering, dodging a knot of kelpies with their great gnarled clubs and dreadlocked manes. Puck had been busy indeed—the frost-giants, their tall blue-peaked caps dripping crystal icicles, were generally held to be free sidhe, but they wrestled with the trolls who had rallied to Summer's banner.

The Queen of Seelie was in the midst of the throng, her handmaidens either cowering or lifting their daggers, but

Robin had no interest in them. Still, they made for the safety of the door, and she had to follow, because Gallow would be here somewhere. He *had* to be, and she could see him defending Summer with her own eyes, and hope the sight would tear the traitorous softness out of her silly half-mortal heart.

Besides, she had a task to accomplish. Not the one Puck had given her, oh no. A personal matter. Once she settled this one account, she could run, and hope none of the Seelie would guess who had offered invitation to Unwinter.

They might even think her dead in the chaos, if she was lucky, and that assumption would grant her a measure of safety.

The Unseelie took no notice of her even in the fray, and those few Seelie who put up resistance had far more to worry about than her sudden reappearance. Robin scrambled for a south passageway, pelted up its length, and found herself before the servant's door to the Great Hall. Summerhome, the great Keep of Seelie, the home of the Jewel, throbbed like an infected tooth, and quick as Robin was, she was not quick enough.

The great doors were flung open and Summer stalked through. The throne-couch, on its dais, blazed with gold, and a shadow to the side was a slim amber sculpture. Robin skidded to a stop, long black bubbling marks blooming on the floor. It wasn't her heels doing the damage, but the scars of Unseelie's attack biting into the heart of Summer's power.

Summer gained her throne and dropped down, spreading her arms slightly. The Jewel, above and between her eyes, filled with poisonous emerald light. Robin gasped for breath, four in, four out, and she could—

"Hold!"

He stalked into the hall. The doors, smoking, were shivered and cast aside, splinters hanging from their shrieking hinges. A pall of sick smoke rose from Unwinter's helm and shoulders, and his step cracked the flooring still further, spiderwebs of dark decay multiplying from each footfall. *"There she is,"* he continued, as Unseelie knights, spattered with blood and other fluids, poured in past him. *"The lady herself."*

At the back of the band, Puck slid along, a shadow with greenyellow eyes. He capered, unable to contain himself.

Summer's gaze flickered over the room, snagged on Robin. She looked surprised for a brief moment, before her dark eyes narrowed and she returned her gaze to Unwinter.

"You have broken the Pact, Unseelie." Her tone sliced the hubbub, and the knights of Unwinter's guard stilled. "And attacked my holdings without provocation."

"I cannot break a bottle you have broken first, Eakanthhe." He spat her name, and Robin's knees almost turned to jelly. *"You did this."*

"I? *I?* Mark my words, you foulness—"

"Give us the cure, and we shall withdraw."

Summer drew herself up. Her handmaidens had no doubt scattered, fleeing or slaughtered. Robin could name every one of them. Some of them had been kind to her, once or twice.

Look how you've repaid them, Robin. And Parsifleur, and others too numerous to count.

Puck melded into the shadows. Did no one else see him there?

"I shall give you naught, oathbreaker." The Jewel flashed. "I shall pronounce doom upon thee, Haahrhne of Unwinter, and soon there will be only Summer."

The words curdled in Robin's throat. She could stop this now, if she—

"Robin Ragged." Summer darted another glance at her. "Sing this oathbreaker into his grave, and I shall restore thy Sean to thee."

The trembling was all through Robin now. Puck, across the room, peering out from behind a pillar, smirked. He watched her as he flitted between the carven trees, and she wondered if it was true, if the one who had sired her was not Seelie at all, but a free sidhe old and cruel and merry, with pipes and a sharp white smile.

Yet she had invited Unwinter in, and now Puck would think to hold her silenced through fear of Summer's reprisal. Games within games, the Fatherless perhaps expecting her to perform as a spy within Seelie halls—or forcing her to other acts.

"If the bird opens her beak, silence her." Unwinter took a single step forward, and his knights moved as one, in Robin's direction.

Then, from behind her, yet another voice, as a silvery shape lengthened beside her. "Cause harm to my lady Ragged, Unwinter, and the Sluagh shall have a new master."

It was Gallow. Rolled in mud and melted ice, his green eyes blazing, he looked every inch the sidhe. Especially since, hanging at his chest from a thick chain of dwarf-forged links, Unwinter's Horn glimmered at her, its true shape trembling underneath its seeming of a simple medallion.

She lost all her breath, staring at him. *How in the name of Stone or Throne... He took Unwinter's Horn? That's not possible!*

It didn't matter. Gallow gazed at the Unseelie King, his mouth a straight line, and suddenly she was not so sure of anything to do with him.

"Robin." Jeremiah didn't look at her, halting just before and to her right. The lance's blade hooked, turning sawtooth-deadly, and flushed with cold iron. "I think we should leave. This does not concern us at all."

Summer spoke over him. "Sing for me, Ragged." She had not moved, but still sat, taut and straight-backed, on her couch.

Next to her, the amber statue glowed with its own inner life. "I shall return him to thee whole and undamaged, I vow it by my Name."

Pulling at her, tugging her in different directions. Caught between impossibles. Sweat stood out on her skin, her mended skirt fluttering on a breeze from nowhere, and Robin Ragged found herself inhaling smoothly as Summer's smile widened, relieved.

A creaking flicker of motion. A shape of yellow-golden, solidified honey, toppling. The statue waltzed on its bare feet, tipping back and forth, and the shadow behind it had yellowgreen eyes and a wide white smile, soft supple leather moving as Puck stepped backward into shadows.

The amber boy... fell.

The sound of his shattering was lost in a sudden cacophony. Seelie knights poured through the door, their gold-chased armor flowing with them, swords flickering and chantments humming as blackwing curses spattered into life. Unwinter turned, and Jeremiah moved forward, the lance flickering. The song swelled inside her throat, tearing chunks of the glossy stone flooring free, grinding them to powder, and she whipped her head aside to keep it from swallowing Gallow whole.

The arrow of destruction boiled over twitching, jagged slivers of amber, each particle exploding under the force of Robin's song. It curved, but Summer was no longer on her throne. Puck danced aside, columns older than mortal history crumbling as the massive noise blasted them.

Clashing, screaming, battle cries, a sudden noisome stench. Unwinter blurred forward, the greatsword that had not been unsheathed in centuries humming as it clove resisting air. Jeremiah leaned back, the same eerie floating speed shaking ice and water droplets free of him. A tearing sound, the lance doubling back, impossible, but Unwinter was past him, and the sword hummed as it descended toward Robin.

She fell, her heels scrabbling, the song dying because she had no more breath to fuel it. Time to think *it's all right, at least it will only hurt for a moment* before Jeremiah crashed into the Unseelie lord from the side, the lanceblade whistling too far away.

Unwinter, light on his mailed feet, whirled with deceptively ponderous grace. His sword was flung wide, clasped in one hand, but the other hand, full of a black-chased hilt, flicked.

Gallow screamed as the short wicked-curved blade pierced his side. Robin had her breath now, and the song rose again, a dreadful wall of force tearing free from the very bottom of her chest. It was tar-black, no sunshine to be found in its glossy thrumming depths, and it threw Unwinter into the knot of fighting knights, Seelie and Unseelie jumbled together like tin soldiers swept from a gameboard.

She gained her feet in a graceless lunge and grabbed Gallow's arm. He almost toppled, but she dragged him, and the chaos behind them as more Seelie came to the aid of their Queen clamored long and loud.

POISON, BREAD, SALT

45

⌖

Stupid, careless, idiotic—he hadn't been thinking, but really, hadn't he? The lance had shown him, clearly enough, what would happen—Unwinter's blade descending, Robin's eyes dimming, the bubbling as her cloven ribs and violated lungs struggled to function.

Everything in him had simply said *no*. Quiet, but final. The Horn had twitched against his chest, and everything had halted for the barest of moments.

A hot nail in his side. It tore with every jolting step, and he had no breath to curse as Robin pulled him along a dusty corridor. He was filthy, and fouling her as he leaned on her slenderness. He helped as much as he could, but the nail twisted, and he fell against the wall.

Robin swore, vile terms he heard through a screen of red agony. It was enough to make his lips try to smile, or was it just a rictus? "Leave...me," he croaked. "Poison...blade..."

"I know, you bastard!" She hauled on his arm. "Unwinter's dagger is always poison, and we have little time. *Move*, Gallow!"

"Jer...emiah. My name. Use...it."

"Shut up and...here. Oh, thank Stone and Throne and

Christ himself." A rattling—there was a door here, perhaps locked, but chantment sparked against Robin's slim fingers as Jeremiah bent into a fish-curve, his body racking against itself. Fire in his veins, he longed for water, for blood, for any liquid to cool it.

The door creaked, and Robin kicked it, then drove her shoulder against it. Battering like a moth against a flame, she grabbed him, yanking even as he screamed at the jolt...

...and they tumbled sideways into a spring morning, thin sunshine scorching faded white paint marching in a thin line.

Parking lot. The Horn hit pavement as he did, but it was still slaved to its chain. It made a low, nasty chiming that sounded like a laugh, and rolled back against his chest. When he died, what would it—

The sun drove the poison back. It could not cure it, but it eased the worst of the cramping, and he simply lay for a few moments, retching. When he could lift his head, he heard light tiptapping, and Robin Ragged was pelting across the acres of parking lot, her skirt flaring and her hair a tangled glory of redcopper.

Had she left him to shift for himself? More charitable than he deserved. His breath was ice; he lay against a streetlight's pylon.

He squinted. It was a supermarket, the door whooshed aside. This early there were few cars in the lot; maybe he could manage to get himself upright and limp for the back. Dumpsters were cold iron, maybe that would...

A sudden blackness, night falling. Or no, his eyelids had slammed shut. When he opened them again he was no doubt hallucinating. The sunshine had strengthened, the parking lines corkscrewing crazily, and another cramping spasm was coming. Hot blood soaking into his side and coat, he wasn't gutsplit but not for lack of trying.

Tiptap tiptap tiptaptiptaptiptap. Running feet. Was she still fleeing him? Time skipped, skewed sideways.

"Hold on." A hoarse sob. "Oh please, Jeremiah, hold on."

Daisy?

No, it was Robin. A prosaic blue paper canister of Morton's salt; she set it down and ripped something—clear plastic, a loaf of fresh French bread from the supermarket's bakery.

I don't think I can eat, thank you.

She cracked the loaf open—it was still warm. Steam rose on the air, and chantment crackled. A swift, efficient yank, and his torn shirt ripped even further. She jammed the bread's torn flesh against the bleeding wound.

Cold relief, a gush of sweat all over him. Her eyes rolled back in her head as syllables dropped from her tongue, the most ancient of languages pouring into the wound. She tore the bread free and cast it aside as it smoked with drawn poison, clapped the other half over the gaping.

Pain retreated. Great panting heaves, the spasming sliding away. A swimming weakness all through him, as if he'd suffered a mortal sickness and heaved up his dinner, that sweat-rimmed moment after vomiting finished and the body knew it had a moment to rest.

She pulled the second half-loaf away from his skin, cast it aside with a muttered word of chantment. It steamed against concrete, sending up foul caustic smoke. Robin grabbed the container of Morton's and ripped it open, then paused, looking down at him.

He lost his breath, again. Sunshine in her hair, her eyes aglow, mud smeared on her cheeks, her nose and eyes red-rimmed from smoke or weeping.

She was glorious.

"This will hurt," she said hoarsely, pouring the salt into her

291

palm. A generous measure indeed, white crystals pattering against the concrete.

"Do it," he husked, and would have told her how beautiful she was. But she slapped her hand against the wound, and a jolt of incredible black agony rolled through him like a thunderbolt, the lightning a cold white star at his chest.

He regained consciousness slowly, aware he was moving. Leaning on her, the two of them weaving like drunks, and her voice soft and low as she spoke to a mortal. Cajoling, a chantment under the words, a door slammed and they were moving without walking.

It was a cab. He wanted to ask where they were going, but she clapped another handful of salt to the wound and he died again, still trying to shape her name with his sick-sour, dry-cracked, stinging mouth.

WHO COULD FORGET
46

>₩₭⊰

A green glimmer, gathering strength as night fell. Black brackish fluid swilled on the marble floor, great scars and gouges torn in the face of Seelie. Pale and perfect, though, the Queen was iron-straight, her snow-white hands clenched-bone fists.

She stood in the shattered hall, before her cushioned bench. The Jewel flamed on her brow, and she closed her black, black eyes. Her green finery hung ragged and soiled, her handmaidens cowering in bowers and her knights occupied in chasing the last stragglers of Unseelie from the borders. Summer was... alone.

Or not quite. A susurration, a whisper, and a flash of white teeth.

Summer's eyes opened halfway. The Jewel gathered strength, glittering dangerously.

"Mischievous one," she murmured. "Have you come to do me an injustice as well?"

"Unwinter has grown brave, and foul." The boyshape sidhe melded from between two shattered columns. "I offer my services, Summer. He has ravaged my holdings as well."

"The mortal?" She considered a moment. "Of science, the one we…"

"We?" Puck Goodfellow laughed, a low musical sound. He did not caper. Instead, he leaned against the ruins of a stone column far older than Rome, or even Babylon. "Unwinter found him."

"Did he?" Summer swayed slightly, a snake's supple movement. "Oh, Goodfellow. How clever you are."

"Not clever enough, it seems." His thumbs in his broad belt, he tilted his sleek head. His ear-tips twitched once. That was all.

"The Gates are open. Summer shall be renewed." The Queen swayed again. "Leave me, Fatherless. I have much to attend to."

"As my lady wishes." He swept a bow, but it was not nearly low enough to be mannerly. His mockery perhaps went unnoticed.

Or perhaps not, for Summer's eyelids lowered a fraction. "After all this time." Her tone was dulcet honey. "He still remembers me."

"Who could forget you, Jewel of the House of Danu?" Puck spun, snapped his long brown fingers, spun again.

"And yet." Her eyes opened fully, and within the tar-black depths every star had winked out. "Where is the Ragged? I wish to see her face."

Did the Goodfellow hesitate? Perhaps he did. In any case, he merely danced another brace of steps, a waltz old when mere huts graced the shore of a muddy river named for a fleetfoot goddess, later to become the crown of an empire the mortal sun never set upon.

Except every empire fell, and every Court as well. Eventually.

Goodfellow finally spoke. "I do not know, my lady. Shall I find her for thee?"

"Do." The Jewel vibrated, a high, sweet ringing beginning to tremble at the edge of even a sidhe's acute hearing. The Queen swayed once more, then stilled, her paleness glowing as the moon might behind thin clouds. "Now get thee hence, *Robin Goodfellow.* I shall brook none within my borders who are not Seelie for some while yet."

Another mocking half-bow, a laugh, and Puck vanished, stepping sideways again.

The Jewel on her forehead filled with radiance. Her head tipped back, her fists turned to bone spurs, and for a single breathless moment the Queen of Seelie's true form shone in the wrack and ruin of her Great Hall. All through Summer's violated dells and fouled rivers, in her ruined orchard and along the flour-white paths, a steady, low hissing gathered strength. The ladies of the Court, handmaidens and fullblood-in-waiting, cowered as they realized what the noise meant. In the forests and fields, each Seelie knight raised his head, a cruel smile playing on thin lips, his armor firing with new gold.

Summer would be renewed, yes.

Come the dawn, she would be hungry. The changelings would be recalled, and the flint knife would loose torrents of nameless blood.

A white-hot flash filled the Jewel. The silent thunderclap rolled through Veil and Seelie alike, the mortal world momentarily full of a hot, uneasy flushing wind, there and gone as soon as tired cops and waitresses working the night shift could think *that's strange, it's still winter.*

When it faded, Summer lay whole and lovely, but pale, so pale, under an indigo night. The stars above field, forest, and dell glittered sharp-dangerous, and in a tall-pillared room in the heart of a white Keep with greenstone towers, a slim sidhe woman was driven to her knees, a green flicker on her forehead fading to dull gray.

The Queen of Seelie looked at her soft, beautiful hands. On her left wrist, a pinprick of black bloomed into a small, hard, calcifying boil.

Her teeth showed in a silent snarl, and Summer sought to gain her feet. It took her two tries. She did not call for her handmaidens yet. When they entered the hall, they would see her gracious and composed, with a rag of her spring-revel finery knotted about her left wrist and the rest of her as naked and innocent as any nymph.

But for now, Summer rocked back and forth on her knees, and hissed a slow, furious song of quiet vengeance that filled the pillared room with the dry, cloying scent of baking apple pie.

FULL NIGHT
47

⟛⊹⟚

He tossed fitfully through most of the afternoon, but the wound had sealed itself. Perhaps she'd drained all the poison. Maybe she should have used more bread?

Too late, now. The wound had closed. If any foulness lingered, she didn't have the skill to draw it.

She roamed the small trailer, her hands finding things and setting them to rights. Laundry, chugging in the washer—she found an ancient box of dryer sheets, and wondered if her sister had sniffed them in the aisle, deciding on this particular scent. *Meadow Fresh!* the label declared, but it smelled like no meadow, mortal or otherwise.

Robin folded the clothes when they were dry, gathered refuse into black trash bags she found under the sink—everything was still arranged in the proper fashion, just where her sister would have put it.

Glancing in on Gallow every quarter-hour. Washing the dishes Puck had not broken—he had crashed around in the kitchen, perhaps offended by its size or the dirty dishes. Chantment eased some of the chores, but she did most of the cleaning by hand, his bathroom sparkling and mildew-free before she stepped into the shower's embrace and stood for a long while in her dress and heels, letting warm mortal water flood her with soothing. When she stepped out, shaking water away with a single crackling word, drying her hair with finger flicks, she stood for a long few moments in front of the mirror. Even a sidhe chantment couldn't get the flyspotting off, but at least there were no toothpaste flecks or smudged fingerprints.

There were bottles in the medicine cabinet. Two prescriptions with Daisy's name on them; her allergies and probably for her back pain. Mama had a bad back, too, a mortal ailment. *Daisy Gallow*, the bottles said. But Jeremiah had put her mortal name on her tombstone, perhaps to keep her even more secret.

Even safer.

The cleaning soothed her. Would he be grateful?

My lady Ragged.

Oh, she could try, she supposed. She could do a Daisy impression, blithe and laughing. The glamour might even become the reality, and Gallow perhaps even grow fond of her.

It was possible. So many things were possible.

The couch was finally cleared off, and she brought his coat there to mend it, needle-chantment pricking her fingers when her attention slipped—when he coughed, or moved in the darkened bedroom. It was like working while Daddy Snowe was sleeping, except without the guilty start every time a car door slammed or a mortal voice called.

Cold iron in his jacket pocket interfered with the mending, so she drew it out. And there was something else.

The Polaroid was ancient, and there on the third step of Mama's trailer were Daisy and Robin. That day had been hot and dusty, she remembered, and the rent was late. But Mama said smile, so they did, Robin's arm around Daisy, who had

298

been promised an ice cream stolen from the corner store if she was good and didn't cry because there was no dinner. The trailer was dark, too, because the power company didn't like it when you didn't pay.

They both knew Mama would let Daddy Snowe come back in when he showed up. Because at least he'd pay the bills, even if his fists flew and Mama could only do things right some of the time. That day, though, it had been just them, and Daisy's sweet warmth nestling beside her.

She heard him moving. The needle-chantment was finished, so she laid the coat gently on the back of the couch and was settled with the Polaroid clasped in her hand when Gallow appeared, moving stiffly as an old man.

His jeans were unbuttoned, dark hair reaching up his chest. A silver medallion winked among the forest, the Horn's camouflage. Muscle moved under his skin, and along his side the angry red scar of Unwinter's poisoned blade. She had done all she could.

It didn't feel like enough. Nothing, in fact, ever did.

He blinked, rubbing at his green eyes. Robin's chest ached, and her throat was full.

When he braced himself against the wall and regarded her again, she was ready. She laid the photograph aside, with one last long, lingering look.

Robin-mama. And all the stars of Summer's dusk. Now dead, dry fires. *You're so warm, Rob.*

Not warm enough to keep mortal death at bay.

"I saw her that day," Robin heard herself say dully. "She... she had come to me. She wanted... to conceive." *Trouble with her lady parts. Who should we blame for that, I wonder? Curse or just bad luck?* "We argued a little, she called it root magic but she wanted it anyhow. I went and bargained for a chantment.

That nonsense, just like Mama called it. She thought I was maybe deluded, but it was worth a try." Was her mouth twisting down bitterly? Maybe. "That night...She...she asked me if I'd stand godmother, if she...I said I would, and I left her. I wish I hadn't. I wish..." She licked her dry lips. "Once I had it, I waited where we usually met, but she didn't come."

He said nothing. So Robin continued. "She said she had a man, and a fine one, and she wanted the rest of it, too. She was...happy. I know she was. You made her happy."

"Robin..." As if he'd been punched.

"When I could leave Summer again I found her buried, and I...I am sorry, Gallow. The chantment...maybe someone saw me speak to her. Maybe..."

"Car accident." He swallowed audibly. He was pale. "A ditch, a tree...It wasn't your fault."

She closed her eyes briefly, sagging. The relief threatened to break a fragile wall between her and more useless weeping.

I will never weep again. When she could, she stood, slowly. Stood in the middle of his mortal trailer, his mortal *life.*

Sister a-broken, Puck sneered inside her head. Yet another account to balance. She braced herself. "You went into Summer. You took her the cure."

"I had to. She would have killed you when you returned, one way or another—"

"Why do you care? Because I look like *her?*"

"She looked like *you.*" Fiercely now. He pushed himself away from the wall and tacked out across the living room. The floor creaked a little. "Robin, I'm not kind, and I'm not asking for—"

"I am not Daisy." Each word a knife. "I will never be your mortal love, Gallow. We are at quits, and I'll not darken your door again."

"Robin." He dug in his jeans pocket, and when he drew the locket out it was barely a surprise. It swung from his fingers, a traitor because it yearned toward him. "I would go with you. I would ask you to stay. I would also give this back to you."

She was a traitor, too, if only with craving. If she stepped across the room, if she let him touch her, she would crumble. Robin's chin came up. "Keep it as weregilt, Armormaster. I am a faithless sidhe bitch, and likely to remain so."

She turned on her heel and stalked for the door. He moved, perhaps to catch her, but Robin was quick, and she had her shoes on. She stepped out into the flow of a warming spring evening, pollen already beginning to float golden on the breeze, and stepped sideways.

And was gone.

>⊩<

Nightfall found her downtown, on the roof of the Savoigh Limited. Tucked between skyscrapers, it was a relic, and had much iron in its construction. The breeze was soft, winter's chill finally fled at last.

The city seethed under its mortal lights. Those who could, sensing the gathering tension, sought any hole to hide in. At dusk Unwinter would have been banished from Summer, if not before, for Summer had the Jewel and no invitation into her lands would stand if she chose to revoke it. It would now be open war between Seelie and Unseelie, and the free sidhe would no doubt make merry hob of it, with Puck Goodfellow's guidance.

If he chose to guide them, that is. Robin thought it very possible indeed.

She waited, perched next to a stone gargoyle's leering, looking at the rubies of brake lights, the diamonds of headlights. Exhaust, and cold iron, a breath of damp from the river. A hint of crackling ozone—lightning about to strike. The faint good smell of a soft spring rain approaching.

He did not keep her waiting long.

"Oh, my darling. What fine merriment we have had." He melded out of the darkness, his boyface alight with glee. "You are the best of children, delighting your sire's heart so ful—"

The golden flood of song hit him squarely, Robin's breathing calm and controlled, and knocked the Fatherless to the ground. She was on her feet in an instant, the stolen crowbar burning in her palms as she lifted it, brought it down with a convulsive crunch. Iron smoked on sidhe flesh, and by the time she ran out of breath and the song died, thick blue ichor spattered the rooftop, steaming and sizzling.

"*You,*" she hissed, between her teeth. "*You* killed her. You pixie-led her car. You killed Sean. *You* did it."

Amazingly, Puck began to laugh. "*Aye!*" he shouted, spitting broken teeth. They gleamed, sharp ivory, ringing against the roof. "Robin, Robin Ragged, I will kill all those close to thy heart. *I will have thy voice!*" He slashed upward with his dagger, a spot of wet green beaded at its tip, but Robin was ready and skipped aside.

Not today. She didn't say it. She'd finished her inhale, and the song burst out again, given free rein.

Smoke, blood, iron, the crowbar stamping time as razor-edged music descended on the Fatherless. Some whispered that he was the oldest of the sidhe; some said he remembered what had caused the Sundering. Others sometimes hinted he was the cause of the division in the children of Danu, the Little Folk, the Blessed.

When the song faded, Robin dropped the crowbar. It clattered on the roof.

The thing lying before her was no longer sidhe. Full-Twisted, it writhed, and its piping little cries struck the ear foully.

She bent, swiftly, and her quick fingers had the pipes and the dagger, Puck Goodfellow's treasures. The Twisted thing swiped at her with a clawed, malformed hand, and its voice was now a growl, warning.

Her breath came high and hard, her ribs flickering. The dagger went into her pocket, its sheath of supple leaf-stamped leather blackened and too finely grained to be animal hide. The pipes—she almost shuddered with revulsion as she poked a finger in each one, and near the bottom, where they were thicker, she touched glass.

Three glass ampoules, like the ones she had bargained Mac-Donnell's kin into making. Decoys within decoys, but this held a sludge that moved grudgingly against its chantment-sealed container. A true cure. Like her, he had decided the only safe place to hide such a thing was in his own pocket.

Like sire, like child, perhaps? Hot, bilious loathing filled her.

The Twisted thing that had been Puck Goodfellow struggled to rise. Morning would find it here, too malformed to speak or walk. It might starve to death; it might cripple out the rest of its existence like Parsifleur Pidge, though she had Twisted it far past that woodwight's ill-luck. Robin looked down at it, tucking the pipes in her other pocket.

They were powerful, and there was no better time to learn their use.

"For Daisy," she said quietly, "and for Sean."

The thing writhed again, trying to rise, the thick shell of bone on its corkscrewed back scraping the roof. Robin turned away. Full night was falling.

I must find a place to hide.

SOON ENOUGH
48

◈╫╬

He was weak from the poison, but he still dragged himself out behind the trailer, onto the trashwood slope. The lance filled his hands, and Jeremiah dropped his second-best backpack. He turned, and listened.

Dusk had folded her robe about her and left the sky, shutting the door of day. From the other side, full night rose in her own indigo splendor, the hard points of stars peeping through racing clouds. The wind was uncertain, flirting, promising rain, and thunder rumbled in the distance. What part of the sound was actual thunder, and what part the approaching battles, he couldn't say.

Nearer, there was a crackling and a rushing. A glitter through the windows, not noticeable from the front yet.

Down at the bottom of the hill there was a stand of young birches, and from there he'd strike out east. Two shackles circled his neck. The locket, its chain too short for his throat, twitched against the notch between his collarbones.

Keep it as weregilt.

Well, maybe he would. But he'd also find her. Sooner or later, she'd listen to him.

The other chain was Unwinter's Horn. He let out a long breath, examining the lance. Solid silver, its leaf-shaped tip, humming expectantly.

Gallow rested the lance-end on the ground, leaned against it. His legs were still a little shaky. Only time would tell if Robin had managed to draw all the poison out. If she hadn't, well.

He didn't have to wait long. Smoke began to billow, and the flames sucked greedily through the windows he'd thoughtfully left open on the back side of the house. Soon after that the entire structure was involved, and the carport buckled, melting. Shouts and running feet, sirens in the distance.

The mortal world already believed him dead. This was simply tidying up loose ends. Weregilt of another kind, perhaps.

Daisy's clothes would be burning already; he'd laid the fire chantment thickest in the bedroom. She was sleeping soundly; there was nothing more to be done.

When the trucks arrived and the mortals began spraying water on the sidhe-fed blaze, he picked up the backpack and shrugged into it. The lance quivered and itched, but it would drink blood soon enough. He might well lead Unwinter to Robin, if he was unlucky.

He didn't care. Selfish, just like a sidhe.

Jeremiah Gallow turned away from his mortal life, again, and vanished into the pale birch trees.

In the distance, the thin threads of silver huntwhistles rose.

>‖‹

All through that long day, the thing on the rooftop smoked and rocked back and forth on its bony shell. Its flaccid limbs flopped uselessly, and the cloudy spring sunshine striped it with steaming weals. It made tiny piping sounds, lost in the noise of traffic below. Horns blared, engines gunned, the murmur of crowds enfolded it.

The sun was cruel, for all it was weak, and the thing's eyes were runnels of black tar pouring down its wasted cheeks. Once proud and capering, it was now a Twisted wreck, its wounds still seeping. She had been thorough, the avenging attacker.

As thorough as he would be, soon. But first he had to survive the assault of the mortal sun. Twisted, iron-poisoned, and wounded as he was, it burned as if he was one of Unwinter's dark-creeping legions. The heavy-misting rain was no balm, full of poisonous exhaust and the stinking effluvia of the metal the foolish salt-sweet mortals used to scar every piece of free soil they found.

Had it been full summer, their sun might have finished the work the daughter had begun.

Below, the Savoigh Limited throbbed. Once its stone facade and plaster walls, ornate fixtures and heavy-framed mirrors had been new, then oudated, then seedy, and now refurbished. The winds of urban gentrification blew erratic but inexorable, and the Savoigh, with its uniformed doormen and its high-rent offices, its tiny cold-water studios for the bohemians and its ancient, growling boiler in the basement, had become that most terrible of things: a fashion-able heap.

Rocking steadily, the rhythm of the thing's shell grinding as it threatened to topple. Its piping sounds became more intense, tiny malformed cries of effort. They soaked through the rooftop's rough surface, burrowing down.

Afterward, if the residents of the Savoigh Limited remembered that chill spring day at all, they remembered an endless string of bad luck. Printers jamming, coffeemakers sputtering, milk and creamer clotted and sour even before its sell-by date. A scented candle shattered on the fifth floor, spilling hot wax across important paperwork and almost catching the drapes on fire, plaster sagged, stray cats wandered in, yowling, and didn't leave until the aroma of their urine soaked the entire building. The boiler sputtered and creaked, moaning, the sound of its displeasure felt through the wooden floors. Fingers jammed in doors, toasters overheating, electrical outlets sparking when the cords were jiggled, four fender-benders out front and the doormen decrying the paucity of tips. Toes catching on carpets, stairs missed and neck-breaking tumbles barely averted, papers scattered and microwaves either not heating anything or scorch-burning it to the container, two mini-fridges inexplicably ceasing to work . . .

All through this, the rocking continued, the creature gaining inches across the roof. Lunchtime came and went, and it became obvious what the thing was aiming for—a pool of shadow in the lee of an HVAC hood, lengthening as the sun tipped past its zenith.

The ill-luck below crested, and one or two of the artists in the studios—their windows facing blank brick walls, their floors humped and buckled as the building settled into gracious decay— saw tiny darts of light in their peripheral vision, gone as soon as they turned their heads. One thought he was having hallucinations, and began to furiously paint the two canvases that would make him world-famous before he slid into a hole of madness and alcohol. The other, her recording equipment suddenly functioning again, began to play cascades of melody on her electric piano, and for the rest of her life never played from sheet music again. Her compositions were said to cause visions, and she retreated from the world years later to a drafty farmhouse in Maine.

Rocking, still. Tipping on the horn-thick edge of the bony shell on its back, sliding into blessed coolness for a moment as the shadow swallowed it, back the other way, teetering on the opposite edge, a sharp whistling cry as it rocked back into the shadow, hesitated on the brink . . .

. . . and toppled over, landing with a flat chiming sound in the shade.

Stillness. Below, paint splashed, music floated down an empty hall, printers suddenly rebooted, the two mini-fridges just as inexplicably started working again. A hush descended on the Savoigh Limited, and as the sun-scarred creature huddled under its shell in its dark almost-hole, a rumble of thunder sounded in the distance.

The spring storms were on their way.

GLOSSARY

Barrow-wight: Fullblood Unseelie wights whose homes are long "barrows." Gold loses its luster in their presence.

Brughnies: House-sidhe; they delight in cooking and cleaning. A well-ordered kitchen is their joy.

The Fatherless: Robin Goodfellow, also called Puck, the nominal leader of the free sidhe.

Folk: Sidhe, or clan within the sidhe, or generally a group, race, or species.

Ghilliedhu: "Birch-girl"; dryads of the birch clan, held to be great beauties.

Grentooth: A jack-wight, often amphibious, with mossy teeth and a septic bite.

Kelpie: A river sidhe, capable of appearing as a black horse and luring its victims to drowning.

Kobolding: A crafty race of sidhe, often amassing great wealth, living underground. Related to goblins, distantly related to the dwarven clans.

Quirpiece: A silver coin, used to hold a particular chantment.

Realmaker: A sidhe whose chantments do not fade at dawn. Very rare.

Seelie: Sidhe of Summer's Court, or holding fealty to Summer.

Selkie: A sealskin sidhe.

Sidhe: The Fair Folk, the Little People, the Children of Danu.

Sluagh: The ravening horde of the unforgiven dead.

Tainted: Possessing mortal blood.

Twisted: A sidhe altered and mutated, often by proximity to cold iron, unable to use sidhe chantments or glamour.

Unseelie: Sidhe of Unwinter's Court, or holding fealty to Unwinter.

Wight: "Being," or "creature"; used to refer to certain classes of sidhe.

Woodwight: A wight whose home or form is a tree, whose blood is resinous.

ACKNOWLEDGMENTS

Thanks must go to Mark Sanders, whose dream provided the impetus for Gallow's world, and to Mel Sanders for telling me I could certainly write it. Additional thanks must go to Miriam Kriss for encouraging me, to Devi Pillai for putting up with me, and to Lindsey Hall for not strangling me when I change things at the very last moment.

Lastly, as always, thank you, dear Reader. Come a little closer, just around this corner, and let me tell you a story...

extras

meet the author

Photo credit: Daron Gildrow

LILITH SAINTCROW was born in New Mexico, bounced around the world as an Air Force brat, and fell in love with writing when she was ten years old. She currently lives in Vancouver, Washington.

introducing

If you enjoyed
TRAILER PARK FAE
look out for the next book in the
Gallow and Ragged series

by Lilith Saintcrow

A Very Thin Shield

Dusk turned to dark well before true nightfall as the storm's wing passed over a small trailer park on Guayahoya Avenue. The sun, as it sank, peered underneath the clouds, turning the west to a furnace of gold and blood. The last streaks and flashes of crimson and yellow faded to indigo dusk. Quiet fell, broken only by cars grinding to a halt and quick bursts of supper-scent puffing out before trailer doors slammed. Evening thickened, swirling under trees whose wet branches now had hard little green nubs, spring bursting out all at once.

A soft breeze rattled droplets from bough and bush. Night tiptoed over the city, thief instead of grand dame.

The cat's hiss brought Robin into wakefulness with a terrified jolt, a taste of bitter almonds on her tongue and every nerve taut-prickling. The cat, her formal black and white disarranged by the puffing of her fur, hissed again, and Robin was off the bed in a flash, instinct driving her toward the closet before she halted, her skirt swinging.

No. Be canny, Ragged.

They were not close, not yet. She shut her eyes, listening, taut as a bard's lutestring, the mortal house a very thin shield indeed. *There.* A silver thrill against the nerves, a faraway ultrasonic thrilling most mortals wouldn't hear. They would *feel* it, though—a cold brush against their backs, a sudden uneasiness.

Huntwhistles. Unwinter's knights rode tonight, perhaps even Unwinter himself. She was no longer stumbling-weary, milk and rest had soothed her aches. She had two pins, the bone comb, her wits, and the music below her thoughts—the massive noise that could kill if she let it loose for long enough. Not to mention the knife at her belt, and the pipes tucked in her secret skirt pocket—a collection of age-blackened and use-lacquered reeds, lashed together with tendons too fine to be animal.

Puck's treasures, now hers.

But it was night, and only spring instead of the full season of glory. Even though Summer had opened the Gates, Unwinter could still ride dusk to dawn if he chose. Slipping into Summer to rest might have been an attractive option, save for the thought of some sidhe remarking upon her and carrying tales to the Queen. Robin did not wish to face *her* again so soon, either.

Did Summer know who had invited the lord of the Hunt into her lands? Could she guess? Goodfellow perhaps had not told her, but Robin could not trust as much. Then there was Sean. All the stars of Summer's dusk ground into shattered amber dust, the child she had cared for gone into whatever awaited mortals after death.

No, when she saw Summer again, Robin wished to be thoroughly prepared.

First, though, she had to survive the night. The silver huntwhistles were far away, but the cat began to growl low in her chest, an amazingly deep noise from such a small animal.

Robin kept breathing. Four in, four out, you could not sing

if you could not breathe, and though her hand wrapped itself about the cold hilt of the loathsome dagger, the song was still her best weapon.

A scratching. Much closer than the huntwhistles. The knights were coursing abroad, probably hoping to find any prey at all, a net she might be able to elude. It was the silent hunters she would have to worry about.

More scritch-scratching, and a desire to laugh rose in Robin's throat, killed by the discipline of breath as soon as it was born. *Who is that nibbling at my house?*

Only the wind, she replied silently, *the child of heaven*. Mortals never realized how much truth was in the old tales. Sometimes they slipped through into the sideways realms—mostly children, but also adults who had not lost the habit of seeing. Usually a swift death awaited them, or a return to the mortal world full of slow lingering illness, not realizing what they pined for. A few survived somewhat unscathed, and their stories passed into myth and fairytale, warning and dream.

Her gaze traveled across the bedroom, to the neat dresser and the invitation card with its tinsel. She ghosted across cheap carpet, still listening to the scratches. Mortals did not bury iron under their doorsteps anymore, or nail up horseshoes to bar ill-wishing. There was salt in the kitchen, she could have poured thin lines over every windowsill and doorstep, but that would simply tell any passerby that someone wished to guard something of value.

Sidhe were a curious, curious folk. Always peering and poking, prying and noticing.

Soft, padding footsteps. More scratching. How many of them? Why had they not broken in already to lay waste to flesh and trailer alike? She was an ill guest indeed, bringing destruction to such a neat, humble home.

The wedding invitation was heavy paper, and inside, written

with purple ink under the printed date and time, was a round, childish hand. *Uncle Eddie, you'd better be there to give me away! Love, Kara.* The moonglow tinsel on the card unraveled under Robin's quick fingers, whispered chantment dropping from her lips. The Old Language slipped and slithered between the strands, the pins and needles of Realmaking spreading into her palms.

Realmaking was precious, but it required something to begin with. She could not simply spin chantment out of empty air, that was a fullblood's trick. When given something, though, she could make something *else*, something that wouldn't fade or turn into leaf and twig come daybreak. It was strange that a tinge of perishable mortal in one's blood was necessary for Realmaking. They were rare, those architects of the real, and no fullblood, highborn or low, had ever been among their number.

A flick of the wrist, another, silver glitters attaching to her fingertips. A full complement of ten, and a swift lance of pain through her temples as a jolting impact crashed into the side of the trailer, rocking it on its foundations.

What in Stone's name is that? She skipped down the hall, past the tiny scrubbed-clean bathroom with its strangely unsmelly litterbox. Her shoes lightened, their chantments waking too as she called upon speed and lightfoot, and by the time the living room window shattered she was in the kitchen, her fingernails throwing hard sharp darts of hungry moonlight as she tweezed open the cabinet near the oven. A blue canister of salt tucked behind other spices, her hand darted in and the small bottles and cans holding pepper, garlic, onion salt, oregano, thyme, swept out in a jumbled mass, falling like rain and most shattering. She whirled, and it was not as bad as it could have been.

Not barrow-wights, with their subtly wrong, noseless faces and their strangler's fingers dripping with gold leached of its daylight lustre. Not fullborn knights either, or Unwinter's narrow-nosed, leaping dogs with their needle-teeth. Instead, it was two lean grace-ful drow and a woodwight, accompanied by a looming silver-necklaced shadow that chilled her clear through until she realized it was a stonetroll on a moonfire leash, making a low, unhappy grum-bling sound as one of the drow poked it with a silver-tipped stick.

None of them were familiar from song or rumor, or known to her. They piled pell-mell into the mortal living room, one of the raven-haired drow leaping atop the couch and hissing, his handsome face distorted as the teeth elongated, rows of serrated pearls. The woodwight swelled, his lean brown frame crackle-heaving between treeshape and biped, living green sprouting from his long, knobbed fingers. Serrated leaves, a dark trunk—an elm, a bad-tempered tree indeed.

The troll heaved forward again, widening the hole in the side of the trailer. Glass shattered, cheap metal buckled and bent, and Robin flicked her right pinkie fingernail with the pad of her thumb.

A silver dart crackled into being, splashing against the wood-wight and scoring deep. Golden, resinous sapblood sprayed, and the wight's knothole mouth opened bellow-wide. A furious scream made of creaking, snapping, thick-groaning branches poured out.

The troll halted, its tiny close-set eyes blinking in confusion. It withdrew slightly, and the second raven-haired drow peered over its shoulder, poking at it afresh with the silvertip stick. Robin flicked her right middle and ring finger, one dart catch-ing in the woodwight's branches and tangling, the other flying true and striking at the troll's eyes. Index finger, another dart made a high keening noise as it streaked for the first drow, who batted it away with contemptuous ease. The spray of sapblood from the woodwight slowed, and the thing hissed a maledic-tion at her, a black-winged curse.

The troll howled, the noise and its stinking breath flutter-ing Robin's skirt, cracking the screen on the ancient television, and batting the flying curse aside. It lashed out, horselike, with each limb in turn, the first its left hind leg, catching the second drow with a crack audible even through the uproar. The first drow leapt forward, shaking out something that glittered gold with flashes of ruby, and Robin's skin chilled all over.

She flicked her thumbnail now, and a high piercing whistle burst between her lips. Ruddy orange flashed, the dart becoming a whip of flame, and it kissed the edge of the woodwight's trunk.

Golden sapblood kindled, and a new layer of noise intruded. Robin ignored it, skipping aside with the canister of salt now in her right hand. *A fine time to wish I had cold iron,* she thought, pointlessly, and dodged, for the gold and ruby glimmer in the first drow's hands was a net, hair-fine metallic strands with red droplets at their junctures, supple-straining as it sensed its holder's quarry. It retreated with a cheated hiss, and the drow snarled at her again.

So *someone* wished her taken alive. Unwinter had sworn to Puck Goodfellow that he would not hunt her, but drow were not of Summer unless they were half something else, whether mortal or another manner of sidhe, and in any case it did not matter.

The Ragged did not mean to let these suitors, or any other, press their attentions *too* closely upon her. The curse, flapping in the living room, vanished under a sheet of flame. Robin's whistle ended and she whooped in a fresh breath, bringing her left hand forward.

The sinister hand. These darts would be more brittle…but far more powerfully malefic.

The troll, fire-maddened and half-blinded, heaved. The entire trailer lifted, foundation to roof, buckling and breaking. The woodwight, screaming and completely alight by now, blundered into the couch, thrusting itself straight into the troll's face as well. The poor creature—stonetrolls were not known for their intelligence—was hopelessly entangled with the side of the trailer, insulation and sharp metal ribboning around its hard hide. It heaved again, and the drow with the net slip-stumbled between carpet and linoleum, his eyes widening as footing became treacherous.

Robin jabbed her left hand forward and the drow dodged aside, crashing into a flimsy closet door—but she hadn't released the darts, and now she flicked them all, fanwise and deadly, a baking draft scouring her from top to toe and her eyes slitted against the blast. Smoke billowed, it would make the air unbreathable after a few more moments. The back door was behind her, she fumbled with her left hand for the knob, her right hand sweeping in a semicircle, scattering salt in an arc that would not halt Unwinter's minion.

But it would delay him, and salt could be fashioned into other things. There was the song, too, her loosening throat scorched with smoke-tang, and just as the drow with the net shook himself free of the ruins of the coat closet and the troll heaved again, the knob turned under her fingers and she half-fell backwards, saving herself with a wrenching, fishlike jump as the wet wooden steps outside splintered.

The troll heaved again, dragging his leash-holder with him, breaking through the remainder of the wall, and instead of backing away from the inferno, plunged forward, crashing entirely through the other side of the trailer. The noise was incredible—mortals would soon take notice. Her heels clattered on a narrow strip of damp pavement. The mortal whose home they had just destroyed had a charcoal grill set here, all rust carefully scrubbed from its legs and black bowl. It went flying as Robin's hip bumped it, clattering and striking gonglike as it rolled.

Did I strike him? Please tell me I did—

The net-bearing drow bulleted out of the burning trailer. The wight's scream had vanished into a snap and crackle of flame, a burst of hot air lifting smoke and sparks heavenward as the fire could now suck on the night air outside the shattered home, window-glass shivered into breaking. Robin kept back-ing up over the small concrete patio, light shuffling skips, and the urge to cough tickled mercilessly at the back of her palate. She denied it, and saw she had, indeed, managed to hit the net-bearer. Thick yellow-greenish ichor threaded with crimson stained his side, his face was a ruin of scratches and soot, his hair full of burning sparks, and one of his feet was tangled with a mass of glittering spikes, fading quickly as they burrowed through his boots, seeking the flesh underneath.

The song burst free of Robin's throat, a low, throbbing orchestral noise. It smashed into the net-bearer head-on, and he flew backwards into the fire, which took another deep breath, finding fresh fuel, and grunted a mass of sparks and blackening smoke skyward. A wet, heavy breeze full of spring-smell and the good greenness of more rain approaching whisked it into a curtain of burning.

Robin halted, her sides heaving. The stonetroll, truly mad-dened now, dragged the other drow into the damp night, its grinding shrieks interspersed with the dark sidhe's screams. It would not be calmed until it had exhausted itself.

She struggled to control her breathing, staring at the flames. *The cat. Stone and Throne, the cat. Is she still inside?*

Sirens in the distance. Some mortal had noticed this, and Robin did not wish to be here when they swarmed. Still, she darted along the back of the house, searching for any unburnt portion. *I am sorry. I am so sorry. I did not mean for this to happen.*

And yet. What else had she expected? She was a Half, mortal and sidhe in equal measure, a faithless sidhe bitch possibly sired by a monstrous ancient, the cause of more trouble and sorrow than any mortal could ever hope to be.

There was no sign of the cat, and Robin, smoke-tarnished, fled before anyone else arrived.

introducing

If you enjoyed
TRAILER PARK FAE
look out for

THE IRON WYRM AFFAIR

Bannon and Clare: Book 1

by Lilith Saintcrow

*Emma Bannon, forensic sorceress in the service of the
Empire, has a mission: to protect Archibald Clare, a failed,
unregistered mentath. His skills of deduction are legendary,
and her own sorcery is not inconsiderable. It doesn't help
much that they barely tolerate each other, or that Bannon's
Shield, Mikal, might just be a traitor himself. Or that the
conspiracy killing registered mentaths and sorcerers
alike will just as likely kill them as seduce them
into treachery toward their Queen.*

*In an alternate London where illogical magic has
turned the Industrial Revolution on its head, Bannon
and Clare now face hostility, treason, cannon fire,*

black sorcery, and the problem of reliably finding hansom cabs.

The game is afoot....

Prelude

A PROMISE OF DIVERSION

When the young dark-haired woman stepped into his parlour, Archibald Clare was only mildly intrigued. Her companion was of more immediate interest, a tall man in a close-fitting velvet jacket, moving with a grace that bespoke some experience with physical mayhem. The way he carried himself, lightly and easily, with a clean economy of movement – not to mention the way his eyes roved in controlled arcs – all but shouted danger. He was hatless, too, and wore curious boots.

The chain of deduction led Clare in an extraordinary direction, and he cast another glance at the woman to verify it.

Yes. Of no more than middle height, and slight, she was in very dark green. Fine cloth, a trifle antiquated, though the sleeves were close as fashion now dictated, and her bonnet perched just so on brown curls, its brim small enough that it would not interfere with her side vision. However, her skirts were divided, her boots serviceable instead of decorative – though of just as fine a quality as the man's – and her jewellery was eccentric, to say the least. Emerald drops worth a fortune at her ears, and the necklace was an amber cabochon large enough to be a baleful eye. Two rings on gloved hands, one with a dull unprecious black stone and the other a star sapphire a royal family might have envied.

The man had a lean face to match the rest of him, strange yellow eyes, and tidy dark hair still dewed with crystal droplets from the light rain falling over Londinium tonight. The moisture, however, did not cling to her. One more piece of evidence, and Clare did not much like where it led.

He set the viola and its bow down, nudging aside a stack of paper with careful precision, and waited for the opening gambit. As he had suspected, *she* spoke.

"Good evening, sir. You are Dr Archibald Clare. Distinguished author of *The Art and Science of Observation*." She paused. Aristocratic nose, firm mouth, very decided for such a childlike face. "Bachelor. And very-recently-unregistered mentath."

"Sorceress." Clare steepled his fingers under his very long, very sensitive nose. Her toilette favoured musk, of course, for a brunette. Still, the scent was not common, and it held an edge of something acrid that should have been troublesome instead of strangely pleasing. "And a Shield. I would invite you to sit, but I hardly think you will."

A slight smile; her chin lifted. She did not give her name, as if she expected him to suspect it. Her curls, if they were not natural, were very close. There was a slight bit of untidiness to them – some recent exertion, perhaps? "Since there is no seat available, *sir*, I am to take that as one of your deductions?"

Even the hassock had a pile of papers and books stacked terrifyingly high. He had been researching, of course. The intersections between musical scale and the behaviour of certain tiny animals. It was the intervals, perhaps. Each note held its own space. He was seeking to determine which set of spaces would make the insects (and later, other things) possibly—

Clare waved one pale, long-fingered hand. Emotion was threatening, prickling at his throat. With a certain rational annoyance he labelled it as *fear*, and dismissed it. There was very little chance she meant him harm. The man was a larger question, but if *she* meant him no harm, the man certainly did not. "If you like. Speak quickly, I am occupied."

She cast one eloquent glance over the room. If not for the efforts of the landlady, Mrs Ginn, dirty dishes would have been stacked on every horizontal surface. As it was, his quarters were cluttered with a full set of alembics and burners, glass jars of various substances, shallow dishes for knocking his pipe clean. The tabac smoke blunted the damned sensitivity in his nose just enough, and he wished for his pipe. The acridity in her scent was becoming more marked, and very definitely not unpleasant.

The room's disorder even threatened the grate, the mantel above it groaning under a weight of books and handwritten journals stacked every which way.

The sorceress, finishing her unhurried investigation, next examined him from tip to toe. He was in his dressing gown, and his pipe had long since grown cold. His feet were in the rubbed-bare slippers, and if it had not been past the hour of reasonable entertaining he might have been vaguely uncomfortable at the idea of a lady seeing him in such disrepair. Red-eyed, his hair mussed, and unshaven, he was in no condition to receive company.

He was, in fact, the picture of a mentath about to implode from boredom. If she knew some of the circumstances behind his recent ill luck, she would guess he was closer to imploding and fusing his faculties into unworkable porridge than was advisable, comfortable... or even sane.

Yet if she knew the circumstances behind his ill luck, would she look so calm? He did not know nearly enough yet. Frustration tickled behind his eyes, the sensation of pounding and seething inside the cup of his skull easing a fraction as he considered the possibilities of her arrival.

Her gloved hand rose, and she held up a card. It was dun-coloured, and before she tossed it – a passionless, accurate flick of her fingers that snapped it through intervening space neat as you please, as if she dealt faro – he had already deduced and verified its provenance.

He plucked it out of the air. "I am called to the service of the Crown. You are to hold my leash. It is, of course, urgent. Does it have to do with an art professor?" For it had been some time since he had crossed wits with Dr Vance, and *that* would distract him most handily. The man was a deuced wonderful adversary.

His sally was only worth a raised eyebrow. She must have practised that look in the mirror; her features were strangely childlike, and the effect of the very adult expression was... odd. "No. It *is* urgent, and Mikal will stand guard while you... dress. I shall be in the hansom outside. You have ten minutes, sir."

With that, she turned on her heel. Her skirts made a low, sweet sound, and the man was already holding the door. She glanced up, those wide dark eyes flashing once, and a ghost of a smile touched her soft mouth.

Interesting. Clare added that to the chain of deduction. He only hoped this problem would last more than a night and provide him further relief. If the young Queen or one of the ministers had sent a summons card, it promised to be very diverting indeed.

It was a delight to have something unknown, but within guessing reach. He sniffed the card. A faint trace of musk, but no violet-water. Not the Queen personally, then. He had not thought it likely – why would Her Majesty trouble herself with *him*? It was a faint joy to find he was correct.

His faculties were, evidently, not porridge *yet*.

The ink was correct as well, just the faintest bitter astringent note as he inhaled deeply. The crest on the front was absolutely genuine, and the handwriting on the back was firm and masculine, not to mention familiar. *Why, it's Cedric.*

In other words, the Chancellor of the Exchequer, Lord Grayson. The Prime Minister was new and inexperienced, since the Queen had banished her lady mother's creatures from her Cabinet, and Grayson had survived with, no doubt, some measure of cunning or because someone thought him incompetent enough to do no harm. Having been at Yton with the man, Clare was inclined to lean towards the former.

And dear old Cedric had exerted his influence so Clare was merely unregistered and not facing imprisonment, a mercy that had teeth. Even more interesting.

Miss Emma Bannon is our representative. Please use haste, and discretion.

Emma Bannon. Clare had never heard the name before, but then a sorceress would not wish her name bruited about overmuch. Just as a mentath, registered or no, would not. So he made a special note of it, adding everything about the woman to the mental drawer that bore her name. She would not take a carved nameplate. No, Miss Bannon's plate would be yellowed parchment, with dragonsblood ink tracing out the letters of her name in a clear, feminine hand.

The man's drawer was featureless blank metal, burnished to

a high gloss. He waited by the open door. Cleared his throat, a low rumble. Meant to hurry Clare along, no doubt.

Clare opened one eye, just a sliver. "There are nine and a quarter minutes left. Do *not* make unnecessary noise, sir."

The man – a sorceress's Shield, meant to guard against physical danger while the sorceress dealt with more arcane perils – remained silent, but his mouth firmed. He did not look amused.

Mikal. His colour was too dark and his features too aquiline to be properly Britannic. Perhaps Tinkerfolk? Or even from the Indus?

For the moment, he decided, the man's drawer could remain metal. He did not know enough about him. It would have to do. One thing was certain: if the sorceress had left one of her Shields with him, she was standing guard against some more than mundane threat outside. Which meant the problem he was about to address was most likely fiendishly complex, extraordinarily important, and worth more than a day or two of his busy brain's feverish working.

Thank God. The relief was palpable.

Clare shot to his feet and began packing.

Chapter One

A PLEASANT EVENING RIDE

Emma Bannon, Sorceress Prime and servant to Britannia's current incarnation, mentally ran through every foul word that would never cross the lips of a lady. She timed them to the clockhorse's steady jogtrot, and her awareness dilated. The simmering cauldron of the streets was just as it always was; there was no breath of ill intent.

Of course, there had not been earlier, either, when she had been a quarter-hour too late to save the *other* unregistered mentath. It was only one of the many things about this situation seemingly designed to try her often considerable patience.

Mikal would be taking the rooftop road, running while she sat at ease in a hired carriage. It was the knowledge that while he did so he could forget some things that eased her conscience, though not completely.

Still, he was a Shield. He would not consent to share a carriage with her unless he was certain of her safety. And there was not room enough to manoeuvre in a two-person conveyance, should he require it.

She was heartily sick of hired carts. Her own carriages were *far* more comfortable, but this matter required discretion. Having it shouted to the heavens that she was alert to the pattern

334

under these occurrences might not precisely frighten her opponents, but it would become more difficult to attack them from an unexpected quarter. Which was, she had to admit, her preferred method.

Even a Prime can benefit from guile, Llew had often remarked. And of course, she would think of him. She seemed constitutionally incapable of leaving well enough alone, and *that* irritated her as well.

Beside her, Clare dozed. He was a very thin man, with a long, mournful face; his gloves were darned but his waistcoat was of fine cloth, though it had seen better days. His eyes were blue, and they glittered feverishly under half-closed lids. An unregistered mentath would find it difficult to secure proper employment, and by the looks of his quarters, Clare had been suffering from boredom for several weeks, desperately seeking a series of experiments to exercise his active brain.

Mentath was like sorcerous talent. If not trained, and *used*, it turned on its bearer.

At least he had found time to shave, and he had brought two bags. One, no doubt, held linens. God alone knew what was in the second. Perhaps she should apply deduction to the problem, as if she did not have several others crowding her attention at the moment.

Chief among said problems were the murderers, who had so far eluded her efforts. Queen Victrix was young, and just recently freed from the confines of her domineering mother's sway. Her new Consort, Alberich, was a moderating influence – but he did not have enough power at Court just yet to be an effective shield for Britannia's incarnation.

The ruling spirit was old, and wise, but Her vessels . . . well, they were not indestructible.

And that, Emma told herself sternly, *is as far as we shall go*

335

with such a train of thought. She found herself rubbing the sardonyx on her left middle finger, polishing it with her opposite thumb. Even through her thin gloves, the stone prickled hotly. Her posture did not change, but her awareness contracted. She felt for the source of the disturbance, flashing through and discarding a number of fine invisible threads.

Blast and bother. Other words, less polite, rose as well. Her pulse and respiration did not change, but she tasted a faint tang of adrenalin before sorcerous training clamped tight on such functions to free her from some of flesh's more…distracting…reactions.

"I say, whatever is the matter?" Archibald Clare's blue eyes were wide open now, and he looked interested. Almost, dare she think it, intrigued. It did nothing for his long, almost ugly features. His cloth was serviceable, though hardly elegant – one could infer that a mentath had other priorities than fashion, even if he had an eye for quality and the means to purchase such. But at least he was cleaner than he had been, and had arrived in the hansom in nine and a half minutes precisely. Now they were on Sarpesson Street, threading through amusement-seekers and those whom a little rain would not deter from their nightly appointments.

The disturbance peaked, and a not-quite-seen starburst of gunpowder igniting flashed through the ordered lattices of her consciousness.

The clockhorse screamed as his reins were jerked, and the hansom yawed alarmingly. Archibald Clare's hand dashed for the door handle, but Emma was already moving. Her arms closed around the tall, fragile man, and she shouted a Word that exploded the cab away from them both. Shards and splinters, driven outwards, peppered the street surface. The glass of the cab's tiny windows broke with a high, sweet tinkle, grinding into crystalline dust.

Shouts. Screams. Pounding footsteps. Emma struggled upright, shaking her skirts with numb hands. The horse had gone avast, rearing and plunging, throwing tiny metal slivers and dribs of oil as well as stray crackling sparks of sorcery, but the traces were tangled and it stood little chance of running loose. The driver was gone, and she snapped a quick glance at the overhanging rooftops before the unhealthy canine shapes resolved out of thinning rain, slinking low as gaslamp gleam painted their slick, heaving sides.

Sootdogs. Oh, how unpleasant. The one that had leapt on the hansom's roof had most likely taken the driver, and Emma cursed aloud now as it landed with a thump, its shining hide running with vapour.

"*Most* unusual!" Archibald Clare yelled. He had gained his feet as well, and his eyes were alight now. The mournfulness had vanished. He had also produced a queerly barrelled pistol, which would be of *no* use against the dog-shaped sorcerous things now gathering. "*Quite* diverting!"

The star sapphire on her right third finger warmed. A globe-shield shimmered into being, and to the roil of smouldering wood, gunpowder and fear was added another scent: the smoke-gloss of sorcery. One of the sootdogs leapt, crashing into the shield, and the shock sent Emma to her knees, holding grimly. Both her hands were outstretched now, and her tongue occupied in chanting.

Sarpesson Street was neither deserted nor crowded at this late hour. The people gathering to watch the outcome of a hansom crash pushed against those onlookers alert enough to note that something entirely different was occurring, and the resultant chaos was merely noise to be shunted aside as her concentration narrowed.

Where is Mikal?

She had no time to wonder further. The sootdogs hunched and wove closer, snarling. Their packed-cinder sides heaved and black tongues lolled between obsidian-chip teeth; they could strip a large adult male to bone in under a minute. There were the onlookers to think of as well, and Clare behind and to her right, laughing as he sighted down the odd little pistol's chunky nose. Only he was not pointing it at the dogs, thank God. He was aiming for the rooftop.

You idiot. The chant filled her mouth. She could spare no words to tell him not to fire, that Mikal was—

The lead dog crashed against the shield. Emma's body jerked as the impact tore through her, but she held steady, the sapphire now a ringing blue flame. Her voice rose, a clear contralto, and she assayed the difficult rill of notes that would split her focus and make another Major Work possible.

That was part of what made a Prime – the ability to concentrate completely on multiple channellings of ætheric force. One's capacity could not be infinite, just like the charge of force carried and renewed every Tideturn.

But one did not need infinite capacity. *One needs only slightly more capacity than the problem at hand calls for,* as her third-form Sophological Studies professor had often intoned.

Mikal arrived.

His dark green coat fluttered as he landed in the midst of the dogs, a Shield's fury glimmering to Sight, bright spatters and spangles invisible to normal vision. The sorcery-made things cringed, snapping; his blades tore through their insubstantial hides. The charmsilver laid along the knives' flats, as well as the will to strike, would be of far more use than Mr Clare's pistol.

Which spoke, behind her, the ball tearing through the shield from a direction the protection wasn't meant to hold. The fabric of the shield collapsed, and Emma had just enough time to deflect the backlash, tearing a hole in the brick-faced fabric of the street and exploding the clockhorse into gobbets of metal and rags of flesh, before one of the dogs turned with stomach-churning speed and launched itself at her – and the man she had been charged to protect.

She shrieked another Word through the chant's descant, her hand snapping out again, fingers contorted in a gesture definitely *not* acceptable in polite company. The ray of ætheric force smashed through brick dust, destroying even more of the road's surface, and crunched into the sootdog.

Emma bolted to her feet, snapping her hand back, and the line of force followed as the dog crumpled, whining and shattering into fragments. She could not hold the forcewhip for very long, but if more of the dogs came—

The last one died under Mikal's flashing knives. He muttered something in his native tongue, whirled on his heel, and stalked toward his Prima. That normally meant the battle was finished.

Yet Emma's mind was not eased. She half turned, chant dying on her lips and her gaze roving, searching. Heard the mutter of the crowd, dangerously frightened. Sorcerous force pulsed and bled from her fingers, a fountain of crimson sparks popping against the rainy air. For a moment the mood of the crowd threatened to distract her, but she closed it away and concentrated, seeking the source of the disturbance.

Sorcerous traces glowed, faint and fading, as the man who had fired the initial shot – most likely to mark them for the dogs – fled. He had some sort of defence laid on him, meant to keep him from a sorcerer's notice.

Perhaps from a sorcerer, but not from a Prime. Not from me, oh no. The dead see all. Her Discipline was of the Black, and it was moments like these when she would be glad of its practicality – if she could spare the attention.

339

Time spun outwards, dilating, as she followed him over roof-tops and down into a stinking alley, refuse piled high on each side, running with the taste of fear and blood in his mouth. Something had injured him.

Mikal? But then why did he not kill the man—

The world jolted underneath her, a stunning blow to her shoulder, a great spiked roil of pain through her chest. Mikal screamed, but she was breathless. Sorcerous force spilled free, uncontained, and other screams rose.

She could possibly injure someone.

Emma came back to herself, clutching at her shoulder. Hot blood welled between her fingers, and the green silk would be ruined. Not to mention her gloves.

At least they had shot her, and not the mentath.

Oh, damn. The pain crested again, became a giant animal with its teeth in her flesh.

Mikal caught her. His mouth moved soundlessly, and Emma sought with desperate fury to contain the force thundering through her. Backlash could cause yet more damage, to the street and to onlookers, if she let it loose.

A Prime's uncontrolled force was nothing to be trifled with.

It was the traditional function of a Shield to handle such overflow, but if he had only wounded the fellow on the roof she could not trust that he was not part of—

"*Let it GO!*" Mikal roared, and the ætheric bonds between them flamed into painful life. She fought it, seeking to contain what she could, and her skull exploded with pain.

She knew no more.